GREAT EXPECTATIONS

CHARLES DICKENS (1812–1870) is one of the recognized celebrities of English literature. His imagination, wit, mastery of the language, and huge creative output single him out as one of the few people who genuinely deserve to be called geniuses.

Like most people, he was driven – haunted by a terrible childhood, some aspects of which he didn't even reveal to his wife. Several of his novels contain episodes of great darkness; but the chances are that these episodes are based on his own childhood experiences.

For some years, the Dickens family lived in increasing poverty in London. In 1824, his father even spent a few months in debtors' prison; during this period, the young Charles was in lodgings on his own, trying to earn a living working long hours in a factory line sticking labels on bottles. His life was squalid, and he was determined to improve himself.

By his early twenties, he had found a job as a parliamentary reporter, and he filled his spare time writing sketches of London life for newspapers and magazines. In 1836, the publication of *Pickwick Papers* shot him to the fame and fortune he had always sought.

Other books followed at an incredible rate. *Great Expectations* was written in 1860–61, and is considered by many to be the best of his novels. The story, which Dickens described as a 'tragi-comedy', is brilliant; the first-person narrative endears Pip to every reader. Dickens created his own extraordinary world in his novels – a world based on the one he was familiar with, and then exaggerated. What saves his books from the faults of exaggeration, however, is that Dickens loved his characters. The Russian author Tolstoy considered this to be Dickens's greatest gift. Dickens enters into every single one of his characters, however minor a part they have to play in a book, and breathes life into them. In his lifetime, he used to give public readings of parts of his books, and he would so thoroughly become each part he played that he could terrify an audience out of its wits. The amount of passion he gave to his work no doubt contributed to his early death.

Some other Puffin Classics to enjoy

OLIVER TWIST
A CHRISTMAS CAROL
Charles Dickens

LORNA DOONE
R. D. Blackmore

CHARLES DICKENS

Great Expectations

Abridged by
LINDA JENNINGS

PUFFIN BOOKS

PUFFIN BOOKS

Published by the Penguin Group
Penguin Books Ltd, 27 Wrights Lane, London W8 5TZ, England
Penguin Putnam Inc., 375 Hudson Street, New York, New York 10014, USA
Penguin Books Australia Ltd, Ringwood, Victoria, Australia
Penguin Books Canada Ltd, 10 Alcorn Avenue, Toronto, Ontario, Canada M4V 3B2
Penguin Books (NZ) Ltd, Private Bag 102902, NSMC, Auckland, New Zealand

Penguin Books Ltd, Registered Offices: Harmondsworth, Middlesex, England

First published 1861
Published in Puffin Books 1991
Published in this edition 1995
7 9 10 8 6

This abridgement copyright © Linda Jennings, 1995
All rights reserved

Typeset by Datix International Limited, Bungay, Suffolk
Set in Monotype Plantin

Made and printed in England by Clays Ltd, St Ives plc

British Library Cataloguing in Publication Data
A CIP catalogue record for this book is available from the British Library

ISBN 0-140-36681-4

1

My father's family name being Pirrip, and my christian
name Philip, I called myself Pip, and came to be called
Pip.

I give Pirrip as my father's family name, on the
authority of his tombstone and my sister – Mrs Joe
Gargery, who married the blacksmith.

My first most vivid and broad impression of the
identity of things, seems to me to have been gained on
a memorable raw afternoon towards evening. At such
a time I found out for certain, that this bleak place
overgrown with nettles was the churchyard; and that
Philip Pirrip and also Georgiana wife of the above,
were dead and buried; and that Alexander, Bartholomew, Abraham, Tobias, and Roger, infant children of the aforesaid, were also dead and buried; and
that the dark flat wilderness beyond the churchyard,
intersected with dykes and mounds and gates, was the
marshes; and that the small bundle of shivers growing
afraid of it all and beginning to cry, was Pip.

'Hold your noise!' cried a terrible voice, as a man
started up from among the graves at the side of the
church porch. 'Keep still, you little devil, or I'll cut
your throat!'

A fearful man, all in coarse grey, with a great iron

on his leg. A man with no hat, and with broken shoes, and with an old rag tied round his head. A man who limped, and shivered, and glared and growled; and whose teeth chattered in his head as he seized me by the chin.

'O! Don't cut my throat, sir,' I pleaded in terror.

'Tell us your name!' said the man. 'Quick!'

'Pip, sir.'

'Once more,' said the man, staring at me. 'Give it mouth!'

'Pip. Pip, sir.'

'Show us where you live,' said the man. 'Pint out the place!'

I pointed to where our village lay, on the flat inshore among the alder-trees and pollards, a mile or more from the church.

The man, after looking at me for a moment, turned me upside-down, and emptied my pockets. There was nothing in them but a piece of bread. When the church came to itself – for he was so sudden and strong that he made it go head over heels before me, and I saw the steeple under my feet – I was seated on a high tombstone, trembling, while he ate the bread ravenously.

'You young dog,' said the man, licking his lips, 'what fat cheeks you ha' got.'

I believe they were fat, though I was at that time undersized for my years, and not strong.

'Darn Me if I couldn't eat em,' said the man, with a threatening shake of his head, 'and if I han't half a mind to't!'

I earnestly expressed my hope that he wouldn't, and held tighter to the tombstone on which he had put me; partly, to keep myself upon it; partly, to keep myself from crying.

'Now lookee here!' said the man. 'Where's your mother?'

'There, sir!' said I.

He started, made a short run, and stopped and looked over his shoulder.

'There, sir!' I timidly explained. 'Also Georgiana. That's my mother.'

'Oh!' said he, coming back. 'And is that your father alonger your mother?'

'Yes, sir,' said I; 'him too; late of this parish.'

'Ha!' he muttered then, considering. 'Who d'ye live with?'

'My sister, sir – Mrs Joe Gargery – wife of Joe Gargery, the blacksmith, sir.'

'Blacksmith, eh?' said he. And looked down at his leg.

After darkly looking at his leg and me several times, he came closer to my tombstone, took me by both arms, and tilted me back as far as he could hold me; so that his eyes looked most powerfully down into mine, and mine looked most helplessly up into his.

'Now lookee here,' he said, 'the question being whether you're to be let to live. You know what a file is?'

'Yes, sir.'

'And you know what wittles is?'

'Yes, sir.'

'You get me a file.' He tilted me again. 'And you get me wittles.' He tilted me again. 'You bring 'em both to me.' He tilted me again. 'Or I'll have your heart and liver out.'

He gave me a most tremendous dip and roll, then, he held me by the arms, in an upright position on the top of the stone, and went on in these fearful terms:

'You bring me, tomorrow morning early, that file and them wittles. You bring the lot to me, at that old Battery over yonder. You do it, and you never dare to say a word or dare to make a sign concerning your having seen such a person as me and you shall be let to live. You fail, or you go from my words in any partickler, and your heart and your liver shall be tore out, roasted and ate. Now, I ain't alone, as you may think I am. There's a young man hid with me, who has a secret way pecooliar to himself, of getting at a boy, and at his heart, and at his liver. It is in wain for a boy to attempt to hide himself from that young man. A boy may lock his door, may be warm in bed, may tuck himself up, may think himself comfortable and safe, but that young man will softly creep and creep his way to him and tear him open. I am a keeping that young man from harming of you at the present moment, with great difficulty. I find it very hard to hold that young man off of your inside. Now, what do you say?'

I said that I would get him the file, and I would get him what broken bits of food I could, and I would come to him at the Battery, early in the morning.

'Say Lord strike you dead if you don't!' said the man.

I said so, and he took me down.

'Now,' he pursued, 'you remember what you've undertook, and you remember that young man, and you get home!'

'Goo-good night, sir,' I faltered.

'Much of that!' said he, glancing about him over the cold wet flat. 'I wish I was a frog. Or a eel!'

At the same time, he hugged his shuddering body in both his arms – clasping himself, as if to hold himself together – and limped towards the low church wall. As I saw him go, picking his way among the nettles, and among the brambles that bound the green mounds, he looked in my young eyes as if he were eluding the hands of the dead people, stretching up cautiously out of their graves, to get a twist upon his ankle and pull him in.

When he came to the low church wall, he got over it, like a man whose legs were numbed and stiff, and then turned round to look for me. When I saw him turning, I set my face towards home, and made the best use of my legs. But presently I looked over my shoulder, and saw him going on again towards the river, still hugging himself in both arms.

On the edge of the river I could faintly make out the only two black things in all the prospect that seemed to be standing upright; one of these was the beacon by which the sailors steered – an ugly thing when you were near it; the other a gibbet, with some chains hanging to it which had once held a pirate. The man was limping on towards this latter, as if he were the pirate come to life, and come down, and going back to hook himself up again. It gave me a terrible turn when I thought so; and as I saw the cattle lifting their heads to gaze after him, I wondered whether they thought so too. I looked all round for the horrible young man, and could see no signs of him. But, now I was frightened again, and ran home without stopping.

2

My sister, Mrs Joe Gargery, was more than twenty years older than I, and had established a great reputation with herself and the neighbours because she had brought me up 'by hand'. Having at that time to find out for myself what the expression meant, and knowing her to have a hard and heavy hand, and to be much in the habit of laying it upon her husband as well as upon me, I supposed that Joe Gargery and I were both brought up by hand.

She was not a good-looking woman, my sister; and I had a general impression that she must have made Joe Gargery marry her by hand. Joe was a fair man, with eyes of such a very undecided blue that they seemed to have somehow got mixed with their own whites. He was a mild, good-natured, sweet-tempered, easy-going, foolish, dear fellow – a sort of Hercules in strength, and also in weakness.

My sister, Mrs Joe, was tall and bony, and almost always wore a coarse apron, fastened over her figure behind with two loops, and having a square impregnable bib in front, that was stuck full of pins and needles. She made it a powerful merit in herself, and a strong reproach against Joe, that she wore this apron so much.

Joe's forge adjoined our house, and when I ran home from the churchyard, the forge was shut up, and Joe was sitting alone in the kitchen. Joe and I being fellow-suffers, and having confidences as such, Joe imparted a confidence to me, the moment I raised the latch of the door and peeped in at him opposite to it, sitting in the chimney corner.

'Mrs Joe has been out a dozen times, looking for you, Pip. And she's out now, making it a baker's dozen; and what's worse, she's got Tickler with her.'

At this dismal intelligence, I twisted the only button on my waistcoat round and round, and looked in great depression at the fire. Tickler was a wax-ended piece of cane, worn smooth by collision with my tickled frame.

'She sat down,' said Joe, 'and she got up, and she made a grab at Tickler, and she rampaged out,' said Joe.

'Has she been gone long, Joe?'

'Well,' said Joe, glancing up at the Dutch clock, 'she's been on the rampage, this last spell, about five minutes, Pip. She's a coming! Get behind the door, old chap, and have the jack-towel betwixt you.'

I took the advice. My sister, Mrs Joe, throwing the door wide open, and finding an obstruction behind it, immediately divined the cause, and applied Tickler to its further investigation. She concluded by throwing me at Joe, who, glad to get hold of me on any terms, passed me on into the chimney and quietly fenced me up there with his great leg.

'Where have you been, you young monkey?' said Mrs Joe, stamping her foot.

'I have only been to the churchyard,' said I, from my stool, crying and rubbing myself.

'Churchyard!' repeated my sister. 'If it warn't for me you'd have been to the churchyard long ago, and stayed there. Who brought you up by hand?'

'You did,' said I.

'And why did I do it, I should like to know?' exclaimed my sister.

I whimpered, 'I don't know.'

'*I* don't!' said my sister. 'I'd never do it again! I know that. It's bad enough to be a blacksmith's wife without being your mother.'

My thoughts strayed from that question as I looked disconsolately at the fire. For, the fugitive out on the marshes with the ironed leg, the mysterious young man, the file, the food, and the dreadful pledge I was under to commit a larceny on those sheltering premises, rose before me in the avenging coals.

'Hah!' said Mrs Joe, restoring Tickler to his station. 'Churchyard, indeed! You'll drive *me* to the church-yard betwixt you, one of these days, and oh, a pr-r-recious pair you'd be without me!'

As she applied herself to set the tea-things, Joe peeped down at me over his leg, as if he were mentally casting me and himself up, and calculating what kind of pair we practically should make, under the grievous circumstances foreshadowed. After that, he sat feeling his right-side flaxen curls and whisker, and following Mrs Joe about with his blue eyes, as his manner always was at squally times.

On the present occasion, though I was hungry, I dared not eat my slice of bread and butter. I felt that I must have something in reserve for my dreadful acquaint-ance, and his ally the still more dreadful young man. I knew Mrs Joe's housekeeping to be of the strictest kind, and that my larcenous researches might find nothing available in the safe. Therefore I resolved to put my hunk of bread-and-butter down the leg of my trousers.

The effort of resolution necessary to the achievement of this purpose was made the more difficult by the unconscious Joe. It was our evening habit to compare the way we bit through our slices, by silently holding them up to each other's admiration now and then – which stimulated us to new exertions. Tonight, Joe several times invited me, by the display of his fast-diminishing slice, to enter upon our usual friendly competition; but he found me, each time, with my yellow mug of tea on one knee, and my untouched bread-and-butter on the other. At last I took advantage of a moment when Joe had just looked at me, and got my bread-and-butter down my leg.

Joe was evidently made uncomfortable by what he supposed to be my loss of appetite, and took a thoughtful bite out of his slice, which he didn't seem to enjoy. He was about to take another bite, when his eye fell on me, and he saw that my bread-and-butter was gone.

The wonder and consternation with which Joe stopped on the threshold of his bite and stared at me, were too evident to escape my sister's observation.

'What's the matter now?' said she, smartly, as she put down her cup.

'I say, you know!' muttered Joe, shaking his head at me in very serious remonstrance. 'Pip, old chap! You'll do yourself a mischief. It'll stick somewhere. You can't have chawed it, Pip.'

'Been bolting his food, has he?' cried my sister.

'You know, old chap,' said Joe, looking at me, and not at Mrs Joe, with his bite still in his cheek, 'I Bolted, myself, when I was your age, but I never see your Bolting equal yet, Pip, and it's a mercy you ain't Bolted dead.'

My sister made a dive at me, and fished me up by the hair: saying nothing more than the awful words, 'You come along and be dosed.'

Some medical beast had revived Tar-water in those days as a fine medicine, and Mrs Joe always kept a supply of it in the cupboard; having a belief in its virtues correspondent to its nastiness. On this particular evening the urgency of my case demanded a pint of this mixture, which was poured down my throat, for my greater comfort, while Mrs Joe held my head under her arm, as a boot would be held in a boot-jack. Joe got off with half a pint; but was made to swallow that (much to his disturbance, as he sat slowly munching and meditating before the fire), 'because he had had a turn.'

Conscience is a dreadful thing when it accuses man or boy; but when, in the case of a boy, that secret burden co-operates with another secret burden down the leg of his trousers, it is a great punishment. The guilty knowledge that I was going to rob Mrs Joe united to the necessity of always keeping one hand on my bread-and-butter as I sat, or when I was ordered about the kitchen on any small errand, almost drove me out of my mind. Then, as the marsh winds made the fire glow and flare, I thought I heard the voice outside, of the man with the iron on his leg who had sworn me to secrecy, declaring that he couldn't and wouldn't starve until tomorrow, but must be fed now. At other times, I thought, What if the young man should yield to a constitutional impatience, or should mistake the time, and should think himself accredited to my heart and liver tonight, instead of tomorrow! If ever anybody's hair stood on end with terror, mine must have done so then. But, perhaps, nobody's ever did?

It was Christmas Eve, and I had to stir the pudding for next day. I tried it with the load upon my leg (and that made me think afresh of the man with the load on *his* leg), and found the tendency of exercise to bring the bread-and-butter out at my ankle, quite unmanageable. Happily, I slipped away, and deposited that part of my conscience in my garret bedroom.

'Hark!' said I, when I had done my stirring, and was taking a final warm in the chimney corner before being sent up to bed; 'was that great guns, Joe?'

'Ah!' said Joe. 'There's another conwict off.'

'What does that mean, Joe?' said I.

Mrs Joe, who always took explanations upon herself, said, snappishly, 'Escaped. Escaped.' Administering the definition like Tar-water.

'There was a conwict off last night,' said Joe, aloud, 'after sunset-gun. And they fired warning of him. And now, it appears they're firing warning of another.'

'*Who's* firing?' said I.

'Drat that boy,' interposed my sister, frowning at me over her work, 'what a questioner he is. Ask no questions, and you'll be told no lies.'

'Mrs Joe,' said I, 'I should like to know – if you wouldn't much mind – where the firing comes from?'

'Lord bless the boy!' exclaimed my sister, as if she didn't quite mean that, but rather the contrary. 'From the Hulks!'

'And please what's Hulks?' said I.

'That's the way with this boy!' exclaimed my sister, pointing me out with her needle and thread, and shaking her head at me. 'Answer him one question, and he'll ask you a dozen directly. Hulks are prison-ships, right 'cross th' meshes.'

'I wonder who's put into prison-ships, and why they're put there?' said I, in a general way, and with quiet desperation.

It was too much for Mrs Joe, who immediately rose. 'I tell you what, young fellow,' said she, 'I didn't bring you up by hand to badger people's lives out. It would be blame to me, and not praise, if I had. People are put in the Hulks because they murder, and because they rob, and forge, and do all sorts of bad; and they always begin by asking questions. Now, you get along to bed!'

I was never allowed a candle to light me to bed, and, as I went upstairs in the dark, I felt fearfully sensible of the great convenience that the Hulks were handy for me. I was clearly on my way there. I had begun by asking questions, and I was going to rob Mrs Joe.

If I slept at all that night, it was only to imagine myself drifting down the river on a strong spring-tide, to the Hulks; a ghostly pirate calling out to me through a speaking-trumpet, as I passed the gibbet-station, that I had better come ashore and be hanged there at once, and not put it off. I was afraid to sleep, for I knew that at the first faint dawn of morning I must rob the pantry.

As soon as the great black velvet pall outside my little window was shot with grey, I got up and went downstairs; every board upon the way, and every crack in every board, calling after me, 'Stop thief!' and 'Get up, Mrs Joe!' In the pantry I stole some bread, some rind of cheese, about half a jar of mincemeat, some brandy from a stone bottle which I decanted into a glass bottle, diluting the stone bottle from a jug in the kitchen cupboard, a meat bone with very little on it, and a beautiful round compact pork pie.

There was a door in the kitchen, communicating with the forge; I unlocked and unbolted that door, and got a file from among Joe's tools. Then, I put the fastenings as I had found them, opened the door at which I had entered when I ran home last night, shut it, and ran for the misty marshes.

3

It was a rimy morning, and very damp. The mist was heavier yet when I got out upon the marshes, so that instead of my running at everything, everything seemed to run at me. This was very disagreeable to a guilty mind. The gates and dykes and banks came bursting at me through the mist, as if they cried as plainly as could be, 'A boy with Somebody-else's pork pie! Stop him!' The cattle came upon me with like suddenness, staring out of their eyes, and steaming out of their nostrils, 'Holloa, young thief!'

All this time, I was getting on towards the river. I knew my way to the Battery, pretty straight, for I had been down there on a Sunday with Joe.

Making my way along here with all despatch, I had just crossed a ditch which I knew to be very near the Battery, and had just scrambled up the mound beyond the ditch, when I saw the man sitting before me. His back was towards me, and he had his arms folded, and was nodding forward, heavy with sleep.

I thought he would be more glad if I came upon him with his breakfast, in that unexpected manner, so I went forward softly and touched him on the shoulder. He instantly jumped up, and it was not the same man, but another man!

And yet this man was dressed in coarse grey, too, and had a great iron on his leg, and was everything that the other man was; except that he had not the same face, and had a flat broad-brimmed low-crowned felt hat on. He swore an oath at me, made a hit at me, and then he ran into the mist, stumbling twice as he went, and I lost him.

'It's the young man!' I thought, feeling my heart shoot as I identified him. I dare say I should have felt a pain in my liver, too, if I had known where it was.

I was soon at the Battery, after that, and there was the right man waiting for me. He was awfully cold, to be sure. His eyes looked so awfully hungry, too, that when I handed him the file and he laid it down on the grass, it occurred to me he would have tried to eat it, if he had not seen my bundle. He did not turn me upside-down, this time, to get at what I had, but left me right side upwards while I opened the bundle and emptied my pockets.

'What's in the bottle, boy?' said he.

'Brandy,' said I.

He was already handing mincemeat down his throat in the most curious manner – more like a man who was putting it away somewhere in a violent hurry, than a man who was eating it – but he left off to take some of the liquor. He shivered all the while, so violently, that it was quite as much as he could do to keep the neck of the bottle between his teeth, without biting it off.

'I think you have got the ague,' said I. 'You've been

lying out on the meshes, and they're dreadful aguish. Rheumatic too.'

'I'll eat my breakfast afore they're the death of me,' said he. 'I'd do that, if I was going to be strung up to that there gallows as there is over there, directly arterwards. I'll beat the shivers so far, *I*'ll bet you.'

He was gobbling mincemeat, meatbone, bread, cheese, and pork pie, all at once: starting distrustfully while he did so at the mist all round us, and often stopping to listen. Some real or fancied sound, some clink upon the river or breathing of beast upon the marsh, now gave him a start, and he said, suddenly:

'You're not a deceiving imp? You brought no one with you?'

'No, sir! No!'

'Well,' said he, 'I believe you. You'd be but a fierce young hound indeed, if at your time of life you could help to hunt a wretched warmint, hunted as near death and dunghill as this poor wretched warmint is!'

Something clicked in his throat, and he smeared his ragged rough sleeve over his eyes.

Pitying his desolation, and watching him as he gradually settled down upon the pie, I made bold to say, 'I am glad you enjoy it.'

'Did you speak?'

'I said I was glad you enjoyed it.'

'Thankee, my boy. I do.'

'I am afraid you won't leave any of it for him,' said I, timidly.

'Leave any for him? Who's him?' said my friend, stopping in his crunching of pie-crust.

'The young man. That you spoke of. That was hid with you.'

'Oh ah!' he returned, with something like a gruff laugh. 'Him? Yes, yes! *He* don't want no wittles.'

'I thought he looked as if he did,' said I.

The man stopped eating, and regarded me with the keenest scrutiny and the greatest surprise.

'Looked? When?'

'Just now.'

'Where?'

'Yonder,' said I, pointing; 'over there, where I found him nodding asleep, and thought it was you.'

He held me by the collar and stared at me so, that I began to think his first idea about cutting my throat had revived.

'Dressed like you, you know, only with a hat,' I explained, trembling; 'and – and' – I was very anxious to put this delicately – 'and with – the same reason for wanting to borrow a file. Didn't you hear the cannon last night?'

'Then, there *was* firing!' he said to himself.

'I wonder you shouldn't have been sure of that,' I returned, 'for we heard it up at home.'

'Why, see now!' said he. 'When a man's alone on these flats, with a light head and a light stomach, perishing of cold and want, he hears nothin' all night, but guns firing, and voices calling. He sees the soldiers, with their red coats lighted up by the torches carried afore, closing in round him. Hears himself challenged, hears the rattle of the muskets, hears the orders "Make ready! Present! Cover him steady, men!" and is laid hands on – and there's nothin'! And as to firing! Why, I see the mist shake with the cannon, arter it was broad day – But this man;' he had said all the rest, as if he had forgotten my being there; 'did you notice anything in him?'

'He had a badly bruised face,' said I, recalling what I hardly knew I knew.

'Where is he?' He crammed what little food was left, into the breast of his grey jacket. 'Show me the way he went. I'll pull him down, like a bloodhound. Curse this iron on my sore leg! Give us hold of the file, boy.'

I indicated in what direction the mist had shrouded the other man, and he looked up at it for an instant. But he was down on the rank wet grass, filing at his iron like a madman, and I told him I must go, but he took no notice, so I thought the best thing I could do was to slip off. The last I saw of him, his head was bent over his knee and he was working hard at his fetter, muttering impatient imprecautions at it and at his leg. The last I heard of him, I stopped in the mist to listen, and the file was still going.

4

I fully expected to find a Constable in the kitchen, waiting to take me up. But not only was there no Constable there, but no discovery had yet been made of the robbery. Mrs Joe was prodigiously busy in getting the house ready for the festivities of the day, and Joe had been put upon the kitchen door-step to keep him out of the dust-pan.

'And where the deuce ha' *you* been?' was Mrs Joe's Christmas salutation, when I and my conscience showed ourselves.

I said I had been down to hear the Carols. 'Ah!

well!' observed Mrs Joe. 'You might ha' done worse. Perhaps if I warn't a blacksmith's wife, and a slave with her apron never off, *I* should have been to hear the Carols. I'm rather partial to Carols, myself, and that's the best of reasons for my never hearing any.'

Joe, who had ventured into the kitchen after me as the dust-pan had retired before us, drew the back of his hand across his nose with a conciliatory air and secretly crossed his two forefingers, and exhibited them to me, as our token that Mrs Joe was in a cross temper.

We were to have a superb dinner, consisting of a leg of pickled pork and greens, and a pair of roast stuffed fowls. A handsome mince-pie had been made yesterday morning (which accounted for the mincemeat not being missed), and the pudding was already on the boil.

My sister having so much to do, was going to church vicariously; that is to say, Joe and I were going. In his working clothes, Joe was a well-knit characteristic-looking blacksmith; in his holiday clothes, he was more like a scarecrow in good circumstances, than anything else. On the present festive occasion he emerged from his room, when the blithe bells were going, the picture of misery, in a full suit of Sunday penitentials. As to me, when I was taken to have a new suit of clothes, the tailor had orders to make them like a kind of Reformatory, and on no account to let me have the free use of my limbs.

Joe and I going to church, therefore, must have been a moving spectacle for compassionate minds. Yet, what I suffered outside, was nothing to what I underwent within. The terrors that had assailed me whenever Mrs Joe had gone near the pantry, or out of the room, were only to be equalled by the remorse with which my mind dwelt on what my hands had done. Under the weight of my wicked secret, I pondered whether the Church would be powerful enough to shield me from the vengeance of the terrible young man, if I divulged to that establishment. I conceived the idea that the time when the banns were read and when the clergyman said, 'Ye are now to declare it!' would be the time for me to rise and propose a private conference in the vestry. I am far from being sure that I might not have astonished our small congregation by resorting to this extreme measure, but for its being Chirstmas Day and no Sunday.

Mr Wopsle, the clerk at church, was to dine with us; and Mr Hubble the wheelwright and Mrs Hubble; and Uncle Pumblechook (Joe's uncle, but Mrs Joe appropriated him), who was a well-to-do corn-chandler in the nearest town, and drove his own chaise-cart. When Joe and I got home, we found the table laid, and Mrs Joe dressed, and the dinner dressing, and the front door unlocked for the company to enter by, and everything most splendid. And still, not a word of the robbery.

The time came, without bringing with it any relief to my feelings, and the company arrived. And I opened the door first to Mr Wopsle, next to Mr and Mrs Hubble, and last of all to Uncle Pumblechook.

'Mrs Joe,' said Uncle Pumblechook: a large hard-breathing middle-aged slow man, with a mouth like a fish, dull staring eyes, and sandy hair standing upright on his head, 'I have brought you, Mum, a bottle of sherry wine – and I have brought you, Mum, a bottle of port wine.'

Every Christmas Day he presented himself, as a

profound novelty, with exactly the same words, and carrying the two bottles like dumb-bells. Every Christmas Day, Mrs Joe replied, as she now replied, 'Oh, Un – cle Pum – ble – chook! This *is* kind!'

My sister was uncommonly lively on the present occasion, and indeed was generally more gracious in the society of Mrs Hubble than in other company. I remember Mrs Hubble as a little curly sharp-edged person in sky-blue, who held a conventionally juvenile position, because she had married Mr Hubble when she was much younger than he. I remember Mr Hubble as a tough high-shouldered stooping old man, of a sawdusty fragrance, with his legs extraordinarily wide apart: so that in my short days I always saw some miles of open country between them when I met him coming up the lane.

Among this good company I should have felt myself, even if I hadn't robbed the pantry, in a false position. Not because I was squeezed in at an acute angle of the table-cloth, with the table in my chest, and the Pumble-chookian elbow in my eye, nor because I was not allowed to speak (I didn't want to speak), no; I should not have minded that, if they would only have left me alone. But they wouldn't leave me alone.

It began the moment we sat down to dinner. Mr Wopsle said grace with theatrical declamation – as it now appears to me, something like a religious cross of the Ghost in *Hamlet* with Richard the Third – and ended with the very proper aspiration that we might be truly grateful.

'Especially,' said Mr Pumblechook, 'be grateful, boy, to them which brought you up by hand.'

Mrs Hubble shook her head, and contemplating me

with a mournful presentiment that I should come to no good, asked, 'Why is it that the young are never grateful?' This moral mystery seemed too much for the company until Mr Hubble tersely solved it by saying, 'Naterally wicious.' Everybody then murmured 'True!' and looked at me in a particularly unpleasant and personal manner.

Joe always aided and comforted me when he could, in some way of his own, and he always did so at dinner-time by giving me gravy, if there were any. There being plenty of gravy today, Joe spooned into my plate, at this point, about half a pint.

A little later on in the dinner, Mr Wopsle reviewed the sermon with some severity, and he remarked that he considered the subject of the day's homily, ill-chosen; which was the less excusable, he added, when there were so many subjects 'going about'.

'True again,' said Uncle Pumblechook. 'A man needn't go far to find a subject. Look at Pork alone. If you want a subject, look at Pork!'

'True, sir. Many a moral for the young,' returned Mr Wopsle; and I knew he was going to lug me in, before he said it; 'might be deduced from that text.'

Joe gave me some more gravy.

'Swine,' pursued Mr Wopsle, in his deepest voice, 'Swine were the companions of the prodigal. The gluttony of Swine is put before us, as an example to the young.' (I thought this pretty well in him who had been praising up the pork for being so plump and juicy.) 'What is detestable in a pig, is more detestable in a boy.'

'Or girl,' suggested Mr Hubble.

'Of course, or girl, Mr Hubble,' assented Mr Wopsle, rather irritably, 'but there is no girl present.'

'Besides,' said Mr Pumblechook, turning sharp on me, 'think what you've got to be grateful for. If you'd been born a Squeaker, would you have been here now? Not you –'

'Unless in that form,' said Mr Wopsle, nodding towards the dish.

'But I don't mean in that form, sir,' returned Mr Pumblechook, 'I mean, enjoying himself with his elders and betters, and rolling in the lap of luxury. Would he have been doing that? No, he wouldn't. And what would have been your destination?' turning on me again, 'Dunstable the butcher would have come up to you as you lay in your straw, and he would have shed your blood and had your life.'

Joe offered me more gravy, which I was afraid to take.

'He was a world of trouble to you, ma'am,' said Mrs Hubble, commiserating my sister.

'Trouble?' echoed my sister; 'trouble?' And then entered on a fearful catalogue of all the illnesses I had been guilty of, and all the times she had wished me in my grave, and I had contumaciously refused to go there.

'Yet,' said Mr Pumblechook, leading the company gently back to the theme from which they had strayed, 'Pork – regarded as biled – is rich, too; ain't it?'

'Have a little brandy, uncle,' said my sister.

O Heavens, it had come at last! He would find it was weak, and I was lost! I held tight to the leg of the table under the cloth, with both hands, and awaited my fate.

My sister went for the stone bottle, came back and poured his brandy out.

I couldn't keep my eyes off him. Holding tight by

the leg of the table with my hands and feet, I saw the miserable creature finger his glass playfully, take it up, smile, throw his head back, and drink the brandy off. Instantly afterwards, the company were seized with unspeakable consternation, owing to his springing to his feet, turning round several times in an appalling spasmodic whooping-cough dance, and rushing out at the door; he then became visible through the window, violently plunging and expectorating, making the most hideous faces, and apparently out of his mind.

I held on tight, while Mrs Joe and Joe ran to him. I didn't know how I had done it, but I had no doubt I had murdered him somehow. In my dreadful situation, it was a relief when he was brought back, and, surveying the company all round as if *they* had disagreed with him, sank down into his chair with the one significant gasp, 'Tar!'

I had filled up the bottle from the tar-water jug. I knew he would be worse by-and-by.

'Tar!' cried my sister, in amazement. 'Why, how ever could Tar come there?'

But, Uncle Pumblechook, who was omnipotent in that kitchen, wouldn't hear the word, wouldn't hear of the subject, imperiously waved it all away with his hand, and asked for hot gin-and-water. For the time at least, I was saved.

By degrees, I became calm enough to release my grasp of the table leg and partake of pudding. Mr Pumblechook partook of pudding. All partook of pudding. The course terminated, and Mr Pumblechook had begun to beam under the genial influence of gin-and-water. I began to think I should get over the day, when my sister said to Joe, 'Clean plates – cold.'

I clutched the leg of the table again. I foresaw what was coming, and I felt that this time I really was gone.

'You must taste,' said my sister, addressing the guests with her best grace, 'You must taste, to finish with, such a delightful and delicious present of Uncle Pumblechook's!'

Must they! Let them not hope to taste it!

'You must know,' said my sister, rising, 'it's a pie; a savoury pork pie.' She went out to get it. I heard her steps proceed to the pantry. I saw Mr Pumblechook balance his knife. I saw re-awakening appetite in the Roman nostrils of Mr Wopsle. I heard Mr Hubble remark that 'a bit of savoury pork pie would lay atop of anything you could mention, and do no harm,' and I heard Joe say, 'You shall have some, Pip.' I felt that I could bear no more, and that I must run away. I released the leg of the table, and ran for my life.

But, I ran no further than the house door, for there I ran head foremost into a party of soldiers with their muskets: one of whom held out a pair of handcuffs to me, saying, 'Here you are, look sharp, come on!'

5

The apparition of a file of soldiers ringing down the butt-ends of their loaded muskets on our door-step, caused the dinner-party to rise from table in confusion, and caused Mrs Joe re-entering the kitchen empty-handed, to stop short and stare, in her wondering lament of 'Gracious goodness gracious me, what's gone – with the – pie!'

It was the sergeant who had spoken to me, and he was now looking round at the company, with his handcuffs invitingly extended towards them in his right hand, and his left on my shoulder.

'Excuse me, ladies and gentlemen,' said the sergeant, 'I am on a chase in the name of the king, and I want the blacksmith.'

'And pray what might you want with *him*?' retorted my sister.

'Missis,' returned the gallant sergeant, 'speaking for myself, I should reply, the honour and pleasure of his fine wife's acquaintance; speaking for the king, I answer, a little job done. You see, blacksmith, we have had an accident with these, and I find the lock of one of 'em goes wrong, and the coupling don't act pretty. As they are wanted for immediate service, will you throw your eye over them?'

Joe pronounced that the job would necessitate the lighting of his forge fire, and would take nearer two hours than one, 'Then will you set about it at once, blacksmith?' said the off-hand sergeant, 'And if my men can bear a hand anywhere, they'll make themselves useful.' With that, he called to his men, who came trooping into the kitchen one after another, and piled their arms in a corner.

All these things I saw without then knowing that I saw them, for I was in an agony of apprehension. But, beginning to perceive that the handcuffs were not for me, and that the military had so far got the better of the pie as to put it in the background, I collected a little more of my scattered wits.

'Would you give me the Time?' said the sergeant, addressing himself to Mr Pumblechook.

'It's just gone half-past two.'

'That's not so bad,' said the sergeant, reflecting; 'even if I was forced to halt here nigh two hours, that'll do. How far might you call yourselves from the marshes, hereabouts?

'Just a mile,' said Mrs Joe.

'That'll do. We begin to close in upon 'em about dusk. A little before dusk, my orders are. That'll do.'

'Convicts, sergeant?' asked Mr Wopsle, in a matter-of-course way.

'Ay!' returned the sergeant, 'two. They're pretty well known to be out on the marshes still, and they won't try to get clear of 'em before dusk. Anybody here seen anything of any such game?'

Everybody, myself excepted, said no, with confidence. Nobody thought of me.

'Well!' said the sergeant, 'they'll find themselves trapped in a circle, I expect, sooner than they count on. Now, blacksmith! If you're ready, his Majesty the King is.'

Joe had got his coat and waistcoat and cravat off, and his leather apron on, and passed into the forge. Then he began to hammer and clink, hammer and clink, and we all looked on.

The interest of the impending pursuit not only absorbed the general attention, but even made my sister liberal. She drew a pitcher of beer from the cask, for the soldiers, and invited the sergeant to take a glass of brandy. But Mr Pumblechook said, sharply, 'Give him wine, Mum. I'll engage there's no Tar in that:' so, the sergeant thanked him and said that as he preferred his drink without tar, he would take wine, if it was equally convenient. When it was given him, he took it all at a mouthful and smacked his lips.

'Good stuff, eh, sergeant?' said Mr Pumblechook.

'I'll tell you something,' returned the sergeant; 'I suspect that stuff's of *your* providing.'

Mr Pumblechook, with a fat sort of laugh, said, 'Ay, ay? Why?'

'Because,' returned the sergeant, clapping him on the shoulder, 'you're a man that knows what's what.'

'D'ye think so?' said Mr Pumblechook, with his former laugh. 'Have another glass!'

'With you. Hob and nob,' returned the sergeant and tossed off his glass again and seemed quite ready for another glass.

At last, Joe's job was done, and the ringing and roaring stopped. As Joe got on his coat, he mustered courage to propose that some of us should go down with the soldiers and see what came of the hunt. Mr Wopsle said he would go, if Joe would. Joe said he was agreeable, and would take me, if Mrs Joe approved. We never should have got leave to go, I am sure, but for Mrs Joe's curiosity to know all about it and how it ended. As it was, she merely stipulated, 'If you bring the boy back with his head blown to bits by a musket, don't look to me to put it together again.'

The sergeant took a polite leave of the ladies, and parted from Mr Pumblechook as from a comrade. His men resumed their muskets and fell in. Mr Wopsle, Joe, and I, received strict charge to keep in the rear, and to speak no word after we reached the marshes. When we were all out in the raw air and were steadily moving towards our business, I treasonably whispered to Joe, 'I hope, Joe, we shan't find them.' And Joe whispered to me, 'I'd give a shilling if they had cut and run, Pip.'

We struck out on the open marshes, through the gate at the side of the churchyard. A bitter sleet came rattling against us here on the east wind, and Joe took me on his back.

Now that we were out upon the dismal wilderness where they little thought I had been within eight or nine hours and had seen both men hiding, I considered for the first time, with great dread, if we should come upon them, would my particular convict suppose that it was I who had brought the soldiers there?

It was of no use asking myself this question now. The soldiers were in front of us, extending into a pretty wide line with an interval between man and man. We were taking the course I had begun with, and from which I had diverged in the mist.

With my heart thumping like a blacksmith at Joe's broad shoulder, I looked all about for any sign of the convicts. I could see none, I could hear none. Mr Wopsle had greatly alarmed me more than once, by his blowing and hard breathing; but I knew the sounds by this time, and could dissociate them from the object of pursuit. I got a dreadful start, when I thought I heard the file still going; but it was only a sheep bell.

The soldiers were moving on in the direction of the old Battery, and we were moving on a little way behind them, when, all of a sudden, we all stopped. For, there had reached us on the wings of the wind and rain, a long shout. Nay, there seemed to be two or more shouts raised together — if one might judge from a confusion in the sound.

To this effect the sergeant and the nearest men were

speaking under their breath, when Joe and I can
The sergeant ordered that the sound should n
answered, but that the course should be changed,
that his men should make towards it 'at the double'.

It was a run indeed now, and what Joe called, in the
only two words he spoke all the time, 'a Winder'.
Down banks and over gates, and splashing into dykes:
no man cared where he went. As we came nearer to the
shouting, it became more and more apparent that it
was made by more than one voice. Sometimes, it
seemed to stop altogether, and then the soldiers
stopped. When it broke out again, the soldiers made
for it at a greater rate than ever, and we after them.
After a while, we had so run it down, that we could
hear one voice calling 'Murder!' and another voice,
'Convicts! Runaways! Guard! This way for the runaway convicts!' Then both voices would seem to be
stifled in a struggle, and then would break out again.

The sergeant ran in first, when we had run the noise
quite down, and two of his men ran in close upon him.
Their pieces were cocked and levelled when we all ran
in.

'Here are both men!' panted the sergeant, struggling
at the bottom of a ditch. 'Surrender, you two! and
confound you for two wild beasts! Come asunder!'

Water was splashing and blows were being struck,
when some more men went down into the ditch to
help the sergeant, and dragged out, separately, my
convict and the other one.

'Mind!' said my convict, wiping blood from his face
with his ragged sleeves, and shaking torn hair from his
fingers: '*I* took him! *I* give him up to you! Mind that!'

'It's not much to be particular about,' said the

sergeant; 'it'll do you small good, my man, being in the same plight yourself.'

'I don't want it to do me more good than it does now,' said my convict, with a greedy laugh. 'I took him. He knows it. That's enough for me.'

The other convict was livid to look at, and, in addition to the old bruised left side of his face, seemed to be bruised and torn all over. He could not so much as get his breath to speak, until they were both separately handcuffed, but leaned upon a soldier to keep himself from falling.

'Take notice, guard – he tried to murder me,' were his first words.

'Tried to murder him?' said my convict, disdainfully. 'Try, and not do it? I took him, and giv' him up. I not only prevented him getting off the marshes, but I dragged him this far on his way back.'

The other one still gasped, 'He tried – he tried – to – murder me. Bear – bear witness.'

'Lookee here!' said my convict to the sergeant. 'Single-handed I got clear of the prison-ship; I made a dash and I done it. I could ha' got clear of these death-cold flats likewise – look at my leg: you won't find much iron on it – if I hadn't made discovery that *he* was here. Let *him* go free? Let *him* profit by the means as I found out? No, no, no. If I had died at the bottom there;' and he made an emphatic swing at the ditch with his manacled hands; 'I'd have held to him with that grip, that you should have been safe to find him in my hold.'

The other fugitive, who was evidently in extreme horror of his companion, repeated, 'He tried to murder me. I should have been a dead man if you had not come up.'

'Enough of this parley,' said the sergeant. 'Light those torches.'

As one of the soldiers, who carried a basket in lieu of a gun, went down on his knee to open it, my convict looked round him for the first time, and saw me. I had alighted from Joe's back on the brink of the ditch when we came up, and had not moved since. I looked at him eagerly when he looked at me, and slightly moved my hands and shook my head. I had been waiting for him to see me, that I might try to assure him of my innocence. It was not at all expressed to me that he even comprehended my intention, for he gave me a look that I did not understand, and it all passed in a moment. But if he had looked at me for an hour or for a day, I could have remembered his face ever afterwards, as having been more attentive.

It had been almost dark before, but now it seemed quite dark. Before we departed from that spot, four soldiers standing in a ring, fired twice into the air. 'All right,' said the sergeant. 'March.'

We had not gone far when three cannon were fired ahead of us with a sound that seemed to burst something inside my ear. 'You are expected on board,' said the sergeant to my convict; 'Don't straggle, my man. Close up here.'

The two were kept apart, and each walked surrounded by a separate guard. Joe carried one of the torches. Mr Wopsle had been for going back, but Joe was resolved to see it out, so we went on with the party. Our lights warmed the air about us with their pitchy blaze, and the two prisoners seemed rather to like that, as they limped along in the midst of the muskets. We could not go fast, because of their lameness; and they were so spent, that two or three times we had to halt while they rested.

After an hour or so of this travelling, we came to a rough wooden hut and a landing-place. There was a guard in the hut, and they challenged, and the sergeant answered. Then, we went into the hut where there was a bright fire, and a lamp, and a stand of muskets, and a drum, and a low wooden bedstead, like an overgrown mangle without the machinery, capable of holding about a dozen soldiers all at once. Three or four soldiers who lay upon it in their great-coats lifted their heads and took a sleepy stare, and then lay down again. The sergeant made some kind of report, and some entry in a book, and then the convict whom I call the other convict was drafted off with his guard, to go on board first.

My convict never looked at me, except that once. While we stood in the hut, he stood before the fire looking thoughtfully at it, and looking thoughtfully at them as if he pitied them for their recent adventures. Suddenly, he turned to the sergeant, and remarked:

'I wish to say something respecting this escape. It may prevent some persons laying under suspicion alonger me.'

'You can say what you like,' returned the sergeant, 'but you have no call to say it here. You'll have opportunity enough to say about it, and hear about it, before it's done with, you know.'

'I know, but this is another pint, a separate matter. A man can't starve; at least *I* can't. I took some wittles, up at the willage over yonder.'

'You mean stole,' said the sergeant.

'And I'll tell you where from. From the blacksmith's.

It was some broken wittles – that's what it was – and a dram of liquor, and a pie.'

'Have you happened to miss such an article as a pie, blacksmith?' asked the sergeant, confidentially.

'My wife did, at the very moment when you came in. Don't you know, Pip?'

'So,' said my convict, turning his eyes on Joe in a moody manner, and without the least glance at me; 'so you're the blacksmith, are you? Then I'm sorry to say, I've eat your pie.'

'God knows you're welcome to it – so far as it was ever mine,' returned Joe, with a saving remembrance of Mrs Joe. 'We don't know what you have done, but we wouldn't have you starved to death for it, poor miserable fellow-creatur – Would us, Pip?'

The boat had returned, and the guard ready, so we followed the convict to the landing-place and saw him put into the boat, which was rowed by a crew of convicts like himself. By the light of the torches, we saw the black Hulk lying out a little way from the mud of the shore, like a wicked Noah's ark. We saw the boat go alongside, and we saw him taken up the side and disappear. Then, the ends of the torches were flung hissing into the water, and went out, as if it were all over with him.

6

I do not recall that I felt any tenderness of conscience in reference to Mrs Joe, when the fear of being found out was lifted off me. But I loved Joe – perhaps for no better reason in those early days than because the dear fellow let me love him – and, as to him, my inner self was not so easily composed. It was much upon my mind that I ought to tell Joe the whole truth. Yet I did not, and for the reason that I mistrusted that if I did, he would think me worse than I was. The fear of losing Joe's confidence, and of thenceforth sitting in the chimney-corner at night staring drearily at my for ever lost companion and friend, tied up my tongue. In a word, I was too cowardly to do what I knew to be right, as I had been too cowardly to avoid doing what I knew to be wrong.

As I was sleepy before we were far away from the prison-ship, Joe took me on his back again and carried me home. He must have had a tiresome journey of it, for Mr Wopsle, being knocked up, was in such a very bad temper that if the Church had been thrown open, he would probably have excommunicated the whole expedition, beginning with Joe and myself. In his lay capacity, he persisted in sitting down in the damp to such an insane extent, that when his coat was taken off to be dried at the kitchen fire, the circumstantial evidence on his trousers would have hanged him if it had been a capital offence.

By that time, I was staggering on the kitchen floor like a little drunkard, through having been fast asleep, and through waking in the heat and lights and noise of tongues. As I came to myself, I found Joe telling them about the convict's confession, and all the visitors suggesting different ways by which he had got into the pantry. Mr Pumblechook made out, after carefully surveying the premises, that he had first got upon the roof of the forge, and had then got upon the roof of the house, and had then let himself down the kitchen chimney by a rope made of his bedding cut into strips; and as Mr Pumblechook was very positive and drove his own chaise-cart – over everybody – it was agreed that it must be so.

This was all I heard that night before my sister assisted me up to bed with such a strong hand that I seemed to have fifty boots on, and to be dangling them all against the edges of the stairs. My state of mind, as I have described it, began before I was up in the morning, and lasted long after the subject had died out, and had ceased to be mentioned saving on exceptional occasions.

7

When I was old enough, I was to be apprenticed to Joe, and until I could assume that dignity I was not to be what Mrs Joe called 'Pompeyed,' or (as I render it) pampered. Therefore, I was not only odd-boy about the forge, but if any neighbour happened to want an extra boy to frighten birds, or pick up stones, or do any such job, I was favoured with the employment. In order, however, that our superior position might not be compromised thereby, a money-box was kept on the kitchen mantel-shelf, into which it was publicly made known that all my earnings were dropped. I have an impression that they were to be contributed eventually towards the liquidation of the National Debt, but I know I had no hope of any personal participation in the treasure.

Mr Wopsle's great-aunt kept an evening school in the village; that is to say, she was a ridiculous old woman of limited means and unlimited infirmity, who used to go to sleep from six to seven every evening, in the society of youth who paid twopence per week each, for the improving opportunity of seeing her do it. She rented a small cottage, and Mr Wopsle had the room upstairs, where we students used to overhear him reading aloud in a most dignified and terrific manner, and occasionally bumping on the ceiling.

Mr Wopsle's great-aunt kept – in the same room as the school – a little general shop. There was a little greasy memorandum-book kept in a drawer, which served as a Catalogue of Prices, and by this oracle Biddy arranged all the shop transactions. Biddy was Mr Wopsle's great-aunt's grandaughter. She was an orphan like myself; like me, too, had been brought up by hand. She was most noticeable, I thought, in respect of her extremities; for, her hair always wanted brushing, her hands always wanted washing, and her shoes always wanted mending and pulling up at heel.

Much of my unassisted self, and more by the help of Biddy than of Mr Wopsle's great-aunt, I struggled through the alphabet as if it had been a bramble-bush; getting considerably worried and scratched by every letter. After that, I fell among those thieves, the nine figures, who seemed every evening to do something new to disguise themselves and baffle recognition. But, at last I began, in a purblind groping way, to read, write, and cipher, on the very smallest scale.

One night, I was sitting in the chimney-corner with my slate, expending great efforts on the production of a letter to Joe. With an alphabet on the hearth at my feet for reference, I contrived in an hour or two to print and smear this epistle:

mI deEr JO i opE U r krWitE wEll i opE i shAl soN B haBelL 4 2 teeDge U JO aN theN wE shOrl b sO glOdd aN wEn i M preNgtD 2 u JO woT larX an blEvE ME inF xn PiP.

I delivered this written communication (slate and all) with my own hand, and Joe received it as a miracle of erudition.

'I say, Pip, old chap!' cried Joe, opening his blue eyes wide, 'what a scholar you are! An't you?'

'I should like to be,' said I.

'Why, here's a J,' said Joe, 'and a O equal to any-think! Here's a J and a O, Pip, and a J-O, Joe.'

I said, 'Ah! But read the rest, Jo.'

'The rest, eh, Pip?' said Joe, looking at it with a slowly searching eye, 'One, two, three. Why, here's three Js, and three Os, and three J-O, Joes in it, Pip!'

I leaned over Joe, and, with the aid of my forefinger, read him the whole letter.

'Astonishing!' said Joe, when I had finished. 'You ARE a scholar.'

'Didn't you ever go to school, Joe, when you were as little as me?' I enquired.

'No, Pip.'

'Why didn't you ever go to school, Joe, when you were as little as me?'

'Well, Pip,' said Joe, taking up the poker, and slowly raking the fire between the lower bars: 'I'll tell you. My father, Pip, he were given to drink, and when he were overtook with drink, he hammered away at my mother, most onmerciful. And he hammered at me with a wigour only to be equalled by the wigour with which he didn't hammer at his anwil. 'Consequence, my mother and me ran away from my father, several times; and then my mother she'd go out to work, and she'd say, "Joe," she'd say, "now, please God, you shall have some schooling, child," and she'd put me to school. But my father were that good in his hart that he couldn't abear to be without us. So, he'd come and make such a row at the doors of the houses where we was, that they used to be obligated to have no more to do with us and to give us up to him. And then he took us home and hammered us. Which, you see, Pip,' said Joe, pausing in his meditative raking of the fire, and looking at me, 'were a drawback on my learning.'

'Certainly, poor Joe!'

'Though mind you, Pip,' said Joe, 'my father were that good in his hart, don't you see?'

I didn't see; but I didn't say so.

'Well!' Joe pursued, 'somebody must keep the pot a biling, Pip, or the pot won't bile, don't you know?'

I saw that, and said so.

'Consequence, my father didn't make objections to my going to work; so I went to work at my present calling, and I worked tolerable hard, I assure you, Pip. In time I were able to keep him, and I kep him till he went off in a purple leptic fit. And it were my intentions to have had put upon his tombstone that Whatsume'er the failings on his part, Remember reader he were that good in his hart.'

Joe recited this couplet with such manifest pride that I asked him if he had made it himself.

'I made it,' said Joe, 'my own self. As I was saying, Pip, it were my intentions to have had it cut over him; but poetry costs money and it were not done. Not to mention bearers, all the money that could be spared were wanted for my mother. She were in poor elth, and quite broke. She weren't long of following, poor soul, and her share of peace come round at last.'

Joe's blue eyes turned a little watery; he rubbed, first one of them, and then the other, in a most uncongenial and uncomfortable manner, with the round knob on the top of the poker.

'It were but lonesome then,' said Joe, 'living here alone, and I got acquainted with your sister. Now, Pip;' Joe looked firmly at me, as if he knew I was not going to agree with him; 'your sister is a fine figure of a woman.'

I could think of nothing better to say than 'I am glad you think so, Joe.'

'When I got acquainted with your sister,' said Joe, 'it were the talk how she was bringing you up by hand. Very kind of her too, all the folks said, and I said, along with all the folks. As to you,' Joe pursued, with a countenance expressive of seeing something very nasty indeed: 'if you could have been aware how small and flabby and mean you was, dear me, you'd have formed the most contemptible opinions of yourself!'

Not exactly relishing this, I said, 'Never mind me, Joe.'

'But I did mind you, Pip,' he returned, with tender simplicity. 'When I offered to your sister to keep company, and to be asked in church at such times as she was willing and ready to come to the forge, I said to her, "And bring the poor little child. There's room for *him* at the forge!"'

I broke out crying and begging pardon, and hugged Joe round the neck.

When this little interruption was over, Joe resumed:

'Well, you see, Pip, and here we are! Now, when you take me in hand in my learning, Pip (and I tell you beforehand I am awful dull, most awful dull), Mrs Joe mustn't see too much of what we're up to. It must be done, as I may say, on the sly. And why on the sly? I'll tell you why, Pip. Your sister an't over partial to having scholars on the premises, and in partickler would not be over partial to my being a scholar, for fear as I might rise. Like a sort of rebel, don't you see?'

I was going to retort with an enquiry, and had got as far as 'Why –' when Joe stopped me.

'Stay a bit. I know what you're a-going to say, Pip; stay a bit! I don't deny that your sister do drop down upon us heavy. At such times as when your sister is on the rampage, Pip,' Joe sank his voice to a whisper and glanced at the door, 'candour compels fur to admit that she is a Buster.'

Joe pronounced this word, as if it began with at least twelve capital Bs.

'Why don't I rise? That were your observation when I broke it off, Pip?'

'Yes, Joe.'

'Well,' said Joe, 'your sister's a master-mind. A master-mind.'

'What's that?' I asked, in some hope of bringing him to a stand. But, Joe was readier with his definition than I had expected, and completely stopped me by arguing circularly, and answering with a fixed look, 'Her.'

'And I an't a master-mind,' Joe resumed, when he had unfixed his look. 'And last of all, Pip – and this I want to say very serous to you, old chap, I'm dead afeerd of going wrong in the way of not doing what's right by a woman, and I'd fur rather of the two go wrong the t'other way, and be a little ill-conwenienced myself. I wish there warn't no Tickler for you, old chap; I wish I could take it all on myself; but this is the up-and-down-and-straight on it, Pip, and I hope you'll overlook shortcomings.'

Young as I was, I believe that I dated a new admiration of Joe from that night. We were equals afterwards, as we had been before; but, afterwards at quiet times when I sat looking at Joe and thinking about him, I had a new sensation of feeling conscious that I was looking up to Joe in my heart.

'However,' said Joe, rising to replenish the fire; 'here's the Dutch-clock a working himself up to being equal to strike Eight of 'em, and she's not come home yet!'

Mrs Joe made occasional trips with Uncle Pumblechook on market-days, to assist him in buying such household stuffs and goods as required a woman's judgement. This was market-day, and Mrs Joe was out on one of these expeditions.

Joe and I went to the door to listen for the chaise-cart. It was a dry cold night, and the wind blew keenly, and the frost was white and hard. A man would die tonight of lying out on the marshes, I thought. And then I looked at the stars, and considered how awful it would be for a man to turn his face up to them as he froze to death, and see no help or pity in all the glittering multitude.

'Here comes the mare,' said Joe, 'ringing like a peal of bells!'

We got a chair out, ready for Mrs Joe's alighting, and she was soon landed, and Uncle Pumblechook was soon down too, covering the mare with a cloth, and we were soon all in the kitchen, carrying so much cold air in with us that it seemed to drive all the heat out of the fire.

'Now,' said Mrs Joe, unwrapping herself with haste and excitement, 'if this boy an't grateful this night, he never will be!'

I looked as grateful as any boy possibly could, who was wholly uninformed why he ought to assume that expression.

'It's only to be hoped,' said my sister, 'that he won't be Pompeyed. But I have my fears.'

'She an't in that line, Mum,' said Mr Pumblechook. 'She knows better.'

She? I looked at Joe, making the motion with my lips and eyebrows, 'She?' Joe looked at me, making the motion with *his* lips and eyebrows, 'She?'

'Well?' said my sister, in her snappish way. 'What are you staring at? Is the house a-fire?'

'– Which some individual,' Joe politely hinted, 'mentioned – she.'

'And she is a she, I suppose?' said my sister. 'Unless you call Miss Havisham a he. And I doubt if even you'll go so far as that.'

'Miss Havisham, up town?' said Joe.

'Is there any Miss Havisham down town?' returned my sister. 'She wants this boy to go and play there. And he had better play there,' said my sister, shaking her head at me as an encouragement to be extremely light and sportive, 'or I'll work him.'

I had heard of Miss Havisham up town as an

immensely rich and grim lady who lived in a large and dismal house barricaded against robbers, and who led a life of seclusion.

'Well to be sure!' said Joe, astounded. 'I wonder how she come to know Pip!'

'Noodle!' cried my sister. 'Who said she knew him?'

'– Which some individual,' Joe again politely hinted, 'mentioned that she wanted him to go and play there.'

'And couldn't she ask Uncle Pumblechook if he knew of a boy to go and play there? Isn't it just barely possible that Uncle Pumblechook may be a tenant of hers, and that he may sometimes go there to pay his rent? And couldn't she then ask Uncle Pumblechook if he knew of a boy to go and play there? And couldn't Uncle Pumblechook, being always considerate and thoughtful for us then mention this boy, standing Prancing here' – which I solemnly declare I was not doing – 'that I have for ever been a willing slave to?'

'Good again!' cried Uncle Pumblechook. 'Good indeed! Now Joseph, you know the case.'

'No, Joseph,' said my sister, still in a reproachful manner, 'you do not yet know the case. You do not know that Uncle Pumblechook has offered to take him into town tonight in his own chaise-cart, and to keep him tonight, and to take him with his own hands to Miss Havisham's tomorrow morning.'

With that, she pounced upon me and my head was put under taps of water-butts, and I was soaped, and kneaded, and towelled, and thumped, and harrowed, and rasped, until I really was quite beside myself.

When my ablutions were completed, I was put into clean linen of the stiffest character, and was trussed up in my tightest and fearfullest suit. I was then delivered over to Mr Pumblechook, who let off upon me the speech that I knew he had been dying to make all along: 'Boy, be for ever grateful to all friends, but especially unto them which brought you up by hand!'

'Goodbye, Joe!'

'God bless you, Pip, old chap!'

I had never parted from him before, and what with my feelings and what with soap-suds, I could at first see no stars from the chaise-cart. But they twinkled out one by one, without throwing any light on the questions why on earth I was going to play at Miss Havisham's and what on earth I was expected to play at.

8

Mr Pumblechook and I breakfasted at eight o'clock the following morning in the parlour behind his corn-chandler's shop, while the shopman took his mug of tea and hunch of bread-and-butter on a sack of peas in the front premises. I considered Mr Pumblechook wretched company. On my politely bidding him Good-morning, he said, pompously, 'Seven times nine, boy?' I was hungry, but before I had swallowed a morsel, he began a running sum that lasted all through the breakfast. 'Seven?' 'And four?' 'And eight?' 'And six?' 'And two?' 'And ten?' And so on. And after each figure was disposed of, it was as much as I could do to get a bite or a sup, before the next came.

For such reasons I was very glad when ten o'clock

came and we started for Miss Havisham's; though I was not at all at my ease regarding the manner in which I should acquit myself under that lady's roof. Within a quarter of an hour we came to Miss Havisham's house, which was of old brick, and dismal, and had a great many iron bars to it. There was a court-yard in front, and that was barred; so, we had to wait, after ringing the bell, until some one should come to open it. While we waited at the gate, I peeped in, and saw that at the side of the house there was a large brewery. No brewing was going on in it, and none seemed to have gone on for a long long time.

A window was raised, and a clear voice demanded 'What name?' To which my conductor replied, 'Pumblechook.' The voice returned, 'Quite right,' and the window was shut again, and a young lady came across the court-yard, with keys in her hand.

'This,' said Mr Pumblechook, 'is Pip.'

'This is Pip, is it?' returned the young lady, who was very pretty and seemed very proud; 'come in, Pip.'

Mr Pumblechook was coming in also, when she stopped him with the gate.

'Oh!' she said. 'Did you wish to see Miss Havisham?'

'If Miss Havisham wished to see me,' returned Mr Pumblechook, discomfited.

'Ah!' said the girl; 'but you see she don't.'

She said it so finally, and in such an undiscussible way, that Mr Pumblechook, though in a condition of ruffled dignity, could not protest. But he eyed me severely – as if I had done anything to him! – and departed with the words reproachfully delivered: 'Boy!

Let your behaviour here be a credit unto them which brought you up by hand!'

My young conductress locked the gate, and we went across the court-yard. It was paved and clean, but grass was growing in every crevice. The brewery buildings had a little lane of communication with it; and the wooden gates of that lane stood open, and all the brewery beyond was empty and disused.

She saw me looking at it, and she said, 'You could drink without hurt all the strong beer that's brewed there now, boy.'

'I should think I could, miss,' said I, in a shy way.

'Not that anybody means to try to brew beer,' she added, 'for that's all done with, and the place will stand as idle as it is, till it falls. As to strong beer, there's enough of it in the cellars already, to drown the Manor House.'

'Is that the name of this house, miss?'

'One of its names, boy.'

'It has more than one, then, miss?'

'One more. Its other name was Satis; which is Greek, or Latin, or Hebrew, or all three – or all one to me – for enough.'

'Enough House,' said I; 'that's a curious name, miss.'

'Yes,' she replied; 'it meant, when it was given, that whoever had this house, could want nothing else. They must have been easily satisfied in those days, I should think. But don't loiter, boy.'

Though she called me 'boy' so often, she was of about my own age. She seemed much older than I, of course, being a girl, and beautiful and self-possessed; and she was as scornful of me as if she had been one-and-twenty, and a queen.

We went into the house by a side door and the first thing I noticed was, that the passages were all dark, and that she had left a candle burning there. She took it up, and we went through more passages and up a staircase.

At last we came to the door of a room, and she said, 'Go in.'

I answered, more in shyness than politeness, 'After you, miss.'

To this, she returned: 'Don't be ridiculous, boy; I am not going in.' And scornfully walked away, and – what was worse – took the candle with her.

This was very uncomfortable, and I was half afraid. However, the only thing to be done being to knock at the door, I knocked, and was told from within to enter. I entered, therefore, and found myself in a pretty large room, well lighted with wax candles. No glimpse of daylight was to be seen in it. It was a dressing-room, as I supposed from the furniture, though much of it was of forms and uses then quite unknown to me. But prominent in it was a draped table with a gilded looking-glass, and that I made out at first sight to be a fine lady's dressing-table.

Whether I should have made out this object so soon, if there had been no fine lady sitting at it, I cannot say. In an arm-chair, with an elbow resting on the table and her head leaning on that hand, sat the strangest lady I have ever seen, or shall ever see.

She was dressed in rich materials – satins, and lace, and silks – all of white. Her shoes were white. And she had a long white veil dependent from her hair, and she had bridal flowers in her hair, but her hair was white. Some bright jewels sparkled on her neck and on her hands, and some other jewels lay sparkling on the table. Dresses, less splendid than the dress she wore, and half-packed trunks, were scattered about. She had not quite finished dressing, for she had but one shoe on – the other was on the table near her hand – her veil was but half arranged, her watch and chain were not put on, and some lace for her bosom lay with those trinkets, and with her handkerchief, and gloves, and some flowers, and a prayer-book, all confusedly heaped about the looking-glass.

I saw that everything within my view which ought to be white, had been white long ago, and had lost its lustre, and was faded and yellow. I saw that the bride within the bridal dress had withered like the dress, and like the flowers, and had no brightness left but the brightness of her sunken eyes. I saw that the dress had been put upon the rounded figure of a young woman, and that the figure upon which it now hung loose, had shrunk to skin and bone.

'Who is it?' said the lady at the table.

'Pip, ma'am.'

'Pip?'

'Mr Pumblechook's boy, ma'am. Come – to play.'

'Come nearer; let me look at you. Come close.'

It was when I stood before her, avoiding her eyes, that I took note of the surrounding objects in detail, and saw that her watch had stopped at twenty minutes to nine, and that a clock in the room had stopped at twenty minutes to nine.

'Look at me,' said Miss Havisham. 'You are not afraid of a woman who has never seen the sun since you were born?'

I regret to state that I was not afraid of telling the enormous lie comprehended in the answer 'No.'

'Do you know what I touch here?' she said, laying her hands, one upon the other, on her left side.

'Yes, ma'am.' (It made me think of the young man.)

'What do I touch?'

'Your heart.'

'Broken!'

She uttered the word with an eager look, and with strong emphasis, and with a weird smile that had a kind of boast in it.

'I sometimes have sick fancies,' said Miss Havisham, 'and I have a sick fancy that I want to see some play. There, there!' with an impatient movement of the fingers of her right hand; 'play, play, play!'

For a moment, with the fear of my sister's working me before my eyes, I had a desperate idea of starting round the room in the assumed character of Mr Pumblechook's chaise-cart. But, I felt myself so unequal to the performance that I gave it up, and stood looking at Miss Havisham in what I suppose she took for a dogged manner, inasmuch as she said, when we had taken a good look at each other:

'Are you sullen and obstinate?'

'No, ma'am, I am very sorry for you, and very sorry I can't play just now. If you complain of me I shall get into trouble with my sister, so I would do it if I could; but it's so new here, and so strange, and so fine – and melancholy.'

Before she spoke again, she turned her eyes from me, and looked at herself in the looking-glass.

'So new to him,' she muttered, 'so old to me; so strange to him, so familiar to me; so melancholy to both of us! Call Estella.'

To stand in the dark in a mysterious passage of an

unknown house, bawling Estella to a scornful young lady neither visible nor responsive, was almost as bad as playing to order. But, she answered at last, and her light came along the dark passage like a star.

Miss Havisham beckoned her to come close, and took up a jewel from the table, and tried its effect upon her fair young bosom and against her pretty brown hair. 'Your own, one day, my dear, and you will use it well. Let me see you play cards with this boy.'

'With this boy! Why, he is a common labouring-boy!'

I thought I overheard Miss Havisham answer – only it seemed so unlikely – 'Well? You can break his heart.'

'What do you play, boy?' asked Estella of myself, with the greatest disdain.

'Nothing but beggar my neighbour, miss.'

'Beggar him,' said Miss Havisham to Estella. So we sat down to cards.

It was then I began to understand that everything in the room had stopped, like the watch and the clock, a long time ago. I noticed that Miss Havisham put down the jewel exactly on the spot from which she had taken it up. As Estella dealt the cards, I glanced at the dressing-table again, and saw that the shoe upon it, once white, now yellow, had never been worn. I glanced down at the foot from which the shoe was absent, and saw that the silk stocking on it, once white, now yellow, had been trodden ragged. Without this arrest of everything, this standing still of all the pale decayed objects, not even the withered bridal dress on the collapsed form could have looked so like grave-clothes, or the long veil so like a shroud.

So she sat, corpse-like, as we played at cards; the frillings and trimmings on her bridal dress, looking like earthy paper.

'He calls the Knaves Jacks, this boy!' said Estella with disdain, before our first game was out. 'And what coarse hands he has! And what thick boots!'

I had never thought of being ashamed of my hands before; but I began to consider them a very indifferent pair. Her contempt for me was so strong, that it became infectious, and I caught it.

She won the game, and I dealt. I misdealt, as was only natural, when I knew she was lying in wait for me to do wrong; and she denounced me for a stupid, clumsy labouring-boy.

'You say nothing of her,' remarked Miss Havisham to me, as she looked on. 'She says many hard things of you, but you say nothing of her. What do you think of her?'

'I think she is very proud,' I replied, in a whisper.

'Anything else?'

'I think she is very pretty.'

'Anything else?'

'I think she is very insulting.'

'Anything else?'

'I think I should like to go home.'

'You shall go soon,' said Miss Havisham, aloud. 'Play the game out.'

I played the game to an end with Estella, and she beggared me. She threw the cards down on the table when she had won them all, as if she despised them for having been won of me.

'When shall I have you here again?' said Miss Havisham. 'Let me think.'

I was beginning to remind her that today was Wednesday, when she checked me with her former impatient movement of the fingers of her right hand.

'There, there! I know nothing of days of the week; I know nothing of weeks of the year. Come again after six days. You hear?'

'Yes, ma'am.'

'Estella, take him down. Let him have something to eat, and let him roam and look about him while he eats. Go, Pip.'

I followed the candle down, and she stood it in the place where we had found it. Until she opened the side entrance, I had fancied that it must necessarily be night-time. The rush of the daylight quite confounded me, and made me feel as if I had been in the candlelight of the strange room many hours.

'You are to wait here, you boy,' said Estella; and disappeared and closed the door.

I took the opportunity of being alone in the court-yard, to look at my coarse hands and my common boots. They had never troubled me before, but they troubled me now, as vulgar appendages. I determined to ask Joe why he had ever taught me to call those picture-cards, Jacks, which ought to be called Knaves. I wished Joe had been rather more genteelly brought up, and then I should have been so too.

She came back, with some bread and meat and a little mug of beer. She put the mug down on the stones of the yard, and gave me the bread and meat without looking at me, as insolently as if I were a dog in disgrace. I was so humiliated, hurt, spurned, of-fended, angry, sorry that tears started to my eyes. The moment they sprang there, the girl looked at me with a quick delight in having been the cause of them. This gave me power to keep them back and to look at her: so, she gave a contemptuous toss – but with a sense, I thought, of having made too sure that I was so wounded – and left me.

But, when she was gone, I looked about me for a place to hide my face in, and got behind one of the gates in the brewery-lane, and leaned my sleeve against the wall there, and leaned my forehead on it and cried. As I cried, I kicked the wall, and took a hard twist at my hair.

I got rid of my injured feelings for the time, by kicking them into the brewery wall, and twisting them out of my hair, and then I smoothed my face with my sleeve, and came from behind the gate.

To be sure, it was a deserted place, down to the pigeon-house in the brewery-yard, which had been blown crooked on its pole by some high wind, and would have made the pigeons think themselves at sea, if there had been any pigeons there to be rocked by it. But, there were no pigeons in the dove-cot, no horses in the stable, no smells of grains and beer in the copper or the vat. All the uses and scents of the brewery might have evaporated with its last reek of smoke. In a by yard, there was a wilderness of empty casks though, which had a certain sour remembrance of better days lingering about them.

Behind the furthest end of the brewery, was a rank garden with an old wall: not so high but that I could struggle up to look over it, and see that the rank garden was the garden of the house, and that it was overgrown with tangled weeds, but that there was a track upon the green and yellow paths, as if some one sometimes walked there, and that Estella was walking away from me even then. But she seemed to be everywhere. For, when I yielded to the temptation presented by the casks, and began to walk on them, I saw *her* walking on them at the end of the yard of casks. She had her back towards me, and held her pretty brown hair spread out in her two hands, and never looked round, and passed out of my view directly. When I first went into the brewery itself, and stood near the door looking about me, I saw her ascend some light iron stairs, and go out by a gallery high overhead, as if she were going out into the sky.

It was in this place, and at this moment, that a strange thing happened to my fancy. I turned my eyes towards a great wooden beam in a low nook of the building near me on my right hand, and I saw a figure hanging there by the neck. A figure all in yellow white, with but one shoe to the feet; and it hung so, that I could see that the faded trimmings of the dress were like earthy paper, and that the face was Miss Havisham's. In the terror of seeing the figure, and in the terror of being certain that it had not been there a moment before, I at first ran from it, and then ran towards it. And my terror was greatest of all, when I found no figure there.

I might not have come to myself as soon as I did, but that I saw Estella approaching with the keys, to let me out. She would have some fair reason for looking down upon me, I thought, if she saw me frightened; and she should have no fair reason.

I was passing out without looking at her, when she touched me with a taunting hand.

'Why don't you cry?'

'Because I don't want to.'

'You do,' said she. 'You have been crying till you are half blind, and you are near crying again now.'

She laughed contemptuously, pushed me out, and locked the gate upon me. I went straight to Mr Pumblechook's, and was immensely relieved to find him not at home. So, leaving word with the shopman on what day I was wanted at Miss Havisham's again, I set off on the four-mile walk to our forge; pondering, as I went along, on all I had seen, and deeply revolving that I was a common labouring-boy; that my hands were coarse; that my boots were thick; that I had fallen into a despicable habit of calling Knaves Jacks; that I was much more ignorant than I had considered myself last night, and generally that I was in a low-lived bad way.

9

When I reached home, my sister was very curious to know all about Miss Havisham's, and asked a number of questions. I felt convinced that if I described Miss Havisham's as my eyes had seen it, I should not be understood. Not only that, but I felt convinced that Miss Havisham too would not be understood; and although she was perfectly incomprehensible to me, I entertained an impression that there would be something coarse and treacherous in my dragging her as she really was (to say nothing of Miss Estella) before the contemplation of Mrs Joe. Consequently, I said as little as I could.

The worst of it was that that bullying old Pumblechook, came gaping over in his chaise-cart at tea-time,
to have the details divulged to him.

'Well, boy,' Uncle Pumblechook began, as soon as
he was seated in the chair of honour by the fire. 'How
did you get on up town?'

I answered, 'Pretty well, sir,' and my sister shook
her fist at me.

'Pretty well?' Mr Pumblechook repeated. 'Tell us
what you mean by pretty well, boy?'

I then answered as if I had discovered a new idea, 'I
mean pretty well.'

My sister with an exclamation of impatience was
going to fly at me when Mr Pumblechook interposed
with 'No! Don't lose your temper. Leave this lad to
me, ma'am; leave this lad to me.' Mr Pumblechook
then turned me towards him, as if he were going to cut
my hair, and said:

'Boy! What like is Miss Havisham?'

'Very tall and dark,' I told him.

'Is she, uncle?' asked my sister.

Mr Pumblechook winked assent; from which I at
once inferred that he had never seen Miss Havisham,
for she was nothing of the kind.

'Good!' said Mr Pumblechook conceitedly. 'Now,
boy! What was she a doing of, when you went in
today?'

'She was sitting,' I answered, 'in a black velvet
coach. And Miss Estella – that's her niece, I think –
handed her in cake and wine at the coach-window, on
a gold plate. And we all had cake and wine on gold
plates. And I got up behind the coach to eat mine,
because she told me to.'

'Was anybody else there?' asked Mr Pumblechook.

'Four dogs,' said I.

'Large or small?'

'Immense,' said I. 'And they fought for veal cutlets out of a silver basket.'

Mr Pumblechook and Mrs Joe stared at one another in utter amazement.

'Where *was* this coach, in the name of gracious?' asked my sister.

'In Miss Havisham's room.' They stared again. 'But there weren't any horses to it.' I added this saving clause, in the moment of rejecting four richly caparisoned coursers which I had had wild thoughts of harnessing.

'Can this be possible, uncle?' asked Mrs Joe. 'What can the boy mean?'

'I'll tell you, Mum,' said Mr Pumblechook. 'My opinion is, it's a sedan-chair.'

'Did you ever see her in it, uncle?' asked Mrs Joe.

'How could I,' he returned, forced to the admission, 'when I never see her in my life? Never clapped eyes upon her!'

'Goodness, uncle! And yet you have spoken to her?'

'Why, don't you know,' said Mr Pumblechook, testily, 'that when I have been there, I have been took up to the outside of her door, and the door has stood ajar, and she has spoke to me that way. Howsever, the boy went there to play. What did you play at, boy?'

'We played with flags,' I said.

'Flags!' echoed my sister.

'Yes,' said I. 'Estella waved a blue flag, and I waved a red one, and Miss Havisham waved one sprinkled all over with little gold stars, out at the coach-window. And then we all waved our swords and hurrahed.'

'Swords!' repeated my sister. 'Where did you get swords from?'

'Out of a cupboard,' said I. 'And there was no daylight in the room, but it was all lighted up with candles.'

'That's true, Mum,' said Mr Pumblechook, with a grave nod. 'That's the state of the case, for that much I've seen myself.'

If they had asked me any more questions I should undoubtedly have betrayed myself, for I was even then on the point of mentioning that there was a balloon in the yard, and a bear in the brewery. They were so much occupied, however, in discussing the marvels I had already presented for their consideration, that I escaped. The subject still held them when Joe came in from his work to have a cup of tea. To whom my sister, more for the relief of her own mind than for the gratification of his, related my pretended experiences.

Now, when I saw Joe open his blue eyes and roll them all round the kitchen in helpless amazement, I was overtaken by penitence; but only as regarded him – not in the least as regarded the other two, who sat debating what results would come to me from Miss Havisham's acquaintance and favour. They had no doubt that Miss Havisham would 'do something' for me. My sister stood out for 'property.' Mr Pumblechook was in favour of a handsome premium for binding me apprentice to some genteel trade. Joe fell into the deepest disgrace with both, for offering the bright suggestion that I might only be presented with one of the dogs who had fought for the veal-cutlets. 'If a fool's head can't express better opinions than that,' said my sister, 'and you have got any work to do, you had better go and do it.' So he went.

After Mr Pumblechook had driven off, I stole into the forge to Joe, and remained by him until he had done for the night. Then I said, 'Before the fire goes out, Joe, I should like to tell you something.'

'Should you, Pip?' said Joe. 'Then tell us. What is it, Pip?'

'Joe,' said I, taking hold of his rolled-up shirt sleeve, and twisting it between my finger and thumb, 'you remember all that about Miss Havisham's?'

'Remember?' said Joe. 'I believe you! Wonderful!'

'It's a terrible thing, Joe; it ain't true. It's all lies.'

'Why sure you don't mean to say, Pip, that there was no black welwet co – eh?' For, I stood shaking my head. 'But at least there was dogs, Pip?'

'No, Joe.'

As I fixed my eyes hopelessly on Joe, Joe contemplated me in dismay. 'Pip, old chap! This won't do, old fellow! I say! Where do you expect to go to?'

'I don't know what possessed me, Joe,' I replied, letting his shirt sleeve go, and sitting down in the ashes at his feet, hanging my head; 'but I wish you hadn't taught me to call Knaves at cards, Jacks; and I wish my boots weren't so thick nor my hands so coarse.'

And then I told Joe that I felt very miserable, and that I hadn't been able to explain myself to Mrs Joe and Pumblechook who were so rude to me, and that there had been a beautiful young lady at Miss Havisham's who had said I was common, and that I wished I was not common, and that the lies had come of it somehow, though I didn't know how.

'There's one thing you may be sure of, Pip,' said Joe, after some rumination, 'namely, that lies is lies. Don't you tell no more of 'em, Pip. *That* ain't the way to get out of being common, old chap. And as to being common, I don't make it out at all clear. You are oncommon in some things. You're oncommon small. Likewise you're a oncommon scholar.'

'No, I am ignorant and backward, Joe.'

'Why, see what a letter you wrote last night! Wrote in print even! I've seen letters – Ah! and from gentle-folks! – that I'll swear weren't wrote in print,' said Joe.

'I have learnt next to nothing, Joe. You think much of me. It's only that.'

'Well, Pip,' said Joe, 'be it so or be it son't, you must be a common scholar afore you can be a oncommon one, I should hope! The king can't sit and write his acts of Parliament in print, without having begun, when he were a unpromoted Prince, with the alphabet – Ah!' added Joe, with a shake of the head that was full of meaning, 'and begun at A too, and worked his way to Z.'

There was some hope in this piece of wisdom, and it rather encouraged me.

'Whether common ones as to callings and earnings,' pursued Joe, reflectively, 'mightn't be the better of continuing for to keep company with common ones, instead of going out to play with oncommon ones – which reminds me to hope that there were a flag, perhaps?'

'No, Joe.'

'(I'm sorry there weren't a flag, Pip.) Whether that might be, or mightn't be, is a thing as can't be looked into now, without putting your sister on the rampage.

Lookee here, Pip, at what is said to you by a true
friend. If you can't get to be oncommon through going
straight, you'll never get to do it through going
crooked. So don't tell no more on 'em, Pip.'

'You are not angry with me, Joe?'

'No, old chap. But bearing in mind that them were
which I meantersay of a stunning and outdacious sort
– alluding to them which bordered on weal-cutlets and
dog-fighting – a sincere well-wisher would adwise,
Pip, their being dropped into your meditations, when
you go upstairs to bed. That's all, old chap, and don't
never do it no more.'

When I got up to my little room and said my
prayers, I did not forget Joe's recommendation, and
yet my young mind was in that disturbed and unthankful state, that I thought long after I laid me down, how
common Estella would consider Joe, a mere blacksmith: how thick his boots, and how coarse his hands.

That was a memorable day to me, for it made great
changes in me. But, it is the same with any life. Pause
you who read this, and think for a moment of the long
chain of iron or gold, of thorns or flowers, that would
never have bound you, but for the formation of the
first link on one memorable day.

10

The felicitous idea occurred to me a morning or two
later when I woke, that the best step I could take
towards making myself uncommon was to get out of

Biddy everything she knew. In pursuance of this lumi-
nous conception I mentioned to Biddy when I went to
Mr Wopsle's great-aunt's at night, that I had a particular reason for wishing to get on in life, and that I
should feel very much obliged to her if she would
impart all her learning to me. Biddy, who was the
most obliging of girls, immediately said she would.

That very evening Biddy entered on our special
agreement, by imparting some information from her
little catalogue of Prices, under the head of moist
sugar, and lending me, to copy at home, a large old
English D which she had imitated from the heading of
some newspaper, and which I supposed, until she told
me what it was, to be a design for a buckle.

Of course there was a public-house in the village,
and of course Joe liked sometimes to smoke his pipe
there. I had received strict orders from my sister to
call for him at the Three Jolly Bargemen, that evening,
on my way from school, and bring him home at my
peril. To the Three Jolly Bargemen, therefore, I directed my steps.

I found the landlord, but as my business was with
Joe and not with him, I merely wished him good-
evening, and passed into the common room at the end
of the passage, where Joe was smoking his pipe in
company with Mr Wopsle and a stranger. Joe greeted
me as usual with 'Halloa, Pip, old chap!' and the
moment he said that, the stranger turned his head and
looked at me.

He was a secret-looking man whom I had never seen
before. His head was all on one side, and one of his
eyes was half shut up, as if he were taking aim at
something with an invisible gun. He had a pipe in his

mouth, and he took it out, and, after slowly blowing all his smoke away and looking hard at me all the time, nodded. So, I nodded, and then he nodded again, and made room on the settle beside him that I might sit down there.

But, as I was used to sit beside Joe whenever I entered that place of resort, I said 'No, thank you, sir,' and fell into the space Joe made for me on the opposite settle.

'You was saying,' said the strange man, turning to Joe, 'that you was a blacksmith.'

'Yes. I said it, you know,' said Joe.

'What'll you drink, Mr——? You didn't mention your name, by-the-bye.'

Joe mentioned it now, and the strange man called him by it. 'What'll you drink, Mr Gargery? At my expense? To top up with?'

'Well,' said Joe, 'to tell you the truth, I ain't much in the habit of drinking at anybody's expense but my own. But I wouldn't wish to be stiff company. Rum.'

'Rum,' repeated the stranger. 'And will the other gentleman originate a sentiment.'

'Rum,' said Mr Wopsle.

'Three Rums!' cried the stranger, calling to the landlord. 'Glasses round!'

'This other gentleman,' observed Joe, by way of introducing Mr Wopsle, 'is our clerk at church.'

'Aha!' said the stranger, quickly, and cocking his eye at me. 'The lonely church, right out on the marshes, with the graves round it!'

'That's it,' said Joe.

The stranger, with a comfortable kind of grunt over his pipe, put his legs up on the settle that he had to himself.

As he looked at the fire, I thought I saw a cunning expression, followed by a half-laugh, come into his face.

'I am not acquainted with this country, gentlemen, but it seems a solitary country towards the river. Do you find any gypsies, now, or tramps, or vagrants of any sort, out there?'

'No,' said Joe; 'none but a runaway convict now and then.'

'Seems you have been out after such?' asked the stranger.

'Once,' returned Joe. 'Not that we wanted to take them, you understand; we went out as lookers on; me, and Mr Wopsle, and Pip. Didn't us, Pip?'

'Yes, Joe.'

The stranger looked at me again and said, 'He's a likely young parcel of bones that. What is it you call him?'

'Pip,' said Joe.

'Son of yours?'

'Well,' said Joe, meditatively – 'well – no. No, he ain't.'

'Nevvy?' said the strange man.

'Well,' said Joe, with the same appearance of profound cogitation, 'he is not – no, not to deceive you, he is *not* – my nevvy.'

'What the Blue Blazes is he?' asked the stranger. Which appeared to me to be an enquiry of unnecessary strength.

Mr Wopsle struck in upon that; and expounded the ties between me and Joe.

And here I may remark that when Mr Wopsle referred to me, he considered it a necessary part of such reference to rumple my hair and poke it into my eyes.

All this while, the strange man looked at nobody but me, and looked at me as if he were determined to have a shot at me at last, and bring me down. But he said nothing until the glasses of rum-and-water were brought; and then he made his shot, and a most extraordinary shot it was.

It was not a verbal remark, but a proceeding in dumb show, and was pointedly addressed to me. He stirred his rum-and-water pointedly at me, and he tasted it: not with a spoon that was brought to him, but *with a file*.

He did this so that nobody but I saw the file; and when he had done it he wiped the file and put it in a breast-pocket. I knew it to be Joe's file, and I knew that he knew my convict, the moment I saw the instrument. I sat gazing at him, spell-bound. But he now reclined on his settle, taking very little notice of me, and talking principally about turnips.

There was a delicious sense of cleaning-up and making a quiet pause before going on in life afresh, in our village on Saturday nights, which stimulated Joe to dare to stay out half an hour longer on Saturdays than at other times. The half hour and the rum-and-water running out together, Joe got up to go, and took me by the hand.

'Stop half a moment, Mr Gargery,' said the strange man. 'I think I've got a bright new shilling somewhere in my pocket, and if I have, the boy shall have it.'

He looked it out from a handful of small change, folded it in some crumpled paper, and gave it to me. 'Yours!' said he. 'Mind! Your own.'

I thanked him, staring at him far beyond the bounds of good manners, and holding tight to Joe. He gave

Joe good-night, and he gave Mr Wopsle good-night, and he gave me only a look with his aiming eye – no, not a look, for he shut it up, but wonders may be done with an eye by hiding it.

My sister was not in a very bad temper when we presented ourselves in the kitchen, and Joe was encouraged by that unusual circumstance to tell her about the bright shilling. 'A bad un, I'll be bound,' said Mrs Joe triumphantly, 'or he wouldn't have given it to the boy! Let's look at it.'

I took it out of the paper, and it proved to be a good one. 'But what's this?' said Mrs Joe, throwing down the shilling and catching up the paper. 'Two One-Pound notes?'

Nothing less than two fat sweltering one-pound notes that seemed to have been on terms of the warmest intimacy with all the cattle markets in the county. Joe caught up his hat again, and ran with them to the Jolly Bargemen to restore them to their owner, but presently, he came back, saying that the man was gone, but that he, Joe, had left word at the Three Jolly Bargemen concerning the notes. Then my sister sealed them up in a piece of paper, and put them in an ornamental teapot on the top of a press in the state parlour. There they remained, a nightmare to me, many and many a night and day.

I had sadly broken sleep when I got to bed, through thinking of the strange man taking aim at me with his invisible gun, and of the guiltily coarse and common thing it was, to be on secret terms of conspiracy with convicts. I was haunted by the file too. A dread possessed me that when I least expected it, the file would reappear. I coaxed myself to sleep by thinking of Miss

Havisham's, next Wednesday; and in my sleep I saw the file coming at me out of a door, without seeing who held it, and I screamed myself awake.

11

At the appointed time I returned to Miss Havisham's, and my hesitating ring at the gate brought out Estella. She locked it after admitting me, as she had done before, and again preceded me into the dark passage where her candle stood. She took no notice of me until she had the candle in her hand, when she looked over her shoulder, superciliously saying, 'You are to come this way today,' and took me to quite another part of the house.

We traversed but one side of the square and at the end of it she stopped, and put her candle down and opened a door. Here, the daylight reappeared, and I found myself in a small paved court-yard, the opposite side of which was formed by a detached dwelling-house, that looked as if it had once belonged to the manager or head clerk of the extinct brewery. There was a clock in the outer wall of this house. Like the clock in Miss Havisham's room, and like Miss Havisham's watch, it had stopped at twenty minutes to nine.

We went in at the door, which stood open, and into a gloomy room with a low ceiling, on the ground floor at the back. There was some company in the room, and Estella said to me as she joined it, 'You are to go and stand there, boy, till you are wanted.' 'There', being the window, I crossed to it, and stood 'there', in a very uncomfortable state of mind, looking out.

I divined that my coming had stopped conversation in the room, and that its other occupants were looking at me. I could see nothing of the room except the shining of the fire in the window glass, but I stiffened in all my joints with the consciousness that I was under close inspection.

There were three ladies in the room and one gentleman. They all had a listless and dreary air of waiting somebody's pleasure, and the most talkative of the ladies had to speak quite rigidly to repress a yawn. This lady, whose name was Camilla, very much reminded me of my sister, with the difference that she was older, and of a blunter cast of features.

'Poor dear soul!' said this lady, with an abruptness of manner quite my sister's. 'Nobody's enemy but his own!'

'It would be much more commendable to be somebody else's enemy,' said the gentleman; 'far more natural.'

'Cousin Raymond,' observed another lady, 'we are to love our neighbour.'

'Sarah Pocket,' returned Cousin Raymond, 'if a man is not his own neighbour, who is?'

Miss Pocket laughed, and Camilla laughed and said (checking a yawn), 'The idea!' But I thought they seemed to think it rather a good idea too. The other lady, who had not spoken yet, said gravely and emphatically, '*Very* true!'

The ringing of a distant bell, combined with the echoing of some cry or call along the passage by which I had come, interrupted the conversation and caused

Estella to say to me, 'Now, boy!' On my turning round, they all looked at me with the utmost contempt, and, as I went out, I heard Sarah Pocket say, 'Well I am sure! What next!' and Camilla add, with indignation, 'Was there ever such a fancy! The i-de-a!'

As we were going with our candle along the dark passage, Estella stopped all of a sudden, and, facing round, said in her taunting manner with her face quite close to mine:

'Well?'

'Well, miss?' I answered, almost falling over her and checking myself.

She stood looking at me, and, of course, I stood looking at her.

'Am I pretty?'

'Yes; I think you are very pretty.'

'Am I insulting?'

'Not so much so as you were last time,' said I.

'Not so much so?'

'No.'

She fired when she asked the last question, and she slapped my face with such force as she had, when I answered it.

'Now?' said she. 'You little coarse monster, what do you think of me now?'

'I shall not tell you.'

'Because you are going to tell, upstairs. Is that it?'

'No,' said I, 'that's not it.'

'Why don't you cry again, you little wretch?'

'Because I'll never cry for you again,' said I. Which was, I suppose, as false a declaration as ever was made; for I was inwardly crying for her then, and I know what I know of the pain she cost me afterwards.

We went on our way upstairs after this episode; and, as we were going up, we met a gentleman groping his way down.

'Whom have we here?' asked the gentleman, stopping and looking at me.

'A boy,' said Estella.

He was a burly man of an exceedingly dark complexion, with an exceedingly large head and a corresponding large hand. He took my chin in his large hand and turned up my face to have a look at me by the light of the candle. He was prematurely bald on the top of his head, and had bushy black eyebrows that wouldn't lie down but stood up bristling. His eyes were set very deep in his head, and were disagreeably sharp and suspicious. He was nothing to me, and I could have had no foresight then, that he ever would be anything to me, but it happened that I had this opportunity of observing him well.

'Boy of the neighbourhood? Hey?' said he.

'Yes, sir,' said I.

'How do *you* come here?'

'Miss Havisham sent for me, sir,' I explained.

'Well! Behave yourself. I have a pretty large experience of boys, and you're a bad set of fellows.'

With those words, he released me – which I was glad of, for his hand smelt of scented soap – and went his way downstairs. I wondered whether he could be a doctor; but no, I thought; he couldn't be a doctor, or he would have a quieter and more persuasive manner. There was not much time to consider the subject, for we were soon in Miss Havisham's room, where she and everything else were just as I had left them. Estella left me standing near the door, and I stood there until Miss Havisham cast her eyes upon me from the dressing-table.

'So!' she said, without being startled or surprised; 'the days have worn away, have they?'

'Yes, ma'am. Today is –'

'There, there, there!' with the impatient movement of her fingers. 'I don't want to know. Are you ready to play?'

I was obliged to answer in some confusion, 'I don't think I am, ma'am.'

'Since this house strikes you old and grave, boy,' said Miss Havisham, impatiently, 'and you are unwilling to play, are you willing to work?'

I could answer this enquiry with a better heart than I had been able to find for the other question, and I said I was quite willing.

'Then go into that opposite room,' said she, pointing at the door behind me with her withered hand, 'and wait there till I come.'

I crossed the staircase landing, and entered the room she indicated. From that room, too, the daylight was completely excluded, and it had an airless smell that was oppressive. Certain wintry branches of candles on the high chimneypiece faintly lighted the chamber. It was spacious, and I dare say had once been handsome, but every discernible thing in it was covered with dust and mould, and dropping to pieces. The most prominent object was a long table with a table-cloth spread on it, as if a feast had been in preparation when the house and the clocks all stopped together. A centre-piece of some kind was in the middle of this cloth; it was so heavily overhung with cobwebs that its form was quite undistinguishable; and, as I looked along the yellow expanse out of which I remember its seeming to grow, like a black fungus, I saw speckled-legged spiders with blotchy bodies running home to it, and running out from it.

I heard the mice too, rattling behind the panels, as if the same occurrence were important to their interests.

These crawling things had fascinated my attention and I was watching them from a distance, when Miss Havisham laid a hand upon my shoulder. In her other hand she had a crutch-headed stick on which she leaned, and she looked like the Witch of the place.

'This,' said she, pointing to the long table with her stick, 'is where I will be laid when I am dead. They shall come and look at me here.'

With some vague misgiving that she might get upon the table then and there and die at once, I shrank under her touch.

'What do you think that is?' she asked me, again pointing with her stick; 'that, where those cobwebs are?'

'I can't guess what it is, ma'am.'

'It's a great cake. A bride-cake. Mine!'

She looked all round the room in a glaring manner, and then said, leaning on me while her hand twitched my shoulder, 'Come, come, come! Walk me, walk me!'

I made out from this, that the work I had to do, was to walk Miss Havisham round and round the room. Accordingly, I started at once, and she leaned upon my shoulder, and we went away at a pace that might have been an imitation of Mr Pumblechook's chaise-cart.

She was not physically strong, and after a little time said, 'Slower!' After a while she said, 'Call Estella!' so

I went out on the landing and roared that name as I had done on the previous occasion. When her light appeared, I returned to Miss Havisham, and we started away again round and round the room.

Estella brought with her the three ladies and the gentleman whom I had seen below. I didn't know what to do. In my politeness, I would have stopped; but, Miss Havisham twitched my shoulder, and we posted on.

'Dear Miss Havisham,' said Miss Sarah Pocket. 'How well you look!'

'I do not,' returned Miss Havisham. 'I am yellow skin and bone.'

Camilla brightened when Miss Pocket met with this rebuff; and she murmured, as she plaintively contemplated Miss Havisham, 'Poor dear soul! Certainly not to be expected to look well, poor thing. The idea!'

'And how are *you*?' said Miss Havisham to Camilla. As we were close to Camilla then, I would have stopped as a matter of course, only Miss Havisham wouldn't stop. We swept on, and I felt that I was highly obnoxious to Camilla.

'Thank you, Miss Havisham,' she returned, 'I am as well as can be expected.'

'Why, what's the matter with you?' asked Miss Havisham, with exceeding sharpness.

'Nothing worth mentioning,' replied Camilla. 'I don't wish to make a display of my feelings, but I have habitually thought of you more in the night than I am quite equal to.'

'Then don't think of me,' retorted Miss Havisham.

'Very easily said!' remarked Camilla, amiably repressing a sob, 'Raymond is a witness what nervous jerkings

I have in my legs. If I could be less affectionate and sensitive, I should have a better digestion and an iron set of nerves. But as to not thinking of you in the night – The idea!' Here, a burst of tears.

The Raymond referred to, I understood to be the gentleman present, and him I understood to be Mr Camilla. He came to the rescue at this point, and said in a consolatory and complimentary voice, 'Camilla, my dear, it is well known that your family feelings are gradually undermining you to the extent of making one of your legs shorter than the other.'

'I am not aware,' observed the grave lady whose voice I had heard but once, 'that to think of any person is to make a great claim upon that person, my dear.'

Miss Sarah Pocket, whom I now saw to be a little dry brown corrugated old woman, supported this position by saying, 'No, indeed, my dear. Hem!'

'Thinking is easy enough,' said the grave lady.

'What is easier, you know?' assented Miss Sarah Pocket.

'Oh, yes, yes!' cried Camilla, whose fermenting feelings appeared to rise from her legs to her bosom. 'It's all very true! It's a weakness to be so affectionate, but I can't help it.' Here another burst of feeling.

Miss Havisham and I had never stopped all this time, but kept going round and round the room: now, brushing against the skirts of the visitors: now, giving them the whole length of the dismal chamber.

'There's Matthew!' said Camilla. 'Never mixing with any natural ties, never coming here to see how Miss Havisham is! I have taken to the sofa with my staylace cut, and have lain there hours, insensible, with my head over the side, and my hair all down, and my feet I don't know where – I have gone off into that state, hours and hours, on account of Matthew's strange and inexplicable conduct, and nobody has thanked me.'

'Really I must say I should think not!' interposed the grave lady.

'Matthew will come and see me at last,' said Miss Havisham, sternly, 'when I am laid on that table. That will be his place – there,' striking the table with her stick, 'at my head! And yours will be there! And your husband's there! And Sarah Pocket's there! And Georgiana's there! Now you all know where to take your stations when you come to feast upon me. And now go!'

'I suppose there's nothing to be done,' exclaimed Camilla, 'but comply and depart. It's something to have seen the object of one's love and duty, for even so short a time. I shall think of it with a melancholy satisfaction when I wake up in the night. I wish Matthew could have that comfort, but he sets it at defiance. I am determined not to make a display of my feelings, but it's very hard to be told one wants to feast on one's relations – as if one was a Giant – and to be told to go. The bare idea!'

Sarah Pocket and Georgiana contended who should remain last; but, Sarah was too knowing to be outdone, and ambled round Georgiana with that artful slipperiness, that the latter was obliged to take precedence. Sarah Pocket then made her separate effect of departing with 'Bless you, Miss Havisham dear!' and with a smile of forgiving pity on her walnut-shell countenance for the weaknesses of the rest.

While Estella was away lighting them down, Miss Havisham walked more and more slowly. At last she stopped before the fire, and said, after muttering and looking at it some seconds:

'This is my birthday, Pip.'

I was going to wish her many happy returns, when she lifted her stick.

'I don't suffer it to be spoken of. I don't suffer those who were here just now, or any one, to speak of it. On this day of the year, long before you were born, this heap of decay,' stabbing with her crutched stick at the pile of cobwebs on the table but not touching it, 'was brought here. It and I have worn away together. The mice have gnawed at it, and sharper teeth than teeth of mice have gnawed at me.'

She held the head of her stick against her heart as she stood looking at the table; she in her once white dress, all yellow and withered; everything around, in a state to crumble under a touch.

'When the ruin is complete,' said she, with a ghastly look, 'and when they lay me dead, in my bride's dress on the bride's table – which shall be done, and which will be the finished curse upon him – so much the better if it is done on this day!'

She stood looking at the table as if she stood looking at her own figure lying there. I remained quiet. Estella returned, and she too remained quiet. In the heavy air of the room, and the heavy darkness that brooded in its remoter corners, I even had an alarming fancy that Estella and I might presently begin to decay.

At length, not coming out of her distraught state by degrees, but in an instant, Miss Havisham said, 'Let me see you two play cards; why have you not begun?'

With that, we returned to her room, and sat down as before; I was beggared, as before; and again, as before, Miss Havisham watched us all the time, directed my attention to Estella's beauty, and made me notice it the more by trying her jewels on Estella's breast and hair.

When we had played some half-dozen games, a day was appointed for my return, and I was taken down into the yard to be fed in the former dog-like manner. There, too, I was again left to wander about as I liked.

I strolled into the garden and strolled all over it. It was quite a wilderness, and there were old melon-frames and cucumber-frames in it, which seemed in their decline to have produced a spontaneous growth of weak attempts at pieces of old hats and boots, with now and then a weedy offshoot into the likeness of a battered saucepan.

When I had exhausted the garden, and a greenhouse with nothing in it but a fallen-down grape-vine and some bottles, I found myself in the dismal corner upon which I had looked out of window. Never questioning for a moment that the house was now empty, I looked in at another window, and found myself, to my great surprise, exchanging a broad stare with a pale young gentleman with red eyelids and light hair.

This pale young gentleman quickly disappeared, and re-appeared beside me.

'Halloa!' said he, 'young fellow! Who let *you* in.'

'Miss Estella.'

'Who gave you leave to prowl about?'

'Miss Estella.'

'Come and fight,' said the pale young gentleman.

What could I do but follow him? His manner was so

final and I was so astonished, that I followed where he led, as if I had been under a spell.

'Stop a minute, though,' he said, wheeling round before we had gone many paces. 'I ought to give you a reason for fighting, too.' In a most irritating manner he instantly slapped his hands against one another, daintily flung one of his legs up behind him, pulled my hair, slapped his hands again, dipped his head, and butted it into my stomach.

I hit out at him and was going to hit out again, when he said, 'Aha! Would you?' and began dancing backwards and forwards in a manner quite unparalleled within my limited experience.

'Laws of the game!' said he. 'Come to the ground, and go through the preliminaries!' Here, he dodged backwards and forwards, and did all sorts of things while I looked helplessly at him.

I was secretly afraid of him when I saw him so dexterous; but, I felt morally and physically convinced that his light head of hair could have had no business in the pit of my stomach. Therefore, I followed him without a word, to a retired nook of the garden. On his asking me if I was satisfied with the ground, and on my replying Yes, he begged my leave to absent himself for a moment, and quickly returned with a bottle of water and a sponge dipped in vinegar. 'Available for both,' he said, placing these against the wall. And then fell to pulling off, not only his jacket and waistcoat, but his shirt too, in a manner at once light-hearted, businesslike, and bloodthirsty.

Although he did not look very healthy – having pimples on his face, and a breaking out at his mouth – these dreadful preparations quite appalled me. I judged him to be about my own age, but he was much taller, and he had a way of spinning himself about that was full of appearance.

My heart failed me when I saw him squaring at me with every demonstration of mechanical nicety, and eyeing my anatomy as if he were minutely choosing his bone. I never have been so surprised in my life, as I was when I let out the first blow, and saw him lying on his back, looking up at me with a bloody nose and his face exceedingly fore-shortened.

But, he was on his feet directly, and after sponging himself with a great show of dexterity began squaring again. The second greatest surprise I have ever had in my life was seeing him on his back again, looking up at me out of a black eye.

He seemed to have no strength, and he never once hit me hard, and he was always knocked down; but, he would be up again in a moment, sponging himself, with the greatest satisfaction in seconding himself according to form, and then came at me with an air and a show that made me believe he really was going to do for me at last. He got heavily bruised, for I am sorry to record that the more I hit him, the harder I hit him; but, he came up again and again and again, until at last he got a bad fall with the back of his head against the wall. Even after that crisis in our affairs, he got up and turned round and round confusedly a few times, not knowing where I was; but finally went on his knees to his sponge and threw it up: at the same time panting out, 'That means you have won.'

He seemed so brave and innocent, that although I had not proposed the contest I felt but a gloomy satisfaction in my victory. I got dressed, darkly wiping my sanguinary face at intervals, and I said, 'Can I help you?' and he said 'No thankee,' and I said 'Good-afternoon,' and *he* said 'Same to you.'

When I got into the court-yard, I found Estella waiting with the keys. But, she neither asked me where I had been, nor why I had kept her waiting; and there was a bright flush upon her face, as though something had happened to delight her. Instead of going straight to the gate, too, she stepped back into the passage, and beckoned me.

'Come here! You may kiss me, if you like.'

I kissed her cheek as she turned it to me. But, I felt that the kiss was given to the coarse common boy as a piece of money might have been, and that it was worth nothing.

What with the birthday visitors, and what with the cards, and what with the fight, my stay had lasted so long, that when I neared home the light on the spit of sand off the point on the marshes was gleaming against a black night-sky, and Joe's furnace was flinging a path of fire across the road.

12

The more I thought of the fight, and recalled the pale young gentleman on his back in various stages of puffy and incrimsoned countenance, the more certain it appeared that something would be done to me. For some days, I even kept close at home, and looked out at the kitchen door with the greatest caution and trepidation

before going on an errand, lest the officers of the
County Jail should pounce upon me. The pale young
gentleman's nose had stained my trousers, and I tried
to wash out that evidence of my guilt in the dead of
night.

When the day came round for my return to the
scene of the deed of violence, my terrors reached their
height. Whether myrmidons of Justice, specially sent
down from London, would be lying in ambush behind
the gate? Whether Miss Havisham, preferring to take
personal vengeance for an outrage done to her house,
might rise in those grave-clothes of hers, draw a pistol,
and shoot me dead?

However, go to Miss Havisham's I must, and go I
did. And behold! nothing came of the late struggle. It
was not alluded to in any way, and no pale young
gentleman was to be discovered on the premises.

On the broad landing between Miss Havisham's
own room and that other room in which the long table
was laid out, I saw a garden-chair – a light chair on
wheels, that you pushed from behind. It had been
placed there since my last visit, and I entered, that
same day, on a regular occupation of pushing Miss
Havisham in this chair round her own room, and
across the landing, and round the other room. Over
and over and over again, we would make these journeys, and sometimes they would last as long as three
hours at a stretch.

As we began to be more used to one another, Miss
Havisham talked more to me, and asked me such
questions as what had I learnt and what was I going to
be? I told her I was going to be apprenticed to Joe, I
believed; and I enlarged upon my knowing nothing

and wanting to know everything, in the hope that she might offer some help towards that desirable end. But, she did not; on the contrary, she seemed to prefer my being ignorant. Neither did she ever give me any money – or anything but my daily dinner – nor even stipulate that I should be paid for my services.

Estella was always about, and always let me in and out, but never told me I might kiss her again. Sometimes, she would coldly tolerate me; sometimes, she would condescend to me; sometimes, she would be quite familiar with me; sometimes, she would tell me energetically that she hated me. Miss Havisham would often ask me in a whisper, or when we were alone, 'Does she grow prettier and prettier, Pip?' And when I said yes (for indeed she did), would seem to enjoy it greedily. And sometimes, when her moods were so many and so contradictory of one another that I was puzzled what to say or do, Miss Havisham would embrace her with lavish fondness, murmuring something in her ear that sounded like 'Break their hearts my pride and hope, break their hearts and have no mercy!'

There was a song Joe used to hum fragments of at the forge, of which the burden was Old Clem. It was a song that imitated the measure of beating upon iron, and was a mere lyrical excuse for the introduction of Old Clem's respected name. Thus, you were to hammer boys round – Old Clem! With a thump and a sound – Old Clem! Beat it out, beat it out – Old Clem! With a clink for the stout – Old Clem! Blow the fire, blow the fire – Old Clem! Roaring dryer, soaring higher – Old Clem! One day, Miss Havisham suddenly saying to me, with the impatient movement of her fingers, 'There, there, there! Sing!' I was surprised into crooning this ditty as I pushed her over the floor. It happened so to catch her fancy, that she took it up in a low brooding voice as if she were singing in her sleep. After that, it became customary with us to have it as we moved about, and Estella would often join in; though the whole strain was so subdued that it made less noise in the grim old house than the lightest breath of wind.

What could I become with these surroundings? Is it to be wondered at if my thoughts were dazed, as my eyes were, when I came out into the natural light from the misty yellow rooms?

That shrinking from having Miss Havisham and Estella discussed, which had come upon me in the beginning, grew much more potent as time went on. I reposed complete confidence in no one but Biddy; but, I told poor Biddy everything. Why it came natural to me to do so, and why Biddy had a deep concern in everything I told her, I did not know then, though I think now.

That ass, Pumblechook, used often to come over of a night for the purpose of discussing my prospects with my sister; and I really do believe that if these hands could have taken a linchpin out of his chaise-cart, they would have done it. He would drag me up from my stool where I was quiet in a corner, and, putting me before the fire as if I were going to be cooked, would begin by saying, 'Now, Mum, here is this boy which you brought up by hand. Hold up your head, boy, and be for ever grateful unto them which so did do.'

Then, he and my sister would pair off in such

nonsensical speculations about Miss Havisham, and about what she would do with me and for me, that I used to want to burst into spiteful tears, fly at Pumble-chook, and pummel him all over.

In these discussions, Joe bore no part. But he was often talked at, by reason of Mrs Joe's perceiving that he was not favourable to my being taken from the forge. When Joe sat with the poker on his knees thoughtfully raking out the ashes between the lower bars, my sister would so distinctly construe that inno-cent action into opposition on his part, that she would dive at him, take the poker out of his hands, shake him, and put it away.

We went on in this way for a long time, when, one day, Miss Havisham stopped short as she and I were walking, she leaning on my shoulder; and said with some displeasure:

'You are growing tall, Pip!'

She said no more at the time; but, she presently stopped and looked at me again; and after that, looked frowning and moody. On the next day of my attend-ance when our usual exercise was over, and I had landed her at her dressing-table, she stayed me with a movement of her impatient fingers:

'Tell me the name again of that blacksmith of yours.'

'Joe Gargery, ma'am.'

'Meaning the master you were to be apprenticed to?'

'Yes, Miss Havisham.'

'You had better be apprenticed at once. Would Gar-gery come here with you, and bring your indentures, do you think?'

I signified that I had no doubt he would take it as an honour to be asked.

'Then let him come.'

When I got home at night, and delivered this message for Joe, my sister 'went on the Rampage', in a more alarming degree than at any previous period. She asked me and Joe whether we supposed she was doormats under our feet, and how we dared to use her so, and what company we graciously thought she *was* fit for? When she had exhausted a torrent of such enquiries, she threw a candle-stick at Joe, burst into a loud sobbing, got out the dustpan – which was always a very bad sign – put on her coarse apron, and began cleaning up to a terrible extent. She cleaned us out of house and home, so that we stood shivering in the back-yard. It was ten o'clock at night before we ventured to creep in again.

13

It was a trial to my feelings, on the next day but one, to see Joe arraying himself in his Sunday clothes to accompany me to Miss Havisham's. However, as he thought his court-suit necessary to the occasion, it was not for me to tell him that he looked far better in his working dress.

At breakfast time my sister declared her intention of going to town with us, and being left at Uncle Pumblechook's, and called for 'when we had done with our fine ladies' – a way of putting the case, from which Joe appeared inclined to augur the worst.

We walked to town, my sister leading the way in a

very large beaver bonnet, and carrying a basket like the Great Seal of England in plaited straw, a pair of pattens, a spare shawl, and an umbrella, though it was a fine bright day.

When we came to Pumblechook's, my sister bounced in and left us. As it was almost noon, Joe and I held straight on to Miss Havisham's house. Estella opened the gate as usual, and, the moment she appeared, Joe took his hat off and stood weighing it by the brim in both his hands: as if he had some urgent reason in his mind for being particular to half a quarter of an ounce.

Estella took no notice of either of us, but led us the way that I knew so well. I followed next to her, and Joe came last.

Estella told me we were both to go in, so I took Joe by the coat-cuff and conducted him into Miss Havisham's presence. She was seated at her dressing-table, and looked round at us immediately.

I could hardly have imagined dear old Joe looking so unlike himself or so like some extraordinary bird; standing, as he did, speechless, with his tuft of feathers ruffled, and his mouth open, as if he wanted a worm.

'You are the husband,' said Miss Havisham, 'of the sister of this boy?'

It was very aggravating; but, throughout the interview Joe persisted in addressing Me instead of Miss Havisham.

'Which I meantersay, Pip,' Joe now observed in a manner that was at once expressive of forcible argumentation, strict confidence, and great politeness, 'as I hup and married your sister, and I were at the time what you might call (if you was anyways inclined) a single man.'

'Well!' said Miss Havisham. 'And you have reared the boy, with the intention of taking him for your apprentice; is that so, Mr Gargery?'

'You know, Pip,' replied Joe, 'if you had ever made objections to the business – such as its being open to black and sut, or such-like – not but what they would have been attended to, don't you see?'

'Has the boy,' said Miss Havisham, 'ever made any objection? Does he like the trade?'

'Which it is well beknown to yourself, Pip,' returned Joe, 'there weren't no objection on your part, and Pip it were the great wish of your hart!'

'Have you brought his indentures with you?' asked Miss Havisham.

'Well, Pip, you know,' replied Joe, as if that were a little unreasonable, 'you yourself see me put 'em in my 'at, and therefore you know as they are here.' With which he took them out, and gave them, not to Miss Havisham, but to me. I am afraid I was ashamed of the dear good fellow when I saw that Estella stood at the back of Miss Havisham's chair, and that her eyes laughed mischievously. I took the indentures out of his hand and gave them to Miss Havisham.

'You expected,' said Miss Havisham, as she looked them over, 'no premium with the boy?'

'Joe!' I remonstrated; for he made no reply at all. 'Why don't you answer –'

'Pip,' returned Joe, cutting me short as if he were hurt, 'which I meantersay that were not a question requiring a answer betwixt yourself and me, and which you know the answer to be full well No. You know it to be No, Pip.'

Miss Havisham glanced at him as if she understood

what he really was, better than I had thought possible, seeing what he was there; and took up a little bag from the table beside her.

'Pip has earned a premium here,' she said, 'and here it is. There are five-and-twenty guineas in this bag. Give it to your master, Pip.'

'This is wery liberal on your part, Pip,' said Joe, 'and it is as such received and grateful welcome, though never looked for. And now, old chap, as may we do our duty! May you and me do our duty, both on us by one and another, and by them which your liberal present – have – conweyed – to be – for the satisfaction of mind – of – them as never –' here Joe showed that he felt he had fallen into frightful difficulties, until he triumphantly rescued himself with the words, 'and from myself far be it!' These words had such a round and convincing sound for him that he said them twice.

'Goodbye, Pip!' said Miss Havisham. 'Let them out, Estella.'

'Am I to come again, Miss Havisham?' I asked.

'No. Gargery is your master now. Gargery! One word!'

Thus calling him back as I went out of the door, I heard her say to Joe, in a distinct emphatic voice, 'The boy has been a good boy here, and that is his reward. Of course, as an honest man, you will expect no other and no more.'

How Joe got out of the room, I have never been able to determine; but, I know that when he did get out he was steadily proceeding upstairs instead of coming down, and was deaf to all remonstrances until I went after him and laid hold of him. In another minute we were outside the gate, and it was locked, and Estella was gone.

I have reason to think that Joe's intellects were brightened by the encounter they had passed through, and that on our way to Pumblechook's he invented a subtle and deep design. My reason is to be found in what took place in Mr Pumblechook's parlour: where my sister sat in conference with that detested seedsman.

'Well?' cried my sister, addressing us both at once. 'And what's happened to *you*?'

'Miss Havisham,' said Joe, with a fixed look at me, like an effort of remembrance, 'made it wery partick'ler that we should give her – were it compliments or respects, Pip?'

'Compliments,' I said.

'And wishing,' pursued Joe, 'that the state of Miss Havisham's elth were sitch as would have – allowed, were it, Pip?'

'Of her having the pleasure,' I added.

'Of ladies' company,' said Joe. And drew a long breath.

'Well!' cried my sister, with a mollified glance at Mr Pumblechook, 'She might have had the politeness to send that message at first, but it's better late than never. And what did she give young Rantipole here?'

'She giv' him,' said Joe, 'nothing.'

Mrs Joe was going to break out, but Joe went on.

'What she giv',' said Joe, 'she giv' to his friends. 'And by his friends,' were her explanation, 'I mean into the hands of his sister Mrs J.Gargery.'

'And how much have you got?' asked my sister, laughing. Positively, laughing!

'What would present company say,' proceeded Joe, 'to twenty pound?'

'Handsome would be the word,' returned my sister.

'Well, then,' said Joe, 'It's more than twenty pound.'

That abject hypocrite, Pumblechook, nodded again, and said, with a patronizing laugh, 'It's more than that, Mum. Good again! Follow her up, Joseph!'

'Then to make an end of it,' said Joe, delightedly handing the bag to my sister; 'it's five-and-twenty pound.'

'It's five-and-twenty pound, Mum,' echoed that basest of swindlers, Pumblechook, rising to shake hands with her; 'and it's no more than your merits (as I said when my opinion was asked), and I wish you joy of the money!'

If the villain had stopped here, his case would have been sufficiently awful, but he blackened his guilt by proceeding to take me into custody, with a right of patronage that left all his former criminality far behind.

'Now you see, Joseph and wife,' said Pumblechook, 'I am one of them that always go right through with what they've begun. This boy must be bound, out of hand.'

'Goodness knows, Uncle Pumblechook,' said my sister (grasping the money), 'we're deeply beholden to you.'

'Never mind me, Mum,' returned that diabolical corn-chandler. 'A pleasure's a pleasure, all the world over.'

The Justices were sitting in the Town Hall near at hand, and we at once went over to have me bound apprentice to Joe in the Magisterial presence. I say, we went over, but I was pushed over by Pumblechook, exactly as if I had that moment picked a pocket or fired a rick; indeed, it was the general impression in Court that I had been taken red-handed, for, as Pumblechook shoved me before him through the crowd, I heard some people say, 'What's he done?' and others, 'He's a young 'un, too, but looks bad, don't he?'

Here, in a corner of the Hall, my indentures were duly signed and attested, and I was 'bound'; Mr Pumblechook holding me all the while as if we had looked in on our way to the scaffold, to have those little preliminaries disposed of.

When we had come out again, we went back to Pumblechook's. And there my sister became so excited by the twenty-five guineas, that nothing would serve her but we must have a dinner out of that windfall, at the Blue Boar, and that Pumblechook must go over in his chaise-cart, and bring the Hubbles and Mr Wopsle.

It was agreed to be done; and a most melancholy day I passed. For, it inscrutably appeared to stand to reason, in the minds of the whole company, that I was an excrescence on the entertainment. And to make it worse, they all asked me from time to time why I didn't enjoy myself. And what could I possibly do then, but say I *was* enjoying myself – when I wasn't?

My only other remembrances of the great festival are, That they wouldn't let me go to sleep, but whenever they saw me dropping off, woke me up and told me to enjoy myself. That, they were all in excellent spirits on the road home, and sang O Lady Fair! Mr Wopsle taking the bass, and asserting with a tremendously strong voice that *he* was the man with his white locks flowing, and that he was upon the whole the weakest pilgrim going.

Finally, I remember that when I got into my little bedroom I was truly wretched, and had a strong conviction on me that I should never like Joe's trade. I had liked it once, but once was not now.

14

It is a most miserable thing to feel ashamed of home. It had never been a very pleasant place to me, because of my sister's temper. But, Joe had sanctified it, and I had believed in it. I had believed in the best parlour as a most elegant saloon; I had believed in the kitchen as a chaste though not magnificent apartment; I had believed in the forge as the glowing road to manhood and independence. Within a single year, all this was changed. Now, it was all coarse and common, and I would not have had Miss Havisham and Estella see it on any account.

Once, it had seemed to me that when I should at last roll up my shirt-sleeves and go into the forge, Joe's 'prentice, I should be distinguished and happy. Now the reality was in my hold, I only felt that I was dusty with the dust of small coal, and that I had a weight upon my daily remembrance to which the anvil was a feather.

I remember that at a later period of my 'time', I used to stand about the churchyard on Sunday evenings comparing my own perspective with the windy marsh view, and making out some likeness between them by thinking how flat and low both were, and how on both there came an unknown way and a dark mist and then the sea. I was quite as dejected on the first working-day of my apprenticeship as in that after-time; but I am glad to know that I never breathed a murmur to Joe while my indentures lasted.

What I wanted, who can say? How can *I* say, when I never knew? What I dreaded was, that in some unlucky hour I, being at my grimiest and commonest, should lift up my eyes and see Estella looking in at one of the wooden windows of the forge. Often after dark, when I was pulling the bellows for Joe, and we were singing Old Clem, and when the thought how we used to sing it at Miss Havisham's would seem to show me Estella's face in the fire, with her pretty hair fluttering in the wind and her eyes scorning me, – often at such a time I would look towards those panels of black night in the wall which the wooden windows then were, and would fancy that I saw her just drawing her face away, and would believe that she had come at last.

After that, when we went in to supper, the place and the meal would have a more homely look than ever, and I would feel more ashamed of home than ever, in my own ungracious breast.

15

As I was getting too big for Mr Wopsle's great-aunt's room, my education under that preposterous female terminated. Not, however, until Biddy had imparted to me everything she knew, from the little catalogue of prices, to a comic song she had once bought for a half-penny.

In my hunger for information, I made proposals to Mr Wopsle to bestow some intellectual crumbs upon me; with which he kindly complied. As it turned out, however, that he only wanted me for a dramatic lay-figure, to be contradicted and embraced and wept over and bullied and stabbed and knocked about in a variety of ways, I soon declined that course of instruction; though not until Mr Wopsle in his poetic fury had severely mauled me.

Whatever I acquired, I tried to impart to Joe. This statement sounds so well, that I cannot in my conscience let it pass unexplained. I wanted to make Joe less ignorant and common, that he might be worthier of my society and less open to Estella's reproach.

The old Battery out on the marshes was our place of study, and a broken slate and a short piece of slate pencil were our educational implements: to which Joe always added a pipe of tobacco. I never knew Joe to remember anything from one Sunday to another, or to acquire, under my tuition, any piece of information whatever. Yet he would smoke his pipe at the Battery with a far more sagacious air than anywhere else as if he considered himself to be advancing immensely.

It was pleasant and quiet, out there with the sails on the river and sometimes, when the tide was low, looking as if they belonged to sunken ships that were still sailing on at the bottom of the water. Whenever I watched the vessels standing out to sea with their white sails spread, I somehow thought of Miss Havisham and Estella, and the strange house and the strange life appeared to have something to do with everything that was picturesque.

One Sunday when Joe, greatly enjoying his pipe, had so plumed himself on being 'most awful dull', that I had given him up for the day, I lay on the earthwork for some time with my chin on my hand, descrying traces of Miss Havisham and Estella all over the prospect, in the sky and in the water, until at last I resolved to mention a thought concerning them that had been much in my head.

'Joe,' said I; 'don't you think I ought to make Miss Havisham a visit?'

'There is some visits, p'r'aps,' said Joe, 'as for ever remains open to the question, Pip. But in regard of visiting Miss Havisham. She might think you wanted something – expected something of her.'

'Don't you think I might say that I did not, Joe?'

'You might, old chap,' said Joe. 'And she might credit it. Similarly she mightn't. You see, Pip, when Miss Havisham done the handsome thing by you, she called me back to say to me as that were all.'

'Yes, Joe. I heard her.'

'Which I meantersay, Pip, it might be that her meaning were – Make a end on it! – As you was! – Me to the North, and you to the South!'

I had thought of that too, and it was very far from comforting to me to find that he had thought of it; for it seemed to render it more probable.

'But Joe, here am I, getting on in the first year of my time, and, since the day of my being bound, I have never thanked Miss Havisham, or asked after her.'

'That's true, Pip; and unless you was to turn her out a set of shoes all four round – and which I meantersay as even a set of shoes all four round might not act acceptable as a present, in a total vacancy of hoofs –'

'I don't mean that sort of remembrance, Joe; I don't mean a present.'

But Joe had got the idea of a present in his head and must harp upon it. 'Or even,' said he, 'if you was helped to knocking her up a new chain for the front door –'

'My dear Joe,' I cried, 'I never thought of making Miss Havisham any present.'

'No, Pip,' Joe assented, as if he had been contending for that, all along; 'and what I say to you is, you are right, Pip.'

'Yes, Joe; but what I wanted to say, was, that as we are rather slack just now, if you would give me a half-holiday tomorrow, I think I would go up-town and make a call on Miss Est – Havisham.'

'Which her name,' said Joe, gravely, 'ain't Estavasham, Pip, unless she have been rechris'ened.'

'I know, Joe, I know. It was a slip of mine. What do you think of it, Joe?'

In brief, Joe thought that if I thought well of it, he thought well of it. But, he was particular in stipulating that if I were not encouraged to repeat my visit as a visit which had no ulterior object but was simply one of gratitude for a favour received, then this experimental trip should have no successor. By these conditions I promised to abide.

Now, Joe kept a journeyman at weekly wages whose name was Orlick. He lodged at a sluice-keeper's out on the marshes, and on working days would come slouching from his hermitage, with his hands in his pockets and his dinner loosely tied in a bundle round his neck and dangling on his back. He always slouched, locomotively, with his eyes on the ground; and, when accosted or otherwise required to raise them, he looked up in a half resentful, half puzzled way, as though the only thought he ever had, was, that it was rather an odd and injurious fact that he should never be thinking.

This morose journeyman had no liking for me. When I became Joe's 'prentice, Orlick was perhaps confirmed in some suspicion that I should displace him. Not that he ever said anything, or did anything, openly importing hospitality; I only noticed that he always beat his sparks in my direction, and that whenever I sang Old Clem, he came in out of time.

Orlick was at work and present, next day, when I reminded Joe of my half-holiday. He said nothing at the moment, he and I was at the bellows; but by-and-by he said, leaning on his hammer:

'Now, master! Sure you're not a going to favour only one of us. If Young Pip has a half-holiday, do as much for Old Orlick.'

'Why, what'll you do with a half-holiday, if you get it?' said Joe.

'What'll *I* do with it! What'll *he* do with it? I'll do as much with it as *him*,' said Orlick.

'Don't lose your temper,' said Joe.

'Shall if I like,' growled Orlick. 'Now, master! Come. No favouring in this shop. Be a man!'

The master refusing to entertain the subject until the journeyman was in a better temper, Orlick plunged at the furnace, drew out a red-hot bar, made at me with it as if he were going to run it through my body, whisked it round my head, laid it on the anvil, hammered it out and finally said, when he had hammered himself hot and the iron cold, and he again leaned on his hammer:

'Now, master!'

'Are you all right now?' demanded Joe.

'Ah! I am all right,' said gruff Old Orlick.

'Then, as in general you stick to your work as well as most men,' said Joe, 'let it be a half-holiday for all.'

My sister had been standing silent in the yard, within hearing – she was a most unscrupulous spy and listener – and she instantly looked in at one of the windows.

'Like you, you fool!' said she to Joe, 'giving holidays to great idle hulkers like that. You are a rich man, upon my life, to waste wages in that way. I wish *I* was his master!'

'You'd be everybody's master, if you durst,' retorted Orlick, with an ill-favoured grin.

('Let her alone,' said Joe.)

'I'd be a match for all noodles and all rogues,' returned my sister, beginning to work herself into a mighty rage. 'And I couldn't be a match for the noodles, without being a match for your master, who's the dunder-headed king of the noodles. And I couldn't be a match for the rogues, without being a match for you, who are the blackest-looking and the worst rogue between this and France. Now!'

'You're a foul shrew, Mother Gargery,' growled the journeyman. 'If that makes a judge of rogues, you ought to be a good'un.'

('Let her alone, will you?' said Joe.)

'What did you say?' cried my sister, beginning to scream. 'What did that fellow Orlick say to me, Pip? What did he call me, with my husband standing by? O! Hold me! O!'

'Ah-h-h!' growled the journeyman, between his

teeth, 'I'd hold you, if you was my wife. I'd hold you under the pump, and choke it out of you.'

('I tell you, let her alone,' said Joe.)

'Oh! To hear him!' cried my sister, with a clap of her hands and a scream together. 'To hear the names he's giving me! That Orlick! In my own house! O! O!' Here my sister, after a fit of clappings and screamings, beat her hands upon her bosom and upon her knees, and threw her cap off, and pulled her hair down. Being by this time a perfect Fury and a complete success, she made a dash at the door, which I had fortunately locked.

What could the wretched Joe do now, after his disregarded parenthetical interruptions, but stand up to his journeyman, and ask him what he meant by interfering betwixt himself and Mrs Joe; and further whether he was man enough to come on? Old Orlick felt that the situation admitted of nothing less than coming on, and was on his defence straightway; so they went at one another, like two giants. But, if any man in that neighbourhood could stand up long against Joe, I never saw the man. Orlick, as if he had been of no more account than the pale young gentleman, was very soon among the coal-dust, and in no hurry to come out of it. Then, Joe unlocked the door and picked up my sister, who had dropped insensible at the window and who was carried into the house and laid down, and who was recommended to revive, and would do nothing but struggle and clench her hands in Joe's hair. Then, came that singular calm and silence which succeed all uproars; and I went upstairs to dress myself.

When I came down again, I found Joe and Orlick

sweeping up, without any other traces of discomposure than a slit in one of Orlick's nostrils. The lull had a sedative and philosophical influence on Joe, who followed me out into the road to say, as a parting observation that might do me good, 'On the rampage, Pip, and off the rampage, Pip – such is Life!'

With what absurd emotions I found myself again going to Miss Havisham's, matters little here. Nor, how I passed and repassed the gate many times before I could make up my mind to ring.

Miss Sarah Pocket came to the gate. No Estella.

'How, then? You here again?' said Miss Pocket. 'What do you want?'

When I said that I only came to see how Miss Havisham was, Sarah evidently deliberated whether or no she should send me about my business. But, unwilling to hazard the responsibility, she let me in, and presently brought the sharp message that I was to 'come up'.

Everything was unchanged, and Miss Havisham was alone. 'Well?' said she, fixing her eyes upon me. 'I hope you want nothing? You'll get nothing.'

'No, indeed, Miss Havisham. I only wanted you to know that I am doing very well in my apprenticeship, and am always much obliged to you.'

'There, there!' with the old restless fingers. 'Come now and then; come on your birthday. – Ay!' she cried suddenly, turning herself and her chair towards me, 'You are looking round for Estella? Hey?'

I had been looking round – in fact, for Estella – and I stammered that I hoped she was well.

'Abroad,' said Miss Havisham; 'educating for a lady; far out of reach; prettier than ever; admired by all who see her. Do you feel that you have lost her?'

There was such a malignant enjoyment in her utterance of the last words, and she broke into such a disagreeable laugh, that I was at a loss what to say. She spared me the trouble of considering, by dismissing me. When the gate was closed upon me by Sarah of the walnut-shell countenance, I felt more than ever dissatisfied with my home and with my trade and with everything; and that was all I took by *that* motion.

As I was loitering along the High-street, looking in disconsolately at the shop windows, and thinking what I would buy if I were a gentleman, who should come out of the bookshop but Mr Wopsle. Mr Wopsle had in his hand the affecting tragedy of George Barnwell, with the view of heaping every word of it on the head of Pumblechook, with whom he was going to drink tea. No sooner did he see me, than he laid hold of me, and insisted on my accompanying him to the Pumblechookian parlour. As I knew it would be miserable at home, and almost any companionship on the road was better than none, I made no great resistance.

The representation of George Barnwell took until half-past nine o'clock that night, and that when Mr Wopsle got into Newgate, I thought he never would go to the scaffold, he became so much slower than at any former period of his disgraceful career. This, however, was a mere question of length and wearisomeness. What stung me, was the identification of the whole affair with my unoffending self. When Barnwell began to go wrong, I declare that I felt positively apologetic, Pumblechook's indignant stare so taxed me with it. Wopsle, too, took pains to present me in the worst light. Even after I was happily hanged and Wopsle had closed the book, Pumblechook sat staring at me, and shaking his head, and saying, 'Take warning, boy, take warning!'

It was a very dark night when it was all over, and when I set out with Mr Wopsle on the walk home. The turnpike lamp was a blur of mist, quite out of the lamp's usual place apparently, and its rays looked solid substance on the fog. We were noticing this, when we came upon a man, slouching under the lee of the turnpike house.

'Halloa!' we said, stopping. 'Orlick, there?'

'Ah!' he answered, slouching out. 'I was standing by, a minute, on the chance of company.'

'You are late,' I remarked.

Orlick not unnaturally answered, 'Well? And *you*'re late.'

'We have been,' said Mr Wopsle, exalted with his late performance, 'we have been indulging, Mr Orlick, in an intellectual evening.'

Old Orlick growled, as if he had nothing to say about that, and we all went on together. I asked him presently whether he had been spending his half-holiday up and down town?

'Yes,' said he, 'all of it. I come in behind yourself. By-the-bye, the guns is going again.'

'At the Hulks?' said I.

'Ay! The guns have been going since dark, about. You'll hear one presently.'

In effect, we had not walked many yards further, when the well-remembered boom came towards us, deadened by the mist, and heavily rolled away along the low grounds by the river.

'A good night for cutting off in,' said Orlick. 'We'd be puzzled how to bring down a jail-bird on the wing, tonight.'

It was very dark, very wet, very muddy, and so we splashed along. Now and then, the sound of the signal cannon broke upon us again. Thus, we came to the village. The way by which we approached it, took us past the Three Jolly Bargemen, which we were surprised to find in a state of commotion. Mr Wopsle dropped in to ask what was the matter, but came running out in a great hurry.

'There's something wrong,' said he, without stopping, 'up at your place, Pip. Run all!'

'What is it?' I asked, keeping up with him. So did Orlick, at my side.

'I can't quite understand. The house seems to have been violently entered when Joe Gargery was out. Supposed by convicts. Somebody has been attacked and hurt.'

We were running too fast to admit of more being said, and we made no stop until we got into our kitchen. It was full of people; the whole village was there, or in the yard; and there was a surgeon, and there was Joe, and there was a group of women, all on the floor in the midst of the kitchen. I became aware of my sister – lying without sense or movement on the bare boards where she had been knocked down by a tremendous blow on the back of the head, dealt by some unknown hand when her face was turned towards the fire – destined never to be on the rampage again, while she was the wife of Joe.

16

Joe had been at the Three Jolly Bargemen, smoking his pipe, from a quarter after eight o'clock to a quarter before ten. While he was there, my sister had been seen standing at the kitchen door, and had exchanged good-night with a farm-labourer going home. When Joe went home at five minutes before ten, he found her struck down on the floor, and promptly called in assistance.

Nothing had been taken away from any part of the house. Neither was there any disarrangement of the kitchen, excepting such as she herself had made, in falling and bleeding. But, there was one remarkable piece of evidence on the spot. She had been struck with something blunt and heavy, on the head and spine; after the blows were dealt, something heavy had been thrown down at her with considerable violence, as she lay on her face. And on the ground beside her, when Joe picked her up, was a convict's leg-iron which had been filed asunder.

Now, Joe, examining this iron with a smith's eye, declared it to have been filed asunder some time ago. The hue and cry going off to the Hulks, and people coming thence to examine the iron, Joe's opinion was corroborated. They did not undertake to say when it had left the prison-ships; but they claimed to know for certain that that particular manacle had not been worn by either of two convicts who had escaped last night.

Further, one of those two was already re-taken, and had not freed himself of his iron.

I believed the iron to be my convict's iron – the iron I had seen and heard him filing at, on the marshes – but my mind did not accuse him of having put it to its latest use. For, I believed one of two other persons to have become possessed of it, and to have turned it to this cruel account. Either Orlick, or the strange man who had shown me the file.

Now, as to Orlick; he had gone to town exactly as he told us when we picked him up at the turnpike, he had been seen about town all the evening, and he had come back with myself and Mr Wopsle. There was nothing against him, save the quarrel; and my sister had quarrelled with him, and with everybody else about her, ten thousand times. As to the strange man; if he had come back for his two bank-notes there could have been no dispute about them, because my sister was fully prepared to restore them. Besides, there had been no altercation; the assailant had come in so silently and suddenly, that she had been felled before she could look round.

It was horrible to think that I had provided the weapon, however undesignedly, but I could hardly think otherwise. I considered and reconsidered whether I should at last dissolve that spell of my childhood, and tell Joe all the story. For months afterwards, I every day settled the question finally in the negative, and re-opened and re-argued it next morning. The contention came, after all, to this; – the secret was such an old one now, had so grown into me and become a part of myself, that I could not tear it away. In addition to the dread that, having led up to so much mischief, it would be now more likely than ever to alienate Joe from me if he believed it. However, I temporized with myself, of course and resolved to make a full disclosure if I should see any such new occasion as a new chance of helping in the discovery of the assailant.

The Constables, and the Bow Street men from London were about the house for a week or two. They took up several obviously wrong people, and they ran their heads very hard against wrong ideas, and persisted in trying to fit the circumstances to the ideas, instead of trying to extract ideas from the circumstances.

Long after these constitutional powers had dispersed, my sister lay very ill in bed. Her sight was disturbed, so that she saw objects multiplied, and grasped at visionary teacups and wine-glasses instead of the realities; her hearing was greatly impaired; her memory also; and her speech was unintelligible. When, at last, she came round so far as to be helped downstairs, it was still necessary to keep my slate always by her, that she might indicate in writing what she could not indicate in speech.

However, her temper was greatly improved, and she was patient. We were at a loss to find a suitable attendant for her, until a circumstance happened conveniently to relieve us. Mr Wopsle's great-aunt conquered a confirmed habit of living into which she had fallen, and Biddy became a part of our establishment.

It may have been about a month after my sister's reappearance in the kitchen, when Biddy came to us, and became a blessing to the household. Above all, she was a blessing to Joe, for the dear old fellow was sadly cut up by the constant contemplation of the wreck of his wife, and had been accustomed, while attending on her of an evening, to turn to me every now and then and say, with his blue eyes moistened, 'Such a fine figure of a woman as she once were, Pip!' Biddy instantly taking the cleverest charge of her, and Joe became able in some sort to appreciate the greater quiet of his life, and to get down to the Jolly Bargemen now and then for a change that did him good.

Biddy's first triumph in her new office, was to solve a difficulty that had completely vanquished me.

Again and again, my sister had traced upon the slate, a character that looked like a curious T, and then with the utmost eagerness had called our attention to it as something she particularly wanted. I had in vain tried everything producible that began with a T, from tar to toast and tub. At length it had come into my head that the sign looked like a hammer, and on my lustily calling that word in my sister's ear, she had begun to hammer on the table and had expressed a qualified assent. Thereupon, I had brought in all our hammers, one after another, but without avail.

When my sister found that Biddy was very quick to understand her, this mysterious sign reappeared on the slate. Biddy looked thoughtfully at it, heard my explanation, looked thoughtfully at my sister, looked thoughtfully at Joe, and ran into the forge, followed by Joe and me.

'Why, of course!' cried Biddy, with an exultant face. 'Don't you see? It's *him*!'

Orlick, without a doubt! She had lost his name, and could only signify him by his hammer. We told him why we wanted him to come into the kitchen, and he came slouching out, with a curious loose vagabond bend in the knees that strongly distinguished him.

I confess that I expected to see my sister denounce him, and that I was disappointed by the different result. She was evidently much pleased by his being at length produced, and motioned that she would have him given something to drink. She watched his countenance as if she were particularly wishful to be assured that he took kindly to his reception. After that day, a day rarely passed without her drawing the hammer on her slate, and without Orlick's slouching in and standing doggedly before her, as if he knew no more than I did what to make of it.

17

On my birthday I paid another visit to Miss Havisham. I found Miss Sarah Pocket still on duty at the gate, I found Miss Havisham just as I had left her, and she spoke of Estella in the very same way, if not in the very same words. The interview lasted but a few minutes, and she gave me a guinea when I was going, and told me to come again on my next birthday.

So unchanging was the dull old house, that I felt as if the stopping of the clocks had stopped Time in that mysterious place, and, while I and everything else outside it grew older, it stood still. Daylight never entered the house as to my thoughts and remembrances of it, any more than as to the actual fact. It bewildered me, and under its influence I continued at heart to hate my trade and to be ashamed of home.

Imperceptibly I became conscious of a change in Biddy, however. Her shoes came up at the heel, her hair grew bright and neat, her hands were always clean. She was not beautiful -- she was common, and could not be like Estella – but she was pleasant and wholesome and sweet-tempered. She had not been with us more than a year, when I observed to myself one evening that she had curiously thoughtful and attentive eyes; eyes that were very pretty and very good.

It came of my lifting up my own eyes from a task I was poring at – writing some passages from a book, to improve myself in two ways at once by a sort of stratagem – and seeing Biddy observant of what I was about.

'How do you manage, Biddy,' said I, 'to learn everything that I learn, and always to keep up with me?' I was beginning to be rather vain of my knowledge, for I spent my birthday guineas on it, and set aside the greater part of my pocket-money for similar investment.

'I might as well ask you,' said Biddy, 'how *you* manage?'

'No; because when I come in from the forge of a night, any one can see me turning to at it. But you never turn to at it, Biddy.'

'I suppose I must catch it – like a cough,' said Biddy, quietly; and went on with her sewing.

I looked at Biddy sewing away with her head on one side and began to think her rather an extraordinary girl. For, I called to mind now, that she was equally accomplished in the terms of our trade, and the names of our different sorts of work, and our various tools. Theoretically, she was already as good a blacksmith as I, or better.

'You are one of those, Biddy,' said I, 'who make the most of every chance. You never had a chance before you came here, and see how improved you are!'

'I was your first teacher though; wasn't I?' said she, as she sewed.

'Biddy!' I exclaimed, in amazement. 'Why, you are crying!'

'No I am not,' said Biddy, looking up and laughing. 'What put that in your head?'

What could have put it in my head, but the glistening of a tear as it dropped on her work? I recalled the hopeless circumstances by which she had been surrounded in the miserable little shop and the miserable little noisy evening school, with that miserable old bundle of incompetence always to be dragged and shouldered. Biddy sat quietly sewing, shedding no more tears, and while I looked at her and thought about it all, it occurred to me that perhaps I had not been sufficiently grateful to Biddy. I might have been too reserved, and should have patronized her more with my confidence.

'Yes, Biddy,' I observed, when I had done turning it over, 'you were my first teacher, and that at a time when we little thought of ever being together like this, in this kitchen.'

'Ah, poor thing!' replied Biddy. It was like her self-forgetfulness, to transfer the remark to my sister, and to get up and be busy about her, making her more comfortable; 'that's sadly true!'

'Well!' said I, 'we must talk together a little more, as we used to do. Let us have a quiet walk on the marshes next Sunday, Biddy, and a long chat.'

My sister was never left alone now; but Joe more than readily undertook the care of her on that Sunday afternoon, and Biddy and I went out together. When we were out on the marshes and began to see the sails of the ships as they sailed on, I began to combine Miss Havisham and Estella with the prospect, in my usual way. When we came to the river-side and sat down on the bank, I resolved that it was a good time and place for the admission of Biddy into my inner confidence.

'Biddy,' said I, after binding her to secrecy, 'I want to be a gentleman.'

'Oh, I wouldn't, if I was you!' she returned.

'Biddy,' said I, with some severity, 'I have particular reasons for wanting to be a gentleman.'

'You know best, Pip; but don't you think you are happier as you are?'

'Biddy,' I exclaimed, impatiently, 'I am disgusted with my calling and with my life. I have never taken to either, since I was bound. Don't be absurd.'

'Was I absurd?' said Biddy, quietly raising her eyebrows; 'I am sorry for that; I only want you to do well, and to be comfortable.'

'Well then, understand once for all that I never shall or can be anything but miserable unless I can lead a very different sort of life from the life I lead now.'

'That's a pity!' said Biddy, shaking her head with a sorrowful air.

'If I could have settled down,' I said, 'Joe and I would perhaps have gone partners when I was out of my time, and I might even have grown up to keep company with you, and we might have sat on this very bank on a fine Sunday, quite different people. I should have been good enough for *you*; shouldn't I, Biddy?'

Biddy sighed, and returned for answer, 'Yes; I am not over-particular.' It scarcely sounded flattering, but I knew she meant well.

'Instead of that,' said I, 'see how I am going on. Dissatisfied, and uncomfortable, and – what would it signify to me, being coarse and common, if nobody had told me so!'

Biddy turned her face suddenly towards mine, and looked far more attentively at me than she had looked at the sailing ships.

'It was neither a very true nor a very polite thing to say,' she remarked. 'Who said it?'

I was disconcerted, for I had broken away without quite seeing where I was going to. It was not to be shuffled off now, however, and I answered, 'The beautiful young lady at Miss Havisham's, and she's more beautiful than anybody ever was, and I admire her dreadfully, and I want to be a gentleman on her account.'

'Do you want to be a gentleman, to spite her or to gain her over?' Biddy quietly asked me, after a pause.

'I don't know,' I moodily answered.

'Because, if it is to spite her,' Biddy pursued, 'that might be better and more independently done by caring nothing for her words. And if it is to gain her over, I should think – but you know best – she was not worth gaining over.'

Exactly what I myself had thought, many times. But how could I, a poor dazed village lad, avoid that wonderful inconsistency into which the best and wisest of men fall every day?

Biddy tried to reason no more with me. She softly patted my shoulder in a soothing way, while my face upon my sleeve I cried a little – exactly as I had done in the brewery yard – and felt vaguely convinced that I was very much ill-used by somebody, or by everybody; I can't say which.

'I am glad of one thing,' said Biddy, 'and that is, that you have felt you could give me your confidence, Pip. And I am glad of another thing, and that is, that of course you know you may depend upon my keeping it and always so far deserving it.' With a quiet sigh for me, Biddy rose from the bank, and said, with a fresh and pleasant change of voice, 'Shall we walk a little further, or go home?'

'Biddy,' I cried, getting up, putting my arm round her neck, and giving her a kiss, 'I shall always tell you everything.'

'Till you're a gentleman,' said Biddy.

'You know I never shall be, so that's always. Not that I have any occasion to tell you anything, for you know everything I know – as I told you at home the other night.'

I said to Biddy we would walk a little further, and we did so, and the summer afternoon toned down into the summer evening, and it was very beautiful. I began to consider whether I was not more naturally and wholesomely situated, after all, in these circumstances, than playing beggar my neighbour by candlelight in the room with the stopped clocks, and being despised by Estella. I thought it would be very good for me if I could get her out of my head, and could go to work determined to relish what I had to do, and stick to it. I asked myself the question whether I did not surely know that if Estella were beside me at that moment instead of Biddy, she would make me miserable? I was obliged to admit that I did know it for a certainty, and I said to myself, 'Pip, what a fool you are!'

We talked a good deal as we walked, and all that Biddy said seemed right. Biddy was never insulting, or capricious; she would have derived only pain, and no pleasure, from giving me pain. How could it be, then, that I did not like her much the better of the two?

'Biddy,' said I, when we were walking homeward, 'I wish you could put me right.'

'I wish I could!' said Biddy.

'If I could only get myself to fall in love with you – you don't mind my speaking so openly to such an old acquaintance?'

'Oh dear, not at all!' said Biddy. 'Don't mind me.'

'If I could only get myself to do it, *that* would be the thing for me.'

'But you never will, you see,' said Biddy.

When we came near the churchyard, we had to cross an embankment, and get over a stile near a sluice gate. There started up, from the gate, or from the rushes, or from the ooze, Old Orlick.

'Halloa!' he growled, 'where are you two going?'

'Where should we be going, but home?'

'Well then,' said he, 'I'm jiggered if I don't see you home!'

Biddy was much against his going with us, and said to me in a whisper. 'Don't let him come; I don't like him.' As I did not like him either, I took the liberty of saying that we thanked him, but we didn't want seeing home. He received that piece of information with a yell of laughter, and dropped back, but came slouching after us at a little distance.

Curious to know whether Biddy suspected him of having had a hand in that murderous attack of which my sister had never been able to give any account, I asked her why she did not like him.

'Oh!' she replied, glancing over her shoulder as he slouched after us, 'because I – I am afraid he likes me.'

'Did he ever tell you he liked you?' I asked, indignantly.

'No,' said Biddy, glancing over her shoulder again, 'he never told me so; but he dances at me, whenever he can catch my eye.'

I did not doubt the accuracy of the interpretation. I was very hot indeed upon Old Orlick's daring to admire her; as hot as if it were an outrage on myself.

I kept an eye on Orlick after that night, and, whenever circumstances were favourable to his dancing at Biddy, got before him, to obscure that demonstration. He had struck root in Joe's establishment, by reason of my sister's sudden fancy for him, or I should have tried to get him dismissed. He quite understood and reciprocated my good intentions, as I had reason to know thereafter.

And now, because my mind was not confused enough before, I complicated its confusion fifty thousand-fold, by having states and seasons when I was clear that Biddy was immeasurably better than Estella, and that the plain honest working life to which I was born offered me sufficient means of self-respect and happiness. At those times, I would decide conclusively that my disaffection to dear old Joe and the forge, was gone, and that I was growing up in a fair way to be partners with Joe and to keep company with

Biddy – when all in a moment some confounding remembrance of the Havisham days would fall upon me, like a destructive missile, and scatter my wits again.

If my time had run out, it would have left me still at the height of my perplexities, I dare say. It never did run out, however, but was brought to a premature end, as I proceed to relate.

18

It was in the fourth year of my apprenticeship to Joe, and it was a Saturday night. There was a group assembled round the fire at the Three Jolly Bargemen, attentive to Mr Wopsle as he read the newspaper aloud. Of that group I was one.

A highly popular murder had been committed, and Mr Wopsle was imbrued in blood to the eyebrows. He gloated over every abhorrent adjective in the description, and identified himself with every witness at the Inquest. The coroner, in Mr Wopsle's hands, became Timon of Athens; the beadle, Coriolanus. He enjoyed himself thoroughly, and we all enjoyed ourselves, and were delightfully comfortable. In this cozy state of mind we came to the verdict Wilful Murder.

Then, and not sooner, I became aware of a strange gentleman leaning over the back of the settle opposite me, looking on. There was an expression of contempt on his face, and he bit the side of a great forefinger as he watched the group of faces.

'Well!' said the stranger to Mr Wopsle, when the

reading was done, 'you have settled it all to your own satisfaction, I have no doubt?'

Everybody started and looked up, as if it were the murderer.

'Guilty, of course?' said he. 'Out with it. Come!'

'Sir,' returned Mr Wopsle, 'without having the honour of your acquaintance, I do say Guilty.'

'I know you do,' said the stranger; 'but now I'll ask you a question. Do you know, or do you not know, that the law of England supposes every man to be innocent, until he is proved to be guilty?'

'Sir,' Mr Wopsle began to reply, 'as an Englishman myself, I –'

'Come!' said the stranger, biting his forefinger at him. 'Don't evade the question. Either you know it, or you don't know it.'

He stood with his head on one side and himself on one side, in a bullying interrogative manner, and he threw his forefinger at Mr Wopsle – as it were to mark him out – before biting it again.

'Now!' said he. 'Do you know it, or don't you know it?'

'Certainly I know it,' replied Mr Wopsle.

'Certainly you know it. Then why didn't you say so at first? Now, I'll ask you another question; *do* you know that none of these witnesses have yet been cross-examined?'

Mr Wopsle hesitated, and we all began to conceive rather a poor opinion of him.

'Come!' said the stranger, 'I'l help you. You don't deserve help, but I'll help you. Look at that paper you hold in your hand. Now, tell me whether it distinctly states that the prisoner expressly said that his legal advisers instructed him altogether to reserve his defence?'

'I read that just now,' Mr Wopsle pleaded.

'Never mind what you read just now, sir; turn to the paper. No, no, no my friend; not to the top of the column; to the bottom, to the bottom. Well? Have you found it?'

'Here it is,' said Mr Wopsle.

'Now, follow that passage with your eye, and tell me whether it distinctly states that the prisoner expressly said that he was instructed by his legal advisers wholly to reserve his defence? Come! Do you make that of it?'

Mr Wopsle answered, 'Those are not the exact words.'

'Not the exact words!' repeated the gentleman, bitterly. 'Is that the exact substance?'

'Yes,' said Mr Wopsle.

'Yes,' repeated the stranger, 'And now I ask you what you say to the conscience of that man who, with that passage before his eyes, can lay his head upon his pillow after having pronounced a fellow-creature guilty, unheard?'

We all began to suspect that Mr Wopsle was not the man we had thought him, and that he was beginning to be found out.

'And the same man, remember,' pursued the gentleman, 'might be summoned as a juryman upon this very trial, and, having thus deeply committed himself, might return to the bosom of his family and lay his head upon his pillow, after deliberately swearing that he would well and truly try the issue joined between Our Sovereign Lord the King and the prisoner at the bar, and would a true verdict give according to the evidence, so help him God!'

The strange gentleman, with an air of authority not to be disputed, left the back of the settle, and came into the space between the two settles, in front of the fire, where he remained standing.

'From information I have received,' said he, looking round at us as we all quailed before him, 'I have reason to believe there is a blacksmith among you, by name Joseph – or Joe – Gargery. Which is the man?'

'Here is the man,' said Joe.

The strange gentleman beckoned him out of his place, and Joe went.

'You have an apprentice,' pursued the stranger, 'commonly known as Pip? Is he here?'

'I am here!' I cried.

The stranger did not recognize me, but I recognized him as the gentleman I had met on the stairs, on the occasion of my second visit to Miss Havisham.

'I wish to have a private conference with you two,' said he, when he had surveyed me at his leisure. 'It will take a little time. Perhaps we had better go to your place of residence.'

Admist a wondering silence, we three walked out of the Jolly Bargemen, and in a wondering silence walked home. While going along, the strange gentleman occasionally looked at me, and occasionally bit the side of his finger. As we neared home, Joe vaguely acknowledging the occasion as an impressive and ceremonious one, went on ahead to open the front door. Our conference was held in the state parlour, which was feebly lighted by one candle.

It began with the strange gentleman's sitting down at the table, drawing the candle to him, and looking over some entries in his pocket-book.

'My name,' he said, 'is Jaggers, and I am a lawyer in London. I am pretty well known. I have unusual business to transact with you, and I commence by explaining that it is not of my originating. If my advice had been asked, I should not have been here. It was not asked, and you see me here. Now, Joseph Gargery, I am the bearer of an offer to relieve you of this young fellow your apprentice. You would not object to cancel his indentures, at his request and for his good? You would want nothing for so doing?'

'Lord forbid that I should want anything for not standing in Pip's way,' said Joe, staring.

I thought Mr Jaggers glanced at Joe, as if he considered him a fool for his disinterestedness. But I was too much bewildered between breathless curiousity and surprise, to be sure of it.

'Very well,' said Mr Jaggers. 'Now, I return to this young fellow. And the communication I have got to make is, that he has great expectations.'

Joe and I gasped, and looked at one another.

'I am instructed to communicate to him,' said Mr Jaggers, throwing his finger at me sideways, 'that he will come into a handsome property. Further, that it is the desire of the present possessor of that property, that he be immediately removed from his present sphere of life and from this place, and be brought up as a gentleman – in a word, as a young fellow of great expectations.'

My dream was out; my wild fancy was surpassed by sober reality; Miss Havisham was going to make my fortune on a grand scale.

'Now, Mr Pip,' pursued the lawyer, 'I address the rest of what I have to say, to you. You are to understand, first, that it is the request of the person from whom I take my instructions, that you always bear the name of Pip. But if you have any objection, this is the time to mention it.' My heart was beating so fast, and there was such a singing in my ears, that I could scarcely stammer I had no objection.

'I should think not! Now you are to understand, secondly, Mr Pip, that the name of the person who is your liberal benefactor remains a profound secret, until the person chooses to reveal it. Now, you are distinctly to understand that you are most positively prohibited from making any enquiry on this head, or any allusion or reference, however distant, to any individual whomsoever as *the* individual, in all the communications you may have with me. If you have a suspicion in your own breast, keep that suspicion in your own breast. The condition is laid down. Your acceptance of it, and your observance of it as binding, is the only remaining condition that I am charged with, by the person from whom I take my instructions. That person is the person from whom you derive your expectations, and the secret is solely held by that person and by me. Now, Mr Pip, I have done with stipulations.' Though he called me Mr Pip, and began rather to make up to me, he still could not get rid of a certain air of bullying suspicion; and even now he occasionally shut his eyes and threw his finger at me while he spoke, as much as to express that he knew all kinds of things to my disparagement. 'We come next, to mere details of arrangement. There is already lodged in my hands, a sum of money amply sufficient for your suitable education and maintenance. You will please consider me your guardian. It is considered that you must be better educated, in accordance with your altered position, and that you will be alive to the importance and necessity of at once entering on that advantage.'

I said I had always longed for it.

'Never mind what you have always longed for, Mr Pip,' he retorted; 'keep to the record. Am I answered that you are ready to be placed at once, under some proper tutor? Is that it?'

I stammered yes, that was it.

'Good. Now, your inclinations are to be consulted. Have you ever heard of any tutor whom you would prefer to another?'

I had never heard of any tutor but Biddy and Mr Wopsle's great-aunt; so, I replied in the negative.

'There is a certain tutor, of whom I have some knowledge, who I think might suit the purpose,' said Mr Jaggers. 'I don't recommend him, observe; because I never recommend anybody. The gentleman I speak of, is one Mr Matthew Pocket.'

Ah! I caught at the name directly. Miss Havisham's relation. The Matthew whose place was to be at Miss Havisham's head, when she lay dead, in her bride's dress on the bride's table.

'You know the name?' said Mr Jaggers.

My answer was, that I had heard of the name.

'Oh!' said he. 'You have heard of the name. But the question is, what do you say of it?'

I said that I was much obliged to him for his mention of Mr Matthew Pocket and that I would gladly try that gentleman.

'Good. You had better try him in his own house. The way shall be prepared for you, and you can see his son first, who is in London. When will you come to London?'

I said (glancing at Joe, who stood looking on, motionless), that I supposed I could come directly.

'First,' said Mr Jaggers, 'you should have some new clothes to come in, and they should not be working clothes. Say this day week. You'll want some money. Shall I leave you twenty guineas?'

He produced a long purse, with the greatest coolness, and counted them out on the table and pushed them over to me.

'Well, Joseph Gargery? You look dumbfoundered?' he said, eyeing Joe.

'I *am*!' said Joe, in a very decided manner.

'It was understood that you wanted nothing for yourself, remember?'

'It were understood,' said Joe. 'And it are understood. And it ever will be similar according.'

'But what,' said Mr Jaggers, swinging his purse, 'what if it was in my instructions to make you a present, as compensation for the loss of his services?'

'Pip is that hearty welcome,' said Joe, 'to go free with his services, to honour and fortun', as no words can tell him. But if you think as Money can make compensation to me for the loss of the little child – what come to the forge – and ever the best of friends! –'

O dear good Joe, whom I was so ready to leave and so unthankful to, I see you again, with your muscular blacksmith's arm before your eyes, and your broad chest heaving, and your voice dying away.

But I encouraged Joe at the time. I was lost in the mazes of my future fortunes, and could not retrace the by-paths we had trodden together. I begged Joe to be comforted, for (as he said) we had ever been the best of friends, and (as I said) we ever would be so.

'Now, Joseph Gargery,' said Mr Jaggers, 'I warn you this is your last chance. If you mean to take a present that I have it in charge to make you, speak out, and you shall have it.' Here to his great amazement, he was stopped by Joe's suddenly working round him with every demonstration of a fell pugilistic purpose.

'Which I meantersay,' cried Joe, 'that if you come into my place bull-baiting and badgering me, come out! Which I meantersay as sech if you're a man, come on!'

I drew Joe away, and he immediately became placable; merely stating to me, in an obliging manner that he were not a going to be bull-baited and badgered in his own place. Mr Jaggers had risen when Joe demonstrated, and had backed near the door. Without evincing any inclination to come in again, he there delivered his valedictory remarks. They were these:

'Well, Mr Pip, I think the sooner you leave here the better. Let it stand for this day week, and you shall receive my printed address in the mean time. You can take a hackney-coach at the stage-coach office in London, and come straight to me. Understand, that I express no opinion on the trust I undertake. I am paid for undertaking it, and I do so. Understand that!'

He was throwing his finger at both of us, and I think would have gone on, but for his seeming to think Joe dangerous, and going off.

Something came into my head which induced me to run after him, as he was going down to the Jolly Bargemen where he had left a hired carriage.

'I beg your pardon, Mr Jaggers.'

'Halloa!' said he, facing round, 'what's the matter?'

'I wish to be quite right, Mr Jaggers, and to keep to

your directions; so I thought I had better ask. Would there be any objection to my taking leave of any one I know, about here, before I go away?'

'No,' said he, looking as if he hardly understood me.

'I don't mean in the village only, but up-town?'

'No,' said he. 'No objection.'

I thanked him and ran home again, and there I found that Joe had already locked the front door, and was seated by the kitchen fire with a hand on each knee, gazing intently at the burning coals. I too sat down before the fire and gazed at the coals, and nothing was said for a long time.

The more I looked into the glowing coals, the more incapable I became of looking at Joe; the longer the silence lasted, the more unable I felt to speak.

At length I got out, 'Joe, have you told Biddy?'

'No, Pip,' returned Joe, still looking at the fire, 'which I left it to yourself, Pip.'

'I would rather you told, Joe.'

'Pip's a gentleman of fortun' then,' said Joe, 'and God bless him in it!'

Biddy dropped her work, and looked at me. Joe held his knees and looked at me. I looked at both of them. After a pause, they both heartily congratulated me; but there was a certain touch of sadness in their congratulations, that I rather resented.

I took it upon myself to impress Biddy to know nothing and say nothing about the maker of my fortune, save that I had come into great expectations from a mysterious patron.

Infinite pains were then taken by Biddy to convey to my sister some idea of what had happened. To the best of my belief, those efforts entirely failed. She laughed and nodded her head a great many times, and even repeated after Biddy, the words 'Pip' and 'Property'. But I doubt if they had more meaning in them than an election cry.

I never could have believed it without experience, but as Joe and Biddy became more at their cheerful ease again, I became quite gloomy. Dissatisfied with my fortune, of course I could not be; but it is possible that I may have been, without quite knowing it, dissatisfied with myself.

I would get up and look out at the door. The very stars to which I then raised my eyes, I am afraid I took to be but poor and humble stars for glittering on the rustic objects among which I had passed my life.

'Saturday night,' said I, when we sat at our supper of bread-and-cheese and beer. 'Five more days, and then the day before *the* day! They'll soon go.'

'Yes, Pip,' observed Joe, whose voice sounded hollow in his beer mug. 'They'll soon go.'

'I have been thinking, Joe, that when I go down on Monday, and order my new clothes, I shall tell the tailor that I'll come and put them on there, or that I'll have them sent to Mr Pumblechook's. It would be very disagreeable to be stared at by all the people here.'

'Mr and Mrs Hubble might like to see you in your new gen-teel figure too, Pip,' said Joe. 'So might Wopsle. And the Jolly Bargemen might take it as a compliment.'

'That's just what I don't want, Joe. They would make such a business of it – such a coarse and common business – that I couldn't bear myself.'

Biddy asked me here, as she sat holding my sister's plate, 'Have you thought about when you'll show yourself to Mr Gargery, and your sister, and me? You will show yourself to us; won't you?'

'If you had waited another moment, Biddy, you would have heard me say that I shall bring my clothes here in a bundle one evening – most likely on the evening before I go away.'

Biddy said no more. Handsomely forgiving her, I soon exchanged an affectionate good-night with her and Joe, and went up to bed. When I got into my little room, I sat down and took a long look at it, as a mean little room that I should soon be parted from and raised above, for ever. It was furnished with fresh young remembrances too, and even at the same moment I fell into much the same confused division of mind between it and the better rooms to which I was going, as I had been in so often between the forge and Miss Havisham's, and Biddy and Estella.

The sun had been shining brightly all day on the roof of my attic, and the room was warm. As I put the window open and stood looking out, I saw Joe come slowly forth at the dark door below, and take a turn or two in the air; and then I saw Biddy come, and bring him a pipe and light it for him. He never smoked so late, and it seemed to hint to me that he wanted comforting, for some reason or other.

He presently stood at the door immediately beneath me, smoking his pipe, and Biddy stood there too, and I knew that they talked of me, for I heard my name mentioned in an endearing tone by both of them. I drew away from the window, and sat down in my one chair by the bedside, feeling it very sorrowful and strange that this first night of my bright fortunes should be the loneliest I had ever known.

19

Joe and Biddy were very sympathetic and pleasant when I spoke of our approaching separation; but they only referred to it when I did. After breakfast, Joe brought out my indentures from the press in the best parlour, and we put them in the fire, and I felt that I was free.

After our early dinner I strolled out alone. As I passed the church, I felt a sublime compassion for the poor creatures who were destined to go there, Sunday after Sunday, all their lives through, and to lie obscurely at last among the low green mounds.

If I had often thought before, with something allied to shame, of my companionship with the fugitive whom I had once seen limping among those graves, what were my thoughts on this Sunday, when the place recalled the wretch, ragged and shivering, with his felon iron and badge! My comfort was, that it happened a long time ago, and that he had doubtless been transported a long way off, and that he was dead to me, and might be veritably dead into the bargain.

No more low wet grounds, no more dykes and sluices, no more of these grazing cattle – though they seemed, in their dull manner, to wear a more respectful air now, and to face round, in order that they might stare as long as possible at the possessor of such great expectations – farewell, monotonous acquaintances of my childhood, henceforth I was for London and greatness. I made my exultant way to the old Battery, and, lying down there to consider the question whether Miss Havisham intended me for Estella, fell asleep.

When I awoke, I was much surprised to find Joe sitting beside me, smoking his pipe. He greeted me with a cheerful smile on my opening my eyes, and said:

'As being the last time, Pip, I thought I'd foller.'

'And Joe, I am very glad you did so.'

'Thankee, Pip.'

'You may be sure, dear Joe,' I went on, after we had shaken hands, 'that I shall never forget you.'

'No, no, Pip!' said Joe, in a comfortable tone, '*I*'m sure of that.'

Somehow, I was not best pleased with Joe's being so mightily secure of me. I should have liked him to have betrayed emotion, or to have said, 'It does you credit, Pip,' or something of that sort.

'It's a pity now, Joe,' said I, 'that you did not get on a little more, when we had our lessons here; isn't it?'

'Well, I don't know,' returned Joe. 'I'm so awful dull. I'm only master of my own trade.'

What I had meant was, that when I came into my property and was able to do something for Joe, it would have been much more agreeable if he had been better qualified for a rise in station. He was so perfectly innocent of my meaning, however, that I thought I would mention it to Biddy in preference.

So, when we had walked home and had had tea, I took Biddy into our little garden by the side of the lane, and said I had a favour to ask of her.

'And it is, Biddy,' said I, 'that you will not omit any opportunity of helping Joe on, a little.'

'How helping him on?' asked Biddy, with a steady sort of glance.

'Well Joe is a dear good fellow but he is rather backward in some things. For instance, Biddy, in his learning and his manners.'

Although I was looking at Biddy as I spoke, and although she opened her eyes very wide when I had spoken, she did not look at me.

'Oh, his manners! won't his manners do, then?' asked Biddy, plucking a black-currant leaf.

'My dear Biddy, they do very well here –'

'Oh! they *do* very well here?' interrupted Biddy.

'Hear me out – but if I were to remove Joe into a higher sphere, they would hardly do him justice.'

'And don't you think he knows that?' asked Biddy.

It was such a very provoking question, that I said, snappishly, 'Biddy, what do you mean?'

Biddy said, 'Have you never considered that he may be proud?'

'Proud?' I repeated, with disdainful emphasis.

'Oh! there are many kinds of pride,' said Biddy, looking full at me and shaking her head; 'pride is not all of one kind. He may be too proud to let any one take him out of a place that he is competent to fill, and fills well and with respect. To tell you the truth, I think he is: though it sounds bold in me to say so, for you must know him far better than I do.'

'Now, Biddy,' said I, 'I am very sorry to see this in you. You are dissatisfied on account of my rise in fortune, and you can't help showing it.'

'If you have the heart to think so,' returned Biddy, 'say so. Say so over and over again.'

'If you have the heart to be so, you mean, Biddy,'

said I, in a virtuous and superior tone; 'don't put it off upon me. I am very sorry to see it, and it's a – it's a bad side of human nature. I did intend to ask you to use any little opportunities you might have after I was gone, of improving dear Joe. But after this, I ask you nothing.'

'Whether you scold me or approve of me,' returned poor Biddy, 'you may equally depend upon my trying to do all that lies in my power, here, at all times. And whatever opinion you take away of me, shall make no difference in my remembrance of you. Yet a gentleman should not be unjust neither,' said Biddy, turning away her head.

I walked down the little path away from Biddy and Biddy went into the house, and I went out at the garden gate and took a dejected stroll until supper-time; again feeling it very sorrowful and strange that this, the second night of my bright fortunes, should be as lonely and unsatisfactory as the first.

But, morning once more brightened my view, and I extended my clemency to Biddy, and we dropped the subject. Putting on the best clothes I had, I went into town as early as I could hope to find the shops open, and presented myself before Mr Trabb, the tailor: who was having his breakfast in the parlour behind his shop.

'Well!' said Mr Trabb, in a hail-fellow-well-met kind of way. 'How are you, and what can I do for you?'

'Mr Trabb,' said I, 'it's an unpleasant thing to have to mention, because it looks like boasting; but I have come into a handsome property.'

A change passed over Mr Trabb. He wiped his fingers on the table-cloth, exclaiming, 'Lord bless my soul!'

'I am going up to my guardian in London,' said I, casually drawing some guineas out of my pocket and looking at them; 'and I want a fashionable suit of clothes to go in. I wish to pay for them,' I added – otherwise I thought he might only pretend to make them – 'with ready money.'

'My dear sir,' said Mr Trabb, 'may I venture to congratulate you? Would you do me the favour of stepping into the shop?'

Mr Trabb's boy was the most audacious boy in all that countryside. When I had entered he was sweeping the shop, and he had sweetened his labours by sweeping over me. He was still sweeping when I came out into the shop with Mr Trabb, and he knocked the broom against all possible corners and obstacles, to express equality with any blacksmith, alive or dead.

'Hold that noise,' said Mr Trabb, with the greatest sternness, 'or I'll knock your head off! Do me the favour to be seated, sir.'

I selected the materials for a suit, and Mr Trabb measured and calculated me, in the parlour, as if I were an estate and he the finest species of surveyor, and gave himself such a world of trouble that I felt that no suit of clothes could possibly remunerate him for his pains. When he had at last done and had appointed to send the articles to Mr Pumblechook's on the Thursday evening, he said, 'I know, sir, that London gentlemen cannot be expected to patronize local work, as a rule; but if you would give me a turn now and then in the quality of a townsman, I should greatly esteem it. Good morning, sir, much obliged. – Door!'

The last word was flung at the boy, who had not the

least notion what it meant. But I saw him collapse as his master rubbed me out with his hands, and my first decided experience of the stupendous power of money, was, that it had morally laid upon his back, Trabb's boy.

After this memorable event, I went to the hatter's, and the bootmaker's, and the hosier's, and felt rather like Mother Hubbard's dog whose outfit required the services of so many trades. When I had ordered everything I wanted, I directed my steps towards Pumblechook's, and, as I approached that gentleman's place of business, I saw him standing at his door.

'My dear friend,' said Mr Pumblechook, taking me by both hands, when he and I and the collation were alone, 'I give you joy of your good fortune. Well deserved, well deserved!'

This was coming to the point, and I thought it a sensible way of expressing himself.

'To think,' said Mr Pumblechook, after snorting admiration at me for some moments, 'that I should have been the humble instrument of leading up to this, is a proud reward.'

I begged Mr Pumblechook to remember that nothing was to be ever said or hinted, on that point.

'My dear young friend,' said Mr Pumblechook, 'if you will allow me to call you so –'

I murmured 'Certainly,' and Mr Pumblechook took me by both hands again.

'But my dear young friend,' said Mr Pumblechook, 'you must be hungry, you must be exhausted. Be seated. Here is a chicken had round from the Boar, here is a tongue had round from the Boar, here's one or two little things had round from the Boar, that I

hope you may not despise. But do I,' said Mr Pumblechook, 'see afore me, him as I ever sported with in his
times of happy infancy? And may I – *may* I –?'

This May I, meant might he shake hands? I con-
sented, and he was fervent, and then sat down again.

'Here is wine,' said Mr Pumblechook. 'Let us drink,
Thanks to Fortune, and may she ever pick out her
favourites with equal judgement! And your sister,' he
resumed, after a little steady eating, 'which had the
honour of bringing you up by hand! It's a sad picter,
to reflect that she's no longer equal to fully understanding the honour.'

'We'll drink her health,' said I.

'Ah!' cried Mr Pumblechook, leaning back in his
chair, quite flaccid with admiration, 'That's the way
you know the noble-minded, sir! Ever forgiving and
ever affable. It might,' said the servile Pumblechook,
putting down his untasted glass in a hurry and getting
up again, 'to a common person, have the appearance of
repeating – but *may* I –?'

When he had done it, he resumed his seat and drank
to my sister. 'Let us never be blind,' said Mr Pumblechook, 'to her faults of temper, but it is to be hoped
she meant well.'

I mentioned to Mr Pumblechook that I wished to
have my new clothes sent to his house, and he was
ecstatic on my so distinguishing him. Then he asked
me tenderly if I remembered how we had gone together
to have me bound apprentice, and, in effect, how he
had ever been my favourite fancy and my chosen
friend? If I had taken ten times as many glasses of
wine as I had, I should have known that he never had
stood in that relation towards me, and should in my

heart of hearts have repudiated the idea. Yet for all that, I remember feeling convinced that I had been much mistaken in him, and that he was a sensible practical good-hearted prime fellow.

We drank all the wine, and Mr Pumblechook made known to me for the first time in my life, and certainly after having kept his secret wonderfully well, that he had always said of me, 'That boy is no common boy and mark me, his fortun' will be no common fortun'.' Finally, I went out into the air, with a dim perception that there was something unwonted in the conduct of the sunshine, and found that I had slumberously got to the turn-pike without having taken any account of the road.

There, I was roused by Mr Pumblechook's hailing me. He was a long way down the sunny street, and was making expressive gestures for me to stop. I stopped, and he came up breathless.

'No, my dear friend,' said he, when he had recovered wind for speech. 'Not if I can help it. This occasion shall not entirely pass without that affability on your part. – May I, as an old friend and well-wisher? *May I?*'

We shook hands yet again, and he blessed me and stood waving his hand to me until I had passed the crook in the road; and then I turned into a field and had a long nap under a hedge before I pursued my way home.

On Friday morning I went to Mr Pumblechook's, to put on my new clothes and pay my visit to Miss Havisham. Mr Pumblechook's own room was given up to me to dress in, and was decorated with clean towels expressly for the event. My clothes were rather a disappointment, but after I had had my new suit on, some half an hour, and had gone through an immensity of posturing with Mr Pumblechook's very limited dressing-glass, in the futile endeavour to see my legs, it seemed to fit me better.

I went circuitously to Miss Havisham's by all the back ways, and rang at the bell. Sarah Pocket came to the gate, and positively reeled back when she saw me so changed; her walnut-shell countenance likewise, turned from brown to green and yellow.

'You?' said she. 'You, good gracious! What do you want?'

'I am going to London, Miss Pocket,' said I, 'and want to say goodbye to Miss Havisham.'

I was not expected, for she left me locked in the yard, while she went to ask if I were to be admitted. After a very short delay, she returned and took me up, staring at me all the way.

Miss Havisham was taking exercise in the room with the long spread table, leaning on her crutch stick. The room was lighted as of yore, and at the sound of our entrance, she stopped and turned. She was then just abreast of the rotted bride-cake.

'Don't go, Sarah,' she said. 'Well, Pip?'

'I start for London, Miss Havisham, tomorrow,' I was exceedingly careful what I said, 'and I thought you would kindly not mind my taking leave of you. I have come into such good fortune since I saw you last,' I murmured. 'And I am so grateful for it, Miss Havisham!'

'Ay, ay!' said she, looking at the discomfited and envious Sarah, with delight. 'I have seen Mr Jaggers. *I* have heard about it, Pip. So you go tomorrow?'

'Yes, Miss Havisham.'

'And you are adopted by a rich person?'

'Yes, Miss Havisham.'

'Not named?'

'No, Miss Havisham.'

'And Mr Jaggers is made your guardian?'

'Yes, Miss Havisham.'

She quite gloated on these questions and answers, so keen was her enjoyment of Sarah Pocket's jealous dismay. 'Well!' she went on; 'you have a promising career before you. Be good – deserve it – and abide by Mr Jaggers's instructions. Goodbye, Pip! – you will always keep the name of Pip, you know.'

'Yes, Miss Havisham.'

'Goodbye, Pip!'

She stretched out her hand, and I went down on my knee and put it to my lips. She looked at Sarah Pocket with triumph in her weird eyes, and so I left my fairy godmother, with both her hands on her crutch stick, standing in the midst of the dimly lighted room beside the rotten bride-cake that was hidden in cobwebs.

As the six evenings dwindled away, to five, to four, to three, to two, I became more and more appreciative of the society of Joe and Biddy. On the last evening, I dressed myself out in my new clothes, for their delight, and sat in my splendour until bedtime. We were all very low, and none the higher for pretending to be in spirits.

All night there were coaches in my broken sleep, going to wrong places instead of to London, and having in the traces, now dogs, now cats, now pigs, now men – never horses. Fantastic failures of journeys occupied me until the day dawned and the birds were singing.

Then, I got up and partly dressed, and sat at the window to take a last look out, and in taking it fell asleep.

Biddy was astir so early to get my breakfast, that, although I did not sleep at the window an hour, I smelt the smoke of the kitchen fire when I started up with a terrible idea that it must be late in the after-noon.

It was a hurried breakfast with no taste in it. I got up from the meal, saying with a sort of briskness, as if it had only just occurred to me, 'Well! I suppose I must be off!' and then I kissed my sister who was laughing and nodding and shaking in her usual chair, and kissed Biddy, and threw my arms around Joe's neck. Then I took up my little portmanteau and walked out. I stopped to wave my hat, and dear old Joe waved his strong right arm above his head, crying huskily 'Hooroar!' and Biddy put her apron to her face.

I walked away at a good pace, thinking it was easier to go than I had supposed it would be. But the village was very peaceful and quiet, and the light mists were solemnly rising, as if to show me the world, and I had been so innocent and little there, and all beyond was so unknown and great, that in a moment with a strong heave and sob I broke into tears.

So subdued I was by those tears, that when I was on the coach, and it was clear of the town, I deliberated with an aching heart whether I would not get down when we changed horses and walk back, and have another evening at home, and a better parting. We changed, and I had not made up my mind, and still reflected for my comfort that it would be quite practica-ble to get down and walk back, when we changed again.

It was now too late and too far to go back, and I went on. And the mists had all solemnly risen now, and the world lay spread before me.

THIS IS THE END OF THE FIRST STAGE OF
PIP'S EXPECTATIONS

20

It was a little past midday when the four-horse stage-coach by which I was a passenger, got into the ravel of traffic frayed out about the Cross Keys, Wood-street, Cheapside, London.

Mr Jaggers had duly sent me his address; it was, Little Britain, and he had written after it on his card, 'just out of Smithfield, and close by the coach-office.' Nevertheless, a hackney-coachman, who seemed to have as many capes to his greasy great-coat as he was years old, packed me up in his coach and hemmed me in with a folding and jingling barrier of steps, as if he were going to take me fifty miles.

I had scarcely had time to enjoy the coach, when I observed the coachman beginning to get down, as if we were going to stop presently. And stop we presently did, in a gloomy street, at certain offices with an open door, whereon was painted MR. JAGGERS.

'How much?' I asked the coachman.

The coachman answered, 'A shilling – unless you wish to make it more.'

I naturally said I had no wish to make it more.

'Then it must be a shilling,' observed the coachman. 'I don't want to get into trouble. *I* know *him!*' He darkly closed an eye at Mr Jaggers's name, and shook his head.

When he had got his shilling, and had got away (which appeared to relieve his mind), I went into the front office with my little portmanteau in my hand and asked, Was Mr Jaggers at home?

'He is not,' returned the clerk. 'He is in Court at present. Am I addressing Mr Pip?'

I signified that he was addressing Mr Pip.

'Mr Jaggers left word would you wait in his room. He couldn't say how long he might be, having a case on. But it stands to reason; that he won't be longer than he can help.'

With those words, the clerk opened a door, and ushered me into an inner chamber at the back.

Mr Jaggers's room was lighted by a skylight only, and was a most dismal place. There were not so many papers about, as I should have expected to see; and there were some odd objects about, that I should not have expected to see – such as an old rusty pistol, a sword in a scabbard, several strange-looking boxes and packages, and two dreadful casts on a shelf, of faces peculiarly swollen, and twitchy about the nose. Mr Jaggers's own high-backed chair was of deadly black horse-hair, with rows of brass nails round it, like a coffin; and I fancied I could see how he leaned back in it, and bit his forefinger at the clients.

I sat down in the cliental chair placed over against Mr Jaggers's chair, and became fascinated by the dismal atmosphere of the place. I wondered how many other clerks there were upstairs, and whether they all claimed to have the same detrimental mastery of their fellow-creatures. I wondered whether the two swollen faces were of Mr Jaggers's family, and, if he were so unfortunate as to have had a pair of such ill-looking relations, why he stuck them on that dusty perch for the blacks and flies to settle on, instead of giving them a place at home. Of course I had no experience of a London summer day, and my spirits may have been oppressed by the hot exhausted air, and by the dust and grit that lay thick on everything. But I sat wondering and waiting in Mr Jaggers's close room, until I really could not bear the two casts on the shelf above Mr Jaggers's chair, and got up and went out.

When I told the clerk that I would take a turn in the air while I waited, he advised me to go round the corner and I should come into Smithfield. So, I came into Smithfield; and the shameful place, being all asmear with filth and fat and blood and foam, seemed to stick to me. So, I turned into a street where I saw the great black dome of Saint Paul's bulging at me from behind a grim stone building which a bystander said was Newgate Prison. Following the wall of the jail, I found the roadway covered with straw to deaden the noise of passing vehicles; and from this, and from the quantity of people standing about, smelling strongly of spirits and beer, I inferred that the trials were on.

While I looked about me here, an exceedingly dirty and partially drunk minister of justice asked me if I would like to step in and hear a trial or so: informing me that he could give me a front place for half-a-crown, whence I should command a full view of the Lord Chief Justice in his wig and robes. As I declined the proposal on the plea of an appointment, he was so good as to take me into a yard and show me where the gallows was kept, and also where people were publicly whipped, and then he showed me the Debtor's Door, out of which culprits came to be hanged: heightening the interest of that dreadful portal by giving me to understand that 'four on 'em' would come out at that door the day after tomorrow at eight in the morning, to be killed in a row. This was horrible, and gave me a sickening idea of London: the more so as the Lord Chief Justice's proprietor wore mildewed clothes, which had evidently not belonged to him originally, and which, I took it into my head, he had bought cheap of the executioner. Under these circumstances I thought myself well rid of him for a shilling.

I dropped into the office to ask if Mr Jaggers had come in yet, and I found he had not, and I strolled out again. This time, I made the tour of Little Britain, and turned into Bartholomew Close; and now I became aware that other people were waiting about for Mr Jaggers, as well as I. There were two men of secret appearance lounging in Bartholomew Close. There was a knot of three men and two women standing at a corner, and one of the women was crying on her dirty shawl, and the other comforted her by saying, as she pulled her own shawl over her shoulders, 'Jaggers is for him, 'Melia, and what more *could* you have?'

As I was looking out at the iron gate of Bartholomew Close into Little Britain, I saw Mr Jaggers coming across the road towards me. All the others who were waiting, saw him at the same time, and there was quite a rush at him. Mr Jaggers, putting a hand on my shoulder and walking me on at his side without saying anything to me, addressed himself to his followers.

First, he took the two secret men.

'Now, I have nothing to say to *you*,' said Mr Jaggers, throwing his finger at them. 'I want to know no more than I know. As to the result, it's a toss-up. I told you from the first it was a toss-up. Have you paid Wemmick?'

'We made the money up this morning, sir,' said one of the men, submissively, while the other perused Mr Jaggers's face.

'I don't ask you when you made it up, or where, or whether you made it up at all. Has Wemmick got it?'

'Yes, sir,' said both the men together.

'Very well; then you may go. Now, I won't have it!' said Mr Jaggers, waving his hand at them to put them behind him. 'If you say a word to me, I'll throw up the case.'

The two men looked at one another as Mr Jaggers waved them behind again, and humbly fell back and were heard no more.

'And now *you*!' said Mr Jaggers, suddenly stopping, and turning on the two women with the shawls, from whom the three men had meekly separated. – 'Oh! Amelia, is it?'

'Yes, Mr Jaggers.'

'And do you remember,' retorted Mr Jaggers, 'that but for me you wouldn't be here and couldn't be here?'

'Oh yes, sir!' exclaimed both women together. 'Lord bless you, sir, well we knows that!'

'Then why,' said Mr Jaggers, 'do you come here?'

'My Bill, sir!' the crying woman pleaded.

'Now, I tell you what!' said Mr Jaggers. 'Once for all. If you don't know that your Bill's in good hands, I know it. And if you come here, bothering about your Bill, I'll make an example of both your Bill and you, and let him slip through my fingers. Have you paid Wemmick?'

'Oh yes, sir! Every farden.'

'Very well. Then you have done all you have got to do. Say another word – one single word – and Wemmick shall give you your money back.'

This terrible threat caused the two women to fall off immediately.

Without further interruption we reached the front office, where we found the clerk. My guardian then took me into his own room, and informed me what arrangements he had made for me. I was to go to 'Barnard's Inn', to young Mr Pocket's rooms, where a bed had been sent in for my accommodation; I was to remain with young Mr Pocket until Monday; on Monday I was to go with him to his father's house on a visit, that I might try how I liked it. Also, I was told what my allowance was to be – it was a very liberal one – and had handed to me from one of my guardian's drawers, the cards of certain tradesmen with whom I was to deal for all kinds of clothes, and such other things as I could in reason want. 'You will find your credit good, Mr Pip,' said my guardian, 'but I shall by this means be able to check your bills, and to pull you up if I find you outrunning the constable. Of course you'll go wrong somehow, but that's no fault of mine.'

After I had pondered a little over this encouraging sentiment, I asked Mr Jaggers if I could send for a coach? He said it was not worth while, I was so near my destination; Wemmick should walk round with me, if I pleased.

I then found that Wemmick was the clerk in the next room. Another clerk was rung down from upstairs to take his place while he was out, and I accompanied him into the street, after shaking hands with my guardian. We found a new set of people lingering outside, but Wemmick made a way among them by saying coolly yet decisively, 'I tell you it's no use; he won't have a word to say to one of you;' and we soon got clear of them, and went on side by side.

21

Casting my eyes on Mr Wemmick as we went along, to see what he was like in the light of day, I found him to be a dry man, rather short in stature, with a square wooden face, whose expression seemed to have been imperfectly chipped out with a dull-edged chisel. I judged him to be a bachelor from the frayed condition of his linen, and he appeared to have sustained a good many bereavements; for, he wore at least four mourning rings, besides a brooch representing a lady and a weeping willow at a tomb with an urn on it. He had glittering eyes – small, keen, and black – and thin wide mottled lips. He had had them, to the best of my belief, from forty to fifty years.

'So you were never in London before?' said Mr Wemmick to me.

'No,' said I.

'*I* was new here once,' said Mr Wemmick. 'Rum to think of now!'

'Is it a very wicked place?' I asked, more for the sake of saying something than for information.

'You may get cheated, robbed, and murdered, in London. But there are plenty of people anywhere, who'll do that for you.'

He wore his hat on the back of his head, and looked straight before him: walking in a self-contained way as if there were nothing in the streets to claim his attention. His mouth was such a post-office of a mouth that he had a mechanical appearance of smiling. We had got to the top of Holborn Hill before I knew that it was merely a mechanical appearance, and that he was not smiling at all.

'Do you know where Mr Matthew Pocket lives?' I asked Mr Wemmick.

'Yes,' said he, nodding in the direction. 'At Hammersmith, west of London.'

'Is that far?'

'Well! Say five miles.'

'Do you know him?'

'Why, you're a regular cross-examiner!' said Mr Wemmick, looking at me with an approving air. 'Yes, I know him. *I* know him!'

There was an air of toleration or depreciation about his utterance of these words, that rather depressed me; and I was still looking sideways at his block of a face in search of any encouraging note to the text, when he said here we were at Barnard's Inn.

We entered this haven through a wicket-gate, and were disgorged by an introductory passage into a melancholy little square that looked to me like a flat burying-ground. I thought it had the most dismal trees in it, and the most dismal houses that I had ever seen. I thought the windows of the sets of chambers into which those houses were divided, were in every stage of dilapidated blind and curtain, cracked glass, dusty decay, and miserable makeshift; while To Let To Let To Let, glared at me from empty rooms, as if no new wretches ever came there.

So imperfect was this realization of the first of my great expectations, that I looked in dismay at Mr Wemmick. 'Ah!' said he, mistaking me; 'the retirement reminds you of the country. So it does me.'

He led me into a corner and conducted me up a flight of stairs – which appeared to me to be slowly collapsing into sawdust, so that one of those days the upper lodgers would look out at their doors and find themselves without the means of coming down – to a set of chambers on the top floor. MR POCKET, JUN., was painted on the door, and there was a label on the letter-box, 'Return shortly.'

'He hardly thought you'd come so soon,' Mr Wemmick explained. 'You don't want me any more?'

'No, thank you,' said I.

'As I keep the cash,' Mr Wemmick observed, 'we shall most likely meet pretty often. Good day.'

'Good day.'

When we had shaken hands and he was gone, I opened the staircase window and had nearly beheaded myself, for, the lines had rotted away, and it came down like the guillotine. After this escape, I was content to take a foggy view of the Inn through the window's encrusting dirt, and to stand dolefully looking out, saying to myself that London was decidedly overrated.

Mr Pocket, Junior's, idea of Shortly was not mine,

for I had nearly maddened myself with looking out for half an hour, before I heard footsteps on the stairs. Gradually there arose before me the hat, head, neck-cloth, waistcoat, trousers, boots, of a member of society of about my own standing. He had a paper-bag under each arm and a pottle of strawberries in one hand, and was out of breath.

'Mr Pip?' said he.

'Mr Pocket?' said I.

'Dear me!' he exclaimed. 'I am extremely sorry; but I knew there was a coach from your part of the country at midday, and I thought you would come by that one. The fact is, I have been out on your account – not that that is any excuse – for I thought, coming from the country, you might like a little fruit after dinner, and I went to Convent Garden Market to get it good. Dear me! This door sticks so!'

As he was fast making jam of his fruit by wrestling with the door while the paper-bags were under his arms, I begged him to allow me to hold them. He relinquished them with an agreeable smile, and com-bated with the door as if it were a wild beast. It yielded so suddenly at last, that he staggered back upon me, and I staggered back upon the opposite door, and we both laughed.

'Pray come in,' said Mr Pocket, Junior.

'I am rather bare here, but I hope you'll be able to make out tolerably well till Monday. My father thought you would get on more agreeably through tomorrow with me than with him, and might like to take a walk about London. As to our table, you won't find that bad, I hope, for it will be supplied from our coffee-house here, and at your expense, such being Mr

Jaggers's directions. As to our lodging, it's not by any means splendid, because I have my own bread to earn, and my father hasn't anything to give me, and I shouldn't be willing to take it, if he had. This is our sitting-room – just such chairs and tables and carpet and so forth, you see, as they could spare from home. This is your bedroom; the furniture's hired for the occasion, but I trust it will answer the purpose; if you should want anything, I'll go and fetch it. Pray let me take these bags from you.'

As I stood opposite to Mr Pocket, Junior, delivering him the bags, One, Two, I saw the starting appearance come into his own eyes that I knew to be in mine, and he said, falling back:

'Lord bless me, you're the prowling boy!'

'And you,' said I, 'are the pale young gentleman!'

22

The pale young gentleman and I stood contemplating one another in Barnard's Inn, until we both burst out laughing. 'Well!' said the pale young gentleman, reaching out his hand good-humouredly, 'it's all over now, I hope, and it will be magnanimous in you if you'll forgive me for having knocked you about so.'

I derived from this speech that Mr Herbert Pocket (for Herbert was the pale young gentleman's name) still rather confounded his intention with his execution. But I made a modest reply, and we shook hands warmly.

'You hadn't come into your good fortune at that time?' said Herbert Pocket.

'No,' said I.

'No,' he acquiesced: 'I heard it had happened very lately. *I* was rather on the look-out for good fortune then.'

'Indeed?'

'Yes. Miss Havisham had sent for me, to see if she could take a fancy to me. But she couldn't – at all events, she didn't.'

I thought it polite to remark that I was surprised to hear that.

'Bad taste,' said Herbert, laughing, 'but a fact. Yes, she had sent for me on a trial visit, and if I had come out of it successfully, I suppose I should have been provided for; perhaps I should have been what-you-may-called it to Estella.'

'What's that?' I asked, with sudden gravity.

'Affianced,' he explained, still busy with the fruit. 'Betrothed. Engaged. What's-his-named. Any word of that sort.'

'How did you bear your disappointment?' I asked.

'Pooh!' said he, 'I didn't care much for it. *She*'s a Tartar.'

'Miss Havisham?'

'I don't say no to that, but I meant Estella. That girl's hard and haughty and capricious to the last degree, and has been brought up by Miss Havisham to wreak revenge on all the male sex.'

'What relation is she to Miss Havisham?'

'None,' said he. 'Only adopted.'

'Why should she wreak revenge on all the male sex? What revenge?'

'Lord, Mr Pip!' said he. 'Don't you know?'

'No,' said I.

'Dear me! It's quite a story, and shall be saved till dinner-time. And now let me take the liberty of asking you a question. How did you come there, that day?'

I told him, and he was attentive until I had finished, and then burst out laughing again, and asked me if I was sore afterwards? I didn't ask him if *he* was, for my conviction on that point was perfectly established.

'Mr Jaggers is your guardian, I understand?' he went on.

'Yes.'

'You know he is Miss Havisham's man of business and solicitor, and has her confidence when nobody else has?'

This was bringing me (I felt) towards dangerous ground. I answered with a constraint I made no attempt to disguise, that I had seen Mr Jaggers in Miss Havisham's house on the very day of our combat, but never at any other time, and that I believed he had no recollection of having ever seen me there.

Herbert Pocker had a frank and easy way with him that was very taking. I had never seen any one then who more strongly expressed to me a natural incapacity to do anything secret and mean. He had not a handsome face, but it was better than handsome: being extremely amiable and cheerful. His figure was a little ungainly, as in the days when my knuckles had taken such liberties with it, but it looked as if it would always be light and young. Whether Mr Trabb's local work would have sat more gracefully on him than on me, may be a question; but I am conscious that he carried off his rather old clothes, much better than I carried off my new suit.

As he was so communicative, I felt that reserve on my part would be a bad return unsuited to our years. I therefore told him my small story, and laid stress on my being forbidden to enquire who my benefactor was. I further mentioned that as I had been brought up a blacksmith in a country place, and knew very little of the ways of politeness, I would take it as a great kindness in him if he would give me a hint whenever he saw me at a loss or going wrong.

'With pleasure,' said he, 'though I venture to prophesy that you'll want very few hints. I dare say we shall be often together, and I should like to banish any needless restraint between us. Will you do me the favour to begin at once to call me by my christian name, Herbert?'

I thanked him, and said I would. I informed him in exchange that my christian name was Philip.

'I don't take to Philip,' said he, smiling. 'I tell you what I should like. We are so harmonious, and you have been a blacksmith. Would you mind Handel for a familiar name? There's a charming piece of music by Handel, called the Harmonious Blacksmith.'

'I should like it very much.'

'Then, my dear Handel,' said he, turning round as the door opened, 'here is the dinner, and I must beg of you to take the top of the table, because the dinner is of your providing.'

This I would not hear of, so he took the top, and I faced him. It was a nice little dinner – seemed to me then, a very Lord Mayor's Feast – and it acquired additional relish from being eaten under those independent circumstances, with no old people by, and with London all around us.

We had made some progress in the dinner, when I reminded Herbert of his promise to tell me about Miss Havisham.

'True,' he replied.'I'll redeem it at once. Miss Havisham, you must know, was a spoilt child. Her mother died when she was a baby, and her father denied her nothing. Mr Havisham was very rich and very proud. So was his daughter.'

'Miss Havisham was an only child?' I hazarded.

'Stop a moment, I am coming to that. No, she was not an only child; she had a half-brother. Her father privately married again - his cook I rather think.'

'I thought he was proud,' said I.

'My good Handel, so he was. He married his second wife privately, because he was proud, and in course of time *she* died. When she was dead, I apprehend he first told his daughter what he had done, and then the son became a part of the family, residing in the house you are acquainted with. As the son grew a young man, he turned out riotous, extravagant, undutiful – altogether bad. At last his father disinherited him; but he softened when he was dying, and left him well off, though not nearly so well off as Miss Havisham. – Take another glass of wine, and excuse my mentioning that society as a body does not expect one to be so strictly conscientious in emptying one's glass, as to turn it bottom upwards with the rim on one's nose.'

I had been doing this, in an excess of attention to his recital. I thanked him, and apologized. He said, 'Not at all,' and resumed.

'Miss Havisham was now an heiress, and you may suppose was looked after as a great match. Her half-brother had now ample means again, but what with

debts and what with new madness wasted them most
fearfully again. There were stronger differences between him and her, than there had been between him
and his father, and it is suspected that he cherished a
deep and mortal grudge against her, as having influ-
enced the father's anger. Now, I come to the cruel part
of the story. There appeared upon the scene – say at
the races, or the public balls, or anywhere else you like
– a certain man, who made love to Miss Havisham. I
have heard my father mention that he was a showy-
man, and the kind of man for the purpose. This man
pursued Miss Havisham closely, and professed to be
devoted to her. I believe she had not shown much
susceptibility up to that time; but all the susceptibility
she possessed, certainly came out then, and she passionately loved him. He practised on her affection in that
systematic way, that he got great sums of money from
her, and he induced her to buy her brother out of a
share in the brewery at an immense price, on the plea
that when he was her husband he must hold and
manage it all. Your guardian was not at that time in
Miss Havisham's councils, and she was too haughty
and too much in love, to be advised by any one. My
father warned her that she was doing too much for this
man, and was placing herself too unreservedly in his
power. She took the first opportunity of angrily order-
ing him out of the house, in his presence, and my
father has never seen her since.'

I thought of her having said, 'Matthew will come
and see me at last when I am laid dead upon that
table;' and I asked Herbert whether his father was so
inveterate against her?

'It's not that,' said he, 'but she charged him, in the

presence of her intended husband, with being disappointed in the hope of fawning upon her for his own advancement, and, if he were to go to her now, it would look true. To return to the man and make an end of him. The marriage day was fixed, the wedding dresses were bought, the wedding guests were invited. The day came, but not the bridegroom. He wrote her a letter –'

'Which she received,' I struck in, 'when she was dressing for her marriage? At twenty minutes to nine?'

'At the hour and minute,' said Herbert, nodding, 'at which she afterwards stopped all the clocks. What was in it, further than that it most heartlessly broke the marriage off, I can't tell you, because I don't know. When she recovered from a bad illness that she had, she laid the whole place waste, as you have seen it, and she has never since looked upon the light of day. I have forgotten one thing. It has been supposed that the man to whom she gave her misplaced confidence, acted throughout in concert with her half-brother; that it was a conspiracy between them; and that they shared the profits.'

'I wonder he didn't marry her and get all the property,' said I.

'He may have been married already, and her cruel mortification may have been a part of her half-brother's scheme,' said Herbert. 'Mind! I don't know that.'

'What became of the two men?' I asked, after again considering the subject.

'They fell into deeper shame and degradation – if there can be deeper – and ruin.'

'Are they alive now?'

'I don't know.'

'You said just now, that Estella was not related to Miss Havisham, but adopted. When adopted?'

Herbert shrugged his shoulders. 'There has always been an Estella, since I have heard of a Miss Havisham. I know no more. And now, Handel,' said he, finally throwing off the story as it were, 'there is a perfectly open understanding between us. All that I know about Miss Havisham, you know.'

'And all that I know,' I retorted, 'you know.'

'I fully believe it. And as to the condition on which you hold your advancement in life, you may be very sure that it will never be encroached upon, or even approached, by me, or by any one belonging to me.'

It had not occurred to me before, that he had led up to the theme for the purpose of clearing it out of our way; but we were so much the lighter and easier for having broached it, that I now perceived this to be the case. We were very gay and sociable, and I asked him, in the course of conversation, what he was? He replied, 'A capitalist – an Insurer of Ships.' I suppose he saw me glancing about the room in search of some tokens of Shipping, or capital, for he added, 'In the City. I shall not rest satisfied though, with merely employing my capital in insuring ships. I shall buy up some good Life Assurance shares, and cut into the Direction. I shall also do a little in the mining way. I think I shall trade to the East Indies, for silks, shawls, spices and precious woods. It's an interesting trade. I think I shall trade, also,' he went on, 'to the West Indies, for sugar, tobacco, and rum.'

'You will want a good many ships,' said I.

'A perfect fleet,' said he.

Quite overpowered by the magnificence of these transactions, I asked him where the ships he insured mostly traded to at present?

'I haven't begun insuring yet,' he replied. 'I am looking about me.'

Somehow, that pursuit seemed more in keeping with Barnard's Inn. I said, 'Ah-h!'

'Yes. I am in a counting-house, and looking about me.'

'Is a counting-house profitable?' I asked.

'Why, n-no: not to me.' He said this with the air of one carefully reckoning up and striking a balance. 'Not directly profitable. That is, it doesn't pay me anything, and I have to – keep myself.'

This certainly had not a profitable appearance, and I shook my head as if I would imply that it would be difficult to lay by much accumulative capital from such a source of income.

'But the thing is,' said Herbert Pocket, 'that you look about you. *That's* the grand thing. You are in a counting-house, you know, and you look about you. Then the time comes when you see your opening. And you go in, and you swoop upon it and you make your capital, and then there you are!'

Having already made his fortune in his own mind, he was so unassuming with it that I felt quite grateful to him for not being puffed up. In the evening we went out for a walk in the streets, and went half-price to the Theatre; and next day we went to church at Westminster Abbey, and in the afternoon we walked in the Parks; and I wondered who shod all the horses there, and wished Joe did.

On a moderate computation, it was many months,

that Sunday, since I had left Joe and Biddy. In the London streets, so crowded with people and so brilliantly lighted in the dusk of evening, there were depressing hints of reproaches for that I had put the poor old kitchen at home so far away; and in the dead of night, the footsteps of some incapable impostor of a porter mooning about Barnard's Inn, under pretence of watching it, fell hollow on my heart.

On the Monday morning at a quarter before nine, Herbert went to the counting-house to report himself – to look about him, too, I suppose – and I bore him company. He was to come away in an hour or two to attend me to Hammersmith, and I was to wait about for him.

I waited about until it was noon, and when Herbert came, we went and had lunch at a celebrated house which I then quite venerated, but now believe to have been the most abject superstition in Europe, and where I could not help noticing, even then, that there was much more gravy on the tablecloths and knives and waiters' clothes, than in the steaks. We then took coach for Hammersmith. We arrived there at two or three o'clock in the afternoon, and had very little way to walk to Mr Pocket's house. Lifting the latch of a gate, we passed direct into a little garden overlooking the river, where Mr Pocket's children were playing about.

Mrs Pocket was sitting on a garden chair under a tree, reading, and Mrs Pocket's two nursemaids were looking about them while the children played. 'Mamma,' said Herbert, 'this is young Mr Pip.' Upon which Mrs Pocket received me with an appearance of amiable dignity.

'Master Alick and Miss Jane,' cried one of the nurses to two of the children, 'if you go a-bouncing up against them bushes you'll fall over into the river and be drownded, and what'll your pa say then?'

At the same time this nurse picked up Mrs Pocket's handkerchief, and said, 'If that don't make six times you've dropped it, Mum!' Upon which Mrs Pocket laughed and said, 'Thank you, Flopson,' and settling herself in one chair only, resumed her book. Before she could have read half a dozen lines, she fixed her eyes upon me, and said, 'I hope your mamma is quite well?' This unexpected inquiry put me into such a difficulty that I began saying in the absurdest way that if there had been any such person I had no doubt she would have been quite well and would have been very much obliged and would have sent her compliments, when the nurse came to my rescue.

'Well!' she cried, picking up the pocket handkerchief, 'if that don't make seven times! What are you a doing of this afternoon, Mum!' Mrs Pocket received her property, at first with a look of unutterable surprise as if she had never seen it before, and then with a laugh of recognition, and said, 'Thank you, Flopson,' and forgot me, and went on reading.

I found, now I had leisure to count them, that there were no fewer than six little Pockets present. I had scarcely arrived at the total when a seventh was heard, as in the region of air, wailing dolefully.

'If there ain't Baby!' said Flopson, appearing to think it most surprising. 'Make haste up, Millers.'

Millers, who was the other nurse, retired into the house, and by degrees the child's wailing was hushed and stopped.

By-and-by Millers came down with the baby, which baby was handed to Flopson, which Flopson was handing it to Mrs Pocket, when she too went fairly head foremost over Mrs Pocket, baby and all, and was caught by Herbert and myself.

'Gracious me, Flopson!' said Mrs Pocket, looking off her book for a moment, 'everybody's tumbling!'

'Gracious you, indeed, Mum!' returned Flopson, very red in the face; 'what have you got there?'

'*I* got here, Flopson?' asked Mrs Pocket.

'Why, if it ain't your footstool!' cried Flopson. 'And if you keep it under your skirts like that, who's to help tumbling? Here! Take the baby, Mum, and give me your book.'

Mrs Pocket acted on the advice, and inexpertly danced the infant a little in her lap, while the other children played about it. This had lasted but a very short time, when Mrs Pocket issued summary orders that they were all to be taken into the house for a nap.

Under these circumstances, when Flopson and Millers had got the children into the house, like a little flock of sheep, and Mr Pocket came out of it to make my acquaintance, I was not much surprised to find that Mr Pocket was a gentleman with a rather perplexed expression of face, and with his very grey hair disordered on his head, as if he didn't quite see his way to putting anything straight.

23

Mr Pocket said he was glad to see me, and he hoped I was not sorry to see him. 'For, I really am not,' he added, with his son's smile, 'an alarming personage.' He was a young-looking man, in spite of his perplexities and his very grey hair, and his manner seemed quite natural. When he had talked with me a little, he said to Mrs Pocket, with a rather anxious contraction of his eyebrows, which were black and handsome, 'Belinda, I hope you have welcomed Mr Pip?' And she looked up from her book, and said, 'Yes.' She then smiled upon me in an absent state of mind, and asked me if I liked the taste of orange-flower water?

I found out that Mrs Pocket was the only daughter of a certain quite accidental deceased Knight, who had invented for himself a conviction that his deceased father would have been made a Baronet but for somebody's determined opposition arising out of entirely personal motives – the Sovereign's, the Prime Minister's, the Archbishop of Canterbury's, – and had tacked himself on to the nobles of the earth in right of this quite supposititious fact. He had directed Mrs Pocket to be brought up from her cradle as one who in the nature of things must marry a title, and who was to be guarded from the acquisition of plebeian domestic knowledge.

So successful a watch and ward had been established over the young lady by this judicious parent, that she had grown up highly ornamental, but perfectly helpless and useless. With her character thus happily formed, she had encountered Mr Pocket: who was also in the first bloom of youth, and not quite decided whether to mount to the Woolsack, or to roof himself in with a mitre. They had married without the knowledge of the judicious parent. The judicious parent, having nothing to bestow or withhold but his blessing, had handsomely settled that dower upon them after a short struggle, and had informed Mr Pocket that his wife was 'a treasure for a Prince'. Mrs Pocket was in general the object of a queer sort of respectful pity, because she had not married a title; while Mr Pocket was the object of a queer sort of forgiving reproach, because he had never got one.

Mr Pocket took me into the house and showed me my room. He then knocked at the doors of two other similar rooms, and introduced me to their occupants, by name Drummle and Startop. Drummle, an old-looking young man of a heavy order of architecture, was whistling. Startop, younger in years and appearance, was reading and holding his head, as if he thought himself in danger of exploding it with too strong a charge of knowledge.

Both Mr and Mrs Pocket had such a noticeable air of being in somebody else's hands, that I wondered who really was in possession of the house and let them live there, until I found this unknown power to be the servants, who felt it a duty they owed to themselves to be nice in their eating and drinking, and to keep a deal of company downstairs. They allowed a very liberal table to Mr and Mrs Pocket, yet it always appeared to me that by far the best part of the house to have boarded in, would have been the kitchen – always supposing the boarder capable of self-defence, for, before I had been there a week, a neighbouring lady with whom the family were personally unacquainted, wrote in to say that she had seen Millers slapping the baby. This greatly distressed Mrs Pocket, who burst into tears on receiving the note, and said that it was an extraordinary thing that the neighbours couldn't mind their own business.

By degrees I learnt, and chiefly from Herbert, that Mr Pocket had been educated at Harrow and at Cambridge, and had then come to London. Here, after gradually failing in loftier hopes, he had 'read' with divers who had lacked opportunities or neglected them, and had refurbished divers others for special occasions, and had turned his acquirements to the account of literary compilation and correction, and on such means, added to some very moderate private resources, still maintained the house I saw.

Mr and Mrs Pocket had a toady neighbour; a widow lady of that highly sympathetic nature that she agreed with everybody, and shed smiles and tears on everybody, according to circumstances. This lady's name was Mrs Coiler, and I had the honour of taking her down to dinner on the day of my installation. She gave me to understand that it was a blow to dear Mrs Pocket that dear Mr Pocket should be under the necessity of receiving gentlemen to read with him. That did not extend to me, she told me; if they were all like Me, it would be quite another thing.

It came to my knowledge, through what passed between Mrs Pocket and Drummle while I was attentive to my knife and fork, spoon, glasses, and other instruments of self-destruction, that Drummle, whose christian name was Bentley, was actually the next heir but one to a baronetcy. Drummle didn't say much, but in his limited way spoke as one of the elect, and recognized Mrs Pocket as a woman and a sister. No one but themselves and Mrs Coiler showed any interest in this part of the conversation, and it appeared to me that it was painful to Herbert; but it promised to last a long time, when the page came in with the announcement of a domestic affliction. It was, in effect, that the cook had mislaid the beef. To my unutterable amazement, I now, for the first time, saw Mr Pocket relieve his mind by going through a performance that struck me as very extraordinary, but which made no impression on anybody else, and with which I soon became as familiar as the rest. He laid down the carving-knife and fork, put his two hands into his disturbed hair, and appeared to make an extraordinary effort to lift himself up by it. When he had done this, and had not lifted himself up at all, he quietly went on with what he was about.

After dinner the children were introduced. There were four little girls, and two little boys, besides the baby who might have been either, and the baby's next successor who was as yet neither. They were brought in by Flopson and Millers, while Mrs Pocket looked at the young Nobles that ought to have been, as if she rather thought she had had the pleasure of inspecting them before, but didn't quite know what to make of them.

One of the little girls, a mere mite who seemed to have prematurely taken upon herself some charge of the others, stepped out of her place by me, and danced to and from the baby until it left off crying, and laughed. Then, all the children laughed, and Mr Pocket laughed, and we all laughed and were glad.

Flopson, by dint of doubling the baby at the joints like a Dutch doll, then got it safely into Mrs Pocket's lap, and gave it the nutcrackers to play with: at the same time recommending Mrs Pocket to take notice that the handles of that instrument were not likely to agree with its eyes, and sharply charging Miss Jane to look after the same. Then, the two nurses left the room, and had a lively scuffle on the staircase with a dissipated page who had clearly lost half his buttons at the gaming-table.

I was made very uneasy in my mind by Mrs Pocket's falling into a discussion with Drummle respecting two baronetcies, and forgetting all about the baby on her lap: who did most appalling things with the nutcrackers. At length, little Jane perceiving its young brains to be imperilled, softly left her place, and with many small artifices coaxed the dangerous weapon away.

In the evening there was rowing on the river. As Drummle and Startop had each a boat, I resolved to set up mine, and to cut them both out. I was pretty good at most exercises in which country-boys are adepts, but, as I was conscious of wanting elegance of style for the Thames, I at once engaged to place myself under the tuition of the winner of a prize-wherry who plied at our stairs, and to whom I was introduced by my new allies. This practical authority confused me very much, by saying I had the arm of a blacksmith. If he could have known how nearly the compliment lost him his pupil, I doubt if he would have paid it.

There was a supper-tray after we got home at night, and I think we should all have enjoyed ourselves, but for a rather disagreeable domestic occurrence. Mr Pocket was in good spirits, when a housemaid came in, and said, 'If you please, sir, I should wish to speak to you.'

'Speak to your master?' said Mrs Pocket, whose dignity was roused again. 'How can you think of such a thing? Go and speak to Flopson. Or speak to me – at some other time.'

'Begging your pardon, ma'am,' returned the house-maid, 'I should wish to speak at once, and to speak to master.'

Hereupon, Mr Pocket went out of the room, and we made the best of ourselves until he came back.

'This is a pretty thing, Belinda!' said Mr Pocket. 'Here's the cook lying insensibly drunk on the kitchen floor, with a large bundle of fresh butter made up in the cupboard ready to sell for grease!'

Mrs Pocket instantly showed much amiable emotion, and said, 'This is that odious Sophia's doing!'

'What do you mean, Belinda?' demanded Mr Pocket.

'Sophia has told you,' said Mrs Pocket. 'Did I not see her with my own eyes and hear her with my own ears, come into the room just now and ask to speak to you?'

'But has she not taken me downstairs, Belinda,' returned Mr Pocket, 'and shown me the woman, and the bundle too?'

'And do you defend her, Matthew,' said Mrs Pocket, 'for making mischief?'

Mr Pocket uttered a dismal groan.

'Am I, grandpapa's granddaughter, to be nothing in the house?' said Mrs Pocket. 'Besides, the cook has always been a very nice respectful woman, and said in the most natural manner when she came to look after the situation, that she felt I was born to be a Duchess.'

There was a sofa where Mr Pocket stood, and he dropped upon it in the attitude of the Dying Gladiator. Still in that attitude he said, with a hollow voice, 'Good-night, Mr Pip,' when I deemed it advisable to go to bed and leave him.

24

After two or three days, when I had established myself in my room and had gone backwards and forwards to London several times, Mr Pocket and I had a long talk together. He knew more of my intended career than I knew myself, for he referred to his having been told by Mr Jaggers that I was not designed for any profession, and that I should be well enough educated for my destiny if I could 'hold my own' with the average of young men in prosperous circumstances.

He advised my attending certain places in London, for the acquisition of such mere rudiments as I wanted, and my investing him with the functions of explainer and director of all my studies. He hoped that with intelligent assistance I should meet with little to discourage me, and should soon be able to dispense with any aid but his.

When these points were settled, and so far carried

out as that I had begun to work in earnest, it occurred to me that if I could retain my bedroom in Barnard's Inn, my life would be agreeably varied, while my manners would be none the worse for Herbert's society. Mr Pocket did not object to this arrangement, but urged that before any step could possibly be taken in it, it must be submitted to my guardian. I felt that his delicacy arose out of the consideration that the plan would save Herbert some expense, so I went off to Little Britain and imparted my wish to Mr Jaggers.

'If I could buy the furniture now hired for me,' said I, 'and one or two other little things, I should be quite at home there.'

'Go it!' said Mr Jaggers, with a short laugh. 'I told you you'd get on. Well! How much do you want?'

I said I didn't know how much.

'Come!' retorted Mr Jaggers. 'How much? Fifty pounds?'

'Oh, not nearly so much.'

'Five pounds?' said Mr Jaggers.

This was such a great fall, that I said in discomfiture, 'Oh! more than that.'

'Come!' said Mr Jaggers. 'Let's get at it. Twice five; will that do? Three times five; will that do? Four times five; will that do?'

I said I thought that would do handsomely.

'Wemmick!' said Mr Jaggers, opening his office door. 'Take Mr Pip's written order, and pay him twenty pounds.'

This strongly marked way of doing business made a strongly marked impression on me, and that not of an agreeable kind. Mr Jaggers never laughed; but he wore great bright creaking boots, and, in poising himself on these boots, awaiting an answer, he sometimes caused the boots to creak, as if *they* laughed in a dry and suspicious way. As he happened to go out now, and as Wemmick was brisk and talkative, I said to Wemmick that I hardly knew what to make of Mr Jaggers's manner.

'Tell him that, and he'll take it as a compliment,' answered Wemmick; 'he don't mean that you *should* know what to make of it.'

Without remarking that man-traps were not among the amenities of life, I said I supposed he was very skilful?

'Deep,' said Wemmick, 'as Australia.' Pointing with his pen at the office floor, to express that Australia was understood to be symmetrically on the opposite spot of the globe. 'If there was anything deeper,' added Wemmick, bringing his pen to paper, 'he'd be it.'

Then, I said I supposed he had a fine business, and Wemmick said, 'Ca-pi-tal!' Then I asked if there were many clerks? to which he replied:

'We don't run much into clerks, because there's only one Jaggers, and people won't have him at second-hand. There are only four of us. Would you like to see 'em? You are one of us, as I may say.'

I accepted the offer. When Mr Wemmick had paid me my money, we went upstairs. In the front first floor, a clerk who looked something between a publican and a rat-catcher was attentively engaged with three or four people of shabby appearance, whom he treated as unceremoniously as everybody seemed to be treated who contributed to Mr Jaggers's coffers. 'Getting evidence together,' said Mr Wemmick, as we came out, 'for the Bailey.' In the room over that, a little flabby terrier of a clerk with dangling hair was similarly engaged with a man with weak eyes, whom Mr Wemmick presented to me as a smelter who kept his pot always boiling, and who would melt me anything I pleased. In a back room, a high-shouldered man with a face-ache tied up in dirty flannel, who was dressed in old black clothes was stooping over his work of making fair copies of the notes of the other two gentlemen, for Mr Jaggers's own use.

This was all the establishment. When we went downstairs again, Wemmick led me into my guardian's room, and said, 'This you've seen already.'

'Pray,' said I, as the two odious casts with the twitchy leer upon them caught my sight again, 'whose likenesses are those?'

'These?' said Wemmick, 'these are two celebrated ones. This chap murdered his master, and, considering that he wasn't brought up to evidence, didn't plan it badly.'

'Is it like him?' I asked, recoiling from the brute, as Wemmick spat upon his eyebrow and gave it a rub with his sleeve.

'Like him? It's himself, you know. The cast was made in Newgate, directly after he was taken down. You had a particular fancy for me, hadn't you, Old Artful?' said Wemmick. He then explained this affectionate apostrophe, by touching his brooch representing the lady and the weeping willow at the tomb with the urn upon it, and saying, 'Had it made for me, express!'

'Is the lady anybody?' said I.

'No,' returned Wemmick. 'Only his game. No; deuce a bit of a lady in the case, Mr Pip, except one – and she wasn't of this slender ladylike sort, and you wouldn't have caught *her* looking after this urn – unless there was something to drink in it.'

'Did that other creature come to the same end?' I asked. 'He has the same look.'

'You're right,' said Wemmick; 'it's the genuine look. Yes, he came to the same end; quite the natural end here, I assure you. He forged wills, this blade did, if he didn't also put the supposed testators to sleep too. You were a gentlemanly Cove, though, and you said you could write Greek. What a liar you were! I never met such a liar as you!' Before putting his late friend on his shelf again, Wemmick touched the largest of his mourning rings, and said, 'Sent out to buy it for me, only the day before.'

While he was putting up the other cast and coming down from the chair, the thought crossed my mind that all his personal jewellery was derived from like sources. I ventured on the liberty of asking him the question, when he stood before me, dusting his hands.

'Oh yes,' he returned, 'these are all gifts of that kind. One brings another, you see; that's the way of it. I always take 'em. They're curiosities. And they're property. It don't signify to you with your brilliant look-out, but as to myself, my guiding-star always is, "Get hold of portable property".'

When I had rendered homage to this light, he went on to say, in a friendly manner:

'If at any odd time when you have nothing better to do, you wouldn't mind coming over to see me at Walworth, I could offer you a bed, and I should consider it an honour.'

I said I should be delighted to accept his hospitality.

'Thankee,' said he; 'then we'll consider that it's to come off, when convenient to you. Have you dined with Mr Jaggers yet?'

'Not yet.'

'Well,' said Wemmick, 'he'll give you wine, and good wine. And I'll tell you something. When you go to dine with Mr Jaggers, look at his housekeeper.'

'Shall I see something very uncommon?'

'Well,' said Wemmick, 'you'll see a wild beast tamed. Not so very uncommon, you'll tell me. I reply, that depends on the original wildness of the beast, and the amount of taming. It won't lower your opinion of Mr Jaggers's powers. Keep your eye on it.'

I told him I would do so, with all the interest and curiosity that his preparation awakened. As I was taking my departure, he asked me if I would like to devote five minutes to seeing Mr Jaggers 'at it?'

For several reasons, and not least because I didn't clearly know what Mr Jaggers would be found to be 'at', I replied in the affirmative. We dived into the City, and came up in a crowded police-court, where a blood-relation (in the murderous sense) of the deceased with the fanciful taste in brooches, was standing at the bar, while my guardian had a woman under examination or cross-examination – I don't know which – and was striking her, and the bench, and everybody present, with awe. If anybody, of whatsoever degree, said a word that he didn't approve of, he instantly required to have it 'taken down.' If anybody wouldn't make an admission, he said, 'I'll have it out of you!' and if anybody made an admission, he said, 'Now I have got you!' Which side he was on, I couldn't make out, for he seemed to me to be grinding the whole place in a mill; I only know that when I stole out on tiptoe, he was not on the side of the bench; for, he was making the legs of the old gentleman who presided, quite convulsive under the table, by his denunciations of his conduct as the representative of British law and justice in that chair that day.

25

Bentley Drummle was a sulky fellow. Heavy in figure, movement, and comprehension, he was idle, proud, niggardly, reserved, and suspicious. He came of rich people down in Somersetshire, who had nursed this combination of qualities until they made the discovery that it was just of age and a blockhead. Thus, Bentley Drummle had come to Mr Pocket when he was a head taller than that gentleman, and half a dozen heads thicker than most gentlemen.

Startop had been spoilt by a weak mother and kept at home when he ought to have been at school, but he was devotedly attached to her, and admired her beyond measure. It was but natural that I should take to him much more kindly than to Drummle, and that, even in the earliest evenings of our boating, he and I should pull homeward abreast of one another, conversing from boat to boat, while Bentley Drummle came up in our wake alone, under the overhanging banks and among the rushes.

When I had been in Mr Pocket's family a month or two, Mr and Mrs Camilla turned up. Camilla was Mr

Pocket's sister. Georgiana, whom I had seen at Miss Havisham's on the same occasion, also turned up. She was a cousin – an indigestive single woman, who called her rigidity religion, and her liver love. These people hated me with the hatred of cupidity and disappointment. Towards Mr Pocket they showed the complacent forbearance I had heard them express. Mrs Pocket they held in contempt; but they allowed the poor soul to have been heavily disappointed in life, because that shed a feeble reflected light upon themselves.

These were the surroundings among which I settled down, and applied myself to my education. I soon contracted expensive habits, and began to spend an amount of money that within a few short months I should have thought almost fabulous; but through good and evil I stuck to my books.

I had not seen Mr Wemmick for some weeks, when I thought I would write him a note and propose to go home with him on a certain evening. He replied that it would give him much pleasure, and that he would expect me at the office at six o'clock. Thither I went, and there I found him, putting the key of his safe down his back as the clock struck.

'Did you think of walking down to Walworth?' said he.

'Certainly,' said I, 'if you approve.'

'Very much,' was Wemmick's reply, 'for I have had my legs under the desk all day, and shall be glad to stretch them.'

'So, you haven't dined with Mr Jaggers yet?' he pursued, as we walked along.

'Not yet.'

'He told me so this afternoon when he heard you

were coming. I expect you'll have an invitation tomorrow. He's going to ask your pals, too. Three of 'em; ain't there?'

Although I was not in the habit of counting Drummle as one of my intimate associates, I answered, 'Yes.'

'Well, he's going to ask the whole gang;' I hardly felt complimented by the word; 'and whatever he gives you, he'll give you good. And there's another rum thing in his house,' proceeded Wemmick, after a moment's pause, as if the remark followed on; 'he never lets a door or window be fastened at night.'

'Is he never robbed?'

'That's it!' returned Wemmick. 'He says, and gives it out publicly, "I want to see the man who'll rob *me*." Lord bless you, I have heard him, a hundred times say to regular cracksmen in our front office, "You know where I live; now, no bolt is ever drawn there; why don't you do a stroke of business with me? Come; can't I tempt you?" Not a man of them, sir, would be bold enough to try it on, for love or moncy.'

'They dread him so much?' said I.

'Dread him,' said Wemmick. 'I believe you they dread him. Not but what he's artful, even in his defiance of them. No silver, sir. Britannia metal, every spoon.'

'So they wouldn't have much,' I observed, 'even if they –'

'Ah! But *he* would have much,' said Wemmick, cutting me short, 'and they know it. He'd have their lives, and the lives of scores of 'em. He'd have all he could get.'

At first with such discourse, and afterwards with conversation of a more general nature, did Mr Wemmick and I beguile the time and the road, until he gave me to understand that we had arrived in the district of Walworth.

Wemmick's house was a little wooden cottage in the midst of plots of garden, and the top of it was cut out and painted like a battery mounted with guns.

'My own doing,' said Wemmick. 'Looks pretty; don't it?'

I highly commended it. I think it was the smallest house I ever saw; with the queerest gothic windows and a gothic door, almost too small to get in at.

'That's a real flagstaff, you see,' said Wemmick, 'and on Sundays I run up a real flag. Then look here. After I have crossed this bridge, I hoist it up – so – and cut off the communication.'

The bridge was a plank, and it crossed a chasm about four feet wide and two deep. But it was very pleasant to see the pride with which he hoisted it up and made it fast; smiling as he did so, with a relish and not merely mechanically.

'At nine o'clock every night, Greenwich time,' said Wemmick, 'the gun fires. There he is, you see! And when you hear him go, I think you'll say he's a Stinger.'

The piece of ordnance referred to, was mounted in a separate fortress, constructed of lattice-work. It was protected from the weather by an ingenious little tarpaulin contrivance in the nature of an umbrella.

'Then, at the back,' said Wemmick, 'there's a pig, and there are fowls and rabbits; then, I knock together my own little frame, you see, and grow cucumbers;

and you'll judge at supper what sort of a salad I can raise.'

Our punch was cooling in an ornamental lake. This piece of water was of a circular form, and he had constructed a fountain in it, which, when you set a little mill going and took a cork out of a pipe, played to that powerful extent that it made the back of your hand quite wet.

'I am my own engineer, and my own carpenter, and my own plumber, and my own gardener, and my own Jack of all Trades,' said Wemmick, in acknowledging my compliments. 'It brushes the Newgate cobwebs away, and pleases the Aged. You wouldn't mind being at once introduced to the Aged, would you? It wouldn't put you out?'

I expressed the readiness I felt, and we went into the castle. There, we found, sitting by a fire, a very old man in a flannel coat: clean, cheerful, comfortable, and well cared for, but intensely deaf.

'Well aged parent,' said Wemmick, shaking hands with him in a cordial and jocose way, 'how am you?'

'All right, John; all right!' replied the old man.

'Here's Mr Pip, aged parent,' said Wemmick, 'Nod away at him, Mr Pip; that's what he likes.'

'This is a fine place of my son's, sir,' cried the old man, while I nodded as hard as I possibly could. This spot and these beautiful works upon it ought to be kept together by the Nation, after my son's time, for the people's enjoyment.'

'You're as proud of it as Punch; ain't you, Aged?' said Wemmick, contemplating the old man, with his hard face really softened; 'there's a nod for you;' giving him a tremendous one; 'there's another for you;' giving him a still more tremendous one. 'If you're not tired, Mr Pip, will you tip him one more?'

I tipped him several more, and he was in great spirits. We left him bestirring himself to feed the fowls, and we sat down to our punch in the arbour; where Wemmick told me that it had taken him a good many years to bring the property up to its present pitch of perfection.

'Is it your own, Mr Wemmick?'

'O yes,' said Wemmick, 'I have got hold of it, a bit at a time.'

'I hope Mr Jaggers admires it?'

'Never seen it,' said Wemmick. 'Never seen the Aged. Never heard of him. No; the office is one thing, and private life is another. When I go into the office, I leave the Castle behind me, and when I come into the Castle, I leave the office behind me. If it's not in any way disagreeable to you, you'll oblige me by doing the same. I don't wish it professionally spoken about.'

Of course I felt my good faith involved in the observance of his request. The punch being very nice, we sat there drinking it and talking, until it was almost nine o'clock. 'Getting near gun-fire,' said Wemmick then, as he laid down his pipe; 'it's the Aged's treat.'

Proceeding into the Castle again, we found the Aged heating the poker, with expectant eyes, as a preliminary to the performance of this great nightly ceremony. Wemmick stood with his watch in his hand, until the moment was come for him to take the red-hot poker from the Aged, and repair to the battery. He took it, and went out, and presently the Stinger went off with a Bang that shook the crazy little box of a cottage as if it must fall to pieces. Upon this, the Aged cried out exultingly, 'He's fired! I heerd him!'

The interval between that time and supper, Wemmick devoted to showing me his collection of curiosities. They were mostly of a felonious character; comprising the pen with which a celebrated forgery had been committed, a distinguished razor or two, some locks of hair, and several manuscript confessions written under condemnation.

The supper was excellent; and though the Castle was rather subject to dry-rot insomuch that it tasted like a bad nut, and though the pig might have been further off, I was heartily pleased with my whole entertainment. Nor was there any drawback on my little turret bedroom, beyond there being such a very thin ceiling between me and the flagstaff, that when I lay down on my back in bed, it seemed as if I had to balance that pole on my forehead all night.

Our breakfast was as good as the supper, and at half-past eight precisely we started for Little Britain. By degrees, Wemmick got dryer and harder as we went along, and his mouth tightened into a post-office again. At last, when we got to his place of business, he looked as unconscious of his Walworth property as if the Castle and the drawbridge and the arbour and the lake and the fountain and the Aged, had all been blown into space together by the last discharge of the Stinger.

26

My guardian was in his room, when I went into the office from Walworth; and he called me to him, and gave me the invitation for myself and friends which Wemmick had prepared me to receive. 'No ceremony,' he stipulated, 'and no dinner dress, and say tomorrow.' I asked him where we should come to, and he replied, 'Come here, and I'll take you home with me.' He had a closet in his room and he would wash his hands with scented soap, and wipe them and dry them all over this towel, whenever he came in from a police-court or dismissed a client from his room. When I and my friends repaired to him at six o'clock next day, we found him with his head butted into this closet, not only washing his hands, but laving his face and gargling his throat.

After we had left the office, he conducted us to Gerrard-street, Soho, to a house on the south side of that street. He took out his key and opened the door, and we all went into a stone hall, bare, gloomy, and little used. So, up a dark brown staircase into a series of three dark brown rooms on the first floor. There were carved garlands on the panelled walls, and as he stood among them giving us welcome, I know what kind of loops I thought they looked like.

The table was comfortably laid in the best of these rooms. At the side of his chair was a capacious dumbwaiter, with a variety of bottles and decanters on it, and four dishes of fruit for dessert.

As Mr Jaggers had scarcely seen my three companions until now – for, he and I had walked together – he stood on the hearth-rug, after ringing the bell, and took a searching look at them. To my surprise, he seemed at once to be principally if not solely interested in Drummle.

'Pip,' said he, putting his large hand on my shoulder and moving me to the window, 'I don't know one from the other. Who's the Spider?'

'The spider?' said I.

'The blotchy, sprawly, sulky fellow.'

'That's Bentley Drummle,' I replied; 'the one with the delicate face is Startop.'

Not making the least account of 'the one with the delicate face', he returned, 'Bentley Drummle is his name, is it? I like the look of that fellow.'

He immediately began to talk to Drummle: not at all deterred by his replying in his heavy reticent way, but apparently led on by it to screw discourse out of him. I was looking at the two, when there came between me and them, the housekeeper, with the first dish for the table.

She was a woman of about forty, I supposed. Rather tall, of a lithe nimble figure, extremely pale, with large faded eyes, and a quantity of streaming hair. I cannot say whether any diseased affection of the heart caused her lips to be parted as if she were panting, and her face to bear a curious expression of suddenness and flutter; but I know that I had been to see *Macbeth* at the theatre, a night or two before, and that her face looked to me as if it were all disturbed by fiery air, like the faces I had seen rise out of the Witches' cauldron.

She set the dish on, touched my guardian quietly on

the arm with a finger to notify that dinner was ready, and vanished. We took our seats at the round table, and my guardian kept Drummle on one side of him, while Startop sat on the other. No other attendant than the housekeeper appeared. She set on every dish; and I always saw in her face, a face rising out of the cauldron.

Induced to take particular notice of the housekeeper, both by her own striking appearance and by Wemmick's preparation, I observed that whenever she was in the room, she kept her eyes attentively on my guardian, and that she would remove her hands from any dish she put before him, hesitatingly, as if she dreaded his calling her back. I fancied that I could detect in his manner a consciousness of this, and a purpose of always holding her in suspense.

Dinner went off gaily, and, although my guardian seemed to follow rather than originate subjects, I knew that he wrenched the weakest part of our dispositions out of us. For myself, I found that I was expressing my tendency to lavish expenditure, and to patronize Herbert, and to boast of my great prospects, before I quite knew that I had opened my lips. It was so with all of us, but with no one more than Drummle: the development of whose inclination to gird in a grudging and suspicious way at the rest, was screwed out of him before the fish was taken off.

It was not then, but when we had got to the cheese, that our conversation turned upon our rowing feats, and that Drummle was rallied for coming up behind of a night in that slow amphibious way of his. Drummle upon this, informed our host that as to strength he could scatter us like chaff.

Now, the housekeeper was at that time clearing the table; my guardian, taking no heed of her, was leaning back in his chair biting the side of his forefinger and showing an interest in Drummle, that, to me, was quite inexplicable. Suddenly, he clapped his large hand on the housekeeper's, like a trap, as she stretched it across the table. So suddenly and smartly did he do this, that we all stopped in our foolish contention.

'If you talk of strength,' said Mr Jaggers, '*I*'ll show you a wrist. Molly, let them see your wrist.'

'Master,' she said, in a low voice, with her eyes attentively and entreatingly fixed upon him. 'Don't.'

'*I*'ll show you a wrist,' repeated Mr Jaggers, with an immovable determination to show it. 'Molly, let them see your wrist.'

'Master,' she again murmured. 'Please!'

'Molly,' said Mr Jaggers, not looking at her, but obstinately looking at the opposite side of the room, 'let them see *both* your wrists. Show them. Come!'

He took his hand from hers, and turned that wrist up on the table. She brought her other hand from behind her, and held the two out side by side. The last wrist was much disfigured – deeply scarred and scarred across and across.

'There's power here,' said Mr Jaggers, coolly tracing out the sinews with his forefinger. 'Very few men have the power of wrist that this woman has. I have had occasion to notice many hands; but I never saw stronger in that respect, man's or woman's, than these. That'll do, Molly, you have been admired, and can go.' She withdrew her hands and went out of the room, and Mr Jaggers, putting the decanters on from his dumb-waiter, filled his glass and passed round the wine.

'At half-past nine, gentlemen,' said he, 'we must break up. Pray make the best use of your time. I am glad to see you all. Mr Drummle, I drink to you.'

If his object in singling out Drummle were to bring him out still more, it perfectly succeeded. In a sulky triumph, Drummle showed his morose depreciation of the rest of us, in a more and more offensive degree until he became downright intolerable.

In our boyish want of discretion I dare say we took too much to drink and I know we talked too much. We became particularly hot upon some boorish sneer of Drummle's, to the effect that we were too free with our money. It led to my remarking, with more zeal than discretion, that it came with a bad grace from him, to whom Startop had lent money in my presence but a week or so before.

'Well,' retorted Drummle; 'he'll be paid.'

'I don't mean to imply that he won't,' said I, 'but it might make you hold your tongue about us and our money, I should think.'

'*You* should think!' retorted Drummle. 'Oh Lord!'

'I dare say,' I went on, meaning to be very severe, 'that you wouldn't lend money to any of us, if we wanted it.'

'You are right,' said Drummle. 'I wouldn't lend one of you a sixpence. I wouldn't lend anybody a sixpence.'

'Rather mean to borrow under those circumtances, I should say.'

'*You* should say,' repeated Drummle. 'Oh Lord!'

This was so very aggravating – the more especially as I found myself making no way against his surly obtuseness – that I said, disregarding Herbert's efforts to check me:

'Come, Mr Drummle, since we are on the subject,

I'll tell you what passed between Herbert here and me, when you borrowed that money.'

'*I* don't want to know what passed between Herbert there and you,' growled Drummle.

'I'll tell you, however,' said I, 'whether you want to know or not. We said that as you put it in your pocket very glad to get it, you seemed to be immensely amused at his being so weak as to lend it.'

Drummle laughed outright, with his hands in his pockets and his round shoulders raised: plainly signifying that he despised us, as asses all.

Hereupon Startop took him in hand, though with a much better grace than I had shown, and tried to turn the discussion aside with some small pleasantry that made us all laugh. Resenting this little success more than anything, Drummle, without any threat or warning, swore, took up a large glass, and would have flung it at his adversary's head, but for our entertainer's dexterously seizing it at the instant when it was raised for that purpose.

'Gentlemen,' said Mr Jaggers, deliberately putting down the glass, and hauling out his gold repeater by its massive chain, 'I am exceedingly sorry to announce that it's half-past nine.'

On this hint we all rose to depart. Before we got to the street door, Startop was cheerily calling Drummle 'old boy', as if nothing had happened. But the old boy was so far from responding, that he would not even walk to Hammersmith on the same side of the way; so, Herbert and I, who remained in town, saw them going down the street on opposite sides; Startop leading, and Drummle lagging behind in the shadow of the houses, much as he was wont to follow in his boat.

As the door was not yet shut, I thought I would leave Herbert there for a moment, and run upstairs again to say a word to my guardian.

I told him I had come up again to say how sorry I was that anything disagreeable should have occurred, and that I hoped he would not blame me much.

'Pooh!' said he, sluicing his face, and speaking through the water-drops; 'it's nothing, Pip. I like that Spider though.'

'I am glad you like him, sir,' said I – 'but I don't.'

'No, no,' my guardian assented; 'don't have too much to do with him. Keep as clear of him as you can. But I like the fellow, Pip; he is one of the true sort. Good-night, Pip.'

'Good-night, sir.'

In about a month after that, the Spider's time with Mr Pocket was up for good, and, to the great relief of all the house but Mrs Pocket, he went home to the family hole.

27

My Dear Mr Pip
I write this by request of Mr Gargery, for to let you know
that he is going to London in company with Mr Wopsle
and would be glad if agreeable to be allowed to see you.
He would call at Barnard's Hotel Tuesday morning at
nine o'clock, when if not agreeable please leave word.
Your poor sister is much the same as when you left. We
talk of you in the kitchen every night, and wonder what
you are saying and doing. No more, dear Mr Pip, from

Your ever obliged, and affectionate servant,
Biddy

P.S. *He wishes me most particular to write* 'what larks'.
*He says you will understand. I hope and do not doubt it
will be agreeable to see him even though a gentleman, for
you had ever a good heart, and he is a worthy worthy
man.*

Let me confess exactly, with what feelings I looked
forward to Joe's coming.

Not with pleasure, though I was bound to him by so
many ties; no; with considerable disturbance, some
mortification, and a keen sense of incongruity. My
greatest reassurance was, that he was coming to Barnard's Inn, not to Hammersmith, and consequently
would not fall in Bentley Drummle's way. I had little
objection to his being seen by Herbert or his father,
for both of whom I had a respect; but I had the
sharpest sensitiveness as to his being seen by
Drummle, whom I held in contempt. By this time, the
rooms were vastly different from what I had found
them, and I enjoyed the honour of occupying a few
prominent pages in the books of a neighbouring uphol-
sterer. I had got on so fast of late, that I had even
started a boy in boots in bondage and slavery to whom
I might have been said to pass my days. For, after I
had made the monster and had clothed him with a
blue coat, canary waistcoat, white cravat, creamy
breeches, and the boots already mentioned, I had to
find him a little to do and a great deal to eat; and with
both of those horrible requirements he haunted my existence.

This avenging phantom was ordered to be on duty at eight on Tuesday morning in the hall, and Herbert suggested certain things for breakfast that he thought Joe would like.

However, I came into town on the Monday night to be ready for Joe, and I got up early in the morning, and caused the sitting-room and breakfast-table to assume their most splendid appearance.

As the time approached I should have liked to run away, but the Avenger pursuant to orders was in the hall, and presently I heard Joe on the staircase. When he stopped outside our door, I could hear his finger tracing over the painted letters of my name, and I afterwards distinctly heard him breathing in at the keyhole. Finally he gave a faint single rap, and Pepper – such was the compromising name of the avenging boy – announced 'Mr Gargery!' I thought he never would have done wiping his feet, and that I must have gone out to lift him off the mat, but at last he came in.

'Joe, how are you, Joe?'

'Pip, how *air* you, Pip?'

With his good honest face all glowing and shining, and his hat put down on the floor between us, he caught both my hands and worked them straight up and down, as if I had been the last-patented Pump.

'I am glad to see you, Joe. Give me your hat.'

But Joe, taking it up carefully with both hands, wouldn't hear of parting with that piece of property, and persisted in standing talking over it in a most uncomfortable way.

'Which you have that growed,' said Joe, 'and that swelled, and that gentle-folked;' Joe considered a little before he discovered this word; 'as to be sure you are a honour to your king and country.'

'And you, Joe, look wonderfully well.'

'Thank God,' said Joe, 'I'm ekerval to most. And your sister, she's no worse than she were. And Biddy, she's ever right and ready. But not Wopsle; he's had a drop.'

'Had a drop, Joe?'

'Why yes,' said Joe, lowering his voice, 'he's left the Church, and went into the playacting. Which the playacting have likeways brought him to London along with me. And his wish were,' said Joe, 'if no offence, as I would 'and you that.'

I took what Joe gave me, and found it to be the crumpled play-bill of a small metropolitan theatre.

'Were you at his performance, Joe?' I enquired.

'I *were*,' said Joe, with emphasis and solemnity.

'Was there a great sensation?'

'Why', said Joe, 'yes, there certainly were a peck of orange-peel. Partickler, when he see the ghost.'

A ghost-seeing effect in Joe's own countenance informed me that Herbert had entered the room. So, I presented Joe to Herbert, who held out his hand; but Joe backed from it.

'Your servant, Sir,' said Joe, 'which I hope as you and Pip' – here his eye fell on the Avenger, who was putting some toast on table, and so plainly denoted an intention to make that young gentleman one of the family, that I frowned it down and confused him more – 'I meantersay, you two gentlemen – which I hope as you get your elths in this close spot? For the present may be a werry good inn, according to London opinions,' said Joe, confidentially, 'and I believe its character do stand; but I wouldn't keep a pig in it myself.'

Having borne this flattering testimony to the merits of our dwelling-place, and having incidentally shown this tendency to call me 'sir', Joe, being invited to sit down to table, looked all round the room for a suitable spot on which to deposit his hat and ultimately stood it on an extreme corner of the chimney-piece, from which it ever afterwards fell off at intervals.

'Do you take tea, or coffee, Mr Gargery?' asked Herbert, who always presided of a morning.

'Thankee, Sir,' said Joe, stiff from head to foot, 'I'll take which ever is most agreeable to yourself.'

'What do you say to coffee?'

'Thankee, Sir,' returned Joe, evidently dispirited by the proposal, 'since you *are* so kind as make chice of coffee, I will not run contrairy to your own opinions. But don't you never find it a little 'eating?'

'Say tea then,' said Herbert, pouring it out.

Here Joe's hat tumbled off the mantel-piece, and he started out of his chair and picked it up, and fitted it to the same exact spot.

'When did you come to town, Mr Gargery?'

'Were it yesterday afternoon?' said Joe, after coughing behind his hand. 'No it were not. Yes it were.'

'Have you seen anything of London, yet?'

'Why, yes, Sir,' said Joe, 'me and Wopsle went off straight to look at the Blacking Ware'us. But we didn't find that it come up to its likeness in the red bills at the shop doors; which I meantersay,' added Joe, in an explanatory manner, 'as it is there drawd too architectooralooral.'

I really believe Joe would have prolonged this word into a perfect Chorus, but for his attention being providentially attracted by his hat, which was toppling.

He made extraordinary play with it, and showed the greatest skill; now, rushing at it and catching it neatly as it dropped; now, merely stopping it midway, beating it up, and humouring it in various parts of the room and against a good deal of the pattern of the paper on the wall, finally, splashing it into the slop-basin, where I took the liberty of laying hands upon it.

Joe had his eyes attracted in such strange directions; was afflicted with such remarkable coughs; sat so far from the table, and dropped so much more than he ate, and pretended that he hadn't dropped it; that I was heartily glad when Herbert left us for the city.

I had neither the good sense nor the good feeling to know that this was all my fault, and that if I had been easier with Joe, Joe would have been easier with me. I felt impatient of him and out of temper with him; in which condition he heaped coals of fire on my head.

'Us two being now alone, Sir,' – began Joe.

'Joe,' I interrupted, pettishly, 'how can you call me, Sir?'

Joe looked at me for a single instant with something faintly like reproach and I was conscious of a sort of dignity in the look.

'Us two being now alone,' resumed Joe, 'and me having the intentions and abilities to stay not many minutes more, I will now conclude to mention what have led to my having had the present honour. This is how it were. I were at the Bargemen t'other night, Pip;' whenever he subsided into affection, he called me Pip, and whenever he relapsed into politeness he called me Sir; 'when there come up in his shay-cart, Pumblechook; and his word were; "Joseph, Miss Havisham she wish to speak to you."'

'Yes, Joe? Go on, please.'

'Next day, Sir,' said Joe, looking at me as if I were a long way off, 'having cleaned myself, I go and I see Miss A.'

'Miss A., Joe? Miss Havisham?'

'Which I say, Sir,' replied Joe, with an air of legal formality, as if he were making his will, 'Miss A., or otherways Havisham. Her expression air then as follering: "Mr Gargery. You air in correspondance with Mr Pip?" Having had a letter from you, I were able to say "I am." "Would you tell him, then," said she, "that which Estella has come home and would be glad to see him." '

I felt my face fire up as I looked at Joe. I hope one remote cause of its firing, may have been my consciousness that if I had known his errand, I should have given him more encouragement.

'Biddy,' pursued Joe, 'when I got home and asked her fur to write the message to you, a little hung back. Biddy says, "I know he will be very glad to have it by word of mouth, it is holiday-time, you want to see him, go!" I have now concluded, Sir,' said Joe, rising from his chair, 'and, Pip, I wish you ever well and ever prospering to a greater and a greater heighth.'

'But you are not going now, Joe?'

'Yes I am,' said Joe.

'But you are coming back to dinner, Joe?'

'No I am not,' said Joe.

Our eyes met, and all the 'Sir' melted out of that manly heart as he gave me his hand.

'Pip, dear old chap, life is made of ever so many partings welded together, as I may say, and one man's a blacksmith, and one's a goldsmith, and one's a

coppersmith. Diwisions among such must come, and
must be met as they come. If there's been any fault at
all today, it's mine. You and me is not two figures to
be together in London. It ain't that I am proud, but
that I want to be right, as you shall never see me no
more in these clothes. I'm wrong in these clothes. I'm
wrong out of the forge, the kitchen, or off th'meshes.
You won't find half so much fault in me if, supposing
as you should ever wish to see me, you come and put
your head in at the forge window and see Joe the
blacksmith, there, at the old anvil, in the old burnt
apron, sticking to the old work. And so God bless you,
dear old Pip, old chap, God bless you!'

I had not been mistaken in my fancy that there was
a simple dignity in him. He touched me gently on the
forehead, and went out. As soon as I could recover
myself sufficiently, I hurried out after him and looked
for him in the neighbouring streets; but he was gone.

28

It was clear that I must repair to our town next day,
and in the first flow of my repentance it was equally
clear that I must stay at Joe's. But I was not by any
means convinced on the last point, and began to invent
reasons and make excuses for putting up at the Blue
Boar. I should be an inconvenience at Joe's; I was not
expected, and my bed would not be ready; I should be
too far from Miss Havisham's, and she was exacting
and mightn't like it.

Having settled that I must go to the Blue Boar, my mind was much disturbed by indecision whether or no to take the Avenger. It was tempting to think of that expensive Mercenary publicly airing his boots in the Blue Boar's posting-yard. But my patroness, too might hear of him, and not approve. On the whole, I resolved to leave the Avenger behind.

It was the afternoon coach by which I had taken my place, and, as winter had now come round, I should not arrive at my destination until two or three hours after dark.

At that time it was customary to carry convicts down to the dockyards by stage-coach. Herbert, meeting me in the yard, came up and told me there were two convicts going down with me. But I had a reason that was an old reason now, for constitutionally faltering whenever I heard the word convict.

'You don't mind them, Handel?' said Herbert.

'Oh no!'

'I thought you seemed as if you didn't like them?'

'I can't pretend that I do like them, and I suppose you don't particularly. But I don't mind them.'

'See! There they are,' said Herbert, 'coming out of the Tap. What a degraded and vile sight it is!'

They had been treating their guard, I suppose, for they had a goaler with them, and all three came out wiping their mouths on their hand. The two convicts were handcuffed together, and had irons on their legs – irons of a pattern that I knew well. They wore the dress that I likewise knew well. One was a taller and stouter man than the other, and appeared as a matter of course, according to the mysterious ways of the world both convict and free, to have had allotted to him the smaller suit of clothes. His arms and legs were like great pincushions of those shapes, and his attire disguised him absurdly; but I knew his half-closed eye at one glance. There stood the man whom I had seen on the settle at the Three Jolly Bargemen on a Saturday night, and who had brought me down with his invisible gun!

It was easy to make sure that as yet he knew me no more than if he had never seen me in his life. He looked across at me, and his eye appraised my watch-chain, and then he incidentally spat and said something to the other convict, and they laughed and slued them-selves round with a clink of their coupling manacle, and looked at something else. The great numbers on their backs, as if they were street doors; their coarse mangy ungainly outer surface, as if they were lower animals; their ironed legs, apologetically garlanded with pocket-handkerchiefs; and the way in which all present looked at them and kept from them; made them (as Herbert had said) a most disagreeable and degraded spectacle.

But this was not the worst of it. It came out that there were no places for the two prisoners but on the seat in front, behind the coachman. Hereupon, a chol-eric gentleman, who had taken the fourth place on that seat, flew into a most violent passion, and said that it was a breach of contract to mix him up with such villainous company. At this time the coach was ready and the coachman impatient, and we were all preparing to get up, and the prisoners had come over with their keeper.

'Don't take it so much amiss, sir,' pleaded the keeper to the angry passenger; 'I'll sit next you myself. I'll put 'em on the outside of the row. They won't interfere with you, sir. You needn't know they're there.'

At length, it was voted that there was no help for the angry gentleman, and that he must either go in his chance company or remain behind. So, he got into his place, still making complaints, and the keeper got into the place next him, and the convicts hauled themselves up as well as they could, and the convict I had recognized sat behind me with his breath on the hair of my head.

'Goodbye, Handel!' Herbert called out as we started. I thought what a blessed fortune it was, that he had found another name for me than Pip.

It is impossible to express with what acuteness I felt the convict's breathing, not only on the back of my head, but all along my spine. He seemed to have more breathing business to do than another man, and to make more noise in doing it; and I was conscious of growing high-shouldered on one side, in my shrinking endeavours to fend him off.

The weather was miserably raw, and the two cursed the cold. I dozed off, in considering the question whether I ought to restore a couple of pounds sterling to this creature before losing sight of him, and how it could best be done. In the act of dipping forward as if I were going to bathe among the horses, I woke in a fright and took the question up again.

But I must have lost it longer than I had thought, since, although I could recognize nothing in the darkness and the fitful lights and shadows of our lamps, I traced marsh country in the cold damp wind that blew at us. Cowering forward for warmth and to make me a screen against the wind, the convicts were closer to me than before. The very first words I heard them interchange as I became conscious were the words of my own thought, 'Two one pound notes.'

'How did he get 'em?' said the convict I had never seen.

'How should I know?' returned the other. 'He had 'em stowed away somehows. Giv him by friends, I expect.'

'I wish,' said the other, with a bitter curse upon the cold, 'that I had 'em here. I'd sell all the friends I ever had, for one, and think it a blessed good bargain. Well? So he says –?'

'So he says,' resumed the convict I had recognized – 'it was all said and done in half a minute: "You're a going to be discharged?" Yes, I was. Would I find out that boy that had fed him and kep his secret, and give him them two one pound notes? Yes, I would. And I did.'

'More fool you,' growled the other. 'He must have been a green one. Mean to say he knowed nothing of you?'

'Not a ha'porth. Different gangs and different ships. He was tried again for prison breaking, and got made a Lifer.'

After overhearing this dialogue, I should assuredly have got down and been left in the solitude and darkness of the highway, but for feeling certain that the man had no suspicion of my identity. Still, the coincidence of our being together on the coach, was sufficiently strange to fill me with a dread that some other coincidence might at any moment connect me, in his hearing, with my name. For this reason, I resolved to alight as soon as we touched the town, and put myself out of his hearing. This device I executed successfully. My little portmanteau was in the boot under my feet; I had but to turn a hinge to get it out; I threw it down before me, got down after it, and was left at the first lamp on the first stones of the town pavement. As to the convicts, they went their way with the coach, and I knew at what point they would be spirited off to the river.

As I walked on to the hotel, I felt that a dread, much exceeding the mere apprehension of a painful or disagreeable recognition, made me tremble. I am confident that it took no distinctness of shape, and that it was the revival for a few minutes of the terror of childhood.

The coffee-room at the Blue Boar was empty, and I had not only ordered my dinner there, but had sat down to it, before the waiter knew me. As soon as he had apologized for the remissness of his memory, he asked me if he should send Boots for Mr Pumble-chook?

'No,' said I, 'certainly not.'

The waiter appeared surprised, and took the earliest opportunity of putting a dirty old copy of a local newspaper so directly in my way, that I took it up and read this paragraph:

Our readers will learn, not altogether without interest, in reference to the recent romantic rise in fortune of a young artificer in iron of this neighbourhood. But that the youth's earliest patron, companion, and friend, was a highly-respected individual not entirely unconnected with the corn and seed trade. It is not wholly irrespective of our personal feelings that we record HIM as the Mentor of our young

Telemachus, for it is good to know that our town produced the founder of the latter's fortunes. Does the thought-contracted brow of the local Sage or the lustrous eye of local Beauty enquire whose fortunes? We believe that Quintin Matsys was the BLACKSMITH of Antwerp. VERB. SAP.

I entertain a conviction that if in the days of my prosperity I had gone to the North Pole, I should have met somebody there who would have told me that Pumblechook was my earliest patron and the founder of my fortunes.

29

Betimes in the morning I was up and out. It was too early yet to go to Miss Havisham's, so I loitered into the country on Miss Havisham's side of town thinking about my patroness, and painting brilliant pictures of her plans for me.

She had adopted Estella, she had as good as adopted me, and it could not fail to be her intention to bring us together. She reserved it for me to restore the desolate house, admit the sunshine into the dark rooms, set the clocks a-going and the cold hearths a-blazing, tear down the cobwebs, destroy the vermin – in short, do all the shining deeds of the young Knight of romance, and marry the Princess. I had stopped to look at the house as I passed; and its seared red brick walls, blocked windows, and strong green ivy clasping even the stacks of chimneys with its twigs and tendons, had made up a rich attractive mystery, of which I was the hero. Estella was the inspiration of it, and the heart of it, of course. But though my fancy and my hope were so set upon her, I did not, even that romantic morning, invest her with any attributes save those she possessed. I loved her simply because I found her irresistible. I knew to my sorrow, often and often, if not always, that I loved her against reason, against promise, against peace, against hope, against happiness, against all discouragement that could be. Once for all; I loved her none the less because I knew it, and it had no more influence in restraining me, than if I had devoutly believed her to be human perfection.

I so shaped out my walk as to arrive at the gate at my old time. I rang at the bell with an unsteady hand, while I tried to get my breath and keep the beating of my heart moderately quiet. I heard steps come across the court-yard; but I pretended not to hear, even when the gate swung on its rusty hinges.

Being at last touched on the shoulder, I started and turned to find myself confronted by the last man I should have expected to see in that place of porter at Miss Havisham's door.

'Orlick!'

'Ah, young master, there's more changes than yours. But come in, come in. It's opposed to my orders to hold the gate open.'

I entered and he swung it, and locked it, and took the key out.

'How did you come here?'

'I come here,' he retorted, 'on my legs. I had my box brought alongside me in a barrow.'

'Are you here for good?'

'I ain't here for harm, young master, I suppose?'

I was not so sure of that. I asked him how long he had left Gargery's forge?

'One day is so like another here,' he replied, 'that I don't know without casting it up. However, I come here some time since you left.'

By this time we had come to the house, where I found his room to be one just within the side door, with a little window in it looking on the court-yard.

'I never saw this room before,' I remarked; 'but there used to be no Porter here.'

'No,' said he; 'not till it got about that there was no protection on the premises, and it come to be considered dangerous, with convicts and Tag and Rag and Bobtail going up and down. And then I was recommended to the place as a man who could give another man as good as he brought, and I took it.'

My eye had been caught by a gun with a brass bound stock over the chimney-piece, and his eye had followed mine.

'Well,' said I, not desirous of more conversation, 'shall I go up to Miss Havisham?'

'Burn me, if I know!' he retorted, first stretching himself and then shaking himself; 'my orders ends here, young master. I give this here bell a rap with this here hammer, and you go on along the passage till you meet somebody.'

'I am expected, I believe?'

'Burn me twice over, if I can say!' said he.

Upon that, I turned down the long passage and he made his bell sound. At the end of the passage I found Sarah Pocket: who appeared to have now become constitutionally green and yellow by reason of me.

'Oh!' said she. 'You, is it, Mr Pip?'

'It is, Miss Pocket. I am glad to tell you that Mr Pocket and family are all well.'

'Are they any wiser?' said Sarah, with a dismal shake of the head; 'they had better be wiser, than well. Ah, Matthew, Matthew! You know your way, sir?'

Tolerably, for I gone up the staircase in the dark, many a time. I ascended it now, in lighter boots than of yore, and tapped in my old way at the door of Miss Havisham's room. 'Pip's rap,' I heard her say, immediately; 'come in, Pip.'

She was in her chair near the old table, in the old dress, with her two hands crossed on her stick. Sitting near her was an elegant lady whom I had never seen.

'Come in, Pip,' Miss Havisham continued to mutter, without looking round or up; 'how do you do, Pip? so you kiss my hand as if I were a queen, eh? – Well?'

She looked up at me suddenly, only moving her eyes, and repeated in a grimly playful manner, Well?'

'I heard, Miss Havisham,' said I, rather at a loss, 'that you were so kind as to wish me to come and see you, and I came directly.'

'Well?'

The lady whom I had never seen before, lifted up her eyes and looked archly at me, and then I saw that the eyes were Estella's eyes. But she was so much changed, was so much more beautiful, so much more womanly. I fancied, as I looked at her, that I slipped hopelessly back into the coarse and common boy again.

She gave me her hand. I stammered something about the pleasure I felt in seeing her again, and about my having looked forward to it for a long, long time.

'Do you find her much changed, Pip?' asked Miss Havisham, with her greedy look.

'When I came in, Miss Havisham, I thought there was nothing of Estella in the face or figure; but now it all settles down so curiously into the old –'

'What? You are not going to say into the old Estella?' Miss Havisham interrupted. 'She was proud and insulting, and you wanted to go away from her. Don't you remember?'

I said confusedly that that was long ago, and that I knew no better then, and the like. Estella smiled with perfect composure, and said she had no doubt of my having been quite right, and of her having been very disagreeable.

'Is *he* changed?' Miss Havisham asked her.

'Very much,' said Estella, looking at me.

It was settled that I should stay there all the rest of the day, and return to the hotel at night, and to London tomorrow. When we had conversed for a while, Miss Havisham sent us two out to walk in the neglected garden: on our coming in by-and-by, she said, I should wheel her about a little as in times of yore.

So, Estella and I went out into the garden by the gate through which I had strayed to my encounter with the pale young gentleman, now Herbert; I, trembling in spirit and worshipping the very hem of her dress; she, quite composed and most decidedly not worshipping the hem of mine. As we drew near to the place of encounter, she stopped and said:

'I must have been a singular little creature to hide and see that fight that day: but I did, and I enjoyed it very much.'

'He and I are great friends now.'

'Are you? I think I recollect though, that you read with his father?'

'Yes.'

I made the admission with reluctance, for it seemed to have a boyish look, and she already treated me more than enough like a boy.

'Since your change of fortune and prospects, you have changed your companions,' said Estella.

'Naturally,' said I.

'And necessarily,' she added, in a haughty tone; 'what was fit company for you once, would be quite unfit company for you now.'

In my conscience, I doubt very much whether I had any lingering intention left, of going to see Joe; but if I had, this observation put it to flight.

The garden was too overgrown and rank for walking in with ease, and after we had made the round of it twice or thrice, we came out again into the brewery yard. I showed her to a nicety where I had seen her walking on the casks, that first old day, and she said, with a cold and careless look in that direction, 'Did I?' I verily believe that her not remembering and not minding in the least, made me cry inwardly – and that is the sharpest crying of all.

'You must know,' said Estella, 'that I have no heart – if that has anything to do with my memory.'

I got through some jargon to the effect that I knew better. That there could be no such beauty without it.

'Oh! I have a heart to be stabbed in or shot in, I have no doubt,' said Estella, 'and, of course, if it ceased to beat I should cease to be. But you know what I mean. I have no softness there, no – sympathy – sentiment – nonsense.'

What *was* it that was borne in upon my mind when she stood still and looked attentively at me? Anything that I had seen in Miss Havisham? No. I could not trace this to Miss Havisham. I looked again, and though she was still looking at me, the suggestion was gone.

What *was* it?

'I am serious,' said Estella, 'if we are to be thrown much together, you had better believe it at once. No!' imperiously stopping me as I opened my lips. 'I have not bestowed my tenderness anywhere. I have never had any such thing.'

We walked round the ruined garden twice or thrice more, and it was all in bloom for me. If the green and yellow growth of weed in the chinks of the old wall had been the most precious flowers that ever blew, it could not have been more cherished in my remembrance.

There was no discrepancy of years between us, to remove her far from me; we were of nearly the same age, but the air of inaccessibility which her beauty and her manner gave her, tormented me in the midst of my delight, and at the height of the assurance I felt that our patroness had chosen us for one another.

At last we went back into the house, and there I heard, with surprise, that my guardian had come down to see Miss Havisham on business, and would come back to dinner. The old wintry branches of chandeliers in the room where the mouldering table was spread, had been lighted while we were out, and Miss Havisham was in her chair and waiting for me.

It was like pushing the chair itself back into the

past, when we began the old slow circuit round about the ashes of the bridal feast. But, in the funereal room, with that figure of the grave fallen back in the chair fixing its eyes upon her, Estella looked more bright and beautiful than before, and I was under stronger enchantment.

The time so melted away, that our early dinner-hour drew close at hand, and Estella left us to prepare herself. We had stopped near the centre of the long table, and Miss Havisham, with one of her withered arms stretched out of the chair, rested that clenched hand upon the yellow cloth. As Estella looked back over her shoulder before going out at the door, Miss Havisham kissed that hand to her, with a ravenous intensity that was of its kind quite dreadful.

Then, Estella being gone and we two left alone, she turned to me, and said in a whisper:

'Is she beautiful, graceful, well-grown? Do you admire her?'

'Everybody must who sees her, Miss Havisham.'

She drew an arm round my neck, and drew my head close down to hers as she sat in the chair. 'Love her, love her, love her! How does she use you?'

Before I could answer (if I could have answered so difficult a question at all), she repeated, 'Love her, love her, love her! If she favours you, love her. If she wounds you, love her. If she tears your heart to pieces, love her, love her, love her!'

Never had I seen such passionate eagerness as was joined to her utterance of these words. I could feel the muscles of the thin arm round my neck, swell with the vehemence that possessed her.

'Hear me, Pip! I adopted her to be loved. I developed

her into what she is, that she might be loved. Love her!'

She said the word often enough, and there could be no doubt that she meant to say it; but if the often repeated word had been hate instead of love – despair – revenge – dire death – it could not have sounded from her lips more like a curse.

'I'll tell you,' said she, in the same hurried passionate whisper, 'what real love is. It is blind devotion, unquestioning self-humiliation, utter submission, trust and belief against yourself and against the whole world, giving up your whole heart and soul to the smiter – as I did!'

When she came to that, and to a wild cry that followed that, I caught her round the waist. For she rose up in the chair, in her shroud of a dress, and struck at the air as if she would as soon have struck herself against the wall and fallen dead.

All this passed in a few seconds. As I drew her down into her chair, I turned and saw my guardian in the room.

Miss Havisham had seen him as soon as I, and was (like everybody else) afraid of him. She made a strong attempt to compose herself, and stammered that he was as punctual as ever.

'As punctual as ever,' he repeated, coming up to us. '(How do you do, Pip? Shall I give you a ride, Miss Havisham? Once round?)'

I told him when I had arrived, and how Miss Havisham had wished me to come and see Estella. To which he replied, 'Ah! Very fine young lady!' Then he pushed Miss Havisham in her chair before him, with one of his large hands, and put the other in his trousers-pocket as if the pocket were full of secrets.

'Well, Pip! How often have you seen Miss Estella before?' said he, when he came to a stop. 'Ten thousand times?'

'Oh! Certainly not so many.'

'Twice?'

'Jaggers,' interposed Miss Havisham, much to my relief; 'leave my Pip alone, and go with him to your dinner.'

He complied, and we groped our way down the dark stairs together. While we were still on our way, he asked me how often I had seen Miss Havisham eat and drink; offering me a breadth of choice, as usual, between a hundred times and once.

I considered, and said, 'Never.'

'And never will, Pip,' he retorted, with a frowning smile. 'She has never allowed herself to be seen doing either, since she lived this present life of hers. She wanders about in the night, and then lays hands on such food as she takes.'

'Pray, sir,' said I, 'may I ask you a question?'

'You may,' said he, 'and I may decline to answer it. Put your question.'

'Estella's name. Is it Havisham or –?' I had nothing to add.

'Or what?' said he.

'Is it Havisham?'

'It is Havisham.'

Anything to equal the determined reticence of Mr Jaggers under that roof, I never saw elsewhere, even in him. He kept his very looks to himself, and scarcely directed his eyes to Estella's face once during dinner. When she spoke to him, he listened, and in due course answered, but never looked at her, that I could see. Throughout dinner he took a dry delight in making Sarah Pocket greener and yellower, by often referring in conversation with me to my expectations; but he showed no consciousness, and even made it appear that he extorted those references out of my innocent self.

I think Miss Pocket was conscious that the sight of me involved her in the danger of being goaded to madness. She did not appear when we afterwards went up to Miss Havisham's room, and we four played at whist. In the interval, Miss Havisham, in a fantastic way, had put some of the most beautiful jewels from her dressing-table into Estella's hair, and about her bosom and arms; and I saw even my guardian look at her from under his thick eyebrows, and raise them a little, when her loveliness was before him, with those rich flushes of glitter and colour in it.

Of the manner and extent to which he took our trumps into custody, and came out with mean little cards at the ends of hands, before which the glory of our Kings and Queens was utterly abased, I say nothing. What I suffered from, was the incompatibility between his cold presence and my feelings towards Estella. It was not that I knew I could never bear to speak to him about her, it was, that my feelings should be in the same place with him – *that*, was the agonizing circumstance.

We played until nine o'clock, and then it was arranged that when Estella came to London I should be forewarned of her coming and should meet her at the coach; and then I took leave of her, and touched her and left her.

My guardian lay at the Boar in the next room to mine. Far into the night, Miss Havisham's words, 'Love her, love her, love her!' sounded in my ears. I adapted them for my own repetition, and said to my pillow, 'I love her, I love her, I love her!' hundreds of times. Then, a burst of gratitude came upon me, that she should be destined for me, once the blacksmith's boy. Then, I thought if she were, as I feared, by no means rapturously grateful for that destiny yet, when would she begin to be interested in me? When should I awaken the heart within her, that was mute and sleeping now?

I never thought there was anything low and small in my keeping away from Joe, because I knew she would be contemptuous of him. It was but a day gone, and Joe had brought the tears into my eyes; they had soon dried, God forgive me! soon dried.

30

After well considering the matter while I was dressing at the Blue Boar in the morning, I resolved to tell my guardian that I doubted Orlick's being the right sort of man to fill a post of trust at Miss Havisham's. It seemed quite to put him into spirits, to find that this particular post was not exceptionally held by the right sort of man, and he listened in a satisfied manner while I told him what knowledge I had of Orlick. 'Very good, Pip,' he observed, when I had concluded, 'I'll go round presently, and pay our friend off.' Rather alarmed by this summary action, I was for a little delay, and even hinted that our friend himself might be difficult to deal with. 'Oh no he won't,' said my guardian, 'I should like to see him argue the question with *me*.'

As we were going back together to London by the midday coach, this gave me an opportunity of saying that I wanted a walk, and that I would go on along the London-road while Mr Jaggers was occupied, if he would let the coachman know that I would get into my place when overtaken. I was thus enabled to fly from the Blue Boar immediately after breakfast. By then making a loop of about a couple of miles into the open country at the back of Pumblechook's premises, I got round into the High-street again, a little beyond that pitfall, and felt myself in comparative security.

It was interesting to be in the quiet old town once more, and it was not disagreeable to be here and there suddenly recognized and stared after. One or two of the tradespeople even darted out of their shops and went a little way down the street before me, that they might turn, as if they had forgotten something, and pass me face to face – on which occasions I don't know whether they or I made the worse pretence; they of not doing it, or I of not seeing it.

The coach, with Mr Jaggers inside, came up in due time, and I took my box-seat again, and arrived in London safe – but not sound, for my heart was gone. As soon as I arrived, I sent a penitential codfish and barrel of oysters to Joe (as reparation for not having gone myself), and then went on to Barnard's Inn.

I found Herbert dining on cold meat, and delighted to welcome me back. Having dispatched the Avenger to the coffee-house for an addition to the dinner, I felt that I must open my breast that very evening to my friend and chum. Dinner done and we sitting with our feet upon the fender, I said to Herbert, 'My dear Herbert, I have something very particular to tell you.'

Herbert crossed his feet, looked at the fire with his head on one side, and having looked at it in vain for some time, looked at me because I didn't go on.

'Herbert,' said I, laying my hand upon his knee, 'I love – I adore – Estella.'

Instead of being transfixed, Herbert replied in an easy matter-of-course way, 'Exactly. Well?'

'Well, Herbert? Is that all you say? Well?'

'What next, I mean?' said Herbert. 'Of course I know *that*.'

'I never told you.'

'Told me! You have never told me when you have got your hair cut, but I have had senses to perceive it. When you told me your own story, you told me plainly that you began adoring her the first time you saw her, when you were very young indeed.'

'Very well, then,' said I, 'I have never left off adoring her. And she has come back, a most beautiful and most elegant creature. And I saw her yesterday. And if I adored her before, I now doubly adore her.'

'Lucky for you then, Handel,' said Herbert, 'that you are picked out for her and allotted to her. Have you any idea yet, of Estella's views on the adoration question?'

I shook my head gloomily. 'Oh! She is thousands of miles away, from me,' said I.

'Patience, my dear Handel: time enough, time enough. But you have something more to say?'

'I am ashamed to say it,' I returned, 'and yet it's no worse to say it than to think it. You call me a lucky fellow. Of course, I am. I was a blacksmith's boy but yesterday; I am – what shall I say I am – today?'

'Say, a good fellow, if you want a phrase,' returned Herbert, smiling, and clapping his hand on the back of mine.

'When I ask what I am to call myself today, Herbert,' I went on, 'I suggest what I have in my thoughts. You say I am lucky. I know that Fortune alone has raised me; that is being very lucky. And yet, when I think of Estella – then, my dear Herbert, I cannot tell you how dependent and uncertain I feel. I may still say that on the constancy of one person (naming no person) all my expectations depend. And at the best, how indefinite and unsatisfactory, only to know so vaguely what they are!'

'Now, Handel,' Herbert replied, in his gay hopeful way, 'it seems to me that in the despondency of the tender passion, we are looking into our gift-horse's mouth with a magnifying-glass. Didn't you tell me that your guardian, Mr Jaggers, told you in the beginning, that you were not endowed with expectations only? And even if he had not told you so – could you believe that of all men in London, Mr Jaggers is the man to hold his present relations towards you unless he were sure of his ground?'

I said I could not deny that this was a strong point. I said it like a rather reluctant concession to truth and justice; – as if I wanted to deny it!

'As to the rest,' said Herbert, 'you must bide your guardian's time, and he must bide his client's time. You'll be one-and-twenty before you know where you

are, and then perhaps you'll get some further enlighten-
ment.'

'What a hopeful disposition you have!' said I, gratefully admiring his cheery ways.

'I ought to have,' said Herbert, 'for I have not much
else. I must acknowledge, by-the-bye, that the good
sense of what I have just said is not my own, but my
father's. The only remark I ever heard him make on
your story, was the final one: "The thing is settled and
done, or Mr Jaggers would not be in it." And now I
want to make myself seriously disagreeable to you for
a moment – positively repulsive.'

'You won't succeed,' said I.

'Oh yes I shall!' said he. 'Handel, my good fellow;'
though he spoke in this light tone, he was very much
in earnest: 'I have been thinking since we have been
talking, that Estella surely cannot be a condition of
your inheritance, if she was never referred to by your
guardian. Am I right in so understanding what you
have told me, as that he never referred to her, directly
or indirectly, in any way? Never even hinted, for
instance, that your patron might have views as to your
marriage ultimately?'

'Never.'

'Now, Handel, I am quite free from the flavour of
sour grapes, upon my soul and honour! Not being
bound to her, can you not detach yourself from her?
Think of her bringing up and think of Miss Havisham.
Think of what she is herself. This may lead to miserable things.'

'I know it, Herbert,' said I, with my head still
turned away, 'but I can't help it.'

'You can't detach yourself?'

'No. Impossible!'

'Well!' said Herbert, getting up with a lively shake as if he had been asleep, and stirring the fire; 'now I'll endeavour to make myself agreeable again!'

'I was going to say a word or two, Handel,' he went on, 'concerning my father and my father's son. I am afraid it is scarcely necessary for my father's son to remark that my father's establishment is not particularly brilliant in its housekeeping.'

'There is always plenty, Herbert,' said I: to say something encouraging.

'Oh yes! and so the dustman says, I believe, with the strongest approval, and so does the marine-store shop in the back street. Gravely, Handel, for the subject is grave enough, you know how it is, as well as I do. I suppose there was a time once when my father had not given matters up; but if ever there was, the time is gone. May I ask you if you have ever had an opportunity of remarking that the children of not exactly suitable marriages, are always most particularly anxious to be married?'

This was such a singular question, that I asked him in return, 'Is it so?'

'I don't know,' said Herbert, 'that's what I want to know. Because it is decidedly the case with us. My poor sister Charlotte who was next me and died before she was fourteen, was a striking example. Little Jane is the same. In her desire to be matrimonially established, you might suppose her to have passed her short existence in the perpetual contemplation of domestic bliss. Little Alick in a frock has already made arrangements for his union with a suitable young person at Kew. And indeed, I think we are all engaged, except the baby.'

'Then you are?' said I.

'I am,' said Herbert; 'but it's a secret.'

'May I ask the name?' I said.

'Name of Clara,' said Herbert.

'Live in London?'

'Yes. Perhaps I ought to mention,' said Herbert, 'that she is rather below my mother's nonsensical family notions. Her father was a species of purser.'

'What is he now?' said I.

'He's an invalid now,' replied Herbert.

'Living on –?'

'On the first floor,' said Herbert. 'I have never seen him, for he has always kept his room overhead, since I have known Clara. But I have heard him constantly. He makes tremendous rows – roars, and pegs at the floor with some frightful instrument.'

He told me that the moment he began to realize Capital, it was his intention to marry this young lady. He added as a self-evident proposition, engendering low spirits, 'But you *can't* marry, you know, while you're looking about you.'

As we contemplated the fire, and as I thought what a difficult vision to realize this same Capital sometimes was, I put my hands in my pockets. A folded piece of paper in one of them attracting my attention, I opened it and found it to be the playbill of *Hamlet* I had received from Joe. 'And bless my heart,' I involuntarily added aloud, 'it's tonight!'

This changed the subject in an instant, and made us hurriedly resolve to go to the play. So, when I had pledged myself to comfort and abet Herbert in the affair of his heart by all practicable and impracticable means, and when Herbert had told me that his affianced already knew me by reputation and that I should be presented to her, we issued forth in quest of Mr Wopsle and Denmark.

31

On our arrival in Denmark, we found the king and queen of that country elevated in two arm-chairs on a kitchen-table, holding a Court. The whole of the Danish nobility were in attendance; consisting of a noble boy in the wash-leather boots of a gigantic ancestor, a venerable Peer with a dirty face, and the Danish chivalry with a comb in its hair and a pair of white silk legs. My gifted townsman stood gloomily apart, with folded arms, and I could have wished that his curls and forehead had been more probable.

The late king of the country not only appeared to have been troubled with a cough at the time of his decease, but to have taken it with him to the tomb, and to have brought it back. The royal phantom also carried a ghostly manuscript round its truncheon, to which it had the appearance of occasionally referring, and that, too, with an air of anxiety and a tendency to lose the place of reference. It was this, I conceive, which led to the Shade's being advised by the gallery to 'turn over!' – a recommendation which it took extremely ill. The Queen of Denmark, a very buxom lady, though no doubt historically brazen, was considered by the public to have too much brass about her; her chin being attached to her diadem by a broad band of that metal, her waist being encircled by another, and each of her arms by another, so that she was openly mentioned as 'the kettledrum'. The noble boy in the ancestral boots, was inconsistent; representing himself, as it were in one breath, as an able seaman, a strolling actor, a grave-digger, a clergyman, and a person of the utmost importance at a Court fencing-match. This gradually led to a want of toleration for him, and even – on his being detected in holy orders, and declining to perform the funeral service – to the general indignation taking the form of nuts. Lastly, Ophelia was a prey to such slow musical madness, that when, in course of time, she had taken off her white muslin scarf, folded it up, and buried it, a sulky man who had been long cooling his impatient nose against an iron bar in the front row of the gallery, growled, 'Now the baby's put to bed let's have supper!'

Upon my unfortunate townsman all these incidents accumulated with playful effect. Whenever that unde-cided Prince had to ask a question or state a doubt, the public helped him out with it. As for example; on the question whether 'twas nobler in the mind to suffer, some roared yes, and some no, and some inclining to both opinions said 'toss up for it;' and quite a Debating Society arose. On his taking the recorders – very like a little black flute that had just been played in the orchestra and handed out at the door – he was called upon unanimously for 'Rule Britannia'. When he re-commended the player not to saw the air thus, the sulky man said, 'And don't *you* do it, neither; you're a deal worse than *him*!' And I grieve to add that peals of laughter greeted Mr Wopsle on every one of these occa-sions.

But his greatest trials were in the churchyard. Mr
Wopsle in a comprehensive black cloak, being descried
entering at the turnpike, the gravedigger was admon-
ished in a friendly way, 'Look out! Here's the under-
taker a-coming, to see how you're a getting on with
your work!' The arrival of the body for interment (in
an empty black box with the lid tumbling open), was
the signal for a general joy which was much enhanced
by the discovery, among the bearers, of an individual
obnoxious to identification. The joy attended Mr
Wopsle through his struggle with Laertes on the brink
of the orchestra and the grave, and slackened no more
until he had tumbled the king off the kitchen-table,
and had died by inches from the ankles upward.

I laughed in spite of myself all the time, the whole
thing was so droll; and yet I had a latent impression
that there was something decidedly fine in Mr
Wopsle's elocution – not for old associations' sake, I
am afraid, but because it was very slow, very dreary,
very up-hill and down-hill, and very unlike any way in
which any man in any natural circumstances of life or
death ever expressed himself about anything. When
the tragedy was over, and he had been called for and
hooted, I said to Herbert, 'Let us go at once, or
perhaps we shall meet him.'

We made all the haste we could downstairs, but we
were not quick enough either. Standing at the door
was a man, who caught my eyes as we advanced, and
said, when we came up with him:

'Mr Pip and friend?'

Identity of Mr Pip and friend confessed.

'Mr Waldengarver,' said the man, 'would be glad to
have the honour.'

'Waldengarver?' I repeated – when Herbert murmured in my ear, 'Probably Wopsle.'

'Oh!' said I. 'Yes. Shall we follow you?'

We all fell through a little dirty swing door, into a sort of hot packing-case immediately behind it. Here Mr Wopsle was divesting himself of his Danish garments, and here there was just room for us to look at him over one another's shoulders, by keeping the packing-case door, or lid, wide open.

'Gentlemen,' said Mr Wopsle, 'I am proud to see you. I hope, Mr Pip, you will excuse my sending round. I had the happiness to know you in former times, and the Drama has ever had a claim which has ever been acknowledged, on the noble and the affluent.'

Meanwhile, Mr Waldengarver, in a frightful perspiration, was trying to get himself out of his princely sables.

'Skin the stockings off, Mr Waldengarver,' said the owner of that property, 'or you'll bust 'em. Keep quiet in your chair now, and leave 'em to me.'

With that, he went upon his knees, and began to flay his victim; who, on the first stocking coming off, would certainly have fallen over backward with his chair, but for there being no room to fall anyhow.

I had been afraid until then to say a word about the play. But then, Mr Waldengarver looked up at us complacently, and said:

'Gentlemen, how did it seem to you, to go, in front?'

Herbert said from behind, 'capitally.' So I said 'capitally.'

'How did you like my reading of the character, gentlemen?' said Mr Waldengarver, almost, if not quite, with patronage.

Herbert said from behind, 'massive and concrete.' So I said boldly, as if I had originated it, and must beg to insist upon it, 'massive and concrete.'

'I am glad to have your approbation, gentlemen,' said Mr Waldengarver, with an air of dignity, in spite of his being ground against the wall at the time, and holding on by the seat of the chair.

Without distinctly knowing whether I should have been more sorry for Mr Wopsle if he had been in despair, I was so sorry for him as it was, that I took the opportunity of his turning round to have his braces put on to ask Herbert what he thought of having him home to supper? Herbert said he thought it would be kind to do so; therefore I invited him, and he went to Barnard's with us, and he sat until two o'clock in the morning, reviewing his success and developing his plans. I forget in detail what they were, but I have a general recollection that he was to begin with reviving the Drama, and to end with crushing it; inasmuch as his decease would leave it utterly bereft and without a chance or hope.

Miserably I went to bed after all, and miserably thought of Estella, and miserably dreamed that my expectations were all cancelled, and that I had to give my hand in marriage to Herbert's Clara, or play Hamlet to Miss Havisham's Ghost, before twenty thousand people, without knowing twenty words of it.

32

One day when I was busy with my books and Mr
Pocket, I received a note by the post, the mere outside
of which threw me into a great flutter; for, though I
had never seen the handwriting in which it was addressed, I divined whose hand it was. It had no set
beginning, as Dear Mr Pip, or Dear Pip, or Dear Sir,
or Dear Anything, but ran thus:

*I am to come to London the day after tomorrow by the midday
coach. I believe it was settled you should meet me? At all events
Miss Havisham has that impression, and I write in obedience
to it. She sends you her regard.*
   Yours, Estella

My appetite vanished instantly, and I knew no peace
or rest until the day arrived. Not that its arrival
brought me either; for, then I was worse than ever,
and began haunting the coach-office in Wood-street,
Cheapside, before the coach had left the Blue Boar in
our town. I had performed the first half-hour of a
watch of four or five hours, when Wemmick ran against
me.

'Halloa, Mr Pip,' said he; 'how do you do? I should
hardly have thought this was *your* beat.'

I explained that I was waiting to meet somebody
who was coming up by coach, and I inquired after the
Castle and the Aged.

'Both flourishing, thankye,' said Wemmick, 'and particularly the Aged. He's in wonderful feather. He'll be eighty-two next birthday. I have a notion of firing eighty-two times, if the neighbourhood shouldn't complain, and that cannon of mine should prove equal to the pressure. However, this is not London talk. Where do you think I am going to?'

'To the office?' said I, for he was tending in that direction.

'Next thing to it,' returned Wemmick, 'I am going to Newgate. We are in a banker's-parcel case just at present, and must have a word or two with our client.'

'Did your client commit the robbery?' I asked.

'Bless your soul and body, no,' answered Wemmick, very drily. 'But he is accused of it. So might you or I be. Either of us might be accused of it, you know.'

'Only neither of us is,' I remarked.

'Yah!' said Wemmick, touching me on the breast with his forefinger; 'you're a deep one, Mr Pip! Would you like to have a look at Newgate? Have you time to spare?'

I had so much time to spare, that the proposal came as a relief, notwithstanding its irreconcilability with my latent desire to keep my eye on the coach-office. Muttering that I would make the enquiry whether I had time to walk with him, I went into the office, and ascertained from the clerk the earliest moment at which the coach could be expected – which I knew beforehand, quite as well as he. I then rejoined Mr Wemmick, and affecting to consult my watch and to be surprised by the information I had received, accepted his offer.

We were at Newgate in a few minutes, and we

passed through the lodge where some fetters were hanging up on the bare walls among the prison rules, into the interior of the jail. It was visiting time when Wemmick took me in; and the prisoners, behind bars in yards, were buying beer, and talking to friends; and a frouzy, ugly, disorderly, depressing scene it was.

Wemmick was highly popular, and I found that he took the familiar department of Mr Jaggers's business: though something of the state of Mr Jaggers hung about him too, forbidding approach beyond certain limits. In one or two instances, there was a difficulty respecting the raising of fees, and then Mr Wemmick said, 'It's no use, my boy. I'm only a subordinate. If you are unable to make up your quantum, my boy, you had better address yourself to a principal; that's my recommendation to you, speaking as a subordinate. Don't try on useless measures. Why should you? Now, who's next?'

Thus, we walked until he turned to me and said, 'Notice the man I shall shake hands with.'

Almost as soon as he had spoken, a portly upright man in a well-worn olive-coloured frock-coat, with a peculiar pallor over-spreading the red in his complexion, came up to a corner of the bars, and put his hand to his hat – which had a greasy and fatty surface like cold broth – with a half-serious and half-jocose military salute.

'Colonel, to you!' said Wemmick; 'how are you, Colonel?'

'All right, Mr Wemmick.'

'Everything was done that could be done, but the evidence was too strong for us, Colonel.'

'Yes, it was too strong, sir – but *I* don't care.'

'No, no,' said Wemmick, coolly, '*you* don't care.' Then, turning to me, 'Served His Majesty this man. Was a soldier in the line and bought his discharge.'

The man's eyes looked at me, and then looked over my head, and then looked all round me, and then he drew his hand across his lips and laughed.

'I think I shall be out of this on Monday, sir,' he said to Wemmick.

'Perhaps,' returned my friend, 'but there's no knowing.'

'I am glad to have the chance of bidding you good-bye, Mr Wemmick,' said the man, stretching out his hand between two bars.

'Thankye,' said Wemmick, shaking hands with him. 'Same to you, Colonel.'

'If what I had upon me when taken, had been real, Mr Wemmick,' said the man, unwilling to let his hand go, 'I should have asked the favour of your wearing another ring – in acknowledgement of your attentions.'

'I'll accept the will for the deed,' said Wemmick. 'By-the-bye; you were quite a pigeon-fancier.' The man looked up at the sky. 'I am told you had a remarkable breed of tumblers. *Could* you commission any friend of yours to bring me a pair, if you've no further use for 'em?'

'It shall be done, sir.'

'All right,' said Wemmick, 'they shall be taken care of. Good afternoon, Colonel. Good-bye!' They shook hands again, and as we walked away Wemmick said to me, 'A Coiner, a very good workman. The Recorder's report is made today, and he is sure to be executed on Monday. Still you see, as far as it goes, a pair of pigeons are portable property, all the same.'

As we came out of the prison through the lodge, I found that the great importance of my guardian was appreciated by the turnkeys, no less than by those whom they held in charge. 'Well, Mr Wemmick,' said the turnkey, who kept us between the two studded and spiked lodge gates, and who carefully locked one before he unlocked the other, 'what's Mr Jaggers going to do with that waterside murder? Is he going to make it manslaughter, or what's he going to make of it?'

'Why don't you ask him?' returned Wemmick.

'Oh yes, I dare say!' said the turnkey.

'Now, that's the way with them here, Mr Pip,' remarked Wemmick, turning to me with his post-office elongated. 'They don't mind what they ask of me, the subordinate; but you'll never catch 'em asking any questions of my principal. Mind you, Mr Pip, I don't know that Mr Jaggers does a better thing than the way in which he keeps himself so high. His constant height is of a piece with his immense abilities. That Colonel durst no more take leave of *him*, than that turnkey durst ask him his intentions respecting a case. Then, between his height and them, he slips in his subordinate – don't you see? – and so he has 'em, soul and body.'

I was very much impressed, and not for the first time, by my guardian's subtlety. To confess the truth, I very heartily wished, and not for the first time, that I had had some other guardian of minor abilities.

Mr Wemmick and I parted at the office in Little Britain, and I returned to my watch in the street of the coach-office, with some three hours on hand. I consumed the whole time in thinking how strange it was that I should be encompassed by all this taint of prison and crime; that, in my childhood out on our lonely marshes on a winter evening I should have first encountered it; that, it should in this new way pervade my fortune and advancement. While my mind was thus engaged, I thought of the beautiful young Estella, proud and refined, coming towards me, and I thought with absolute abhorrence of the contrast between the gaol and her. I wished that Wemmick had not met me, or that I had not yielded to him and gone with him, so that, of all days in the year on this day, I might not have had Newgate in my breath and on my clothes. I beat the prison dust off my feet as I sauntered to and fro, and I shook it out of my dress, and I exhaled its air from my lungs. So contaminated did I feel, remembering who was coming, that the coach came quickly after all, and I saw her face at the coach window and her hand waving to me.

What *was* the nameless shadow which again in that one instant had passed?

33

In her furred travelling-dress, Estella seemed more delicately beautiful than she had ever seemed yet, even in my eyes. Her manner was more winning than she had cared to let it be to me before, and I thought I saw Miss Havisham's influence in the change.

'I am going to Richmond,' she told me. 'I am to have a carriage, and you are to take me. This is my purse, and you are to pay my charges out of it. We have no choice, you and I, but to obey our instructions. We are not free to follow our own devices, you and I.'

As she looked at me in giving me the purse, I hoped there was an inner meaning in her words. She said them slightingly, but not with displeasure.

She drew her arm through mine, as if it must be done, and I requested a waiter who had been staring at the coach like a man who had never seen such a thing in his life, to show us a private sitting-room. He took my order: which, proving to be merely 'Some tea for the lady,' and I sent him out of the room.

'Where are you going to, at Richmond?' I asked Estella.

'I am going to live,' said she, 'with a lady there, who has the power of taking me about, and introducing me, and showing people to me and showing me to people.'

'I suppose you will be glad of variety and admiration?'

'Yes, I suppose so.'

She answered so carelessly, that I said, 'You speak of yourself as if you were someone else.'

'Where did you learn how I speak of others? Come, come,' said Estella, smiling delightfully, 'you must not expect me to go to school to *you*; I must talk in my own way. How do you thrive with Mr Pocket?'

'I live quite pleasantly there; at least –' It appeared to me that I was losing a chance.

'At least?' repeated Estella.

'As pleasantly as I could anywhere, away from you.'

'You silly boy,' said Estella, quite composedly, 'how can you talk such nonsense? Your friend Mr Matthew, I believe, is superior to the rest of his family?'

'Very superior indeed. He is nobody's enemy –'

'Don't add but his own,' interposed Estella, 'for I hate that class of man. But he really is disinterested, and above small jealousy and spite, I have heard?'

'I am sure I have every reason to say so.'

'You have not every reason to say so of the rest of his people,' said Estella, 'for they beset Miss Havisham with reports and insinuations to your disadvantage. They watch you, misrepresent you, write letters about you (anonymous sometimes), and you are the torment and the occupation of their lives. You can scarcely realize to yourself the hatred those people feel for you.'

'They do me no harm, I hope?'

Instead of answering, Estella burst out laughing. When she left off – and she had not laughed languidly, but with real enjoyment – I said, in my diffident way with her:

'I hope I may suppose that you would not be amused if they did me any harm.'

'No, no, you may be sure of that,' said Estella. 'You may be certain that I laugh because they fail. It is not easy for even you to know what satisfaction it gives me to see those people thwarted, for you were not brought up in that strange house from a mere baby. – I was. You had not your little wits sharpened by their intriguing against you, suppressed and defenceless, under the mask of sympathy and pity and what not that is soft and soothing. – I had.'

It was no laughing matter with Estella now, nor was she summoning these remembrances from any shallow place. I would not have been the cause of that look of hers, for all my expectations in a heap.

'Two things I can tell you,' said Estella. 'First, you

may set your mind at rest that these people never will impair your ground with Miss Havisham, in any particular, great or small. Second, I am beholden to you as the cause of their being so busy and so mean in vain, and there is my hand upon it.'

As she gave it me playfully, I held it and put it to my lips. 'You ridiculous boy,' said Estella, 'will you never take warning? Or do you kiss my hand in the same spirit in which I once let you kiss my cheek?'

'What spirit was that?' said I.

'I must think a moment. A spirit of contempt for the fawners and plotters.'

'If I say yes, may I kiss the cheek again?'

'You should have asked before you touched the hand. But, yes, if you like.'

I leaned down, and her calm face was like a statue's. 'Now,' said Estella, gliding away the instant I touched her cheek, 'you are to take care that I have some tea, and you are to take me to Richmond.'

I rang for the tea, and the waiter brought in by degrees some fifty adjuncts to that refreshment, but of tea not a glimpse. A teaboard, cups and saucers, plates, knives and forks, spoons, salt-cellars, a meek little muffin confined under a strong iron cover, Moses in the bullrushes typified by a soft bit of butter in a quantity of parsley, a pale loaf with a powdered head, two proof impressions of the bars of the kitchen fireplace on triangular bits of bread, and ultimately a fat family urn.

The bill paid, and the waiter remembered, we got into our post-coach and drove away. Turning into Cheapside and rattling up Newgate-street, we were soon under the walls of which I was so ashamed.

'What place is that?' Estella asked me.

I made a foolish pretence of not at first recognizing it, and then told her. As she looked at it, and drew in her head again, murmuring 'Wretches!' I would not have confessed to my visit for any consideration.

'Mr Jaggers,' said I, by way of putting it neatly on somebody else, 'has the reputation of being more in the secrets of that dismal place than any man in London.'

'He is more in the secrets of every place, I think,' said Estella, in a low voice.

'You have been accustomed to see him often, I suppose?'

'I have been accustomed to see him at uncertain intervals, ever since I can remember. But I know him no better now, than I did before I could speak plainly. What is your own experience of him? Do you advance with him?'

'Once habituated to his distrustful manner,' said I, 'I have done very well.'

I should have been chary of discussing my guardian too freely even with her; but I should have gone on with the subject so far as to describe the dinner in Gerrard-street, if we had not then come into a sudden glare of gas. It seemed, while it lasted, to be all alight and alive with that inexplicable feeling I had had before; and when we were out of it, I was as much dazed for a few moments as if I had been in Lightning.

It was impossible for me to avoid seeing that she cared to attract me; that she made herself winning; and would have won me even if the task had needed pains. Yet this made me none the happier, for, even if she had not taken that tone of our being disposed of by others, I should have felt that she held my heart in her hand because she wilfully chose to do it, and not because it would have wrung any tenderness in her, to crush it and throw it away.

When we passed through Hammersmith, I showed her where Mr Matthew Pocket lived, and said it was no great way from Richmond, and that I hoped I should see her sometimes.

'Oh yes, you are to see me; you are to come when you think proper; you are to be mentioned to the family; indeed you are already mentioned.'

'I wonder Miss Havisham could part with you again so soon.'

'It is a part of Miss Havisham's plans for me, Pip,' said Estella, with a sigh, as if she were tired; 'I am to write to her constantly and see her regularly, and report how I go on.'

It was the first time she had ever called me by my name. Of course she did so, purposely, and knew that I should treasure it up.

We came to Richmond all too soon, and our destination there, was a staid old house, where hoops and powder and patches, embroidered coats, rolled stockings, ruffles and swords, had had their court days many a time. Two cherry-coloured maids came fluttering out to receive Estella. The doorway soon absorbed her boxes, and she gave me her hand and a smile, and said good-night, and was absorbed likewise.

I got into the carriage to be taken back to Hammersmith, and I got in with a bad heart-ache, and I got out with a worse heart-ache.

Mr Pocket being justly celebrated for giving most

excellent practical advice, and for having a clear and sound perception of things and a highly judicious mind, I had some notion in my heart-ache of begging him to accept my confidence. But, happening to look up at Mrs Pocket as she sat reading her book of dignities after prescribing Bed as a sovereign remedy for baby, I thought – Well – No, I wouldn't.

34

As I had grown accustomed to my expectations, I had insensibly begun to notice their effect upon myself and those around me. I lived in a state of chronic uneasiness respecting my behaviour to Joe. My conscience was not by any means comfortable about Biddy. When I woke up in the night – like Camilla – I used to think, with a weariness on my spirits, that I should have been happier and better if I had never seen Miss Havisham's face, and had risen to manhood content to be partners with Joe in the honest old forge. Many a time of an evening, when I sat alone looking at the fire, I thought, after all, there was no fire like the forge fire and the kitchen fire at home.

Yet Estella was so inseparable from all my restlessness and disquiet of mind, that I really fell into confusion as to the limits of my own part in its production. That is to say, supposing I had had no expectations, and yet had had Estella to think of, I could not make out to my satisfaction that I should have done much better. Now, concerning the influence of my position

on others, I was in no such difficulty, and so I perceived – though dimly enough perhaps – that it was
not beneficial to anybody, and, above all, that it was
not beneficial to Herbert. My lavish habits led his easy
nature into expenses that he could not afford, cor-
rupted the simplicity of his life, and disturbed his
peace with anxieties and regrets. It often caused me a
twinge to think that I had done him evil service in
crowding his sparely-furnished chambers with incon-
gruous upholstery work, and placing the canary-
breasted Avenger at his disposal.

So now, as an infallible way of making little ease
great ease, I began to contract a quantity of debt. I
could hardly begin but Herbert must begin too, so he
soon followed. At Startop's suggestion, we put ourselves down for election into a club called The Finches
of the Grove: the object of which institution I have
never divined, if it were not that the members should
dine expensively once a fortnight, to quarrel among
themselves as much as possible after dinner, and to
cause six waiters to get drunk on the stairs.

The Finches spent their money foolishly, and the
first Finch I saw, when I had the honour of joining the
Grove, was Bentley Drummle: at that time floundering
about town in a cab of his own, and doing a great deal
of damage to the posts at the street corners.

In my confidence in my own resources, I would
willingly have taken Herbert's expenses on myself; but
Herbert was proud, and I could make no such proposal
to him. So, he got into difficulties in every direction,
and continued to look about him.

When I was at Hammersmith I haunted Richmond:
whereof separately by-and-by. Herbert would often

come to Hammersmith when I was there, and I think at those seasons his father would occasionally have some passing perception that the opening he was looking for, had not appeared yet. In the mean time Mr Pocket grew greyer, and tried oftener to lift himself out of his perplexities by the hair. While Mrs Pocket tripped up the family with her footstool, read her book of dignities, lost her pocket-handkerchief, told us about her grandpapa, and taught the young idea how to shoot, by shooting it into bed whenever it attracted her notice.

We spent as much money as we could, and got as little for it as people could make up their minds to give us. We were always more or less miserable, and most of our acquaintance were in the same condition.

Every morning, with an air ever new, Herbert went into the City to look about him. He had nothing else to do, poor fellow, except at a certain hour of every afternoon to 'go to Lloyd's' – in observance of a ceremony of seeing his principal, I think. He never did anything else in connection with Lloyd's that I could find out, except come back again. When he felt his case unusually serious, and that he positively must find an opening, he would go on 'Change at a busy time, and walk in and out, among the assembled magnates. 'For,' says Herbert to me, coming home to dinner on one of those special occasions, 'I find the truth to be, Handel, that an opening won't come to one, but one must go to it – so I have been.'

As we got more and more into debt, breakfast became a hollower and hollower form, and, being on one occasion at breakfast-time threatened (by letter) with legal proceedings, I went so far as to seize the

Avenger by his blue collar and shake him off his feet for presuming to suppose that we wanted a roll.

At certain times I would say to Herbert, as if it were a remarkable discovery:

'My dear Herbert, we are getting on badly.'

'My dear Handel,' Herbert would say to me, in all sincerity, 'if you will believe me, those very words were on my lips, by a strange coincidence.'

'Then, Herbert,' I would respond, 'let us look into our affairs.'

Dinner over, we produced a bundle of pens, a copious supply of ink, and a goodly show of writing and blotting paper. For, there was something very comfortable in having plenty of stationery.

I would then take a sheet of paper, and write across the top of it, in a neat hand, the heading, 'Memorandum of Pip's debts'; with Barnard's Inn and the date very carefully added. Herbert would also take a sheet of paper, and write across it with similar formalities, 'Memorandum of Herbert's debts'.

When we had written a little while, I would ask Herbert how he got on? Herbert probably would have been scratching his head in a most rueful manner at the sight of his accumulating figures.

'They are mounting up, Handel,' Herbert would say; 'upon my life, they are mounting up.'

'Be firm, Herbert,' I would retort, plying my own pen with great assiduity. 'Look the thing in the face. Look into your affairs. Stare them out of countenance.'

'So I would, Handel, only they are staring *me* out of countenance.'

However, my determined manner would have its effect, and Herbert would fall to work again.

I established with myself on these occasions, the reputation of a first-rate man of business – prompt, decisive, energetic, clear, cool-headed. When I had got all my responsibilities down upon my list, I compared each with the bill, and ticked it off. My self-approval when I ticked an entry was quite a luxurious sensation. When I had no more ticks to make, I folded all my bills up uniformly, docketed each on the back, and tied the whole into a symmetrical bundle. Then I did the same for Herbert, and felt that I had brought his affairs into a focus for him.

There was a calm, a rest, a virtuous hush, consequent on these examinations of our affairs that gave me, for the time, an admirable opinion of myself. Soothed by my exertions, my method, and Herbert's compliments, I would sit with his symmetrical bundle and my own on the table before me among the stationery, and feel like a Bank of some sort, rather than a private individual.

We shut our outer door on these solemn occasions, in order that we might not be interrupted. I had fallen into my serene state one evening, when we heard a letter dropped through the slit in the said door, and fall on the ground. 'It's for you, Handel,' said Herbert, going out and coming back with it, 'and I hope there is nothing the matter.' This was in allusion to its heavy black seal and border.

The letter was signed TRABB & Co., and its contents were simply, that I was an honoured sir, and that they begged to inform me that Mrs J. Gargery had departed this life on Monday last, at twenty minutes past six in the evening, and that my attendance was requested at the interment on Monday next at three o'clock in the afternoon.

35

It was the first time that a grave had opened in my road of life, and the gap it made in the smooth ground was wonderful. The figure of my sister in her chair by the kitchen fire, haunted me night and day. That the place could possibly be, without her, was something my mind seemed unable to compass; and whereas she had seldom or never been in my thoughts of late, I had now the strangest ideas that she was coming towards me in the street, or that she would presently knock at the door.

Whatever my fortunes might have been, I could scarcely have recalled my sister with much tenderness. But I suppose there is a shock of regret which may exist without much tenderness. I was seized with a violent indignation against the assailant from whom she had suffered so much; and I felt that on sufficient proof I could have revengefully pursued Orlick, or any one else, to the last extremity.

Having written to Joe, to offer consolation, and to assure him that I should come to the funeral, I passed the intermediate days in the curious state of mind I have glanced at. I went down early in the morning, and alighted at the Blue Boar in good time to walk over to the forge.

It was fine summer weather again, as I walked along, the times when I was a little helpless creature, and my sister did not spare me, vividly returned, with a gentle tone upon them.

At last I came within sight of the house, and saw that Trabb and Co. had put in a funeral execution and taken possession. Two dismally absurd persons, each ostentatiously exhibiting a crutch done up in a black bandage were posted at the front door.

All the children of the village, and most of the women, were admiring these sable warders and the closed windows of the house and forge; and as I came up, one of the two warders knocked at the door – implying that I was far too much exhausted by grief, to have strength remaining to knock for myself.

Poor dear Joe, entangled in a little black cloak tied in a large bow under his chin, was seated apart at the upper end of the room; where, as chief mourner, he had evidently been stationed by Trabb. When I bent down and said to him, 'Dear Joe, how are you?' he said, 'Pip, old chap, you knowed her when she were a fine figure of a –' and clasped my hand and said no more.

Biddy, looking very neat and modest in her black dress, went quietly here and there, and was very help-ful. When I had spoken to Biddy, as I thought it not a time for talking I went and sat down near Joe, and there began to wonder in what part of the house it – she – my sister – was. The air of the parlour being faint with the smell of sweet cake, I looked about for the table of refreshments; it was scarcely visible until one had got accustomed to the gloom, but there was a cut-up plum-cake upon it, and there were cut-up oranges, and sandwiches, and biscuits, and two decanters, one full of port, and one of sherry. Standing at this table, I became conscious of the servile Pumble-chook in a black cloak and several yards of hatband,

who was alternately stuffing himself, and making obse-
quious movements to catch my attention. The moment
he succeeded, he came over to me, and said in a
subdued voice, 'May I, dear sir?' and did. I then
descried Mr and Mrs Hubble; the last-named in a
decent speechless paroxysm in a corner. We were all
going to 'follow', and were all in course of being tied
up separately (by Trabb) into ridiculous bundles.

'Which I meantersay, Pip,' Joe whispered me, as we
were being what Mr Trabb called 'formed' in the
parlour, two and two, 'which I meantersay, sir, as I
would in preference have carried her to the church
myself, along with three or four friendly ones wot
come to it with willing harts and arms, but it were
considered as it were wanting in respect.'

We filed out two and two; Joe and I; Biddy and
Pumblechook; Mr and Mrs Hubble. The remains of
my poor sister had been brought round by the kitchen
door, and, it being a point of Undertaking ceremony
that the six bearers must be stifled and blinded under
a horrible black velvet housing with a white border,
the whole looked like a blind monster with twelve
human legs, shuffling and blundering along, under the
guidance of two keepers.

The neighbourhood, however, highly approved of
these arrangements, and we were much admired as we
went through the village. The more exuberant among
them called out in an excited manner on our emergence
round some corner of expectancy, '*Here* they come!'
'*Here* they are!' and we were all but cheered.

And now, the range of marshes lay clear before us,
with the sails of the ships on the river growing out of
it; and we went into the churchyard, close to the

graves of my unknown parents. And there, my sister was laid quietly in the earth while the larks sang high above it, and the light wind strewed it with beautiful shadows of clouds and trees.

When we got back, Pumblechook had the hardihood to tell me that he wished my sister could have known I had done her so much honour, and to hint that she would have considered it reasonably purchased at the price of her death. After that, he drank all the rest of the sherry, and Mr Hubble drank the port, and the two talked as if they were of quite another race from the deceased, and were notoriously immortal. Finally, he went away with Mr and Mrs Hubble – to make an evening of it, I felt sure, and to tell the Jolly Bargemen that he was the founder of my fortunes and my earliest benefactor.

Soon afterwards, Biddy, Joe, and I, had a cold dinner together; but we dined in the best parlour, not in the old kitchen, and Joe was so exceedingly particular what he did with his knife and fork and the salt-cellar and what not, that there was great restraint upon us. But after dinner, when I made him take his pipe, we got on better.

He was very much pleased by my asking if I might sleep in my own little room, and I was pleased too; for, I felt that I had done rather a great thing in making the request. When the shadows of evening were closing in, I took an opportunity of getting into the garden with Biddy for a little talk.

'Biddy,' said I, 'I think you might have written to me about these sad matters.'

'Do you, Mr Pip?' said Biddy. 'I should have written if I had thought that.'

She was so quiet, and had such an orderly, good, and pretty way with her, that I did not like the thought of making her cry again. After looking a little at her downcast eyes as she walked beside me, I gave up that point.

'I suppose it will be difficult for you to remain here now, Biddy dear?'

'Oh! I can't do so, Mr Pip,' said Biddy, in a tone of regret, but still of quiet conviction. 'I have been speaking to Mrs Hubble, and I am going to her tomorrow. I hope we shall be able to take some care of Mr Gargery, together, until he settles down.'

'How are you going to live, Biddy? If you want any mo –'

'How am I going to live?' repeated Biddy, striking in, with a momentary flush upon her face. 'I'll tell you, Mr Pip. I am going to try to get the place of mistress in the new school nearly finished here. You know, Mr Pip,' pursued Biddy, with a smile, as she raised her eyes to my face, 'the new schools are not like the old, but I learnt a good deal from you after that time, and have had time since then to improve.'

I walked a little further with Biddy, looking silently at her downcast eyes.

'I have not heard the particulars of my sister's death, Biddy.'

'They are very slight, poor thing. She had been in one of her bad states for four days, when she came out of it in the evening, just at teatime, and said quite plainly, "Joe." As she had never said any word for a long while, I ran and fetched in Mr Gargery from the forge. She made signs to me that she wanted him to sit down close to her, and wanted me to put her arms round his neck. So I put them round his neck, and she laid her head down on his shoulder quite content and satified. And so she presently said "Joe" again, and once "Pardon", and once "Pip". And so she never lifted her head up any more, and it was just an hour later when we laid it down on her own bed, because we found she was gone.'

Biddy cried; the darkening garden, and the lane, and the stars that were coming out, were blurred in my own sight.

'Nothing was ever discovered, Biddy?'

'Nothing.'

'Do you know what is become of Orlick?'

'I should think from the colour of his clothes that he is working in the quarries.'

'Of course you have seen him then? – Why are you looking at that dark tree in the lane?'

'I saw him there, on the night she died.'

'That was not the last time either, Biddy?'

'No; I have seen him there, since we have been walking here.'

It revived my utmost indignation to find that she was still pursued by this fellow, and I told her so, and told her that I would spend any money or take any pains to drive him out of that country. By degrees she led me into more temperate talk, and she told me how Joe loved me, and how Joe never complained of anything – she didn't say, of me; she had no need; I knew what she meant – but ever did his duty in his way of life, with a strong hand, a quiet tongue, and a gentle heart.

'Indeed, it would be hard to say too much for him,' said I; 'and Biddy, we must often speak of these things, for of course I shall be often down here now. I am not going to leave poor Joe alone.'

Biddy said never a single word.

'Biddy, don't you hear me?'

'Yes, Mr Pip.'

'Biddy,' said I, 'I made a remark respecting my coming down here often, to see Joe, which you received with a marked silence. Have the goodness, Biddy, to tell me why.'

'Are you quite sure, then, that you *will* come to see him often?' asked Biddy.

'Oh dear me!' said I, as if I found myself compelled to give up Biddy in despair. 'This really is a very bad side of human nature! Don't say any more, if you please, Biddy. This shocks me very much.'

For which cogent reason I kept Biddy at a distance during supper, and, when I went up to my own old little room, took as stately a leave of her as I could. As often as I was restless in the night, and that was every quarter of an hour, I reflected what an unkindness, what an injury, what an injustice, Biddy had done me.

Early in the morning, I was to go. Early in the morning, I stood, for minutes, looking at Joe, already at work with a glow of health and strength upon his face that made it show as if the bright sun of the life in store for him were shining on it.

'Goodbye, dear Joe! – No, don't wipe it off – for God's sake, give me your blackened hand! – I shall be down soon, and often.'

'Never too soon, sir,' said Joe, 'and never too often, Pip!'

Biddy was waiting for me at the kitchen door, with a mug of new milk and a crust of bread. 'Biddy,' said I, when I gave her my hand at parting, 'I am not angry, but I am hurt.'

'No, don't be hurt,' she pleaded quite pathetically; 'let only me be hurt, if I have been ungenerous.'

Once more, the mists were rising as I walked away. If they disclosed to me, as I suspect they did, that I should not come back, and that Biddy was quite right, all I can say is – they were quite right too.

36

Herbert and I went on from bad to worse, in the way of increasing our debts, looking into our affairs, and Time went on, and I came of age – in fulfilment of Herbert's prediction, that I should do so before I knew where I was.

I had taken care to have it well understood in Little Britain, when my birthday was. On the day before it, I received an official note from Wemmick, informing me that Mr Jaggers would be glad if I would call upon him at five in the afternoon of the auspicious day. This convinced us that something great was to happen, and threw me into an unusual flutter when I repaired to my guardian's office, a model of punctuality.

In the outer office Wemmick offered me his congratulations, and incidentally rubbed the side of his nose with a folded piece of tissue-paper that I liked the look of. But he said nothing respecting it, and motioned me with a nod into my guardian's room. It was November, and my guardian was standing before his fire leaning his back against the chimney-piece, with his hands under his coat-tails.

'Well, Pip,' said he, 'I must call you Mr Pip today. Congratulations, Mr Pip. Take a chair.'

As I sat down, and he preserved his attitude and bent his brows at his boots, I felt at a disadvantage, which reminded me of that old time when I had been put upon a tombstone. The two ghastly casts on the shelf were not far from him, and their expression was as if they were making a stupid apoplectic attempt to attend to the conversation.

'Now my young friend,' my guardian began, as if I were a witness in the box, 'I am going to have a word or two with you.'

'If you please, sir.'

'What do you suppose,' said Mr Jaggers, bending forward to look at the ground, and then throwing his head back to look at the ceiling, 'what do you suppose you are living at the rate of?'

Reluctantly, I confessed myself quite unable to answer the question. This reply seemed agreeable to Mr Jaggers, who said, 'I thought so!' and blew his nose with an air of satisfaction.

'Now, I have asked *you* a question, my friend,' said Mr Jaggers. 'Have you anything to ask *me*?'

'Of course it would be a great relief to me to ask you several questions, sir; but I remember your prohibition.'

'Ask one,' said Mr Jaggers.

'Is my benefactor to be made known to me today?'

'No. Ask another.'

'Is that confidence to be imparted to me soon?'

'Waive that, a moment,' said Mr Jaggers, 'and ask another.'

'Have – I – anything to receive, sir?' On that, Mr Jaggers said, triumphantly, 'I thought we should come to it!' and called to Wemmick to give him that piece of paper. Wemmick appeared, handed it in, and disappeared.

'Now, Mr Pip,' said Mr Jaggers, 'attend, if you please. You have been drawing pretty freely here; your name occurs pretty often in Wemmick's cash-book; but you are in debt, of course?'

'I am afraid I must say yes, sir.'

'I don't ask you what you owe, because you don't know; and if you did know, you wouldn't tell me; you would say less. Now, take this piece of paper in your hand. You have got it? Very good. Now, unfold it and tell me what it is.'

'This is a bank-note,' said I, 'for five hundred pounds.'

'You consider it, undoubtedly, a handsome sum of money. Now, that handsome sum of money, Pip, is your own. It is a present to you on this day, in earnest of your expectations. And at the rate, of that handsome sum of money per annum, and at no higher rate, you are to live until the donor of the whole appears. That is to say, you will now take your money affairs entirely into your own hands, and you will draw from Wemmick one hundred and twenty-five pounds per quarter, until you are in communication with the fountain-head. As I have told you before, I am the mere agent. I execute my instructions, and I am paid for doing so.'

After a pause, I hinted:

'There was a question just now, Mr Jaggers, which you desired me to waive for a moment. I hope I am doing nothing wrong in asking it again?'

'What is it?' said he.

'Is it likely,' I said, after hesitating, 'that my patron, the fountain-head you have spoken of, Mr Jaggers, will soon –' there I delicately stopped.

'Will soon what?' asked Mr Jaggers. 'That's no question as it stands, you know.'

'Will soon come to London,' said I, after casting about for a precise form of words, 'or summon me anywhere else?'

'Now here,' replied Mr Jaggers, fixing me for the first time with his dark deep-set eyes, 'we must revert to the evening when we first encountered one another in your village. What did I tell you then, Pip?'

'You told me, Mr Jaggers, that it might be years hence when that person appeared.'

'Just so,' said Mr Jaggers; 'that's my answer.'

'Do you suppose it will still be years hence, Mr Jaggers?'

Mr Jaggers shook his head - not in negativing the question, but in altogether negativing the notion that he could anyhow be got to answer it - and the two horrible casts of the twitched faces looked, when my eyes strayed up to them, as if they had come to a crisis in their suspended attention, and were going to sneeze.

'Come!' said Mr Jaggers, warming the backs of his legs with the backs of his warmed hands, 'I'll be plain with you, my friend Pip. That's a question I must not be asked. You'll understand that better, when I tell you it's a question that might compromise *me*. When that person discloses,' he went on, 'you and that person will settle your own affairs. When that person discloses, my part in this business will cease and determine. When that person discloses, it will not be necessary for me to know anything about it. And that's all I have got to say.'

From this last speech I derived the notion that Miss Havisham, for some reason or no reason, had not taken him into her confidence as to her designing me for Estella; that he resented this, and felt a jealousy about it; or that he really did object to that scheme, and would have nothing to do with it.

'If that is all you have to say, sir,' I remarked, 'there can be nothing left for me to say.'

He nodded assent, and asked me where I was going to dine? I replied at my own chambers, with Herbert. As a necessary sequence, I asked him if he would favour us with his company, and he promptly accepted the invitation. But he insisted on walking home with me, in order that I might make no extra preparation for him, and first he had a letter or two to write, and (of course) had his hands to wash. So, I said I would go into the outer office and talk to Wemmick.

The fact was, that when the five hundred pounds had come into my pocket, a thought had come into my head which had been often there before; and it appeared to me that Wemmick was a good person to advise with, concerning such thought.

He had already locked up his safe, and made preparations for going home. He had put his hat and greatcoat ready, and was beating himself all over the chest with his safe-key, as an athletic exercise after business.

'Mr Wemmick,' said I, 'I want to ask your opinion. I am very desirous to serve a friend.'

Wemmick tightened his post-office and shook his head, as if his opinion were dead against any fatal weakness of that sort.

'This friend,' I pursued, 'is trying to get on in commercial life, but has no money, and finds it difficult and disheartening to make a beginning. Now, I want somehow to help him to a beginning.'

'With money down?' said Wemmick, in a tone drier than any sawdust.

'With *some* money down,' I replied, 'and perhaps some anticipation of my expectations.'

'Mr Pip,' said Wemmick, 'I should like just to run over with you on my fingers, if you please, the names of the various bridges up as high as Chelsea Reach. Let's see; there's London, one; Southwark, two; Blackfriars, three; Waterloo, four; Westminster, five; Vauxhall, six.' He had checked off each bridge in its turn, with the handle of his safe-key on the palm of his hand. 'There's as many as six, you see, to choose from.'

'I don't understand you,' said I.

'Choose your bridge, Mr Pip,' returned Wemmick, 'and take a walk upon your bridge, and pitch your money into the Thames over the centre arch of your bridge, and you know the end of it. Serve a friend with it, and you may know the end of it too – but it's a less pleasant and profitable end.'

'This is very discouraging,' said I.

'Meant to be so,' said Wemmick.

'Then is it your opinion,' I enquired, with some little indignation, 'that a man should never –'

'– Invest portable property in a friend?' said Wemmick. 'Certainly he should not. Unless he wants to get rid of the friend – and then it becomes a question how much portable property it may be worth to get rid of him.'

'And that,' said I, 'is your deliberate opinion, Mr Wemmick?'

'That,' he returned, 'is my deliberate opinion in this office.'

'Ah!' said I, pressing him, for I thought I saw him near a loophole here; 'but would that be your opinion at Walworth?'

'Mr Pip,' he replied, with gravity, 'Walworth is one place, and this office is another. My Walworth sentiments must be taken at Walworth; none but my official sentiments can be taken in this office.'

'Very well,' said I, much relieved, 'then I shall look you up at Walworth, you may depend upon it.'

'Mr Pip,' he returned, 'you will be welcome there, in a private and personal capacity.'

We had held this conversation in a low voice, well knowing my guardian's ears to be the sharpest of the sharp. As he now appeared in his doorway, towelling his hands, Wemmick got on his great-coat and stood by to snuff out the candles. We all three went into the street together, and from the door-step Wemmick turned his way, and Mr Jaggers and I turned ours.

I could not help wishing more than once that evening, that Mr Jaggers had had an Aged in Gerrard-street, or a Stinger, or a Something, or a Somebody, to unbend his brows a little. He was a thousand times better informed and cleverer than Wemmick, and yet I would a thousand times rather have had Wemmick to dinner. And Mr Jaggers made not me alone intensely melancholy, because, after, he was gone, Herbert said of himself, with his eyes fixed on the fire, that he thought he must have committed a felony and forgotten the details of it, he felt so dejected and guilty.

37

Deeming Sunday the best day for taking Mr Wemmick's Walworth sentiments, I devoted the next ensu-
ing Sunday afternoon to a pilgrimage to the Castle. On
arriving before the battlements, I found the Union
Jack flying and the drawbridge up. I rang at the gate,
and was admitted in a most pacific manner by the
Aged.

'My son, sir,' said the old man, after securing the
drawbridge, 'rather had it in his mind that you might
happen to drop in, and he left word that he would
soon be home from his afternoon's walk.'

I nodded at the old gentleman as Wemmick himself
might have nodded, and we went in and sat down by
the fireside.

'You made acquaintance with my son, sir,' said the
old man, 'at his office, I expect?' I nodded. 'Hah! I
have heerd that my son is a wonderful hand at his
business, sir?' I nodded hard. 'Yes; so they tell me.
His business is the Law?' I nodded harder. 'Which
makes it more surprising in my son,' said the old man,
'for he was not brought up to the Law, but to the
Wine-Coopering.'

Curious to know how the old gentleman stood informed concerning the reputation of Mr Jaggers, I
roared that name at him. He threw me into the greatest
confusion by laughing heartily and replying in a very
sprightly manner, 'No, to be sure; you're right.' And

to this hour I have not the faintest notion what he meant, or what joke he thought I had made.

I was startled by a sudden click in the wall on one side of the chimney, and the ghostly tumbling open of a little wooden flap with 'JOHN' upon it. The old man, following my eyes, cried with great triumph, 'My son's come home!' and we both went out to the drawbridge.

It was worth any money to see Wemmick waving a salute to me from the other side of the moat, when we might have shaken hands across it with the greatest ease. The Aged was so delighted to work the drawbridge, that I made no offer to assist him, but stood quiet until Wemmick had come across, and had presented me to Miss Skiffins: a lady by whom he was accompanied.

Miss Skiffins was of a wooden appearance. She might have been some two or three years younger than Wemmick, and I judged her to stand possessed of portable property. The cut of her dress from the waist upward, both before and behind, made her figure very like a boy's kite; and I might have pronounced her gown a little too decidedly orange, and her gloves a little too intensely green. But she seemed to be a good sort of fellow, and showed a high regard for the Aged. I was not long in discovering that she was a frequent visitor at the Castle; for, on our going in, and my complimenting Wemmick on his ingenious contrivance for announcing himself to the Aged, he begged me to give my attention for a moment to the other side of the chimney, and disappeared. Presently another click came, and another little door tumbled open with 'Miss Skiffins' on it; then Miss Skiffins shut up and John tumbled open; then Miss Skiffins and John both tumbled open together, and finally shut up together. On Wemmick's return from working these mechanical appliances, I expressed the great admiration with which I regarded them, and he said, 'Well, you know, they're both pleasant and useful to the Aged. And by George, sir, the secret of those pulls is only known to the Aged, Miss Skiffins, and me!'

While Miss Skiffins was taking off her bonnet, Wemmick invited me to take a walk with him round the property, and see how the island looked in wintertime. Thinking that he did this to give me an opportunity of taking his Walworth sentiments, I seized the opportunity as soon as we were out of the Castle.

Having thought of the matter with care, I approached my subject as if I had never hinted at it before. I informed Wemmick that I was anxious in behalf of Herbert Pocket, and I told him how we had first met, and how we had fought. I alluded to the advantages I had derived in my first rawness and ignorance from his society, and I confessed that I feared I had but ill repaid them, and that he might have done better without me and my expectations. Keeping Miss Havisham in the background at a great distance, I still hinted at the possibility of my having competed with him in his prospects, and at the certainty of his possessing a generous soul, and being far above any mean distrusts, retaliations, or designs. For all these reasons and because he was my young companion and friend, and I had a great affection for him, I wished my own good fortune to reflect some rays upon him. I begged Wemmick, in conclusion, to understand that my help be rendered without Herbert's knowledge or suspicion, and that there was no one else in the world with whom I could advise.

Wemmick was silent for a little while, and then said with a kind of start, 'Well you know, Mr Pip, I must tell you one thing. This is devilish good of you.'

'Say you'll help me to be good then,' said I.

'Mr Pip, I'll put on my considering-cap, and I think all you want to do, may be done by degrees. Skiffins (that's her brother) is an accountant and agent. I'll look him up and go to work for you.'

'I thank you ten thousand times.'

After a little further conversation to the same effect, we returned into the Castle where we found Miss Skiffins preparing tea. The responsible duty of making the toast was delegated to the Aged, and he prepared such a haystack of buttered toast, that I could scarcely see him over it as it simmered on an iron stand hooked on to the top-bar; while Miss Skiffins brewed such a jorum of tea, that the pig in the back premises became strongly excited, and repeatedly expressed his desire to participate in the entertainment.

We ate the whole of the toast, and drank tea in proportion, and it was delightful to see how warm and greasy we all got after it. After a short pause of repose, Miss Skiffins washed up the tea-things, in a trifling lady-like amateur manner that compromised none of us. Then, she put on her gloves again, and we drew round the fire, and Wemmick said, 'Now Aged Parent, tip us the paper.'

Wemmick explained to me while the Aged got his spectacles out, that it gave the old gentleman infinite satisfaction to read the news aloud.

The Aged's reading reminded me of the classes at

Mr Wopsle's great-aunt's, with the pleasanter peculiarity that it seemed to come through a keyhole. As he wanted the candles close to him, and as he was always on the verge of putting either his head or the newspaper into them, he required as much watching as a powder-mill. But Wemmick was equally untiring and gentle in his vigilance, and the Aged read on, quite unconscious of his many rescues.

As Wemmick and Miss Skiffins sat side by side, and as I sat in a shadowy corner, I observed a slow and gradual elongation of Mr Wemmick's mouth, powerfully suggestive of his slowly and gradually stealing his arm round Miss Skiffins's waist. In course of time I saw his hand appear on the other side of Miss Skiffins; but at that moment Miss Skiffins neatly stopped him with the green glove, unwound his arm again as if it were an article of dress, and with the greatest deliberation laid it on the table before her. Miss Skiffins's composure while she did this was one of the most remarkable sights I have ever seen, and if I could have thought the act consistent with abstraction of mind, I should have deemed that Miss Skiffins performed it mechanically.

At last, the Aged read himself into a light slumber. This was the time for Wemmick to produce a little kettle, a tray of glasses, and a black bottle with a porcelain-topped cork. With the aid of these appliances we all had something warm to drink: including the Aged, who was soon awake again. Miss Skiffins mixed, and I observed that she and Wemmick drank out of one glass. Of course I knew better than to offer to see Miss Skiffins home, and under the circumstances I thought I had best go first: which I did, taking a cordial leave of the Aged, and having passed a pleasant evening.

Before a week was out, I received a note from Wemmick, dated Walworth, stating that he hoped he had made some advance in that matter appertaining to our private and personal capacities, and that he would be glad if I could come and see him again upon it. The upshot was, that we found a worthy young merchant or shipping-broker, not long established in business, who wanted intelligent help, and who wanted capital, and who in due course of time and receipt would want a partner. Between him and me, secret articles were signed of which Herbert was the subject, and I paid him half of my five hundred pounds down, and engaged for sundry other payments: some, to fall due at certain dates out of my income: some, contingent on my coming into my property. Miss Skiffins's brother conducted the negotiation. Wemmick pervaded it throughout, but never appeared in it.

The whole business was so cleverly managed, that Herbert had not the least suspicion of my hand being in it. I never shall forget the radiant face with which he came home one afternoon, and told me, as a mighty piece of news, of his having fallen in with one Clarriker (the young merchant's name), and of Clarriker's having shown an extraordinary inclination towards him, and of his belief that the opening had come at last. At length, the thing being done, and he having that day entered Clarriker's House, I did really cry in good earnest when I went to bed, to think that my expectations had done some good to somebody.

A great event in my life, the turning-point of my life, now opens on my view. But, before I proceed to narrate it, I must give one chapter to Estella. It is not much to give to the theme that so long filled my heart.

38

If that staid old house near the Green at Richmond should ever come to be haunted when I am dead, it will be haunted, surely, by my ghost. O the many, many nights and days through which the unquiet spirit within me haunted that house when Estella lived there!

The lady with whom Estella was placed, Mrs Brandley by name, was a widow, with one daughter several years older than Estella.

In Mrs Brandley's house and out of Mrs Brandley's house, I suffered every kind and degree of torture that Estella could cause me. She made use of me to tease other admirers, and she turned the very familiarity between herself and me, to the account of putting a constant slight on my devotion to her.

She had admirers without end. No doubt my jealousy made an admirer of every one who went near her; but there were more than enough of them without that.

I saw her often at Richmond, I heard of her often in town, and I used often to take her and the Brandleys on the water; there were picnics, fête days, plays, operas, concerts, parties, all sorts of pleasures, through which I pursued her – and they were all miseries to me.

'Pip, Pip,' she said one evening, when we sat apart at a darkening window of the house in Richmond; 'will you never take warning?'

'Warning not to be attracted by you, do you mean, Estella?'

'Do I mean! If you don't know what I mean, you are blind.'

I should have replied that Love was commonly reputed blind, but for the reason that I always was restrained by a feeling that it was ungenerous to press myself upon her, when she knew that she could not choose but obey Miss Havisham. My dread always was, that this knowledge on her part laid me under a heavy disadvantage with her pride, and made me the subject of a rebellious struggle in her bosom.

'At any rate,' said I, 'I have no warning given me just now, for you wrote to me to come to you, this time.'

'That's true,' said Estella, with a cold careless smile that always chilled me.

After looking at the twilight without, for a little while, she went on to say:

'The time has come round when Miss Havisham wishes to have me for a day at Satis. You are to take me there, and bring me back, if you will. Can you take me?'

'Can I take you, Estella!'

'You can then? The day after tomorrow, if you please.'

This was all the preparation I received for that visit. We went down on the next day but one, and we found her in the room where I had first beheld her, and it is needless to add that there was no change in Satis House.

Miss Havisham was even more dreadfully fond of Estella than she had been when I last saw them together; I repeat the word advisedly, for there was something positively dreadful in the energy of her looks and embraces.

From Estella she looked at me, with a searching glance that seemed to pry into my heart and probe its wounds. 'How does she use you, Pip; how does she use you?' she asked me again, with her witch-like eagerness, even in Estella's hearing. But, when we sat by her flickering fire at night, she was most weird; for then, keeping Estella's hand drawn through her arm, and clutched in her own hand, she extorted from her the names and conditions of the men whom she had fascinated; and as Miss Havisham dwelt upon this roll, with the intensity of a mind mortally hurt and diseased, she sat with her other hand on her crutch stick, and her chin on that, and her wan bright eyes glaring at me, a very spectre.

I saw in this, that Estella was set to wreak Miss Havisham's revenge on men, and that she was not to be given to me until she had gratified it for a term. I saw in this, a reason for her being beforehand assigned to me. Sending her out to attract and torment and do mischief, Miss Havisham sent her with the malicious assurance that she was beyond the reach of all admirers, and that all who staked upon that cast were secured to lose. I saw in this, the reason for my being staved off so long, and the reason for my late guardian's declining to commit himself to the formal knowledge of such a scheme. I saw in this, the distinct shadow of the darkened and unhealthy house, in which Miss Havisham's life was hidden from the sun.

It happened on the occasion of this visit that some sharp words arose between Estella and Miss Havisham.

We were seated by the fire, and Miss Havisham still had Estella's arm drawn through her own, and still clutched Estella's hand in hers, when Estella gradually began to detach herself.

'What!' said Miss Havisham, flashing her eyes upon her, 'are you tired of me?'

'Only a little tired of myself,' replied Estella, disengaging her arm, and moving to the great chimneypiece, where she stood looking down at the fire.

'Speak the truth, you ingrate!' cried Miss Havisham, passionately striking her stick upon the floor; 'you are tired of me.'

Estella looked at her with perfect composure, and again looked down at the fire. Her graceful figure and her beautiful face expressed a self-possessed indifference to the wild heat of the other, that was almost cruel.

'You stock and stone!' exclaimed Miss Havisham. 'You cold, cold heart!'

'What?' said Estella, 'do you reproach me for being cold? You?'

'Are you not?' was the fierce retort.

'You should know,' said Estella. 'I am what you have made me.'

'O, look at her, look at her!' cried Miss Havisham, bitterly; 'Look at her, so hard and thankless, on the hearth where she was reared! Where I took her into this wretched breast when it was first bleeding from its stabs, and where I have lavished years of tenderness upon her!'

'At least I was no party to the compact,' said Estella, 'for if I could walk and speak, when it was made, it was as much as I could do. But what would you have? You have been very good to me, and I owe everything to you. What would you have?'

'Love,' replied the other.

'You have it.'

'I have not,' said Miss Havisham.

'Mother by adoption,' retorted Estella, never departing from the easy grace of her attitude, never raising her voice as the other did, never yielding either to anger or tenderness, 'I have said that I owe everything to you. But if you ask me to give you what you never gave me, my gratitude and duty cannot do impossibilities.'

'So hard, so hard!' moaned Miss Havisham, pushing away her grey hair with both her hands.

'Who taught me to be hard?' returned Estella. 'Who praised me when I learnt my lesson?'

'But to be hard to *me*!' Miss Havisham quite shrieked, as she stretched out her arms. 'Estella, Estella, Estella, to be hard to *me*!'

Estella looked at her for a moment with a kind of calm wonder, but was not otherwise disturbed; when the moment was past, she looked down at the fire again.

'I cannot think,' said Estella, raising her eyes after a silence, 'why you should be so unreasonable when I come to see you after a separation. I have never forgotten your wrongs and their causes. I have never shown any weakness that I can charge myself with. I must be taken as I have been made. The success is not mine, the failure is not mine, but the two together make me.'

Miss Havisham had settled down, I hardly knew how, upon the floor, among the faded bridal relics with which it was strewn. I took advantage of the moment to leave the room, after beseeching Estella's attention to her, with a movement of my hand. When I left, Estella was yet standing by the great chimney-piece, just as she had stood throughout. Miss Havisham's grey hair was all adrift upon the ground, among the other bridal wrecks, and was a miserable sight to see.

It was with a depressed heart that I walked in the starlight for an hour and more, about the court-yard, and about the brewery, and about the ruined garden. When I at last took courage to return to the room, I found Estella sitting at Miss Havisham's knee, taking up some stitches in one of those old articles of dress that were dropping to pieces. Afterwards, Estella and I played at cards, and so the evening wore away, and I went to bed.

It was the first time I had ever lain down to rest in Satis House, and sleep refused to come near me. A thousand Miss Havishams haunted me. She was on this side of my pillow, on that, at the head of the bed, at the foot, in the dressing-room, in the room overhead, in the room beneath – everywhere. At last, when the night was slow to creep on towards two o'clock, I felt that I absolutely could no longer bear the place as a place to lie down in. I therefore got up and put on my clothes, and went out across the yard into the long stone passage, designing to gain the outer court-yard and walk there for the relief of my mind. But, I was no sooner in the passage than I extinguished my candle; for, I saw Miss Havisham going along it in a ghostly manner, making a low cry. I followed her at a distance, and saw her go up the staircase. She carried a bare candle in her hand. Standing at the bottom of the staircase, I felt the mildewed air of the feast-chamber, without seeing her open the door, and I heard her walking there, and so across into her own room, and so across again into that, never ceasing the low cry. After a time, I tried in the dark both to get out, and to go back, but I could do neither until some streaks of day strayed in and showed me where to lay my hands. During the whole interval, whenever I went to the bottom of the staircase, I heard her footstep, saw her light pass above and heard her ceaseless low cry.

Before we left next day, there was no revival of the difference between her and Estella. Nor, did Miss Havisham's manner towards Estella in anywise change, except that I believed it to have something like fear infused among its former characteristics.

It is impossible to turn this leaf of my life, without putting Bentley Drummle's name upon it; or I would, very gladly.

On a certain occasion when the Finches were assembled in force, the presiding Finch called the Grove to order, forasmuch as Mr Drummle had not yet toasted a lady; which, according to the solemn constitution of the society, it was the brute's turn to do that day. What was my indignant surprise when he called upon the company to pledge him to 'Estella!'

'Estella who?' said I.

'Never you mind,' retorted Drummle.

'Estella of where?' said I. 'You are bound to say of where.'

'Of Richmond, gentlemen,' said Drummle, putting me out of the question, 'and a peerless beauty.'

'I know that lady,' said Herbert, across the table, when the toast had been honoured.

'*Do* you?' said Drummle.

'And so do I,' I added, with a scarlet face.

'*Do* you?' said Drummle. '*Oh*, Lord!'

I immediately rose in my place and said that I could not but regard it as being like the honourable Finch's impudence to come down to that Grove, proposing a lady of whom he knew nothing. Mr Drummle upon this, starting up, demanded what I meant by that? Whereupon, I made him the extreme reply that I believed he knew where I was to be found.

It was decided that if Mr Drummle would bring never so slight a certificate from the lady, importing that he had the honour of her acquaintance, Mr Pip must express his regret, as a gentleman and a Finch, for 'having been betrayed into a warmth which.' Next day was appointed for the production, and next day Drummle appeared with a polite little avowal in Estella's hand, that she had had the honour of dancing with him several times. This left me no course but to regret that I had been 'betrayed into a warmth which', and the whole to repudiate, as untenable, the idea that I was to be found anywhere.

I cannot adequately express what pain it gave me to think that Estella should show any favour to a contemptible, clumsy, sulky booby, so very far below the average. It was easy for me to find out, and I did soon find out, that Drummle had begun to follow her closely, and that she allowed him to do it. A little while, and he was always in pursuit of her, and he and I crossed one another every day. He held on, in a dull persistent way, and Estella held him on; now with encouragement, now with discouragement, now almost flattering him, now openly despising him, now knowing him very well, now scarcely remembering who he was.

The Spider, as Mr Jaggers had called him, was used to lying in wait, however, and had the patience of his tribe. Added to that, he had a blockhead confidence in his money and in his family greatness, which sometimes did him good service. So, the Spider, doggedly watching Estella, outwatched many brighter insects, and would often uncoil himself and drop at the right nick of time.

At a certain Assembly Ball at Richmond, where Estella had outshone all other beauties, this blundering Drummle so hung about her, and with so much toleration on her part, that I resolved to speak to her concerning him and I took the next opportunity.

'Are you tired, Estella?'

'Rather, Pip.'

'You should be.'

'Say rather, I should not be; for I have my letter to Satis House to write, before I go to sleep.'

'Recounting tonight's triumph?' said I. 'Surely a very poor one, Estella.'

'What do you mean? I didn't know there had been any.'

'Estella,' said I, 'do look at that fellow in the corner yonder, who is looking over here at us.'

'Why should I look at him?' returned Estella, with her eyes on me instead. 'What is there in that fellow in the corner yonder – to use your words – that I need look at?'

'Indeed, that is the very question I want to ask you,' said I. 'For he has been hovering about you all night.'

'Moths, and all sorts of ugly creatures,' replied Estella, with a glance towards him, 'hover about a lighted candle. Can the candle help it?'

'But, Estella, do hear me speak. It makes me wretched that you should encourage a man so generally despised as Drummle.'

'Well?' said she.

'You know he is as ungainly within, as without. A deficient, ill-tempered, lowering, stupid fellow. You know he has nothing to recommend him but money, and a ridiculous roll of addle-headed predecessors; now, don't you?'

'Well?' said she again.

To overcome the difficulty of getting past that monosyllable, I took it from her, and said, repeating it with emphasis, 'Well! Then, that is why it makes me wretched.'

'Pip,' said Estella, casting her glance over the room, 'don't be foolish about its effect on you. It may have its effect on others, and may be meant to have. It's not worth discussing.'

'Yes it is,' said I, 'because I cannot bear that people should say, "she throws away her graces and attractions on a mere boor, the lowest in the crowd."'

'I can bear it,' said Estella.

'Oh! don't be so proud, Estella, and so inflexible.'

'Calls me proud and inflexible in this breath!' said Estella, opening her hands. 'And in his last breath reproached me for stooping to a boor!'

'There is no doubt you do,' said I, something hurriedly, 'for I have seen you give him looks and smiles this very night, such as you never give to – me.'

'Do you want me then,' said Estella, turning

suddenly with a fixed and serious, if not angry, look, 'to deceive and entrap you?'

'Do you deceive and entrap him, Estella?'

'Yes, and many others – all of them but you. Here is Mrs Brandley. I'll say no more.'

And now that I have given the one chapter to the theme that so filled my heart, I pass on, unhindered, to the event that had impended over me longer yet; the event that had begun to be prepared for, before I knew that the world held Estella, and in the days when her baby intelligence was receiving its first distortions from Miss Havisham's wasting hands.

39

I was three-and-twenty years of age. Not another word had I heard to enlighten me on the subject of my expectations, and my twenty-third birthday was a week gone. We had left Barnard's Inn more than a year, and lived in the Temple. Our chambers were in Garden-court, down by the river.

Mr Pocket and I had for some time parted company as to our original relations, though we continued on the best terms. That matter of Herbert's was still progressing, and everything with me was as I have brought it down to the close of the last preceding chapter.

Business had taken Herbert on a journey to Marseilles. I was alone, and had a dull sense of being alone.

We lived at the top of the house, and the wind rushing up the river shook it that night, like discharges of cannon, or breakings of a sea. When I set the doors open and looked down the staircase, the staircase lamps were blown out; and when I shaded my face with my hands and looked through the black windows I saw that the lamps in the court were blown out, and that the lamps on the bridges and the shore were shuddering, and that the coal fires in barges on the river were being carried away before the wind like red-hot splashes in the rain.

I read with my watch upon the table, purposing to close my book at eleven o'clock. As I shut it, Saint Paul's, and all the many church-clocks in the City struck that hour. The sound was curiously flawed by the wind; and I was listening, and thinking how the wind assailed and tore it, when I heard a footstep on the stair.

What nervous folly made me start, and awfully connect it with the footstep of my dead sister, matters not. It was past in a moment, and I listened again, and heard the footstep stumble in coming on. Remembering then, that the staircase-lights were blown out, I took up my reading-lamp and went out to the stairhead.

'There is some one down there, is there not?' I called out, looking down.

'Yes,' said a voice from the darkness beneath.

'What floor do you want?'

'The top. Mr Pip.'

'That is my name. – There is nothing the matter?'

'Nothing the matter,' returned the voice. And the man came on.

I stood with my lamp held out over the stair-rail, and he came slowly within its light. It was a shaded lamp, to shine upon a book, and its circle of light was very contracted; so that he was in it for a mere instant, and then out of it. In the instant, I had seen a face that was strange to me, looking up with an incomprehensible air of being touched and pleased by the sight of me.

Moving the lamp as the man moved, I made out that he was substantially dressed, but roughly; like a voyager by sea. That he had long iron-grey hair. That his age was about sixty. That he was a muscular man, strong on his legs, and that he was browned and hardened by exposure to weather. As he ascended the last stair or two, and the light of my lamp included us both, I saw, with a stupid kind of amazement, that he was holding out both his hands to me.

'Pray what is your business?' I asked him.

'My business?' he repeated, pausing. 'Ah! Yes. I will explain my business, by your leave.'

'Do you wish to come in?'

'Yes,' he replied; 'I wish to come in, Master.'

I took him into the room I had just left and, having set the lamp on the table, asked him as civilly as I could, to explain himself.

He looked about him with the strangest air – an air of wondering pleasure, as if he had some part in the things he admired – and he pulled off a rough outer coat, and his hat. Then, I saw that his head was furrowed and bald, and that the long iron-grey hair grew only on its sides. But, I saw nothing that in the least explained him.

He stopped in his looking at me, and slowly rubbed

his right hand over his head. 'It's disapinting to a man,' he said, in a coarse broken voice, 'arter having looked for'ard so distant, and come so fur; but you're not to blame for that. I'll speak in half a minute. Give me half a minute, please.'

He sat down on a chair that stood before the fire, and covered his forehead with his large brown veinous hands. I looked at him attentively then, and recoiled a little from him; but I did not know him.

'There's no one nigh,' said he, looking over his shoulder; 'is there?'

'Why do you, a stranger coming into my rooms at this time of the night, ask that question?' said I.

'You're a game one,' he returned, shaking his head at me with a deliberate affection, at once most unintelligible and most exasperating; 'I'm glad you've grow'd up, a game one! But don't catch hold of me. You'd be sorry arterwards to have done it.'

I relinquished the intention he had detected, for I knew him! Even yet, I could not recall a single feature, but I knew him! If the wind and the rain had driven away the intervening years, had swept us to the churchyard where we first stood face to face on such different levels, I could not have known my convict more distinctly than I knew him now, as he sat in the chair before the fire. No need to take a file from his pocket and show it to me; no need to take the handkerchief from his neck and twist it round his head, I knew him before he gave me one of those aids.

He came back to where I stood, and again held out both his hands. Not knowing what to do – for, in my astonishment I had lost my self-possession – I reluctantly gave him my hands. He grasped them heartily, raised them to his lips, kissed them, and still held them.

'You acted noble, my boy,' said he. 'Noble, Pip! And I have never forgot it!'

At a change in his manner as if he were even going to embrace me, I laid a hand upon his breast and put him away.

'Stay!' said I. 'Keep off! If you are grateful to me for what I did when I was a little child, I hope you have shown your gratitude by mending your way of life. If you have come here to thank me, it was not necessary. Still, however you have found me out, there must be something good in the feeling that has brought you here, and I will not repulse you; but surely you must understand that – I –'

'You was a saying,' he observed, when we had confronted one another in silence, 'that surely I must understand. What, surely must I understand?'

'That I cannot wish to renew that chance intercourse with you of long ago, under these different circumstances. I am glad to believe you have repented and recovered yourself. I am glad to tell you so. But our ways are different ways, none the less. You are wet, and you look weary. Will you drink something before you go?'

'I think,' he answered, 'that I *will* drink (I thank you) afore I go.'

I made him some hot rum and water. I tried to keep my hand steady while I did so, but his look at me as he leaned back in his chair – made my hand very difficult to master. When at last I put the glass to him, I saw with amazement that his eyes were full of tears.

Up to this time I had remained standing, not to

disguise that I wished him gone. But I was softened by the softened aspect of the man, and felt a touch of reproach. 'I hope,' said I, 'that you will not think I spoke harshly to you just now. I had no intention of doing it, and I am sorry for it if I did. I wish you well, and happy!'

He stretched out his hand. I gave him mine, and then he drank, and drew his sleeve across his eyes and forehead.

'How are you living?' I asked him.

'I've been a sheep-farmer, stock-breeder, other trades besides, away in the new world,' said he.

'I hope you have done well?'

'I've done wonderful well. There's others went out alonger me as has done well too, but no man has done nigh as well as me. I'm famous for it.'

'I am glad to hear it.'

'I hope to hear you say so, my dear boy.'

Without stopping to try to understand those words or the tone in which they were spoken, I turned off to a point that had just come into my mind.

'Have you ever seen a messenger you once sent to me,' I enquired, 'since he undertook that trust?'

'Never set eyes upon him. I warn't likely to it.'

'He came faithfully, and he brought me the two one-pound notes. I was a poor boy then, as you know, and to a poor boy they were a little fortune. But, like you, I have done well since, and you must let me pay them back.' I took out my purse.

He watched me as I laid my purse upon the table and opened it, and he watched me as I separated two one-pound notes from its contents. I spread them out and handed them over to him. Still watching me, he laid them one upon the other, folded them long-wise, gave them a twist, set fire to them at the lamp, and dropped the ashes into the tray.

'May I make so bold,' he said then, with a smile that was like a frown, and with a frown that was like a smile, 'as ask you *how* you have done well, since you and me was out on them lone shivering marshes?'

He emptied his glass, got up, and stood at the side of the fire. He put a foot up to the bars, to dry and warm it, and the wet boot began to steam; but, he neither looked at it, nor at the fire, but steadily looked at me. It was only now that I began to tremble.

When my lips had parted, and had shaped some words that were without sound, I forced myself to tell him that I had been chosen to succeed to some property.

'Might a mere warmint ask what property?' said he.

I faltered, 'I don't know.'

'Might a mere warmint ask whose property?' said he.

I faltered again, 'I don't know.'

'Could I make a guess, I wonder,' said the convict, 'at your income since you come of age! As to the first figure now. Five?'

With my heart beating like a heavy hammer of disordered action, I rose out of my chair, and stood with my hand upon the back of it, looking wildly at him.

'Concerning a guardian,' he went on. 'There ought to have been some guardian, or such-like, whiles you was a minor. Some lawyer, maybe. As to the first letter of that lawyer's name now. Would it be J?'

All the truth of my position came flashing on me; and its disappointments, dangers, disgraces, consequences of all kinds, rushed in in such a multitude that I was borne down by them and had to struggle for every breath I drew.

'Put it,' he resumed, 'as the employer of that lawyer whose name begun with a J, and might be Jaggers – put it as he had come over sea to Portsmouth, and had landed there, and had wanted to come on to you. 'However, you have found me out,' you says just now. Well! However did I find you out? Why, I wrote from Portsmouth to a person in London, for particulars of your address. That person's name? Why, Wemmick.'

I could not have spoken one word, though it had been to save my life. I stood looking wildly at him, until I grasped at the chair, when the room began to surge and turn. He caught me, drew me to the sofa, put me up against the cushions, and bent on one knee before me: bringing the face that I now well remembered, and that I shuddered at, very near to mine.

'Yes, Pip, dear boy, I've made a gentleman on you! It's me wot has done it! I swore that time, sure as ever I earned a guinea, that guinea should go to you. I swore arterwards, sure as ever I spec'lated and got rich, you should get rich. I lived rough, that you should live smooth; I worked hard, that you should be above work. What odds, dear boy? Do I tell it, fur you to feel a obligation? Not a bit. I tell it, fur you to know as that there hunted dunghill dog wot you kep life in, got his head so high that he could make a gentleman – and, Pip, you're him!'

The abhorrence in which I held the man, the dread I had of him, the repugnance with which I shrank from him, could not have been exceeded if he had been some terrible beast.

'Look'ee here, Pip. I'm your second father. You're my son – more to me nor any son. I've put away money, only for you to spend. When I was a hired-out shepherd in a solitary hut, not seeing no faces but faces of sheep till I half forgot wot men's and women's faces wos like, I see yourn. I drops my knife many a time in that hut when I was a-eating my dinner or my supper, and I says, 'Here's the boy again, a looking at me whiles I eats and drinks!' I see you there a many times, as plain as ever I see you on them misty marshes. 'Lord strike me dead!' I says each time but wot if I gets liberty and money, I'll make that boy a gentleman!' And I done it. Why, look at you, dear boy! Look at these here lodgings o'yourn, fit for a lord!'

Again he took both my hands and put them to his lips, while my blood ran cold within me.

'Don't you mind talking, Pip,' said he, after again drawing his sleeve over his eyes and forehead, 'you can't do better nor keep quiet, dear boy. You ain't looked slowly forward to this as I have; you wosn't prepared for this, as I wos. But didn't you never think it might be me?'

'O no, no, no,' I returned. 'Never, never!'

'Well, you see it *wos* me, and single-handed. Never a soul in it but my own self and Mr Jaggers.'

'Was there no one else?' I asked.

'No,' said he, with a glance of surprise: 'who else should there be? And, dear boy, how good looking you have growed! There's bright eyes somewheres – eh? Isn't there bright eyes somewheres, wot you love the thoughts on?'

O Estella, Estella!

'They shall be yourn, dear boy, if money can buy

'em. Let me finish wot I was a telling you, dear boy. From that there hut and that there hiring-out, I got money left me by my master and got my liberty and went for myself. In every single thing I went for, I went for you. It all prospered wonderful. It was the money left me, and the gains of the first few year wot I sent home to Mr Jaggers – all for you – when he first come arter you, agreeable to my letter.'

O, that he had never come! That he had left me at the forge – far from contented, yet, by comparison, happy!

'And then, dear boy, it was a recompense to me, look'ee here, to know in secret that I was making a gentleman.'

He laid his hand on my shoulder. I shuddered at the thought that for anything I knew, his hand might be stained with blood.

'It warn't easy, Pip, for me to leave them parts, nor yet it warn't safe. But I held to it, and the harder it was, the stronger I held, for I was determined, and my mind firm made up. At last I done it. Dear boy, I done it!'

I tried to collect my thoughts, but I was stunned. Throughout, I had seemed to myself to attend more to the wind and the rain than to him; even now, I could not separate his voice from those voices, though those were loud and his was silent.

'Where will you put me?' he asked, presently. 'I must be put somewheres, dear boy. To sleep long and sound, for I've been sea-tossed and sea-washed, months and months.'

'My friend and companion,' said I, rising from the sofa, 'is absent; you must have his room.'

'He won't come back tomorrow; will he?'

'No,' said I, answering almost mechanically, in spite of my utmost efforts; 'not tomorrow.'

'Because, look'ee here, dear boy,' he said, dropping his voice, and laying a long finger on my breast in an impressive manner, 'caution is necessary.'

'How do you mean? Caution?'

'I was sent for life. It's death to come back. There's been overmuch coming back of late years, and I should of a certainty be hanged if took.'

Nothing was needed but this; the wretched man, after loading wretched me with his gold and silver chains for years, had risked his life to come to me, and I held it there in my keeping! If I had been attracted to him by the strongest admiration and affection, instead of shrinking from him with the strongest repugnance; it could have been no worse. On the contrary, it would have been better, for his preservation would then have naturally and tenderly addressed my heart.

My first care was to close the shutters, so that no light might be seen from without, and then to close and make fast the doors.

When I had gone into Herbert's room, and had shut off any other communication between it and the staircase than through the room in which our conversation had been held, I asked him if he would go to bed? He said yes, but asked me for some of my 'gentleman's linen' to put on in the morning. I brought it out, and laid it ready for him, and my blood again ran cold when he again took me by both hands to give me good-night.

For an hour or more I remained too stunned to think; and it was not until I began to think, that I began fully to know how wrecked I was, and how the ship in which I had sailed was gone to pieces.

Miss Havisham's intentions towards me, all a mere dream; Estella not designed for me; I only suffered in Satis House as a convenience, a sting for the greedy relations, a model with a mechanical heart to practise on when no other practice was at hand; those were the first smarts I had. But, sharpest and deepest pain of all – it was for the convict, guilty of I knew not what crimes, and liable to be taken out of those rooms where I sat thinking, and hanged at the Old Bailey door, that I had deserted Joe.

I would not have gone back to Joe now, I would not have gone back to Biddy now, for any consideration: simply, I suppose, because my sense of my own worthless conduct to them was greater than every consideration. I could never, never, never, undo what I had done.

In every rage of wind and rush of rain, I heard pursuers. Twice, I could have sworn there was a knocking and whispering at the outer door.

Crowding up with these reflections came the reflection that I had seen him with my childish eyes to be a desperately violent man; that I had heard that other convict reiterate that he had tried to murder him; that I had seen him down in the ditch tearing and fighting like a wild beast. Out of such remembrances I brought into the light of the fire, a half-formed terror that it might not be safe to be shut up there with him in the dead of the wild solitary night. This dilated until it filled the room, and impelled me to take a candle and go in and look at my dreadful burden.

He was asleep, and quietly too, though he had a

pistol lying on the pillow. Assured of this, I softly removed the key to the outside of his door, and turned it on him before I again sat down by the fire. Gradually I slipped from the chair and lay on the floor. When I awoke, without having parted in my sleep with the perception of my wretchedness, the clocks of the East-ward churches were striking five, the candles were wasted out, the fire was dead, and the wind and rain intensified the thick black darkness.

THIS IS THE END OF THE SECOND STAGE OF
PIP'S EXPECTATIONS.

40

It was fortunate for me that I had to take precautions to ensure (so far as I could) the safety of my dreaded visitor; for, this thought pressing on me when I awoke, held other thoughts in a confused concourse at a distance.

The impossibility of keeping him concealed in the chambers was self-evident. I was looked after by an inflammatory old female, assisted by an animated rag-bag whom she called her niece, and to keep a room secret from them would be to invite curiosity and exaggeration. Not to get up a mystery with these people, I resolved to announce in the morning that my uncle had unexpectedly come from the country.

This course I decided on while I was yet groping about in the darkness for the means of getting a light.

Not stumbling on the means after all, I was fain to go out to the adjacent Lodge and get the watchman there to come with his lantern. Now, in groping my way down the black staircase I fell over something, and that something was a man crouching in a corner.

As the man made no answer when I asked him what he did there, but eluded my touch in silence, I ran to the Lodge and urged the watchman to come quickly: telling him of the incident on the way back. We examined the staircase from the bottom to the top and found no one there. It then occurred to me as possible that the man might have slipped into my rooms; so, lighting my candle at the watchman's, and leaving him standing at the door, I examined them carefully, including the room in which my dreaded guest lay asleep. All was quiet, and assuredly no other man was in those chambers.

It troubled me that there should have been a lurker on the stairs, on that night of all nights in the year, and I asked the watchman, whether he had admitted at his gate any gentleman who had perceptibly been dining out? Yes, he said; at different times of the night, three. One lived in Fountain Court, and the other two lived in the Lane, and he had seen them all go home. Again, the only other man who dwelt in the house of which my chambers formed a part, had been in the country for some weeks; and he certainly had not returned in the night, because we had seen his door with his seal on it as we came upstairs.

'Besides them three gentlemen that I have named, I don't call to mind another since about eleven o'clock, when a stranger asked for you,' said the watchman.

'My uncle,' I muttered. 'Yes.'

'You saw him, sir?'

'Yes. Oh yes.'

'Likewise the person with him?'

'Person with him!' I repeated.

'I judged the person to be with him,' returned the watchman. 'The person stopped, when he stopped to make enquiry of me, and the person took this way when he took this way.'

'What sort of person?'

The watchman had not particularly noticed; he should say a working person; to the best of his belief, he had a dust-coloured kind of clothes on, under a dark coat. The watchman made more light of the matter than I did, and naturally; not having my reason for attaching weight to it.

When I had got rid of him, my mind was much troubled by these two circumstances taken together. Whereas they were easy of innocent solution apart – as, for instance, some diner-out might have strayed to my staircase and dropped asleep there – and my nameless visitor might have brought some one with him to show him the way – still, joined, they had an ugly look to one as prone to distrust and fear as the changes of a few hours had made me.

All this time I had never been able to consider my own situation, nor could I do so yet. When I opened the shutters and looked out at the wet wild morning, all of a leaden hue, I thought how miserable I was, but hardly knew why, or how long I had been so, or on what day of the week I made the reflection, or even who I was that made it.

At last, the old woman and the niece came in and

testified surprise at sight of me and the fire. To whom I imparted how my uncle had come in the night and was then asleep, and how the breakfast preparations were to be modified accordingly. Then, I washed and dressed while they knocked the furniture about and made a dust; and so, in a sort of dream or sleep-waking, I found myself sitting by the fire again, waiting for – Him – to come to breakfast.

By-and-by, his door opened and he came out. I could not bring myself to bear the sight of him, and I thought he had a worse look by daylight.

'I do not even know,' said I, speaking low as he took his seat at the table, 'by what name to call you. I have given out that you are my uncle.'

'That's it, dear boy! Call me uncle.'

'You assumed some name, I suppose, on board ship? Do you mean to keep that name?'

'Why, yes, dear boy, it's as good as another – unless you'd like another.'

'What is your real name?' I asked him in a whisper.

'Magwitch,' he answered, in the same tone; 'chrisen'd Abel.'

'When you came into the Temple last night –' said I, pausing to wonder whether that could really have been last night, which seemed so long ago.

'Yes, dear boy?'

When you came into the gate and asked the watchman the way here, had you any one with you?'

'With me? No, dear boy.'

'But there was some one there?'

'I didn't take particular notice,' he said, dubiously, 'not knowing the ways of the place. But I think there *was* a person, too, come in alonger me.'

'Are you known in London?'

'I hope not!' said he, giving his neck a jerk with his forefinger that made me turn hot and sick.

'Were you – tried – in London?'

'Which time?' said he, with a sharp look.

'The last time.'

He nodded. 'First knowed Mr Jaggers that way. Jaggers was for me.'

It was on my lips to ask him what he was tried for, but he took up a knife, gave it a flourish, and with the words, 'And what I done is worked out and paid for!' fell to at his breakfast.

'I'm a heavy grubber, dear boy,' he said, as a polite kind of apology when he had made an end of his meal, 'but I always was. If it had been in my constitution to be a lighter grubber, I might ha' got into lighter trouble. Similarly, I must have my smoke.'

As he said so, he got up from table, and putting his hand into the breast of the pea-coat he wore, brought out a short black pipe, and a handful of loose tobacco. Having filled his pipe, he put the surplus tobacco back again, as if his pocket were a drawer. Then, he took a live coal from the fire with the tongs, and lighted his pipe at it, and then turned round on the hearth-rug with his back to the fire, and went through his favourite action of holding out both his hands for mine.

'And this,' said he, dandling my hands up and down in his, as he puffed at his pipe; 'and this is the gentleman what I made! The real genuine One! It does me good fur to look at you, Pip.'

I released my hands as soon as I could, and found that I was beginning slowly to settle down to the contemplation of my condition. What I was chained to, and how heavily, became intelligible to me, as I heard his hoarse voice, and sat looking up at his furrowed bald head with its iron grey hair at the sides.

'I mustn't see my gentleman a-footing it in the mire of the streets; there mustn't be no mud on *his* boots. My gentleman must have horses, Pip! Horses to ride, and horses to drive, and horses for his servant to ride and drive as well.'

He took out of his pocket a great thick pocket-book, bursting with papers, and tossed it on the table.

'There's something worth spending in that there book, dear boy. It's yourn. All I've got ain't mine; it's yourn. Don't you be afeerd on it. There's more where that come from. I've come to the old country fur to see my gentleman spend his money *like* a gentleman. That'll be *my* pleasure.'

'Stop!' said I, almost in a frenzy of fear and dislike, 'I want to speak to you. I want to know how you are to be kept out of danger, how long you are going to stay, what projects you have. First, what precautions can be taken against your being recognized and seized?'

'Well, dear boy, the danger ain't so great. Without I was informed agen, the danger ain't so much to signify. There's Jaggers, and there's Wemmick, and there's you Who else is there to inform?'

'Is there no chance person who might identify you in the street?' said I.

'Well,' he returned, 'there ain't many. Not yet I don't intend to advertise myself in the newspapers by the name of A.M. come back from Botany Bay; and years have rolled away, and who's to gain by it? Still, look'ee here, Pip. If the danger had been fifty times as great, I should ha' come to see you, mind you, just the same.'

'And how long do you remain?'

'How long?' said he, 'I'm not a-going back. I've come for good.'

'Where are you to live?' said I. 'Where will you be safe?'

'Dear boy,' he returned, 'there's disguising wigs can be bought for money, and there's hair powder, and spectacles, and black clothes – shorts and what not. As to the where and how of living, dear boy, give me your own opinions on it.'

'You take it smoothly now,' said I, 'but you were very serious last night, when you swore it was Death.'

'And so I swear it is Death,' said he, 'and Death by the rope, in the open street not fur from this, and it's serious that you should fully understand it to be so. What then, when that's once done? Here I am. To go back now, 'ud be as bad as to stand ground – worse. Besides, Pip, I'm here, because I've meant it by you, years and years.'

It appeared to me that I could do no better than secure him some quiet lodging hard by, of which he might take possession when Herbert returned: whom I expected in two or three days. That the secret must be confided to Herbert as a matter of unavoidable necessity, was plain to me. But it was by no means so plain to Mr Provis (I resolved to call him by that name), who reserved his consent to Herbert's participation until he should have seen him and formed a favourable judgement of his physiognomy. 'And even then, dear boy,' said he, pulling a greasy little clasped black Testament out of his pocket, 'we'll have him on his oath.'

As he was at present dressed in a seafaring slop suit,

in which he looked as if he had some parrots and cigars to dispose of, I next discussed with him what dress he should wear. He had in his own mind sketched a dress for himself that would have made him something between a dean and a dentist. It was with considerable difficulty that I won him over to the assumption of a dress more like a prosperous farmer's; and we arranged that he should cut his hair close, and wear a little powder. Lastly, as he had not yet been seen by the laundress or her niece, he was to keep himself out of their view until his change of dress was made.

It would seem a simple matter to decide on these precautions; but in my dazed, not to say distracted, state, it took so long, that I did not get out to further them, until two or three in the afternoon. He was to remain shut up in the chambers while I was gone, and was on no account to open the door.

There being to my knowledge a respectable lodging-house in Essex-street, I first of all repaired to that house, and was so fortunate as to secure the second floor for my uncle, Mr Provis. I then went from shop to shop, making such purchases as were necessary to the change in his appearance. This business transacted, I turned my face, on my own account, to Little Britain. Mr Jaggers was at his desk, but, seeing me enter, got up immediately and stood before his fire.

'Now, Pip,' said he, 'be careful.'

'I will, sir,' I returned. For, coming along I had thought well of what I was going to say.

'Don't commit yourself,' said Mr Jaggers, 'and don't commit any one. You understand – any one. Don't tell me anything: I am not curious.'

Of course I saw that he knew the man was come.

'I merely want, Mr Jaggers,' said I, 'to assure myself that what I have been told, is true. I have no hope of its being untrue, but at least I may verify it.'

Mr Jaggers nodded. 'But did you say "told" or "informed"?' he asked me. 'Told would seem to imply verbal communication. You can't have verbal communication with a man in New South Wales, you know.'

'I will say, informed, Mr Jaggers.'

'Good.'

'I have been informed by a person named Abel Magwitch, that he is the benefactor so long unknown to me.'

'That is the man,' said Mr Jaggers, '– in New South Wales.'

'I am not so unreasonable, sir, as to think you at all responsible for my mistakes and wrong conclusions; but I always supposed it was Miss Havisham.'

'As you say, Pip,' returned, Mr Jaggers, turning his eyes upon me cooly, and taking a bite at his forefinger, 'I am not at all responsible for that.'

'I have no more to say,' said I, with a sigh, after standing silent for a little while. 'I have verified my information, and there's an end.'

'And Magwitch – in New South Wales – having at last disclosed himself,' said Mr Jaggers, 'you will comprehend, Pip, how rigidly throughout my communication with you, I have always adhered to the strict line of fact. I communicated to Magwitch when he first wrote to me – from New South Wales. He appeared to me to have obscurely hinted in his letter at some distant idea he had of seeing you in England here. I cautioned him that he was not at all likely to obtain a pardon; that he was expatriated for the term of his natural life; and that his presenting himself in this country would be an act of felony, rendering him liable to the extreme penalty of the law. I gave Magwitch that caution,' said Mr Jaggers, looking hard at me; 'He guided himself by it, no doubt.'

'No doubt,' said I.

'I have been informed by Wemmick,' pursued Mr Jaggers, still looking hard at me, 'that he has received a letter, under date Portsmouth, from a colonist of the name of Provis, asking for the particulars of your address, on behalf of Magwitch. Wemmick sent him the particulars, I understand, by return of post. Probably it is through Provis that you have received the explanation of Magwitch – in New South Wales?'

'It came through Provis,' I replied.

'Good day, Pip,' said Mr Jaggers, offering his hand; 'glad to have seen you. In writing by post to Magwitch – in New South Wales – or in communicating with him through Provis, have the goodness to mention that the particulars and vouchers of our long account shall be sent to you, together with the balance; for there is still a balance remaining. Good day, Pip!'

We shook hands, and he looked hard at me as long as he could see me. I turned at the door, and he was still looking hard at me, while the two vile casts on the shelf seemed to be trying to get their eyelids open, and to force out of their swollen throats, 'O, what a man he is!'

Next day the clothes I had ordered, all came home, and Provis put them on. Whatever he put on, became him less than what he had worn before. The more I dressed him and the better I dressed him, the more he looked like the slouching fugitive on the marshes. This effect on my anxious fancy was partly referable, no doubt, to his old face and manner growing more familiar to me: but I believe too that he dragged one of his legs as if there were still a weight of iron on it, and that from head to foot there was convict in the very grain of the man.

It had been his own idea to wear a touch of powder. But I can compare the effect of it, when on, to nothing but the probable effect of rouge upon the dead; so awful was the manner in which everything in him that it was most desirable to repress, started through that thin layer of pretence, and seemed to come blazing out at the crown of his head. It was abandoned as soon as tried, and he wore his grizzled hair cut short.

Words cannot tell what a sense I had, at the same time, of the dreadful mystery that he was to me. When he fell asleep of an evening, with his knotted hands clenching the sides of the easy-chair, and his bald head tattooed with deep wrinkles falling forward on his breast, I would sit and look at him, wondering what he had done, and loading him with all the crimes in the Calendar, until the impulse was powerful on me to start up and fly from him. Once, I actually did start out of bed in the night, and begin to dress myself in my worst clothes, hurriedly intending to leave him there with everything else I possessed, and enlist for India as a private soldier.

I doubt if a ghost could have been more terrible to me, up in those lonely rooms in the long evenings and long nights, with the wind and the rain always rushing by. A ghost could not have been taken and hanged on my account, and the consideration that he could be, and the dread that he would be, were no small addition to my horrors.

This is written of, as if it had lasted a year. It lasted about five days. Expecting Herbert all the time, I dared not go out, except when I took Provis for an airing after dark. At length, one evening when dinner was over and I had dropped into a slumber quite worn out, I was roused by the welcome footstep on the staircase. Provis, who had been asleep too, staggered up at the noise I made, and in an instant I saw his jack-knife shining in his hand.

'Quiet! It's Herbert!' I said; and Herbert came bursting in, with the airy freshness of six hundred miles of France upon him.

'Handel, my dear fellow, how are you? I seem to have been gone a twelvemonth! Why, so I must have been, for you have grown quite thin and pale! Handel, my – Halloa! I beg your pardon.'

He was stopped in his running on and in his shaking hands with me, by seeing Provis. Provis, regarding him with a fixed attention, was slowly putting up his jack-knife, and groping in another pocket for something else.

'Herbert, my dear friend,' said I, while Herbert stood staring and wondering, 'something very strange has happened. This is – a visitor of mine.'

'It's all right, dear boy!' said Provis coming forward, with his little clasped black book, and then addressing himself to Herbert. 'Take it in your right hand. Lord strike you dead on the spot, if ever you split in any way sumever! Kiss it!'

'Do so, as he wishes it,' I said to Herbert. So, Herbert, looking at me with a friendly uneasiness and amazement, complied, and Provis immediately shaking hands with him, said, 'Now you're on your oath, you

know. And never believe me on mine, if Pip shan't
make a gentleman on you!'

41

In vain should I attempt to describe the astonishment
and disquiet of Herbert, when he and I and Provis sat
down before the fire, and I recounted the whole of the
secret. Enough, that I saw my own feelings reflected
in Herbert's face, and, not least among them, my
repugnance towards the man who had done so much
for me.

What would alone have set a division between that
man and us, if there had been no other dividing circumstance, was his triumph in my story. His boast that he
had made me a gentleman, and that he had come to see
me support the character on his ample resources, was
made for me quite as much as for himself; and that it
was a highly agreeable boast to both of us, and that we
must both be very proud of it, was a conclusion quite
established in his own mind.

It was midnight before I took Provis round to
Essex-street, and saw him safely in at his own dark
door. When it closed upon him, I experienced the first
moment of relief I had known since the night of his arrival.

Never quite free from an uneasy remembrance of
the man on the stairs, I had always looked about me in
taking my guest out after dark, and in bringing him
back; and I looked about me now. The street was

empty when I turned back into the Temple. Nobody had come out at the gate with us, nobody went in at the gate with me. As I crossed by the fountain, I saw his lighted back windows looking bright and quiet, and, when I stood for a few moments in the doorway of the building where I lived, before going up the stairs, Garden-court was as still and lifeless as the staircase was when I ascended it.

Herbert received me with open arms, and I had never felt before, so blessedly, what it is to have a friend. When he had spoken some sound words of sympathy and encouragement, we sat down to consider the question,

'What,' said I to Herbert, 'what is to be done?'

'My poor dear Handel,' he replied, holding his head, 'I am too stunned to think.'

'So was I, Herbert, when the blow first fell. Still, something must be done. He is intent upon various new expenses – horses, and carriages, and lavish appearance of all kinds. He must be stopped somehow.'

'You mean that you can't accept –'

'How can I?' I interposed, as Herbert paused. 'Think of him! Look at him!'

An involuntary shudder passed over both of us.

'Yet I am afraid the dreadful truth is, Herbert, that he is attached to me, strongly attached to me. Think what I owe him already.'

'My poor dear Handel,' Herbert repeated.

'Then,' said I, 'I am heavily in debt – very heavily for me, who have now no expectations – and I have been bred to no calling, and I am fit for nothing.'

'Well, well, well!' Herbert remonstrated. 'Don't say fit for nothing.'

'What am I fit for? I know only one thing that I am fit for, and that is, to go for a soldier. And I might have gone my dear Herbert, but for the prospect of taking counsel with your friendship and affection.'

Of course I broke down there: and of course Herbert, beyond seizing a warm grip of my hand, pretended not to know it.

'But there is another question,' said Herbert. 'This is an ignorant determined man, who has long had one fixed idea. More than that, he seems to me to be a man of a desperate and fierce character.'

'I know he is,' I returned. And I told him what I had not mentioned in my narrative; of that encounter with the other convict.

'See, then,' said Herbert; 'think of this! He comes here at the peril of his life, for the realization of his fixed idea. In the moment of realization, after all his toil and waiting, you cut the ground from under his feet, destroy his idea, and make his gains worthless to him. Do you see nothing that he might do, under the disappointment?'

'I have seen it, Herbert, and dreamed of it, ever since the fatal night of his arrival. Nothing has been in my thoughts so distinctly, as his putting himself in the way of being taken.'

'Then you may rely upon it,' said Herbert, 'that there would be great danger of his doing it.'

I was so struck by the horror of this idea, which had weighed upon me from the first, and the working out of which would make me regard myself, in some sort, as his murderer, that I could not rest in my chair but began pacing to and fro. I said to Herbert, meanwhile, that even if Provis were recognized and taken, in spite of himself, I should be wretched as the cause, however innocently.

'Handel,' said Herbert, 'you feel convinced that you can take no further benefits from him; do you?'

'Fully. Surely you would, too, if you were in my place?'

'And you feel convinced that you must break with him?'

'Herbert, can you ask me?'

'And you have, and are bound to have, that tenderness for the life he has risked on your account, that you must save him, if possible, from throwing it away. Then you must get him out of England. You will have to go with him. That done, extricate yourself, in Heaven's name, and we'll see it out together, dear old boy.'

'Now, Herbert,' said I, 'with reference to gaining some knowledge of his history. There is but one way that I know of. I must ask him point-blank.'

'Yes. Ask him,' said Herbert, 'when we sit at breakfast in the morning.'

He came round at the appointed time, took out his jack-knife, and sat down to his meal. He was full of plans 'for his gentleman's coming out strong, and like a gentleman,' and urged me to begin speedily upon the pocket-book, which he had left in my possession. When he had made an end of his breakfast, I said to him, without a word of preface:

'After you were gone last night, I told my friend of the struggle that the soldiers found you engaged in on the marshes, when we came up. You remember?'

'Remember!' said he. 'I think so!'

'We want to know something about that man – and

about you. Is not this as good a time as another for our knowing more?'

'Well!' he said, after consideration. 'You're on your oath, you know, Pip's comrade?'

'Assuredly,' replied Herbert.

'As to anything I say, you know,' he insisted. 'The oath applies to all.'

'I understand it to do so.'

'And look'ee here! Wotever I done, is worked out and paid for,' he insisted again.

'So be it.'

He turned an angry eye on the fire for a few minutes, looked round at us, and said what follows:

42

'Dear boy and Pip's comrade. I am not a going fur to tell you my life, like a song or a story-book. But to give it you short and handy, I'll put it at once into a mouthful of English. In gaol and out of gaol, in gaol and out of gaol, in gaol and out of gaol.

'I know'd my name to be Magwitch, chrisen'd Abel. So fur as I could find, there warn't a soul that see young Abel Magwitch, with as little on him as in him, but wot caught fright at him, and either drove him off, or took him up. I was took up, took up, took up, to that extent that I reg'larly grow'd up took up.

'This is the way it was, that when I was a ragged little creetur as much to be pitied as ever I see, I got the name of being hardened. "This is a terrible hardened one," they says to prison wisitors, picking out me. "May be said to live in gaols, this boy." They always went on agen me about the Devil. But what the Devil was I to do? I must put something into my stomach, mustn't I?

'Tramping, begging, thieving, working sometimes when I could, I got to be a man. I warn't locked up as often now as formerly, but I wore out my good share of key-metal still.

'At Epsom races, a matter of over twenty years ago, I got acquainted wi' a man whose name was Compeyson; and that's the man, dear boy, what you see me a-pounding in the ditch, according to what you truly told your comrade arter I was gone last night.

'He set up fur a gentleman, this Compeyson. He was good-looking too. It was the night afore the great race, when I found him on the heath, in a booth that I know'd on. Him and some more was a-sitting among the tables when I went in, and the landlord called him out, and said, "I think this is a man that might suit you" – meaning I was.

'Compeyson, he looks at me very noticing, and I look at him.

'"To judge from appearances, you're out of luck," says Compeyson to me.

'"Yes, master, and I've never been in it much."

'"Luck changes," says Compeyson; "perhaps yours is going to change."

'I says, "I hope it may be so. There's room."

'"What can you do?" says Compeyson.

'"Eat and drink," I says; "if you'll find the materials."

'Compeyson laughed, looked at me again very

noticing, giv me five shillings, and appointed me for next night. Same place.

'I went to Compeyson next night, same place, and Compeyson took me on to be his man and pardner. Compeyson's business was the swindling, handwriting forging, stolen bank-note passing, and such-like. He'd no more heart than a iron file, he was as cold as death, and he had the head of the Devil afore mentioned.

'Not to go into the things that Compeyson planned, and I done – which 'ud take a week – I'll simply say to you, that that man got me into such nets as made me his black slave. I was always in debt to him, always under his thumb. He'd got craft, and he'd got learning, and he overmatched me five hundred times told and no mercy. The time wi' Compeyson was a'most as hard a time as ever I had; that said, all's said. Did I tell you as I was tried, alone, for misdemeanour, while with Compeyson?'

I answered, No.

'Well!' he said, 'I *was* – me and Compeyson was both committed for felony – on a charge of putting stolen notes in circulation – and there was other charges behind. Compeyson says to me, "Separate defences, no communication," and that was all. And I was so miserable poor, that I sold all the clothes I had, except what hung on my back, afore I could get Jaggers.

'When we was put in the dock, I noticed first of all what a gentleman Compeyson looked, and what a common sort of a wretch I looked. When the evidence was giv in the box, I noticed how it was always me that had come for'ard, and could be swore to, how it was always me that the money had been paid to, how it was always me that had seemed to work the thing and get the profit. But, when the defence come on, then I see the plan plainer; for, says the counsellor for Compeyson, "My lord and gentlemen, here you has afore you, two persons as your eyes can separate wide; one, the younger, well brought up, one, the elder, ill brought up, who will be spoke to as such; one, the younger, seldom if ever seen in these here transactions, and only suspected; t'other, the elder, always seen in 'em and always wi' his guilt brought home. Can you doubt, if there is but one in it, which is the one, and, if there is two in it, which is much the worst one?" And when the verdict come, warn't it Compeyson as was recommended to mercy on account of good character and bad company, and giving up all the information he could agen me, and warn't it me as got never a word but Guilty? And when I says to Compeyson, "Once out of this court, I'll smash that face of yourn!" ain't it Compeyson as prays the Judge to be protected, and gets two turnkeys stood betwixt us? And when we're sentenced, ain't it him as gets seven year, and me fourteen, and ain't it him as the Judge is sorry for, because he might a done so well, and ain't it me as the Judge perceives to be a old offender of violent passion, likely to come to worse?'

He had so heated himself that he took out his hand-kerchief and wiped his face and head and neck and hands, before he could go on.

'I had said to Compeyson that I'd smash that face of his, and I swore Lord smash mine! to do it. We was in the same prison-ship, but I couldn't get at him for long, though I tried. At last I come behind him and hit him on the cheek to turn him round and get a smashing one at him, when I was seen and seized. The black-hole of that ship warn't a strong one. I escaped to the shore, and I was a hiding among the graves there, envying them as was in 'em and all over, when I first see my boy!'

He regarded me with a look of affection that made him almost abhorrent to me again, though I had felt great pity for him.

'By my boy, I was giv to understand as Compeyson was out on them marshes too. I hunted him down. I smashed his face. "And now," says I, "as the worst thing I can do, caring nothing for myself, I'll drag you back." And I'd have swum off, towing him by the hair, if it had come to that, and I'd a got him aboard without the soldiers.

'Of course he'd much the best of it to the last – his character was so good. He had escaped when he was made half-wild by me and my murderous intentions; and his punishment was light. I was put in irons, brought to trial again, and sent for life. I didn't stop for life, dear boy and Pip's comrade, being here.'

'Is he dead?' I asked, after a silence.

'He hopes *I* am, if he's alive, you may be sure,' with a fierce look. 'I never heerd no more of him.'

Herbert had been writing with his pencil in the cover of a book.

He softly pushed the book over to me, as Provis stood smoking with his eyes on the fire, and I read in it:

Compeyson is the man who professed to be Miss Havisham's lover.

I shut the book and nodded slightly to Herbert, and put the book by; but we neither of us said anything, and both looked at Provis as he stood smoking by the fire.

43

Why should I pause to ask how much of my shrinking from Provis might be traced to Estella? Why should I loiter on my road, to compare the state of mind in which I had tried to rid myself of the stain of the prison before meeting her at the coach-office, with the state of mind in which I now reflected on the abyss between Estella in her pride and beauty, and the returned transport whom I harboured?

Never would I breathe a word of Estella to Provis. But, I said to Herbert that before I could go abroad, I must see both Estella and Miss Havisham. I resolved to go out to Richmond next day, and I went.

On my presenting myself at Mrs Brandley's, Estella's maid was called to tell me that Estella had gone into the country. Where? To Satis House, as usual. Not as usual, I said, for she had never yet gone there without me; when was she coming back? There was an air of reservation in the answer which increased my perplexity, and the answer was, that her maid believed she was only coming back at all for a little while. I could make nothing of it, and I went home again in complete discomfiture.

Next day, I had the meanness to feign that I was

under a binding promise to go down to Joe; but I was capable of almost any meanness towards Joe or his name. Provis was to be strictly careful while I was gone, and Herbert was to take the charge of him that I had taken. I was to be absent only one night, and, on my return, the gratification of his impatience for my starting as a gentleman on a greater scale, was to be begun. It occurred to me then, and as I afterwards found to Herbert also, that he might be best got away across the water, on that pretence – as, to make purchases, or the like.

I set off by the early morning coach before it was yet light. When we drove up to the Blue Boar after a drizzly ride, whom should I see come out under the gateway, toothpick in hand, to look at the coach, but Bentley Drummle!

As he pretended not to see me, I pretended not to see him. It was a very lame pretence on both sides; the lamer, because we both went into the coffee-room, where he had just finished his breakfast, and where I ordered mine. It was poisonous to me to see him in the town, for I very well knew why he had come there.

I sat at my table while he stood before the fire. By degrees it became an enormous injury to me that he stood before the fire, and I got up, determined to have my share of it. I had to put my hands behind his legs for the poker when I went up to the fire-place to stir the fire, but still pretended not to know him.

'Is this a cut?' said Mr Drummle.

'Oh!' said I, poker in hand; 'it's you, is it? How do you do? I was wondering who it was, who kept the fire off.'

'You have just come down?' said Mr Drummle, edging me a little away with his shoulder.

'Yes,' said I, edging *him* a little away with *my* shoulder.

'Beastly place,' said Drummle. – 'Your part of the country, I think?'

'Yes,' I assented. 'I am told it's very like your Shropshire.'

'Not in the least like it,' said Drummle.

'Have you been here long?' I asked, determined not to yield an inch of the fire.

'Long enough to be tired of it,' returned Drummle.

I felt here, through a tingling in my blood, that if Mr Drummle's shoulder had claimed another hair's breadth of room, I should have jerked him into the window; equally, that if my own shoulder had urged a similar claim, Mr Drummle would have jerked me into the nearest box. He whistled a little. So did I.

'Large tract of marshes about here, I believe?' said Drummle and laughed.

'Are you amused, Mr Drummle?'

'No,' said he, 'not particularly. I am going out for a ride in the saddle. I mean to explore those marshes for amusement. Waiter! Is that horse of mine ready?'

'Brought round to the door, sir.'

'I say. Look here, you sir. The lady won't ride today; the weather won't do. And I don't dine, because I'm going to dine at the lady's.'

Then, Drummle glanced at me, with an insolent triumph on his great-jowled face that cut me to the heart, dull as he was, and so exasperated me, that I felt inclined to take him in my arms and seat him on the fire.

The horse was visible outside in the drizzle at the

door, my breakfast was put on table, Drummle's was cleared away, the waiter invited me to begin, I nodded, we both stood our ground.

'Have you been to the Grove since?' said Drummle.

'No,' said I, 'I had quite enough of the Finches the last time I was there.'

'Was that when we had a difference of opinion?'

'Yes,' I replied, very shortly.

'Come, come!' sneered Drummle. 'You shouldn't have lost your temper.'

'Mr Drummle,' said I, 'you are not competent to give advice on that subject. When I lose my temper I don't throw glasses.'

'I do,' said Drummle.

Again glancing at him once or twice, in an increased state of smouldering ferocity, I said:

'Mr Drummle, I did not seek this conversation, and I don't think it an agreeable one.'

'I am sure it's not,' said he, superciliously over his shoulder; 'I don't think anything about it.'

'And therefore,' I went on, 'with your leave, I will suggest that we hold no kind of communication in future.'

'Quite my opinion,' said Drummle. 'But don't lose your temper. Haven't you lost enough without that?'

'What do you mean, sir?'

'Wai-ter!' said Drummle, by way of answering me.

The waiter reappeared.

'Look here, you sir. You quite understand that the young lady don't ride today, and that I dine at the young lady's?'

'Quite so, sir!'

When the waiter had felt my fast cooling tea-pot

with the palm of his hand, and had gone out, Drummle took a cigar from his pocket and bit the end off, but showed no sign of stirring. How long we might have remained in this ridiculous position it is impossible to say, but for the incursion of three thriving farmers who came into the coffee-room and before whom, as they charged at the fire, we were obliged to give way.

I saw him through the window, seizing his horse's mane, and mounting in his blundering brutal manner, and sidling and backing away. I thought he was gone, when he came back, calling for a light for the cigar in his mouth, which he had forgotten. A man in a dust-coloured dress appeared with what was wanted and as Drummle leaned down from the saddle and lighted his cigar and laughed, the slouching shoulders and ragged hair of this man, whose back was towards me, re-minded me of Orlick.

Too heavily out of sorts to care much at the time whether it were he or no, I went out to the memorable old house that it would have been so much the better for me never to have entered, never to have seen.

44

In the room where the dressing-table stood, and where the wax candles burnt on the wall, I found Miss Havisham and Estella; Estella was knitting and Miss Havisham was looking on.

'And what wind,' said Miss Havisham, 'blows you here, Pip?'

Though she looked steadily at me, I saw that she was rather confused. Estella, pausing a moment in her knitting with her eyes upon me, and then going on, I fancied that I read in the action of her fingers, that she perceived I had discovered my real benefactor.

'Miss Havisham,' said I, 'I went to Richmond yesterday, to speak to Estella; and finding that some wind had blown *her* here, I followed.'

I took the chair by the dressing-table, which I had often seen her occupy. With all that ruin at my feet and about me, it seemed a natural place for me, that day.

'What I had to say to Estella, Miss Havisham, I will say before you, presently – in a few moments. It will not surprise you, it will not displease you. I am as unhappy as you can ever have meant me to be. I have found out who my patron is. It is not a fortunate discovery, and is not likely ever to enrich me in reputation, station, fortune, anything. There are reasons why I must say no more of that. It is not my secret, but another's. When you first caused me to be brought here, Miss Havisham; I suppose I did really come here, as any other chance boy might have come – as a kind of servant, to gratify a want or a whim, and to be paid for it?'

'Ay, Pip,' replied Miss Havisham, steadily nodding her head; 'you did.'

'And that Mr Jaggers –'

'Mr Jaggers,' said Miss Havisham, taking me up in a firm tone, 'had nothing to do with it, and knew nothing of it. His being my lawyer, and his being the lawyer of your patron, is a coincidence.'

'But when I fell into the mistake I have so long remained in, at least you led me on?' said I.

'Yes,' she returned, again nodding steadily, 'I let you go on.'

'Was that kind?'

'Who am I,' cried Miss Havisham, striking her stick upon the floor and flashing into wrath so suddenly that Estella glanced up at her in surprise, 'who am I, for God's sake, that I should be kind?'

'I was liberally paid for my old attendance here,' I said, to soothe her, 'in being apprenticed, and I have asked these questions only for my own information. In humouring my mistake, Miss Havisham, you punished your self-seeking relations?'

'I did. Why, they would have it so! So would you. What has been my history, that I should be at the pains of entreating either them, or you, not to have it so! You made your own snares. *I* never made them.'

Waiting until she was quiet again, I went on.

'I have been thrown among one family of your relations, Miss Havisham, and have been constantly among them since I went to London. I know them to have been as honestly under my delusion as I myself. And I should be false and base if I did not tell you that you deeply wrong both Mr Matthew Pocket and his son Herbert, if you suppose them to be otherwise than generous, upright, open, and incapable of anything designing or mean.'

'What do you want for them?' she asked.

'I am not so cunning, you see,' I said, in answer, conscious that I reddened a little, 'as that I could hide from you, even if I desired, that I do want something. Miss Havisham, if you would spare the money to do my friend Herbert a lasting service in life, but which from the nature of the case must be done without his knowledge, I could show you how.'

'Why must it be done without his knowledge?' she asked.

'Because,' said I, 'I began the service myself, more than two years ago, without his knowledge, and I don't want to be betrayed. Why I fail in my ability to finish it, I cannot explain. It is a part of the secret which is another person's and not mine.'

She gradually withdrew her eyes from me, and turned them on the fire. After watching it for a long time, she looked towards me again — at first, vacantly — then, with a gradually concentrating attention. When Miss Havisham had fixed her attention on me, she said, speaking as if there had been no lapse in our dialogue:

'What else?'

'Estella,' said I, turning to her now, and trying to command my trembling voice, 'you know that I have loved you long and dearly.'

She raised her eyes to my face, on being thus addressed, and her fingers plied their work, and she looked at me with an unmoved countenance.

'I know, I have no hope that I shall ever call you mine, Estella. I am ignorant what may become of me very soon, how poor I may be, or where I may go. Still, I love you. I have loved you ever since I first saw you in this house.'

Looking at me perfectly unmoved and with her fingers busy, she shook her head.

'It would have been cruel in Miss Havisham, horribly cruel, to practise on the susceptibility of a poor boy, and to torture me through all these years with a vain hope and an idle pursuit, if she had reflected on the gravity of what she did. But I think she did not. I think that in the endurance of her own trial, she forgot mine, Estella.'

I saw Miss Havisham put her hand to her heart and hold it there, as she sat looking by turns at Estella and at me.

'When you say you love me,' said Estella, very calmly, 'I know what you mean, as a form of words; but nothing more. You address nothing in my breast, you touch nothing there. I have tried to warn you of this; now, have I not?'

I said in a miserable manner, 'Yes.'

'Yes. But you would not be warned, for you thought I did not mean it.'

'I thought and hoped you could not mean it. Surely it is not in Nature.'

'It is in *my* nature,' she returned. 'I make a great difference between you and all other people when I say so much. I can do no more.'

'Is it not true,' said I, 'that Bentley Drummle is in town here, and pursuing you?'

'It is quite true,' she replied, referring to him with the indifference of utter contempt.

'That you encourage him, and ride out with him, and that he dines with you this very day?'

She seemed a little surprised that I should know it, but again replied, 'Quite true.'

'You cannot love him, Estella!'

She looked toward Miss Havisham, and considered for moment with her work in her hands. Then she said, 'Why not tell you the truth? I am going to be married to him.'

I dropped my face into my hands, but was able to control myself better than I could have expected, considering what agony it gave me to hear her say those words. When I raised my face again, there was such a ghastly look upon Miss Havisham's, that it impressed me, even in my passionate hurry and grief.

'Estella, dearest dearest Estella, do not let Miss Havisham lead you into this fatal step. Miss Havisham gives you to him, as the greatest slight and injury that could be done to the many far better men who admire you, and to the few who truly love you. Among those few, there may be one who loves you even as dearly, as I. Take him, and I can bear it better, for your sake!'

My earnestness awoke a wonder in her that seemed as if it would have been touched with compassion, if she could have rendered me at all intelligible to her own mind.

'I am going,' she said again, in a gentler voice,'to be married to him. Why do you injuriously introduce the name of my mother by adoption? It is my own act.'

'Your own act, Estella, to fling yourself away upon a brute?'

'On whom should I fling myself away?' she retorted, with a smile. 'Should I fling myself away upon the man who would the soonest feel that I took nothing to him? I shall do well enough, and so will my husband.'

'O Estella!' I answered, as my bitter tears fell fast, do what I would to restrain them; 'even if I remained in England, how could I see you Drummle's wife?'

'You will get me out of your thoughts in a week.'

'Out of my thoughts! You are part of my existence, part of myself. You have been in every line I have ever read, since I first came here, the rough common boy whose poor heart you wounded even then. Estella, to the last hour of my life, you cannot choose but remain part of my character, but, in this separation I associate you only with the good, and I will faithfully hold you to that always, for you must have done me far more good than harm, let me feel now what sharp distress I may. O God bless you, God forgive you!'

In what ecstasy of unhappiness I got these broken words out of myself, I don't know. I held her hand to my lips some lingering moments, and so I left her. But ever afterwards, I remembered – and soon afterwards with stronger reason – that while Estella looked at me merely with incredulous wonder, the spectral figure of Miss Havisham, her hand still covering her heart, seemed all resolved into a ghastly stare of pity and remorse.

So much was done and gone, that when I went out at the gate, the light of the day seemed of a darker colour than when I went in. For a while, I hid myself among some lanes and by-paths, and then struck off to walk all the way to London.

It was past midnight when I crossed London Bridge. As it seldom happened that I came in that Whitefriars gate after the Temple was closed, and as I was very muddy and weary, I did not take it ill that the night-porter examined me with much attention as he held the gate a little way open for me to pass in. To help his memory I mentioned my name.

'I was not quite sure, sir, but I thought so. Here's a note, sir. The messenger that brought it, said would you be so good as read it by my lantern?'

Much surprised by the request, I took the note. It was directed to Philip Pip, Esquire. I opened it, the watchman holding up his light, and read inside, in Wemmick's writing: DON'T GO HOME.

45

Turning from the Temple gate as soon as I had read the warning, I made the best of my way to Fleet-street, and there got a late hackney chariot and drove to the Hummums in Covent Garden. In those times a bed was always to be got there at any hour of the night, and the chamberlain lighted the candle next in order on his shelf, and showed me straight into the bedroom next in order on his list.

As I had asked for a night-light, the chamberlain had brought me in, before he left me, the good old constitutional rush-light of those virtuous days – which was placed in solitary confinement at the bottom of a high tin tower, perforated with round holes that made a staringly wide-awake pattern on the walls. When I had got into bed, and lay there footsore, weary, and wretched, I found that I could no more close my own eyes than I could close the eyes of this foolish Argus.

What a doleful night! How anxious, how dismal, how long! When I had lain awake a little while, those extraordinary voices with which silence teems, began to make themselves audible. The closet whispered, the fireplace sighed, the little washing-stand ticked. At about the same time, the eyes on the wall acquired a new expression, and in every one of those staring rounds I saw written, DON'T GO HOME.

Whatever night-fancies and night-noises crowded on me, they never warded off this DON'T GO HOME. Even when I thought of Estella, and how we had parted that day for ever – even then I was pursuing, here and there and everywhere the caution Don't go home. When at last I dozed, in sheer exhaustion of mind and body, it became a vast shadowy verb which I had to conjugate. Do not thou go home, let him not go home, let us not go home, let not them go home until I felt that I was going distracted, and rolled over on the pillow, and looked at the staring rounds upon the wall again.

I had left directions that I was to be called at seven; for it was plain that I must see Wemmick before seeing any one else, and equally plain that this was a case in which his Walworth sentiments only, could be taken.

The Castle battlements arose upon my view at eight o'clock. I crossed the drawbridge, and so came without announcement into the presence of Wemmick as he was making tea for himself and the Aged. An open door afforded a perspective view of the Aged in bed.

'Halloa, My Pip!' said Wemmick. 'You did come home then?'

'Yes,' I returned; 'but I didn't go home.'

'That's all right,' said he, rubbing his hands. 'I left a note for you at each of the Temple gates, on the chance. Which gate did you come to?'

I told him.

'I'll go round to the others in the course of the day and destroy the notes,' said Wemmick; 'it's a good rule never to leave documentary evidence if you can help it, because you don't know when it may be put in.'

I thanked him for his friendship and caution, and our discourse proceeded in a low tone, while I toasted the Aged's sausage and he buttered the crumb of the Aged's roll.

'I accidentally heard, yesterday morning,' said Wemmick, 'that a certain person not altogether of uncolonial pursuits, and not unpossessed of portable property – I don't know who it may really be – we won't name this person –'

'Not necessary,' said I.

'– had made some little stir in a certain part of the world where a good many people go, not always in gratification of their own inclinations, and not quite irrespective of the government expense by disappearing from such place, and being no more heard of thereabouts. I also heard that you at your chambers in Garden-court, Temple, had been watched, and might be watched again.'

'By whom?' said I.

'I wouldn't go into that,' said Wemmick, evasively, 'it might clash with official responsibilities. I heard it, as I have in my time heard other curious things in the same place. I don't tell it you on information received. I heard it.'

He set forth the Aged's breakfast neatly on a little tray and went into the Aged's room with a clean white cloth, and tied the same under the old gentleman's chin, and propped him up. Then, he placed his breakfast before him with great care, and said, 'All right, ain't you, Aged P.?' To which the cheerful Aged replied, 'All right, John, my boy, all right!'

'This watching of me at my chambers,' I said to Wemmick when he came back, 'is inseparable from the person to whom you have adverted; is it?'

Wemmick looked very serious. 'I couldn't undertake to say that, of my own knowledge. But it either is, or it will be, or it's in great danger of being.'

As I saw that he was restrained by fealty to Little Britain from saying as much as he could, and as I knew with thankfulness to him how far out of his way he went to say what he did, I could not press him. But I told him that I would like to ask him a question. He paused in his breakfast, and crossing his arms, and pinching his shirt-sleeves he nodded to me once, to put my question.

'You have heard of a man of bad character, whose true name is Compeyson?'

He answered with one other nod.

'Is he living?'

One other nod.

'Is he in London?'

He gave me one last nod, and went on with his breakfast.

'Now,' said Wemmick, 'questioning being over;' which he emphasized and repeated for my guidance; 'I come to what I did, after hearing what I heard. I went to Garden-court to find you; not finding you, I went to Clarriker's to find Mr Herbert.'

'And him you found?' said I, with great anxiety.

'And him I found. Without mentioning any names or going into any details, I gave him to understand that if he was aware of anybody – Tom, Jack, or Richard – being about the chambers, or about the immediate neighbourhood, he had better get Tom, Jack, or Richard, out of the way while you were out of the way.'

'He would be greatly puzzled what to do?'

'He *was* puzzled what to do; not the less, because I gave him my opinion that it was not safe to try to get Tom, Jack, or Richard, too far out of the way at present. Mr Pip, I'll tell you something. Don't break cover too soon. Lie close. Wait till things slacken, before you try the open, even for foreign air.'

I thanked him for his valuable advice, and asked him what Herbert had done?'

'Mr Herbert,' said Wemmick, 'struck out a plan. He mentioned to me as a secret, that he is courting a young lady who has, as no doubt you are aware, a bedridden Pa. Which Pa, having been in the Purser line of life, lies a-bed in a bow-window where he can see the ships sail up and down the river. The house being by the river-side, down the Pool there between Limehouse and Greenwich, and being kept, it seems, by a very respectable widow who has a furnished upper floor to let, Mr Herbert put it to me, what did I think of that as a temporary tenement for Tom, Jack, or Richard? Now, I thought very well of it, for three reasons I'll give you. That is to say. Firstly. It's altogether out of all your beats. Secondly. Without going near it yourself, you could always hear of the safety of Tom, Jack, or Richard, through Mr Herbert. Thirdly. After a while and when it might be prudent, if you should want to slip Tom, Jack, or Richard, on board a foreign packet-boat, there he is – ready.'

Much comforted by these considerations, I thanked Wemmick again and again, and begged him to proceed.

'Well, sir! Mr Herbert threw himself into the business with a will, and by nine o'clock last night he housed Tom, Jack, or Richard quite successfully. Now, another great advantage of all this, is, that it was done without you, and when you must be known to be ever so many miles off and quite otherwise engaged. This diverts suspicion and confuses it; and for the same reason I recommended that even if you came back last night, you should not go home. It brings in more confusion, and you want confusion.'

Wemmick, having finished his breakfast, here looked at his watch, and began to get his coat on.

'And now, Mr Pip,' said he, with his hands still in the sleeves, 'I have probably done the most I can do; but if I can ever do more from a Walworth point of view, I shall be glad to do it. Here's the address. There can be no harm in your going here tonight and seeing for yourself that all is well with Tom, Jack, or Richard, before you go home. He laid his hands upon my shoulders, and added in a solemn whisper: 'Avail yourself of this evening to lay hold of his portable property. You don't know what may happen to him. Don't let anything happen to the portable property.'

Quite despairing of making my mind clear to Wemmick on this point, I forbore to try.

'Time's up,' said Wemmick, 'and I must be off. If you had nothing more pressing to do than to keep here till dark, that's what I should advise. You look very much worried, and it would do you good to have a perfectly quiet day with the Aged – he'll be up presently. Good-bye, Aged Parent!' in a cheery shout.

I soon fell asleep before Wemmick's fire, and the Aged and I enjoyed one another's society by falling asleep before it more or less all day. When it was quite dark, I left the Aged preparing the fire for toast; and I inferred from the number of teacups, as well as from

his glances at the two little doors in the wall, that Miss
Skiffins was expected.

46

Eight o'clock had struck before I got into the air that
was scented, not disagreeably, by the chips and shav-
ings of the long-shore boat-builders, and mast oar and
block makers. I found that the spot I wanted was not
where I had supposed it to be, and was anything but
easy to find. It was called Mill Pond Bank, Chinks's
Basin; and I had no other guide to Chinks's Basin than
the Old Green Copper Rope-Walk. After several times
falling short of my destination and as often over-shoot-
ing it, I came unexpectedly round a corner, upon Mill
Pond Bank.

Selecting from the few queer houses upon Mill
Pond Bank, a house with a wooden front and three
stories of bow-window, I looked at the plate upon the
door, and read there, Mrs Whimple. That being the
name I wanted, I knocked, and an elderly woman of a
pleasant and thriving appearance responded. She was
immediately deposed, however, by Herbert, who silently led me into the parlour and shut the door.

'All is well, Handel,' he said. 'My dear girl is with
her father; and if you'll wait till she comes down, I'll
make you known to her, and then we'll go upstairs. –
That's her father.'

I had become aware of an alarming growling overhead,
and had probably expressed the fact in my countenance.

'I am afraid he is a sad old rascal,' said Herbert, smiling, 'but I have never seen him. Don't you smell rum? He is always at it.'

'At rum?' said I.

'Yes,' returned Herbert.

'He persists, too, in keeping all the provisions upstairs in his room, and serving them out. His room must be like a chandler's shop.'

While he thus spoke, the growling noise became a prolonged roar, and then died away.

'To have Provis for an upper lodger is quite a godsend to Mrs Whimple,' said Herbert, 'for of course people in general won't stand that noise. A curious place, Handel; isn't it?'

It was a curious place, indeed; but remarkably well kept and clean.

'Mrs Whimple,' said Herbert, when I told him so, 'is the best of housewives, and I really do not know what my Clara would do without her motherly help. For, Clara has no mother of her own, Handel, and no relation in the world but old Gruffandgrim - that's my name for him. His name is Mr Barley.'

As we were thus conversing in a low tone while Old Barley's sustained growl vibrated in the beam that crossed the ceiling, the room door opened, and a very pretty slight dark-eyed girl of twenty or so, came in with a basket in her hand: whom Herbert tenderly relieved of the basket, and presented blushing, as 'Clara'. She really was a most charming girl, and might have passed for a captive fairy, whom that truculent Ogre, Old Barley, had pressed into his service.

There was something so gentle in Clara, so much

needing protection on Mill Pond Bank, by Chinks's Basin, and the Old Green Copper Rope-Walk, with Old Barley growling in the beam – that I would not have undone the engagement between her and Herbert, for all the money in the pocket-book I had never opened.

I was looking at her with pleasure and admiration, when suddenly the growl swelled into a roar again, and a frightful bumping noise was heard above, as if a giant with a wooden leg were trying to bore it through the ceiling to come at us. Upon this Clara said to Herbert, 'Papa wants me, darling!' and ran away.

She returned soon afterwards, and Herbert accompanied me upstairs to see our charge. As we passed Mr Barley's door, he was heard hoarsely muttering within, in a strain that rose and fell like wind, the following Refrain; in which I substitute good wishes for something quite the reverse.

'Ahoy! Bless your eyes, here's old Bill Barley. Here's old Bill Barley on the flat of his back, by the Lord. Lying on the flat of his back, like a drifting old dead flounder, here's your old Bill Barley, bless your eyes. Ahoy! Bless you.'

In his two cabin rooms at the top of the house, which were fresh and airy, I found Provis comfortably settled. He expressed no alarm, and seemed to feel none that was worth mentioning; but it struck me that he was softened – indefinably, for I could not have said how, and could never afterwards recall how when I tried; but certainly. When Herbert and I sat down with him by his fire, I asked him first of all whether he relied on Wemmick's judgement and sources of information?

'Ay, ay, dear boy!' he answered, with a grave nod, 'Jaggers knows.'

'Then, I have talked with Wemmick,' said I, 'and have come to tell you what caution he gave me and what advice.'

This I did accurately, and I told him how Wemmick had heard, in Newgate prison, that he was under some suspicion, and that my chambers had been watched; how Wemmick had recommended his keeping close for a time, and my keeping away from him; and what Wemmick had said about getting him abroad. I added, that of course, when the time came, I should go with him, or should follow close upon him, as might be safest in Wemmick's judgement. What was to follow that, I did not touch upon; neither indeed was I at all clear or comfortable about it in my own mind, now that I saw him in that softer condition, and in declared peril for my sake. As to altering my way of living, by enlarging my expenses, I put it to him whether in our present unsettled and difficult circumstances, it would not be simply ridiculous, if it were no worse?

He could not deny this, and indeed was very reasonable throughout. His coming back was a venture, he said. He would do nothing to make it a desperate venture, and he had very little fear of his safety with such good help.

Herbert, who had been looking at the fire and pondering, here said that something had come into his thoughts arising out of Wemmick's suggestion, which it might be worth while to pursue. 'We are both good watermen, Handel, and could take him down the river ourselves when the right time comes. Don't you think it might be a good thing if you began at once to keep a boat at the Temple stairs, and were in the habit of rowing up and down the river? Do it twenty or fifty times, and there is nothing special in your doing it the twenty-first or fifty-first.'

I liked this scheme, and Provis was quite elated by it. We agreed that it should be carried into execution, and that Provis should never recognize us if we came below Bridge and rowed past Mill Pond Bank. But, we further agreed that he should pull down the blind in that part of his window which gave upon the east, when ever he saw us and all was right.

Our conference being now ended, and everything arranged, I rose to go; remarking to Herbert that he and I had better not go home together, and that I would take half an hour's start of him. 'I don't like to leave you here,' I said to Provis, 'though I cannot doubt your being safer here than near me. Good-bye!'

We thought it best that he should stay in his own rooms, and we left him on the landing outside his door, holding a light over the stair-rail to light us down stairs. Looking back at him, I thought of the first night of his return when our positions were re-versed, and when I little supposed my heart could ever be as heavy and anxious at parting from him as it was now.

When I had taken leave of the pretty gentle dark-eyed girl, and of the motherly woman who had not outlived her honest sympathy with a little affair of true love, I felt as if the Old Green Copper Rope-Walk had grown quite a different place.

I walked past the fountain twice or thrice before I descended the steps that were between me and my rooms, but I was quite alone. Herbert coming to my bedside when he came in, made the same report. Opening one of the windows after that, he looked out into the moonlight, and told me that the pavement was as solemnly empty as the pavement of any Cathedral at that same hour.

Next day, I set myself to get the boat. It was soon done, and the boat was brought round to the Temple stairs, and lay where I could reach her within a minute or two. Then, I began to go out as for training and practice: sometimes alone, sometimes with Herbert. The first time I passed Mill Pond Bank, Herbert and I were pulling a pair of oars; and, both in going and returning, we saw the blind towards the east come down. Herbert was rarely there less frequently than three times in a week, and he never brought me a single word of intelligence that was at all alarming. Herbert had sometimes said to me that he found it pleasant to stand at one of our windows after dark, when the tide was running down, and to think that it was flowing, with everything it bore, towards Clara. But I thought with dread that it was flowing towards Magwitch, and that any black mark on its surface might be his pursuers, going swiftly, silently, and surely, to take him.

47

Some weeks passed without bringing any change. We waited for Wemmick, and he made no sign.

My worldly affairs began to wear a gloomy

appearance, and I was pressed for money by more than one creditor. But I had quite determined that it would be a heartless fraud to take more money from my patron in the existing state of my uncertain thoughts and plans. Therefore, I had sent him the unopened pocket-book by Herbert, to hold in his own keeping, and I felt a kind of satisfaction in not having profited by his generosity since his revelation of himself.

It was an unhappy life that I lived, and its one dominant anxiety never disappeared from my view. Still, no new cause for fear arose. Condemned to inaction and a state of constant restlessness and suspense, I rowed about in my boat, and waited, waited, waited, as I best could.

One afternoon, late in the month of February, I came ashore at the wharf at dusk. I had pulled down as far as Greenwich with the ebb tide, and had turned with the tide. Both in going and returning, I had seen the signal in his window, All well.

As it was a raw evening and I was cold, I thought I would comfort myself with dinner at once; and as I had hours of dejection and solitude before me if I went home to the Temple, I thought I would afterwards go to the play. The theatre where Mr Wopsle had achieved his questionable triumph, was in that waterside neighbourhood, and to that theatre I resolved to go.

I dined at a chop-house and wore out the time in dozing over crumbs, staring at gas, and baking in a hot blast of dinners. By-and-by, I roused myself and went to the play.

There, I found a virtuous boatswain in his Majesty's service who knocked all the little men's hats over their eyes, though he was very generous and brave, and who wouldn't hear of anybody's paying taxes, though he was very patriotic. He had a bag of money in his pocket, and on that property married a young person in bed-furniture, with great rejoicings. A certain dark-complexioned Swab, however, whose heart was openly stated to be as black as his figure-head, proposed to two other Swabs to get all mankind into difficulties; which was so effectually done that it took half the evening to set things right. This led to Mr Wopsle's (who had never been heard of before) coming in with a star and garter on, as a plenipotentiary of great power direct from the Admiralty, to say that the Swabs were all to go to prison on the spot, and that he had brought the boatswain down the Union Jack, as a slight acknowledgement of his public services. The boatswain, respectfully dried his eyes on the Jack, and then cheering up and addressing Mr Wopsle as Your Honour, solicited permission to take him by the fin. Mr Wopsle conceding his fin with a gracious dignity, was immediately shoved into a dusty corner while everybody danced a hornpipe, and from that corner, surveying the public with a discontented eye, became aware of me. And I observed with great surprise, that he devoted himself to staring in my direction as if he were lost in amazement.

There was something so remarkable in the increasing glare of Mr Wopsle's eye, that I could not make it out.

I was still thinking of it when I came out of the theatre an hour afterwards, and found him waiting for me near the door.

'How do you do?' said I, shaking hands with him as we turned down the street together. 'I saw that you saw me.'

'Saw you, Mr Pip!' he returned. 'Yes, of course I saw you. But who else was there?'

'Who else?'

'It is the strangest thing,' said Mr Wopsle, drifting into his lost look again; 'and yet I could swear to him.'

Becoming alarmed, I entreated Mr Wopsle to explain in his meaning.

'Whether I should have noticed him at first but for your being there,' said Mr Wopsle, going on in the same lost way, 'I can't be positive; yet I think I should.'

Involuntarily I looked round me, as I was accustomed to look round me when I went home; for, these mysterious words gave me a chill.

'I had a ridiculous fancy that he must be with you, Mr Pip, till I saw that you were quite unconscious of him, sitting behind you there, like a ghost.'

I was resolved not to speak yet, for it was quite consistent with his words that he might be set on to induce me to connect these references with Provis. Of course, I was perfectly sure and safe that Provis had not been there.

'I dare say you wonder at me, Mr Pip; indeed I see you do. But it is so very strange! You'll hardly believe what I am going to tell you.'

'Indeed?' said I.

'No, indeed. Mr Pip, you remember in old times a certain Christmas Day, when you were quite a child, and I dined at Gargery's, and some soldiers came to the door to get a pair of handcuffs mended?'

'I remember it very well.'

'And you remember that there was a chase after two convicts, and that we joined in it, and that Gargery took you on his back, and that I took the lead and you kept up with me as well as you could? And you remember that we came up with the two in a ditch, and that there was a scuffle between them, and that one of them had been severely handled and much mauled about the face, by the other?'

'I see it all before me.'

'Then, Mr Pip, one of those two prisoners sat behind you tonight. I saw him over your shoulder.'

'Steady!' I thought. I asked him then, 'Which of the two do you suppose you saw?'

'The one who had been mauled,' he answered readily, 'and I'll swear I saw him! The more I think of him, the more certain I am of him.'

'This is very curious!' said I, with the best assumption I could put on, of its being nothing more to me. 'Very curious indeed!'

I cannot exaggerate the enhanced disquiet into which this conversation threw me, or the special and peculiar terror I felt at Compeyson's having been behind me 'like a ghost'. For, if he had ever been out of my thoughts for a few moments together since the hiding had begun, it was in those very moments when he was closest to me.

I put such questions to Mr Wopsle as, When did the man come in? He could not tell me that; he saw me, and over my shoulder he saw the man. He had from the first vaguely associated him with me, and known him as somehow belonging to me in the old village time. How was he dressed? He thought, in black. Was his face at all disfigured? No, he believed not.

When Mr Wopsle had imparted to me all that he could recall or I extract, and when I had treated him to a little appropriate refreshment after the fatigues of the evening, we parted. It was between twelve and one o'clock when I reached the Temple, and the gates were shut. No one was near me when I went in and went home.

Herbert had come in, and we held a very serious council by the fire. But there was nothing to be done, saving to communicate to Wemmick what I had that night found out, and to remind him that we waited for his hint. I made this communication by letter. I wrote it before I went to bed, and went out and posted it; and again no one was near me. Herbert and I agreed that we could do nothing else but be very cautious. I for my part never went near Chinks's Basin, except when I rowed by, and then I only looked at Mill Pond Bank as I looked at anything else.

48

The second of the two meetings referred to in the last chapter, occurred about a week after the first. I was strolling along Cheapside, when a large hand was laid upon my shoulder, by some one overtaking me. It was Mr Jaggers's hand, and he passed it through my arm.

'As we are going in the same direction, Pip, we may walk together. Where are you bound for?'

'For the Temple, I think,' said I.

'Don't you know?' said Mr Jaggers.

'Well,' I returned, glad for once to get the better of him in cross-examination, 'I do *not* know, for I have not made up my mind.'

'You are going to dine?' said Mr Jaggers. 'You don't mind admitting that, I suppose?'

'No,' I returned, 'I don't mind admitting that.'

'Then,' said Mr Jaggers, 'come and dine with me.'

I was going to excuse myself, when he added, 'Wemmick's coming.' So, I changed my excuse into an acceptance.

At the office in Little Britain there was the usual letter-writing, hand-washing, candle-snuffing, and safe-locking, that closed the business of the day. As I stood idle by Mr Jaggers's fire, its rising and falling flame made the two casts on the shelf look as if they were playing a diabolical game at bo-peep with me.

We went to Gerrard-street, all three together, in a hackney-coach: and as soon as we got there, dinner was served. Although I should not have thought of making, in that place, the most distant reference by so much as a look to Wemmick's Walworth sentiments, yet I should have had no objection to catching his eye now and then in a friendly way. But it was not to be done. He turned his eyes on Mr Jaggers whenever he raised them from the table, and was as dry and distant to me as if there were twin Wemmicks and this was the wrong one.

'Did you send that note of Miss Havisham's to Mr Pip, Wemmick?' Mr Jaggers asked, soon after we began dinner.

'No, sir,' returned Wemmick; 'it was going by post, when you brought Mr Pip into the office. Here it is.' He handed it to his principal, instead of to me.

'It's a note of two lines, Pip,' said Mr Jaggers, handing it on, 'sent up to me by Miss Havisham, on account of her not being sure of your address. She tells me that she wants to see you on a little matter of business you mentioned to her. You'll go down?'

'Yes,' said I, casting my eyes over the note, which was exactly in those terms.

'If Mr Pip has the intention of going at once,' said Wemmick to Mr Jaggers, 'he needn't write an answer, you know.'

Receiving this as an intimation that it was best not to delay, I settled that I would go tomorrow, and said so.

'So, Pip! Our friend the Spider,' said Mr Jaggers, 'has played his cards. He has won the pool.'

It was as much as I could do to assent.

'Hah! He is a promising fellow – in his way – but he may not have it all his own way. The stronger will win in the end, but the stronger has to be found out first. If he should turn to, and beat her –'

'Surely,' I interrupted, with a burning face and heart, 'you do not seriously think that he is scoundrel enough for that, Mr Jaggers?'

'I didn't say so, Pip. I am putting a case. If he should turn to and beat her, he may possibly get the strength on his side; if it should be a question of intellect, he certainly will not. It's a toss-up between two results.'

'May I ask what they are?'

'A fellow like our friend the Spider,' answered Mr Jaggers, 'either beats, or cringes. Ask Wemmick *his* opinion.'

'Either beats or cringes,' said Wemmick, not at all addressing himself to me.

'So, here's to Mrs Bentley Drummle,' said Mr Jaggers, taking a decanter of choicer wine from his dumbwaiter, and filling for each of us and for himself, 'and may the question of supremacy be settled to the lady's satisfaction! Now, Molly, Molly, Molly, Molly, how slow you are today!'

She was at his elbow when he addressed her, putting a dish upon the table. As she withdrew her hands from it, she fell back a step or two, nervously muttering some excuse. And a certain action of her fingers as she spoke arrested my attention.

'What's the matter?' said Mr Jaggers.

'Nothing. Only the subject we were speaking of,' said I, 'was rather painful to me.'

The action of her fingers was like the action of knitting. She stood looking at her master, not under-standing whether she was free to go, or whether he had more to say to her and would call her back if she did go. Her look was very intent. Surely, I had seen exactly such eyes and such hands, on a memorable occasion very lately!

He dismissed her, and she glided out of the room. But she remained before me, as plainly as if she were still there. I looked at those hands, I looked at those eyes, I looked at that flowing hair; and I compared them with other hands, other eyes, other hair, that I knew of, and with what those might be after twenty years of a brutal husband and a stormy life. I looked again at those hands and eyes of the housekeeper, and thought of the inexplicable feeling that had come over me when I last walked – not alone – in the ruined garden, and through the deserted brewery. I thought how the same feeling had come back when I saw a face looking at me, and a hand waving to me, from a stage-coach window; and how it had come back again and had flashed about me like Lightning, when I had passed in a carriage – not alone – through a sudden glare of light in a dark street. And I felt absolutely certain that this woman was Estella's mother.

Mr Jaggers had seen me with Estella, and was not likely to have missed the sentiments I had been at no pains to conceal. He nodded when I said the subject was painful to me, clapped me on the back, put round the wine again, and went on with his dinner.

Only twice more, did the housekeeper reappear, and then her stay in the room was very short, and Mr Jaggers was sharp with her. But her hands were Estella's hands, and her eyes were Estella's eyes, and if she had re-appeared a hundred times I could have been neither more sure nor less sure that my conviction was the truth.

We took our leave early, and Wemmick and I left together. Even when we were groping among Mr Jaggers's stock of boots for our hats, I felt that the right twin was on his way back; and we had not gone half a dozen yards down Gerrard-street in the Walworth direction before I found that I was walking arm-in-arm with the right twin, and that the wrong twin had evaporated into the evening air.

I asked him if he had ever seen Miss Havisham's adopted daughter, Mrs Bentley Drummle? He said no. To avoid being too abrupt, I then spoke of the Aged, and of Miss Skiffins. He looked rather sly when I mentioned Miss Skiffins, and stopped in the street to blow his nose, with a roll of the head and a flourish not quite free from latent boastfulness.

'Wemmick,' said I, 'do you remember telling me before I first went to Mr Jaggers's private house, to notice that housekeeper?'

'Did I?' he replied. 'Ah, I dare say I did.'

'A wild beast tamed, you called her.'

'And what do *you* call her?'

'The same. How did Mr Jaggers tame her, Wemmick?'

'That's his secret. She has been with him many a long year.'

'I wish you would tell me her story. I feel a particular interest in being acquainted with it.'

'Well!' Wemmick replied, 'I don't know her story – that is, I don't know all of it. But what I do know, I'll tell you.'

'Of course.'

'A score or so of years ago, that woman was tried at the Old Bailey for murder, and was acquitted. Mr Jaggers was for her and he worked it to general admiration; in fact, it may almost be said to have made him. The murdered person was a woman; a woman, a very much larger, and very much stronger. It was a case of jealousy. They both led tramping lives, and this woman in Gerrard-street here had been married very young, to a tramping man, and was a perfect fury in point of jealousy. The murdered woman was found dead in a barn near Hounslow Heath. There had been a violent struggle, perhaps a fight. She was bruised and scratched and torn, and had been held by the throat at last and choked. Now, there was no reasonable evidence to implicate any person but this woman, and, on the improbabilities of her having been able to do it, Mr Jaggers principally rested his case.

'Well, sir!' Wemmick went on; 'it happened that this woman was so very artfully dressed from the time of her apprehension, that she looked much slighter than she really was.' She had only a bruise or two about her but the backs of her hands were lacerated, and the question was, was it with finger-nails? Now, Mr Jaggers showed that she had struggled through a great lot of brambles which were not as high as her face; but which she could not have got through and kept her hands out of; and bits of those brambles were actually found in her skin and put in evidence. But the boldest point he made, was this. It was attempted to be set up in proof of her jealousy, that she was under strong suspicion of having, at about the time of the murder, frantically destroyed her child by this man – some three years old – to revenge herself upon him. Mr Jaggers worked that, in this way. "We say these are not marks of finger-nails, but marks of brambles, and we show you the brambles. You say they are marks of finger-nails, and you set up the hypothesis that she destroyed her child. You must accept all consequences of that hypothesis. For anything we know, she may have destroyed her child, and the child in clinging to her may have scratched her hands. What then? You are not trying her for the murder of her child; why don't you? As to this case, if you *will* have scratches, we say that, for anything we know, you may have accounted for them, assuming for the sake of argument that you have not invented them?" To sum up, sir,' said Wemmick, 'Mr Jaggers was altogether too many for the Jury, and they gave in.'

'Has she been in his service ever since?'

'Yes; but not only that,' said Wemmick. 'She went into his service immediately after her acquittal, tamed as she is now.'

'Do you remember the sex of the child?'

'Said to have been a girl.'

'You have nothing more to say to me tonight?'

'Nothing. I got your letter and destroyed it. Nothing.'

We exchanged a cordial good-night, and I went home, with new matter for my thoughts, though with no relief from the old.

49

Putting Miss Havisham's note in my pocket, that it might serve as my credentials for so soon reappearing at Satis House, I went down again by the coach next day.

The best light of the day was gone when I passed along the quiet echoing courts behind the High-street. The cathedral chimes had at once a sadder and a more remote sound to me, as I hurried on avoiding observation, than they had ever had before; so, the swell of the old organ was borne to my ears like funeral music; and the rooks, as they hovered about the grey tower and swung in the bare high trees of the priory-garden, seemed to call to me that the place was changed, and that Estella was gone out of it for ever.

An elderly woman opened the gate. The lighted candle stood in the dark passage within, as of old, and I took it up and ascended the staircase alone. Miss Havisham was in the larger room across the landing. Looking in at the door, after knocking in vain, I saw her sitting on the hearth in a ragged chair, close before, and lost in the contemplation of, the ashy fire.

Doing as I had often done, I went in, and stood, touching the old chimney-piece, where she could see me when she raised her eyes. She stared, and said in a low voice, 'Is it real?'

'It is I, Pip. Mr Jaggers gave me your note yesterday, and I have lost no time.'

As I brought another of the ragged chairs to the hearth and sat down, I remarked a new expression on her face, as if she were afraid of me.

'I want,' she said, 'to pursue that subject you mentioned to me when you were last here, and to show you that I am not all stone. But perhaps you can never believe, now, that there is anything human in my heart?'

When I said some reassuring words, she stretched out her tremulous right hand, as though she was going to touch me; but she recalled it again before I understood the action, or knew how to receive it.

'You said, speaking for your friend, that you could tell me how to do something useful and good. Something that you would like done, is it not?'

I began explaining to her that secret history of the partnership. I had not got far into it, when I judged from her looks that she was thinking in a discursive way of me, rather than of what I said. It seemed to be so, for, when I stopped speaking, many moments passed before she showed that she was conscious of the fact.

'Do you break off,' she asked then, 'because you hate me too much to bear to speak to me?'

'No, no,' I answered, 'how can you think so, Miss Havisham! I stopped because I thought you were not following what I said.'

'Perhaps I was not,' she answered, putting a hand to her head. 'Begin again, and let me look at something else. Stay! Now tell me.'

She set her hand upon her stick, in the resolute way that sometimes was habitual to her, and looked at the fire with a strong expression of forcing herself to attend. I went on with my explanation, and told her how I had hoped to complete the transaction out of my means, but how in this I was disappointed.

'So!' said she, 'and how much money is wanting to complete the purchase?'

'Nine hundred pounds.'

'If I give you the money for this purpose, will you keep my secret as you have kept your own?'

'Quite as faithfully.'

'And your mind will be more at rest?'

'Much more at rest.'

'Are you very unhappy now?'

'I am far from happy, Miss Havisham; but I have other causes of disquiet than any you know of. They are the secrets I have mentioned.'

'Can I only serve you, Pip, by serving your friend? Regarding that as done, is there nothing I can do for you yourself?'

'Nothing. I thank you for the question. I thank you even more for the tone of the question. But, there is nothing.'

She took from her pocket a yellow set of ivory tablets, mounted in tarnished gold, and wrote upon them with a pencil in a case of tarnished gold that hung from her neck.

'You are still on friendly terms with Mr Jaggers?'

'Quite. I dined with him yesterday.'

'This is an authority to him to pay you that money, to lay out at your irresponsible discretion for your friend. I keep no money here; but if you would rather Mr Jaggers knew nothing of the matter, I will send it to you.'

'Thank you, Miss Havisham; I have not the least objection to receiving it from him.'

I took the tablets from her hand, and it trembled again, and it trembled more as she took off the chain to which the pencil was attached, and put it in mine. All this she did, without looking at me.

'My name is on the first leaf. If you can ever write under my name, "I forgive her", though ever so long after my broken heart is dust – pray do it!'

'O Miss Havisham,' said I, 'I can do it now. There have been sore mistakes; and my life has been a blind and thankless one; and I want forgiveness and direction far too much, to be bitter with you.'

She turned her face to me for the first time since she had averted it, and, to my amazement dropped on her knees at my feet.

To see her with her white hair and her worn face kneeling at my feet, gave me a shock through all my frame. I entreated her to rise, and got my arms about her to help her up; but she only pressed that hand of mine which was nearest to her grasp, and hung her head over it and wept.

'O!' she cried, despairingly. 'What have I done! What have I done!'

'If you mean, Miss Havisham, what have you done to injure me, let me answer. Very little. I should have loved her under any circumstances. – Is she married?'

'Yes.'

It was a needless question, for a new desolation in the desolate house had told me so.

'What have I done! What have I done!' She wrung her hands, and crushed her white hair, and returned to this cry over and over again. 'What have I done!'

I knew not how to answer, or how to comfort her. That she had done a grievous thing in taking an impressionable child to mould into the form that her wild resentment, spurned affection, and wounded pride, found vengeance in, I knew full well. But that, in shutting out the light of day, she had shut out infinitely more; that, in seclusion, she had secluded herself from a thousand natural and healing influences; that, her mind had grown diseased.

'Until you spoke to her the other day, and until I saw in you a looking-glass that showed me what I once felt myself, I did not know what I had done. What have I done! What have I done!'

'Miss Havisham,' I said, when her cry had died away, 'you may dismiss me from your mind and con- science. But Estella is a different case, and if you can ever undo any scrap of what you have done amiss in keeping a part of her right nature away from her, it will be better to do that, than to bemoan the past through a hundred years.'

'Yes, yes, I know it. But, Pip – my Dear! When she first came to me, I meant to save her from misery like my own. At first I meant no more. But as she grew, and promised to be very beautiful, I gradually did worse. I stole her heart away and put ice in its place.'

'Better,' I could not help saying, 'to have left her a natural heart, even to be bruised or broken.'

With that, Miss Havisham looked distractedly at me for a while, and then burst out again, What had she done!

'If you knew all my story,' she pleaded, 'you would have some compassion for me and a better understanding of me.'

'Miss Havisham,' I answered, as delicately as I could, 'I believe I may say that I do know your story, and have known it ever since I first left this neighbourhood.'

She was seated on the ground, with her arms on the ragged chair, and her head leaning on them. She looked full at me when I said this, and replied, 'Go on.'

'Whose child was Estella?'

She shook her head.

'You don't know?'

She shook her head again.

'But Mr Jaggers brought her here, or sent her here?'

'Brought her here.'

'Will you tell me how that came about?'

She answered in a low whisper and with caution: 'I had been shut up in these rooms a long time when I told him that I wanted a little girl to rear and love, and save from my fate. He told me that he would look about him for such an orphan child. One night he brought her here asleep, and I called her Estella.'

'Might I ask her age then?'

'Two or three. She herself knows nothing, but that she was left an orphan and I adopted her.'

So convinced I was of that woman's being her mother, that I wanted no evidence to establish the fact in my own mind.

What more could I hope to do by prolonging the

interview? I had succeeded on behalf of Herbert, Miss Havisham had told me all she knew of Estella, I had said and done what I could to ease her mind. No matter with what other words we parted.

Twilight was closing in when I went downstairs into the natural air. I called to the woman who had opened the gate when I entered, that I would walk round the place before leaving.

I made my way to the ruined garden. I went all round it; round by the corner where Herbert and I had fought our battle; round by the paths where Estella and I had walked. So cold, so lonely, so dreary all!

Taking the brewery on my way back, I raised the rusty latch of a little door at the garden end of it, and walked through. I was going out at the opposite door when I turned my head to look back. A childish association revived with wonderful force in the moment of the slight action, and I fancied that I saw Miss Havisham hanging to the beam. So strong was the impression, that I stood under the beam shuddering from head to foot before I knew it was a fancy – though to be sure I was there in an instant.

The mournfulness of the place and time, and the great terror of this illusion, caused me to feel an indescribable awe as I came out between the open wooden gates where I had once wrung my hair after Estella had wrung my heart. Passing on into the front court-yard, I hesitated whether to call the woman to let me out at the locked gate of which she had the key, or first to go upstairs and assure myself that Miss Havisham was as safe and well as I had left her. I took the latter course and went up.

I looked into the room where I had left her, and I

saw her seated in the ragged chair upon the hearth close to the fire, with her back towards me. In the moment when I was withdrawing my head to go quietly away, I saw a great flaming light spring up. In the same moment, I saw her running at me, shrieking, with a whirl of fire blazing all about her, and soaring at least as many feet above her head as she was high.

I had a double-caped great-coat on, and over my arm another thick coat. That I got them off, closed with her, threw her down, and got them over her; that I dragged the great cloth from the table for the same purpose, and with it dragged down the heap of rottenness in the midst, and all the ugly things that sheltered there; that we were on the ground struggling like desperate enemies, and that the closer I covered her, the more wildly she shrieked and tried to free herself, I knew nothing until I knew that we were on the floor by the great table, and that patches of tinder yet alight were floating in the smoky air, which, a moment ago, had been her faded bridal dress.

She was insensible, and I was afraid to have her moved, or even touched. Assistance was sent for and I held her until it came, as if I unreasonably fancied (I think I did) that if I let her go, the fire would break out again and consume her. When I got up, on the surgeon's coming to her with other aid, I was astonished to see that both my hands were burnt; for, I had no knowledge of it through the sense of feeling.

On examination it was pronounced that she had received serious hurts, but that they of themselves were far from hopeless; the danger lay mainly in the nervous shock. By the surgeon's directions, her bed was carried into that room and laid upon the great table: which happened to be well suited to the dressing of her injuries. When I saw her again, an hour afterwards, she lay indeed where I had seen her strike her stick, and had heard her say that she would lie one day.

Though every vestige of her dress was burnt, as they told me, she still had something of her old ghastly bridal appearance; for, they had covered her to the throat with white cotton-wool, and as she lay with a white sheet loosely overlying that, the phantom air of something that had been and was changed, was still upon her.

I found, on questioning the servants, that Estella was in Paris, and I got a promise from the surgeon that he would write to her by the next post. Miss Havisham's family I took upon myself; intending to communicate with Mr Matthew Pocket only, and leave him to do as he liked about informing the rest. This I did next day, through Herbert, as soon as I returned to town.

There was a stage, that evening, when she spoke collectedly of what had happened, though with a certain terrible vivacity. Towards midnight she began to wander in her speech, and after that it gradually set in that she said innumerable times in low solemn voice, 'What have I done!' And then, 'When she first came, I meant to save her from misery like mine.' And then, 'Take the pencil and write under my name, "I forgive her!"'

I decided in the course of the night that I would return by the early morning coach: walking on a mile or so, and being taken up clear of the town. At about six o'clock of the morning, therefore, I leaned over her and touched her lips with mine, just as they said, not stopping for being touched, 'Take the pencil and write under my name, "I forgive her".'

50

My left arm was a good deal burned to the elbow, and less severely, as high as the shoulder. My right hand was not so badly burnt but that I could move the fingers. I could only wear my coat like a cloak, loose over my shoulders and fastened at the neck. My hair had been caught by the fire, but not my head or face.

When Herbert had been down to Hammersmith and seen his father, he came back to me at our chambers, and devoted the day to attending on me.

At first, as I lay quiet on the sofa, I found it painfully difficult, I might say impossible, to get rid of the impression of the glare of the flames, their hurry and noise, and the fierce burning smell. If I dozed for a minute, I was awakened by Miss Havisham's cries, and by her running at me with all that height of fire above her head. This pain of the mind was much harder to strive against than any bodily pain I suffered; and Herbert, seeing that, did his utmost to hold my attention engaged.

My first question when I saw Herbert had been of course, whether all was well down the river? As he replied in the affirmative, with perfect confidence and cheerfulness, we did not resume the subject until the day was wearing away. But then, as Herbert changed the bandages, more by the light of the fire than by the outer light, he went back to it spontaneously.

'I sat with Provis last night, Handel, two good hours.'

'Where was Clara?'

'Dear little thing!' said Herbert. 'She was up and down with Gruffandgrim all the evening. He was perpetually pegging at the floor, the moment she left his sight. I doubt if he can hold out long though.'

'And then you will be married, Herbert?'

'How can I take care of the dear child otherwise? I was speaking of Provis. Do you know, Handel, he improves?'

'I said to you I thought he was softened when I last saw him.'

'So you did. And so he is. He was very communicative last night, and told me more of his life. You remember his breaking off here about some woman that he had had great trouble with. – Did I hurt you?'

I had started, but not under his touch. His words had given me a start.

'I had forgotten that, Herbert, but I remember it now you speak of it.'

'Well! He went into that part of his life, and a dark wild part it is. Shall I tell you? Or would it worry you just now?'

'Tell me by all means. Every word.'

'It seems,' said Herbert, that the woman was a young woman, and a jealous woman, and a revengeful woman; revengeful, Handel, to the last degree.'

'To what last degree?'

'Murder. – Does it strike too cold on that sensitive place?'

'I don't feel it. How did she murder? Whom did she murder?'

'Why, the deed may not have merited quite so terrible a name,' said Herbert, 'but, she was tried for it, and Mr Jaggers defended her, and the reputation of that defence first made his name known to Provis. It was another and a stronger woman who was the victim, and there had been a struggle – in a barn. Who began it, or how fair it was, or how unfair, may be doubtful; but how it ended, is certainly not doubtful, for the victim was found throttled.'

'Was the woman brought in guilty?'

'No; she was acquitted. – My poor Handel, I hurt you!'

'It is impossible to be gentler, Herbert. Yes? What else?'

'This acquitted young woman and Provis had a little child of whom Provis was exceedingly fond. On the evening of the very night when the object of her jealousy was strangled, the young woman presented herself before Provis for one moment, and swore that she would destroy the child, and he should never see it again; then, she vanished.'

'Did the woman keep her oath?'

'There comes the darkest part of Provis's life. She did.'

'That is, he says she did.'

'Why, of course, my dear boy,' returned Herbert, in a tone of surprise, and again bending forward to get a nearer look at me. 'He says it all. I have no other information.'

'No, to be sure.'

'Now, whether,' pursued Herbert, 'he had used the

child's mother ill, or whether he had used the child's mother well, Provis doesn't say; but, she had shared some four or five years of the wretched life he described to us at this fireside, and he seems to have felt pity for her, and forbearance towards her. Therefore, fearing he should be called upon to depose about this destroyed child, and so be the cause of her death, he hid himself out of the way and out of the trial, and was only vaguely talked of as a certain man called Abel, out of whom the jealousy arose. After the acquittal she disappeared, and thus he lost the child and the child's mother. That evil genius, Compeyson, knowing of his keeping out of the way at that time, and of his reasons for doing so, of course afterwards held the knowledge over his head as a means of keeping him poorer, and working him harder.'

'I want to know,' said I, 'and particularly, Herbert, whether he told you when this happened?'

'Particularly? Let me remember, then, what he said as to that. His expression was, "a round score o' year ago, and a'most directly after I took up wi' Compeyson." How old were you when you came upon him in the little churchyard?'

'I think in my seventh year.'

'Ay. It had happened some three or four years then, he said, and you brought into his mind the little girl so tragically lost, who would have been about your age.'

'Herbert,' said I, after a short silence, in a hurried way, 'can you see me best by the light of the window, or the light of the fire?'

'By the firelight,' answered Herbert, coming close again.

'Look at me.'

'I do look at you, my dear boy.'

'You are not afraid that I am in any fever, or that my head is much disordered by the accident of last night?'

'N-no, my dear boy,' said Herbert, after taking time to examine me. 'You are rather excited, but you are quite yourself.'

'I know I am quite myself. And the man we have in hiding down the river, is Estella's Father.'

51

When Herbert and I had held our momentous conversation, I was seized with a feverish conviction that I ought to hunt the matter down – that I ought not to let it rest, but that I ought to see Mr Jaggers, and come at the bare truth.

Early next morning we went out together, and at the corner of Giltspur-street by Smithfield, I left Herbert to go his way into the City, and took my way to Little Britain.

There were periodical occasions when Mr Jaggers and Wemmick went over the office accounts, and checked off the vouchers, and put all things straight. On these occasions Wemmick took his books and papers into Mr Jaggers's room, and one of the upstairs clerks came down into the outer office. Finding such clerk on Wemmick's post that morning, I knew what was going on; but, I was not sorry to have Mr Jaggers and Wemmick together, as Wemmick would then hear for himself that I said nothing to compromise him.

My appearance with my arm bandaged and my coat loose over my shoulders, favoured my object. Although I had sent Mr Jaggers a brief account of the accident as soon as I had arrived in town, yet I had to give him all the details now. While I described the disaster, Mr Jaggers stood, according to his wont, before the fire. Wemmick leaned back in his chair, staring at me, with his hands in the pockets of his trousers, and his pen put horizontally into the post. The two brutal casts, always inseparable in my mind from the official proceedings, seemed to be congestively considering whether they didn't smell fire at the present moment.

My narrative finished, and their questions exhausted, I then produced Miss Havisham's authority to receive the nine hundred pounds for Herbert. Mr Jaggers's eyes retired a little deeper into his head when I handed him the tablets, but he presently handed them over to Wemmick, with instructions to draw the cheque for his signature.

As I thought the time was now come for pursuing the theme I had at heart, I said, turning on Mr Jaggers:

'I asked Miss Havisham to give me some information relative to her adopted daughter, and she gave me all she possessed.'

'Did she?' said Mr Jaggers, 'Hah! I don't think I should have done so, if I had been Miss Havisham. But *she* ought to know her own business best.'

'I know more of the history of Miss Havisham's adopted child, than Miss Havisham herself does, sir. I know her mother.'

Mr Jaggers looked at me enquiringly, and repeated 'Mother?'

'I have seen her mother within these three days. And so have you, sir. And you have seen her still more recently.'

'Yes?' said Mr Jaggers.

'Perhaps I know more of Estella's history than even you do,' said I. 'I know her father too.'

A certain stop that Mr Jaggers came to in his manner assured me that he did not know who her father was.

'So! You know the young lady's father, Pip?' said Mr Jaggers.

'Yes,' I replied, 'and his name is Provis – from New South Wales.'

Even Mr Jaggers started when I said those words. How Wemmick received the announcement I am unable to say, for I was afraid to look at him just then, lest Mr Jaggers's sharpness should detect that there had been some communication unknown to him between us.

'And on what evidence, Pip,' asked Mr Jaggers, very coolly, as he paused with his handkerchief half way to his nose, 'does Provis make this claim?'

'He does not make it,' said I, 'and has never made it, and has no knowledge or belief that his daughter is in existence.'

Then I told him all I knew, and how I knew it; with the one reservation that I left him to infer that I knew from Miss Havisham what I in fact knew from Wemmick. I was very careful indeed as to that.

'Hah!' said Mr Jaggers at last, as he moved towards the papers on the table. '– What item was it you were at, Wemmick, when Mr Pip came in?'

But I could not submit to be thrown off in that way, and I made a passionate, almost an indignant, appeal to him to be more frank and manly with me. I reminded him of the false hopes into which I had lapsed, the length of time they had lasted, and the discovery I had made. I represented myself as being surely worthy of some little confidence from him, in return for the confidence I had just now imparted. And if he asked me why I wanted it and why I thought I had any right to it, I would tell him, little as he cared for such poor dreams, that I had loved Estella dearly and long, and that, although I had lost her, whatever concerned her was still nearer and dearer to me than anything else in the world. And seeing that Mr Jaggers stood quite still and silent, and apparently quite obdurate, under this appeal, I turned to Wemmick, and said, 'Wemmick, I know you to be a man with a gentle heart. I have seen your pleasant home, and your old father, and all the innocent cheerful playful ways with which you refresh your business life. And I entreat you to say a word for me to Mr Jaggers, and to represent to him that, all circumstances considered, he ought to be more open with me!'

I have never seen two men look more oddly at one another than Mr Jaggers and Wemmick did after this apostrophe. At first, a misgiving crossed me that Wemmick would be instantly dismissed from his employment; but, it melted as I saw Mr Jaggers relax into something like a smile, and Wemmick become bolder.

'What's all this?' said Mr Jaggers. 'You with an old father, and you with pleasant and playful ways?'

'Well!' returned Wemmick. 'If I don't bring 'em here, what does it matter?'

'Pip,' said Mr Jaggers, laying his hand upon my arm, and smiling openly, 'this man must be the most cunning impostor in all London.'

'Not a bit of it,' returned Wemmick, growing bolder and bolder. 'I think you're another.'

Again they exchanged their former odd looks, each apparently still distrustful that the other was taking him in.

'*You* with a pleasant home?' said Mr Jaggers.

'Since it don't interfere with business,' returned Wemmick, 'let it be so. Now, I look at you, sir, I shouldn't wonder if *you* might be planning and contriving to have a pleasant home of your own, one of these days, when you're tired of all this work.'

Mr Jaggers nodded his head retrospectively two or three times, and actually drew a sigh. 'Pip,' said he, 'we won't talk about "poor dreams"; but about this other matter. I'll put a case to you. Mind! I admit nothing. Put the case that a woman, under such circumstances as you have mentioned, held her child concealed, and was obliged to communicate the fact to her legal adviser. Put the case that at the same time he held a trust to find a child for an eccentric rich lady to adopt and bring up. Put the case that he often saw children solemnly tried at a criminal bar, where they were held up to be seen; put the case that he habitually knew of their being imprisoned, whipped, transported, neglected, cast out, qualified in all ways for the hangman, and growing up to be hanged.'

'I follow you, sir.'

'Put the case, Pip, that here was one pretty little child out of the heap, who could be saved; whom the father believed dead, and dared make no stir about; as to whom, over the mother, the legal adviser had this power: "I know what you did, and how you did it. I have tracked you through it all, and I tell it you all.

Give the child into my hands, and I will do my best to bring you off. If you are saved, your child is saved too; if you are lost, your child is still saved.'' Put the case that this was done, and that the woman was cleared.'

'I understand you perfectly.'

'Put the case, Pip, that passion and the terror of death had a little shaken the woman's intellects, and that when she was set at liberty, she was scared out of the ways of the world and went to him to be sheltered. Put the case that he took her in, and that he kept down the old wild violent nature whenever he saw an inkling of its breaking out, by asserting his power over her in the old way. Do you comprehend the imaginary case?'

'Quite.'

'Put the case that the child grew up, and was married for money. That the mother was still living. That the father was still living. That the secret was still a secret, except that you had got wind of it. Put that last case to yourself very carefully.'

'I do.'

'I ask Wemmick to put it to *him*self very carefully.'

And Wemmick said, 'I do.'

'For whose sake would you reveal the secret? For the father's? I think he would not be much the better for the mother. For the mother's? I think if she had done such a deed she would be safer where she was. For the daughter's? I think it would hardly serve her, to establish her parentage for the information of her husband, and to drag her back to disgrace, after an escape of twenty years, pretty secure to last for life. But, add the case that you had loved her, Pip, then I tell you that you had better chop off that bandaged left hand of yours with your bandaged right hand, and

then pass the chopper on to Wemmick there, to cut
that off, too.'

I looked at Wemmick, whose face was very grave.
He gravely touched his lips with his forefinger. I did
the same. Mr Jaggers did the same. 'Now, Wemmick,'
said the latter then, resuming his usual manner, 'what
item was it you were at, when Mr Pip came in?'

52

From Little Britain, I went, with my cheque in my
pocket, to Miss Skiffins's brother, the accountant; and
Miss Skiffins's brother, the accountant, going straight
to Clarriker's and bringing Clarriker to me, I had the
great satisfaction of concluding that arrangement.

Clarriker informing me on that occasion that the
affairs of the House were steadily progressing, that he
would now be able to establish a small branch-house
in the East which was much wanted for the extension
of the business, and that Herbert in his new partnership capacity would go out and take charge of it, I
found that I must have prepared for a separation from
my friend, even though my own affairs had been more
settled. And now indeed I felt as if my last anchor
were loosening its hold, and I should soon be driving
with the winds and waves.

We had now got into the month of March. My left
arm took in the natural course so long to heal that I
was still unable to get a coat on. My right arm was
tolerably restored; – disfigured, but fairly serviceable.

On a Monday morning, when Herbert and I were at breakfast, I received the following letter from Wemmick by the post.

Walworth. Burn this as soon as read. Early in the week, or say Wednesday, you might do what you know of, if you felt disposed to try it. Now burn.

When I had shown this to Herbert and had put it in the fire, we considered what to do.

'I have thought it over, again and again,' said Herbert, 'and I think I know a better course than taking a Thames waterman. Take Startop. A good fellow, a skilled hand, fond of us, and enthusiastic and honourable.'

'But how much would you tell him, Herbert?'

'It is necessary to tell him very little. Let him suppose it a mere freak, but a secret one, until the morning comes: then let him know that there is urgent reason for your getting Provis aboard and away. You go with him?'

'No doubt.'

'Where?'

It had seemed to me, in the many anxious considerations I had given the point, almost indifferent what port we made for – Hamburg, Rotterdam, Antwerp – the place signified little, so that he was got out of England. I had always proposed to myself to get him well down the river in the boat. As foreign steamers would leave London at about the time of high-water, our plan would be to get down the river by a previous ebb-tide, and lie by in some quiet spot until we could pull off to one.

Herbert assented to all this, and we went out immediately after breakfast to pursue our investigations. We found that a steamer for Hamburg was likely to suit our purpose best, and we directed our thoughts chiefly to that vessel. But we noted down what other foreign steamers would leave London with the same tide, and we satisfied ourselves that we knew the build and colour of each. We then separated for a few hours; I, to get at once such passports as were necessary; Herbert, to see Startop at his lodgings. When we met again at one o'clock we reported it done. I, for my part, was prepared with passports; Herbert had seen Startop, and he was more than ready to join.

Those two should pull a pair of oars, we settled, and I would steer; our charge would be sitter, and keep quiet; as speed was not our object, we should make way enough. We arranged that Herbert should not come home to dinner before going to Mill Pond Bank that evening; that he should prepare Provis to come down to some stairs hard by the house, on Wednesday, when he saw us approach, and not sooner; that all the arrangements with him should be concluded that Monday night.

These precautions well understood by both of us, I went home.

On opening the outer door of our chambers with my key, I found a letter in the box, directed to me; a very dirty letter, though not ill-written. Its contents were these:

If you are not afraid to come in the old marshes tonight or tomorrow night at Nine, and to come to the little sluice-house by the limekiln, you had better come. If you want information regarding *your uncle Provis*, you had much better come and tell no one and lose no time. *You must come alone*. Bring this with you.

I had had load enough upon my mind before the receipt of this strange letter. And the worst was, that I must decide quickly, or I should miss the afternoon coach, which would take me down in time for tonight. Tomorrow night I could not think of going, for it would be too close upon the time of the flight. And again, for anything I knew, the proffered information might have some important bearing on the flight itself.

Having hardly any time for consideration – my watch showing me that the coach started within half an hour – I resolved to go. I left a note in pencil for Herbert, telling him that as I should be so soon going away, I knew not for how long, I had decided to hurry down and back, to ascertain for myself how Miss Havisham was faring. I caught the coach just as it came out of the yard. I was the only inside passenger, jolting away knee-deep in straw, when I came to myself.

For, I really had not been myself since the receipt of the letter. The morning hurry and flutter had been great, for, long and anxiously as I had waited for Wemmick, his hint had come like a surprise at last. And now, I began to wonder at myself for being in the coach, and to doubt whether I had sufficient reason for being there. Still, the reference to Provis by name, mastered everything. I reasoned as I had reasoned already without knowing it, in case any harm should befall him through my not going, how could I ever forgive myself!

It was dark before we got down, and the journey

seemed long and dreary to me who could see little of it inside, and who could not go outside in my disabled state. Avoiding the Blue Boar, I put up at an inn of minor reputation down the town, and ordered some dinner. While it was preparing, I went to Satis House and inquired for Miss Havisham; she was still very ill, though considered something better.

My inn had once been a part of an ancient ecclesiastical house, and I dined in a little octagonal common-room, like a font. As I was not able to cut my dinner, the old landlord with a shining bald head did it for me. This bringing us into conversation, he was so good as to entertain me with my own story – of course with the popular feature that Pumblechook was my earliest benefactor and the founder of my fortunes.

'Do you know the young man?' said I.

'Know him!' repeated the landlord. 'Ever since he was – no height at all.'

'Does he ever come back to his neighbourhood?'

'Ay, he comes back,' said the landlord, 'to his great friends, now and again, and gives the cold shoulder to the man that made him.'

'What man is that?'

'Him that I speak of,' said the landlord, 'Mr Pumblechook, who has done everything for him.'

'Does Pumblechook say so?'

'It would turn a man's blood to white wine winegar to hear him tell of it, sir,' said the landlord.

I thought, 'Yet Joe, dear Joe, *you* never tell of it. Long-suffering and loving Joe, *you* never complain. Nor you, sweet-tempered Biddy!'

I had never been struck at so keenly, for my thank-lessness to Joe, as through the brazen impostor

Pumblechook. The falser he, the truer Joe; the meaner he, the nobler Joe.

I got up and had my coat fastened round my neck, and went out. I had previously sought in my pockets for the letter, that I might refer to it again, but I could not find it, and was uneasy to think that it must have been dropped in the straw of the coach. I knew very well, however, that the appointed place was the little sluice-house by the limekiln on the marshes, and the hour nine. Towards the marshes I now went straight, having no time to spare.

53

It was a dark night, though the full moon rose as I left the enclosed lands, and passed out upon the marshes.

I knew the limekiln as well as I knew the old Battery, but they were miles apart; so that if a light had been burning at each point that night, there would have been a long strip of the blank horizon between the two bright specks.

It was another half-hour before I drew near to the kiln. Hard by, was a small stone-quarry. It lay directly in my way, and had been worked that day, as I saw by the tools and barrows that were lying about.

Coming up again to the marsh level out of this excavation I saw a light in the old sluice-house. I quickened my pace, and knocked at the door with my hand. There was no answer, and I knocked again. No answer still, and I tried the latch.

It rose under my hand, and the door yielded. Looking in, I saw a lighted candle on a table, a bench, and a mattress on a truckle bedstead. As there was a loft above, I called, 'Is there any one here?' but no voice answered. Then, I looked at my watch, and, finding that it was past nine, called again, 'Is there any one here?' There being still no answer, I went out at the door, irresolute what to do.

It was beginning to rain fast. Seeing nothing save what I had seen already, I turned back into the house, and stood just within the shelter of the doorway, looking out into the night. While I was considering that some one must have been there lately and must soon be coming back, or the candle would not be burning, it came into my head to look if the wick were long. I turned round to do so, and had taken up the candle in my hand, when it was extinguished by some violent shock, and the next thing I comprehended, was, that I had been caught in a strong running noose, thrown over my head from behind.

'Now,' said a suppressed voice with an oath, 'I've got you!'

'What is this?' I cried, struggling. 'Who is it? Help, help, help!

Not only were my arms pulled close to my sides, but the pressure on my bad arm caused me exquisite pain. Sometimes, a strong man's hand, sometimes a strong man's breast, was set against my mouth to deaden my cries, and with a hot breath always close to me, I struggled ineffectually in the dark, while I was fastened tight to the wall. 'And now,' said the suppressed voice with another oath, 'call out again, and I'll make short work of you!'

The sudden exclusion of the night and the substitution of black darkness in its place, warned me that the man had closed a shutter. After groping about for a little, he found the flint and steel he wanted, and began to strike a light. The tinder was damp – no wonder there – and one after another the sparks died out.

The man was in no hurry, and struck again with the flint and steel. As the sparks fell thick and bright about him, I could see his hands, and touches of his face, and could make out that he was seated and bending over the table; but nothing more. Presently I saw his blue lips breathing on the tinder, and then a flare of light flashed up, and showed me Orlick.

Whom I had looked for, I don't know. I had not looked for him. Seeing him, I felt that I was in a dangerous strait indeed, and I kept my eyes upon him.

'Now,' said he, when we had surveyed one another for some time, 'I've got you.'

'Unbind me. Let me go!'

'Ah!' he returned, '*I'll* let you go. I'll let you go to the moon, I'll let you go to the stars. All in good time.'

'Why have you lured me here?'

'Don't you know?' said he, with a deadly look.

'Why have you set upon me in the dark?'

'Because I mean to do it all myself. One keeps a secret better than two. Oh you enemy, you enemy!'

His enjoyment of the spectacle I furnished, as he sat with his arms folded on the table, shaking his head at me and hugging himself, had a malignity in it that made me tremble. As I watched him in silence, he put his hand into the corner at his side, and took up a gun with a brass-bound stock.

'Do you know this?' said he, making as if he would take aim at me. 'Do you know where you saw it afore? Speak, wolf!'

'Yes,' I answered.

'You cost me that place. You did. Speak!'

'What else could I do?'

'You did that, and that would be enough, without more. How dared you to come betwixt me and a young woman I liked?'

'When did I?'

'When didn't you? It was you as always give Old Orlick a bad name to her.'

'You gave it to yourself; I could have done you no harm, if you had done yourself none.'

'You're a liar. And you'll take any pains, and spend any money, to drive me out of this country, will you?' said he, repeating my words to Biddy in the last interview I had with her. 'Now, I'll tell you a piece of information. It was never so well worth your while to get me out of this country as it is tonight. Ah! If it was all your money twenty times told, to the last brass farden!'

'What are you going to do to me?'

'I'm a-going,' said he, bringing his fist down upon the table with a heavy blow, and rising as the blow fell, to give it greater force, 'I'm a-going to have your life!'

He leaned forward staring at me, slowly unclenched his hand and drew it across his mouth as if his mouth watered for me, and sat down again.

'You was always in Old Orlick's way since ever you was a child. You goes out of his way, this present night. He'll have no more on you. You're dead. More than that,' said he, folding his arms on the table again, 'I won't have a rag of you, I won't have a bone of you, left on earth. I'll put your body in the kiln and let people suppose what they may of you, they shall never know nothing.'

My mind, with inconceivable rapidity, followed out all the consequences of such a death. Estella's father would believe I had deserted him, would be taken, would die accusing me; even Herbert would doubt me, when he compared the letter I had left for him, with the fact that I had called at Miss Havisham's gate for only a moment; Joe and Biddy would never know how sorry I had been that night; none would ever know how true I had meant to be, what an agony I had passed through. The death close before me was terrible, but far more terrible than death was the dread of being misremembered after death.

'Now, wolf,' said he, 'afore I kill you like any other beast – I'll have a good look at you and a good goad at you. Oh, you enemy!'

He had been drinking, and his eyes were red and bloodshot. Around his neck was slung a tin bottle, as I had often seen his meat and drink slung about him in other days. He brought the bottle to his lips, and took a fiery drink from it; and I smelt the strong spirits that I saw flash into his face.

'Wolf!' said he, folding his arms again, 'Old Orlick's a-going to tell you somethink. It was you as did for your shrew sister. I come upon her from behind, as I come upon you tonight. I giv' it her! I left her for dead, and if there had been a limekiln as nigh her as there is now nigh you, she shouldn't have come to life again. But it warn't Old Orlick as did it; it was you. You was favoured, and he was bullied and beat. Old Orlick bullied and beat, eh? Now you pays for it.'

He drank again, and became more ferocious. I saw by his tilting of the bottle that there was no great quantity left in it. I distinctly understood that he was working himself up with its contents, to make an end of me. I knew that every drop it held, was a drop of my life.

When he had drunk this second time, he rose from the bench on which he sat, and pushed the table aside. Then, he took up the candle, and shading it with his murderous hand so as to throw its light on me, stood before me, looking at me and enjoying the sight.

'Wolf, I'll tell you something more. It was Old Orlick as you tumbled over on your stairs that night. And why was Old Orlick there? You and her *have* pretty well hunted me out of this country, so far as getting a easy living in it goes, and I've took up with new companions, and new masters. Some of 'em writes my letters when I wants 'em wrote. They writes fifty hands; they're not like sneaking you, as writes but one. I've had a firm mind and a firm will to have your life, since you was down here at your sister's burying. For, says Old Orlick to himself, "Somehow or another I'll have him!" What! When I looks for you, I finds your uncle Provis, eh?'

Mill Pond Bank, and Chinks's Basin, and the Old Green Copper Rope-Walk, all so clear and plain! Provis in his rooms, the signal whose use was over, pretty Clara, the good motherly woman, old Bill Barley on his back, all drifting by, as on the swift stream of my life fast running out to sea!

'*You* with a uncle too! Why, I know'd you at Gargery's when you was so small a wolf that I could have took your weazen betwixt this finger and thumb and chucked you away dead and you hadn't found no uncles then. No, not you! But when Old Orlick come for to hear that your uncle Provis had mostlike wore the leg-iron wot Old Orlick had picked up, filed asunder, on these meshes ever so many year ago, and wot he kep by him till he dropped your sister with it, like a bullock, as he means to drop you – hey? – when he come for to hear that – hey? –'

In his savage taunting, he flared the candle so close at me, that I turned my face aside, to save it from the flame.

'Ah!' he cried, laughing, after doing it again, 'the burnt child dreads the fire! Old Orlick knowed you was burnt, Old Orlick knowed you was a smuggling your uncle Provis. Now I'll tell you something more, wolf, and this ends it. There's them that's as good a match for your uncle Provis as Old Orlick has been for you. Let him 'ware them, when he's lost his nevvy! Let him 'ware them, when no man can't find a rag of his dear relation's clothes, nor yet a bone of his body. There's them that can't and that won't have Magwitch alive in the same land with them! 'Ware Compeyson, Magwitch, and the gallows!'

There was a clear space of a few feet between the table and the opposite wall. Within this space, he now slouched backwards and forwards. I had no grain of hope left. I could yet clearly understand that unless he had resolved that I was within a few moments of surely perishing out of all human knowledge, he would never have told me what he had told.

Of a sudden, he stopped, took the cork out of his bottle, and tossed it away. He swallowed slowly, tilting up the bottle by little and little, and now he looked at me no more. Then, with a sudden hurry of violence and swearing horribly, he threw the bottle from him, and stopped; and I saw in his hand a stone-hammer with a long heavy handle.

I shouted out with all my might, and struggled with all my might. In the same instant I heard responsive shouts, saw figures and a gleam of light dash in at the door, heard voices and tumult, and saw Orlick emerge from a struggle of men, clear the table at a leap, and fly out into the night.

After a blank, I found that I was lying unbound, on the floor, in the same place, with my head on some one's knee.

Too indifferent at first, even to look round and ascertain who supported me, I was lying looking at the ladder, when there came between me and it, a face. The face of Trabb's boy!

'I think he's all right!' said Trabb's boy, in a sober voice; 'but ain't he just pale though!'

The face of him who supported me looked over into mine, and I saw my supporter to be –

'Herbert! Great Heaven!'

'Softly,' said Herbert. 'Gently, Handel. Don't be too eager.'

'And our old comrade, Startop!' I cried, as he too bent over me.

'Remember what he is going to assist us in,' said Herbert, 'and be calm.'

The allusion made me spring up. 'The time has not gone by, Herbert, has it?' For, I had a strange and strong misgiving that I had been lying there a long time – a day and a night – two days and nights – more.

'The time has not gone by. It is still Monday night.'

'Thank God!'

'And you have all tomorrow, Tuesday, to rest in,' said Herbert. 'Can you stand?'

'Yes, yes,' said I, 'I can walk. I have no hurt but in this throbbing arm.'

I could scarcely endure to have it touched. But, they tore up their handkerchiefs to make fresh bandages, and carefully replaced it in the sling, until we could get to the town and obtain some cooling lotion to put upon it. In a little while we had shut the door of the dark and empty sluice-house, and were passing through the quarry on our way back. The white vapour of the kiln was passing from us as we went by, and, as I had thought a prayer before, I thought a thanksgiving now.

Entreating Herbert to tell me how he had come to my rescue, I learnt that I had in my hurry dropped the letter, open, in our chambers, where he, coming home to bring with him Startop whom he had met in the street on his way to me, found it, very soon after I was gone. Its tone made him uneasy, and the more so because of the inconsistency between it and the hasty letter I had left for him. His uneasiness increasing instead of subsiding after a quarter of an hour's consideration, he set off with Startop. They duly arrived at the Blue Boar, fully expecting there to find me, or tidings of me; but, finding neither, went on to Miss Havisham's, where they lost me. Hereupon they went back to the hotel to refresh themselves and to get some one to guide them out upon the marshes. Among the loungers under the Boar's archway, happened to be Trabb's boy, he and Trabb's boy had seen me passing from Miss Havisham's in the direction of my dining-place. Thus, Trabb's boy became their guide, and with him they went out to the sluice-house. Herbert left his guide and Startop on the edge of the quarry, and went on by himself, and stole round the house two or three times, endeavouring to ascertain whether all was right within. As he could hear nothing but indistinct sounds of one deep rough voice, he even at last began to doubt whether I was there, when suddenly I cried out loudly, and he answered the cries, and rushed in, closely followed by the other two.

When I told Herbert what had passed within the house, he was for our immediately going before a magistrate in the town, and getting out a warrant. But, I had already considered that such a course, by detaining us there, or binding us to come back, might be fatal to Provis. There was no gainsaying this difficulty, and we relinquished all thoughts of pursuing Orlick at that time. Wednesday being so close upon us, we determined to go back to London that night. It was daylight when we reached the Temple, and I went at once to bed, and lay in bed all day. No precaution could have been more obvious than our refraining from communication with Provis that day; yet this again increased my restlessness. I started at every footstep and every sound, believing that he was discovered and taken, and this was the messenger to tell me so. My burning arm throbbed, and my burning head throbbed, and I fancied I was beginning to wander.

They kept me very quiet all day, and kept my arm constantly dressed, and gave me cooling drinks. Whenever I fell asleep, I awoke with the notion that a long time had elapsed and the opportunity to save him was gone. About midnight I got out of bed and went to

Herbert, with the conviction that I had been asleep for four-and-twenty hours, and that Wednesday was past. It was the last self-exhausting effort of my fretfulness, for, after that, I slept soundly.

Wednesday morning was dawning when I looked out of window. The winking lights upon the bridges were already pale, the coming sun was like a marsh of fire on the horizon.

Herbert lay asleep in his bed, and our old fellow-student lay asleep on the sofa. I could not dress myself without help, but I made up the fire, which was still burning, and got some coffee ready for them. In good time we admitted the sharp morning air at the windows, and looked at the tide that was still flowing towards us.

'When it turns at nine o'clock,' said Herbert, cheerfully, 'look out for us, and stand ready, you over there at Mill Pond Bank!'

54

It was one of those March days when the sun shines hot and the wind blows cold: when it is summer in the light, and winter in the shade. We had our pea-coats with us, and I took a bag. Of all my worldly possessions I took no more than the few necessaries that filled the bag. I wondered for the passing moment, as I stopped at the door and looked back, under what altered circumstances I should next see those rooms, if ever.

We loitered down to the Temple stairs, and stood loitering there, as if we were not quite decided to go upon the water at all. After a little show of indecision, we went on board and cast off; Herbert in the bow, I steering. It was then about high-water – half-past eight.

Our plan was this. The tide, beginning to run down at nine, and being with us until three, we intended still to creep on after it had turned, and row against it until dark. We should then be well in those long reaches below Gravesend, between Kent and Essex, where the river is broad and solitary, and where lone public-houses are scattered here and there, of which we could choose one for a resting-place. There, we meant to lie by, all night. The steamer for Hamburg, and the steamer for Rotterdam, would start from London at about nine on Thursday morning. We should know at what time to expect them, according to where we were, and would hail the first; so that if by any accident we were not taken aboard, we should have another chance.

Early as it was, there were plenty of scullers going here and there that morning, and plenty of barges dropping down with the tide.

Old London Bridge was soon passed, and old Bill-ingsgate market with its oyster-boats and Dutchmen, and the White Tower and Traitor's Gate, and we were in among the tiers of shipping. And now I, sitting in the stern, could see with a faster beating heart, Mill Pond Bank and Mill Pond stairs.

'Is he there?' said Herbert.

'Not yet.'

'Right! He was not to come down till he saw us. Can you see his signal?'

'Not well from here; but I think I see it. – Now, I see him! Pull both. Easy, Herbert. Oars!'

We touchèd the stairs lightly for a single moment, and he was on board and we were off again. He had a boat-cloak with him, and a black canvas bag, and he looked as like a river-pilot as my heart could have wished.

'Dear boy!' he said, putting his arm on my shoulder as he took his seat. 'Faithful dear boy, well done. Thankye, thankye!'

Again among the tiers of shipping, in and out, avoiding rusty chain-cables, frayed hempen hawsers and bobbing buoys, in and out, under the figure-head of the John of Sunderland making a speech to the winds, in and out, hammers going in ship-builders' yards, saws going at timber, ships going out to sea, in and out – out at last upon the clearer river, where the ships' boys might take their fenders in, and where the festooned sails might fly out to the wind.

We certainly had not been, and at that time as certainly we were not, either attended or followed by any boat. We held our own, without any appearance of molestation.

Provis looked a natural part of the scene. It was remarkable that he was the least anxious of any of us.

'If you knowed, dear boy,' he said to me, 'what it is to sit here alonger my dear boy and have my smoke, arter having been day by day betwixt four walls, you'd envy me. But you don't know what it is.'

'I think I know the delights of freedom,' I answered.

'Ah,' said he, shaking his head gravely. 'But you don't know it equal to me. You must have been under lock and key, dear boy, to know it equal to me – but I ain't a-going to be low. You see, dear boy, when I was over yonder, t'other side the world, I was always a-looking to this side; and it come flat to be there, for all I was a-growing rich. Everybody knowed Magwitch, and Magwitch could come, and Magwitch could go, and nobody's head would be troubled about him. They ain't so easy concerning me here, dear boy – wouldn't be, leastwise, if they knowed where I was.'

'If all goes well,' said I, 'you will be perfectly free and safe again, within a few hours.'

'Well,' he returned, drawing a long breath, 'I hope so.'

'But for your face, I should think you were a little despondent,' said I.

'Not a bit on it, dear boy! It comes of flowing on so quiet, and of that there rippling at the boat's head making a sort of a Sunday tune. Maybe I'm a growing a trifle old besides.'

He put his pipe back in his mouth with an undisturbed expression of face, and sat as composed and contented as if we were already out of England. Yet he was as submissive to a word of advice as if he had been in constant terror, for, when we ran ashore to get some bottles of beer into the boat, I hinted that I thought he would be safest where he was, and he said, 'Do you, dear boy?' and quietly sat down.

The air felt cold upon the river, but it was a bright day, and the sunshine was very cheering. The tide ran strong, I took care to lose none of it, and our steady stroke carried us on thoroughly well. The tide was yet with us when we were off Gravesend. As our charge was wrapped in his cloak, I purposely passed within a boat or two's length of the floating Custom House, and so out to catch the stream, alongside of two emigrant ships, and under the bows of a large transport with troops on the forecastle looking down at us.

Our oarsmen were so fresh, by dint of having occasionally let her drive with the tide for a minute or two, that a quarter of an hour's rest proved full as much as they wanted. We got ashore among some slippery stones while we ate and drank what we had with us, and looked about. It was like my own marsh country, flat and monotonous, and with a dim horizon; while the winding river turned and turned, and the great floating buoys upon it turned and turned, and everything else seemed stranded and still.

We pushed off again, and made what way we could. It was much harder work now, but Herbert and Startop persevered, and rowed, and rowed, and rowed, until the sun went down. As the night was fast falling, we held a little council: a short one, for clearly our course was to lie by at the first lonely tavern we could find. So, they plied their oars once more, and I looked out for anything like a house. Thus we held on, speaking little, for four or five dull miles.

At length we descried a light and a roof, and presently afterwards ran alongside a little causeway made of stones that had been picked up hard by. Leaving the rest in the boat, I stepped ashore, and found the light to be in a window of a public-house. It was a dirty place enough, and I dare say not unknown to smuggling adventurers; but there was a good fire in the kitchen, and there were eggs and bacon to eat, and various liquors to drink. No other company was in the house than the landlord, his wife, and a grizzled male creature, the 'Jack' of the little causeway, who was as slimy and smeary as if he had been low-water mark too.

With this assistant, I went down to the boat again, and we all came ashore. We made a very good meal by the kitchen fire, and then apportioned the bedrooms: Herbert and Startop were to occupy one; I and our charge the other.

While we were comforting ourselves by the fire after our meal, the Jack – who was sitting in a corner – asked me if we had seen a four-oared galley going up with the tide? When I told him No, he said she must have gone down then, and yet she 'took up too', when she left there.

'They must ha' thought better on't for some reason or another,' said the Jack, 'and gone down.'

'A four-oared galley, did you say?' said I.

'A four,' said the Jack, 'and two sitters.'

'Did they come ashore here?'

'They put in with a stone two-gallon jar, for some beer. I'd ha' been glad to pison the beer myself,' said the Jack, 'or put some rattling physic in it.'

'Why?'

'*I* know why,' said the Jack. He spoke in a slushy voice, as if much mud had washed into his throat.

'He thinks,' said the landlord, 'he thinks they was, what they wasn't.'

'I knows what I thinks,' observed the Jack.

'You thinks Custum 'Us, Jack?' said the landlord.

'I do,' said the Jack.

'Why, what do you make out that they done with their buttons then, Jack?' asked the landlord, vacillating weakly.

'Done with their buttons?' returned the Jack. 'Chucked 'em overboard. Done with their buttons!'

'Don't be cheeky, Jack,' remonstrated the landlord, in a melancholy and pathetic way.

'A four and two sitters don't go hanging and hovering, up with one tide and down with another, and both with and against another, without there being Custum 'Us at the bottom of it,' said the Jack and went out in disdain; and the landlord, having no one to reply upon, found it impracticable to pursue the subject.

This dialogue made us all uneasy, and me very uneasy. A four-oared galley hovering about in so unusual a way as to attract this notice, was an ugly circumstance that I could not get rid of. When I had induced Provis to go up to bed, I went outside with my two companions (Startop by this time knew the state of the case), and held another council. Whether we should remain at the house until near the steamer's time, which would be about one in the afternoon; or whether we should put off early in the morning; was the question we discussed. On the whole we deemed it the better course to lie where we were, until within an hour or so of the steamer's time, and then to get out in her track, and drift easily with the tide. Having settled to do this, we returned into the house and went to bed.

I lay down and slept well for a few hours. When I awoke, the wind had risen, and the sign of the house (the Ship) was creaking and banging about, with noises that startled me. Rising softly, for my charge lay fast asleep, I looked out of the window. It commanded the causeway where we had hauled up our boat, and, as my eyes adapted themselves to the light of the clouded moon, I saw two men looking into her. They passed by under the window, looking at nothing else, and they did not go down to the landing-place which I could discern to be empty, but struck across the marsh in the direction of the Nore.

My first impulse was to call up Herbert, and show him the two men going away. But, reflecting before I got into his room, which was at the back of the house and adjoined mine, that he and Startop had had a harder day than I, and were fatigued, I forbore. Going back to my window, I could see the two men moving over the marsh. In that light, however, I soon lost them, and feeling very cold, lay down to think of the matter, and fell asleep again.

We were up early. As we walked to and fro, I deemed it right to recount what I had seen. Again our charge was the least anxious of the party. It was very likely that the men belonged to the Custom House, he said quietly, and that they had no thought of us. I tried to persuade myself that it was so – as, indeed, it might easily be. However, I proposed that Provis and I should walk away together to a distant point we could see, and that the boat should take us aboard there, or as near there as might prove feasible, at about noon: This being considered a good precaution, soon after breakfast he and I set forth, without saying anything at the tavern.

We spoke very little. As we approached the point, I begged him to remain in a sheltered place, while I went on to reconnoitre; for, it was towards it that the men had passed in the night. He complied, and I went on alone.

When he looked out from his shelter in the distance, and saw that I waved my hat to him to come up, he rejoined me, and there we waited; sometimes moving about to warm ourselves: until we saw our boat coming round. We got aboard easily, and rowed out into the track of the steamer. It was half-past one before we saw her smoke, and soon afterwards we saw behind it the smoke of another steamer. As they were coming on at full speed, we got the two bags ready, and took that opportunity of saying good-bye to Herbert and Startop. We had all shaken hands cordially, and neither Herbert's eyes nor mine were quite dry, when I saw a four-oared galley shoot out from under the bank but a little way ahead of us, and row out into the same track.

The galley, which was very skilfully handled, crossed us, let us come up with her, and fell alongside. Leaving just room enough for the play of the oars, she kept alongside, drifting when we drifted, and pulling a stroke or two when we pulled. Of the two sitters, one held the rudder lines, and looked at us attentively – as did all the rowers; the other sitter was wrapped up, much as Provis was, and seemed to shrink, and whisper some instruction to the steerer as he looked at us. Not a word was spoken in either boat.

Startop could make out, after a few minutes, which steamer was first, and gave me the word 'Hamburg', in a low voice as we sat face to face. She was nearing us very fast, and the beating of her paddles grew louder and louder. I felt as if her shadow were absolutely upon us, when the galley hailed us.

'You have a returned Transport there,' said the man who held the lines. 'That's the man, wrapped in the cloak. His name is Abel Magwitch, otherwise Provis. I apprehend that man, and call upon him to surrender, and you to assist.'

At the same moment, without giving any audible direction to his crew, he ran the galley aboard of us. They had pulled one sudden stroke ahead, had got their oars in, had run athwart us, and were holding on to our gunwale, before we knew what they were doing. In the same moment I saw the steersman of the galley lay his hand on Provis's shoulder, and saw that both boats were swinging round with the force of the tide, and saw that all hands on board the steamer were running forward quite frantically. Still in the same moment, I saw Provis start up, lean across his captor, and pull the cloak from the neck of the shrinking sitter in the galley. Still in the same moment, I saw that the face disclosed, was the face of the other convict of long ago. Still in the same moment, I saw the face tilt backward with a white terror on it that I shall never forget, and heard a great cry on board the steamer and a loud splash in the water, and felt the boat sink from under me.

It was but for an instant that I seemed to struggle; that instant past, I was taken on board the galley. Herbert was there, and Startop was there; but our boat was gone, and the two convicts were gone.

I could not at first distinguish sky from water or shore from shore; but, the crew of the galley righted her with great speed, and pulling certain swift strong strokes ahead, lay upon their oars, every man looking silently and eagerly at the water astern. Presently a dark object was seen in it, bearing towards us on the tide. No man spoke, but the steersman held up his hand, and all softly backed water, and kept the boat straight and true before it. As it came nearer, I saw it to be Magwitch, swimming, but not swimming freely. He was taken on board, and instantly manacled at the wrists and ankles.

The galley was kept steady, and the silent eager look-out at the water was resumed. But, the Rotterdam steamer now came up, and apparently not understanding what had happened, came on at speed. By the time she had been hailed and stopped, both steamers were drifting away from us, and we were rising and falling in a troubled wake of water. The look-out was kept, long after all was still again and the two steamers were gone; but, everybody knew that it was hopeless now.

At length we gave it up, and pulled under the shore towards the tavern we had lately left, where we were received with no little surprise. Here, I was able to get some comforts for Magwitch – Provis no longer – who had received some very severe injury in the chest and a deep cut in the head.

He told me that he believed himself to have gone under the keel of the steamer, and to have been struck on the head in rising. The injury to his chest he thought he had received against the side of the galley. He added that he did not pretend to say what he might or might not have done to Compeyson, but, that in the moment of his laying his hand on his cloak to identify him, that villain had staggered up and staggered back, and they had both gone overboard together; that there had been a struggle under water, and that he had disengaged himself, struck out, and swum away.

When I asked this officer's permission to change the prisoner's wet clothes by purchasing any spare garments I could get at the public-house, he gave it readily: merely observing that he must take charge of everything his prisoner had about him. So the pocketbook which had once been in my hands, passed into the officer's. He further gave me leave to accompany the prisoner to London.

The Jack at the Ship was instructed where the

drowned man had gone down, and undertook to search for the body in the places where it was likeliest to come ashore.

We remained at the public-house until the tide turned, and then Magwitch was carried down to the galley and put on board. Herbert and Startop were to get to London by land, as soon as they could. We had a doleful parting, and when I took my place by Magwitch's side, I felt that that was my place henceforth while he lived.

For now, my repugnance to him had all melted away, and in the hunted wounded shackled creature who held my hand in his, I only saw a man who had meant to be my benefactor, and who had felt affectionately, gratefully, and generously, towards me with great constancy through a series of years. I only saw in him a much better man than I had been to Joe.

I tried to rest him on the arm I could use, in any easy position; but, it was dreadful to think that I could not be sorry at heart for his being badly hurt, since it was unquestionably best that he should die. That he would be leniently treated, I could not hope. He who had been presented in the worst light at his trial, who had since broken prison and had been tried again, who had returned from transportation under a life sentence, and who had occasioned the death of the man who was the cause of his arrest.

As we returned towards the setting sun we had yesterday left behind us, I told him how grieved I was to think that he had come home for my sake.

'Dear boy,' he answered, 'I'm quite content to take my chance. I've seen my boy, and he can be a gentleman without me.'

No. I had thought about that, while we had been there side by side. No. Apart from any inclinations of my own, I understood Wemmick's hint now. I foresaw that, being convicted, his possessions would be forfeited to the Crown.

'Lookee here, dear boy,' said he. 'It's best as a gentleman should not be knowed to belong to me now. Only come to see me as if you come by chance alonger Wemmick. Sit where I can see you when I am swore to, for the last o' many times, and I don't ask no more.'

'I will never stir from your side,' said I, 'when I am suffered to be near you. Please God, I will be as true to you, as you have been to me!'

I felt his hand tremble as it held mine, and he turned his face away as he lay in the bottom of the boat. It was a good thing that he had touched this point, for it put into my mind what I might not otherwise have thought of until too late: That he need never know how his hopes of enriching me had perished.

55

He was taken to the Police Court next day, and would have been immediately committed for trial, but that it was necessary to send down for an old officer of the prison-ship from which he had once escaped, to speak to his identity. I had gone direct to Mr Jaggers at his private house, on my arrival over night, to retain his assistance, and Mr Jaggers on the prisoner's behalf would admit nothing. It was the sole resource, for he told me that the case must be over in five minutes when the witness was there, and that no power on earth could prevent its going against us.

I imparted to Mr Jaggers my design of keeping him in ignorance of the fate of his wealth. Mr Jaggers was querulous and angry with me for having 'let it slip through my fingers', and said we must memorialize by-and-by, and try at all events for some of it. But, he did not conceal from me that although there might be many cases in which the forfeiture would not be exacted, there were no circumstances in this case to make it one of them.

There appeared to be reason for supposing that the drowned informer had hoped for a reward out of this forfeiture, and had obtained some accurate knowledge of Magwitch's affairs. When his body was found, many miles from the scene of his death, and so horribly disfigured that he was only recognizable by the contents of his pockets, notes were still legible. Among these, were the name of a banking-house in New South Wales where a sum of money was, and the designation of certain lands of considerable value. Both these heads of information were in a list that Magwitch, while in prison, gave to Mr Jaggers, of the possessions he supposed I should inherit. His ignorance, poor fellow, at last served him; he never mistrusted but that my inheritance was quite safe, with Mr Jaggers's aid.

After three days' delay, during which the crown prosecution stood over for the production of the witness from the prison-ship, the witness came, and completed the easy case. He was committed to take his trial at the next Sessions, which would come on in a month.

It was at this dark time of my life that Herbert returned home one evening, a good deal cast down, and said:

'My dear Handel, I fear I shall soon have to leave you.'

His partner having prepared me for that, I was less surprised than he thought.

'We shall lose a fine opportunity if I put off going to Cairo, and I am very much afraid I must go, Handel, when you most need me.'

'Herbert, I shall always need you, because I shall always love you; but my need is no greater now, than at another time.'

'You will be so lonely.'

'I have not leisure to think of that,' said I. 'You know that I am always with him to the full extent of the time allowed, and that I should be with him all day long, if I could. And when I come away from him, you know that my thoughts are with him.'

'My dear fellow,' said Herbert, 'let the near prospect of our separation – for, it is very near – be my justification for troubling you about yourself. Have you thought of your future?'

'No, for I have been afraid to think of any future.'

'But yours cannot be dismissed; indeed, my dear dear Handel, it must not be dismissed. I wish you would enter on it now, as far as a few friendly words go, with me.'

'I will,' said I.

'In this branch house of ours, Handel, we must have a –'

I saw that his delicacy was avoiding the right word, so I said, 'A clerk.'

'A clerk. And I hope it is not at all unlikely that he may expand into a partner. Now, Handel – in short, my dear boy, will you come to me? Clara and I have talked about it again and again,' Herbert pursued, 'and the dear little thing begged me only this evening to say to you that if you will live with us when we come together, she will do her best to make you happy. We should get on so well, Handel!'

I thanked him heartily, but said I could not yet make sure of joining him as he so kindly offered. Firstly, my mind was too preoccupied to be able to take in the subject clearly. Secondly – Yes! Secondly, there was a vague something lingering in my thoughts that will come out very near the end of this slight narrative.

'But if you thought, Herbert, that you could, without doing any injury to your business, leave the question open for a little while –'

'For any while,' cried Herbert. 'Six months, a year!' Herbert was highly delighted when we shook hands on this arrangements, and said he could now take courage to tell me that he believed he must go away at the end of the week.

'And Clara?' said I.

'The dear little thing,' returned Herbert, 'holds dutifully to her father as long as he lasts; but he won't last long. Mrs Whimple confides to me that he is certainly going and then I shall come back for the dear little thing, and the dear little thing and I will walk quietly into the nearest church.'

On the Saturday in that same week, I took my leave of Herbert as he sat on one of the seaport mail coaches and then went to my lonely home.

On the stairs I encountered Wemmick, who was

coming down. I had not seen him alone, since the disastrous issue of the attempted flight; and he had come, in his private and personal capacity, to say a few words of explanations in reference to that failure.

'The late Compeyson,' said Wemmick, 'had by little and little got at the bottom of half of the regular business now transacted, and it was from the talk of some of his people in trouble that I heard what I did. I can only suppose now, that it was a part of his policy, as a very clever man, habitually to deceive his own instruments. You don't blame me, I hope, Mr Pip? I am sure I tried to serve you, with all my heart.'

'I am as sure of that, Wemmick, as you can be, and I thank you most earnestly for all your interest and friendship.'

'Thank you, thank you very much. It's a bad job,' said Wemmick, scratching his head, 'and I assure you I haven't been so cut up for a long time. What I look at, is the surface of so much portable property. Dear me!'

'What *I* think of, Wemmick, is the poor owner of the property.'

'Yes, to be sure,' said Wemmick. 'Of course there can be no objection to your being sorry for him, and I'd put down a five-pound note myself to get him out of it But what I look at, is this. The late Compeyson having been beforehand with him in intelligence of his return, and being so determined to bring him to book, I do not think he could have been saved. Whereas, the portable property certainly could have been saved.'

I invited Wemmick to come upstairs, and refresh himself with a glass of grog before walking to Walworth. He accepted the invitation. While he was drinking his moderate allowance, he said, 'What do you think of my meaning to take a holiday on Monday, Mr Pip?'

'Why, I suppose you have not done such a thing these twelve months.'

'These twelve years, more likely,' said Wemmick. 'Yes. I'm going to take a holiday. More than that; I'm going to take a walk. More than that; I'm going to ask you to take a walk with me.'

I was about to excuse myself, as being but a bad companion just then, when Wemmick anticipated me.

'I know your engagements,' said he. 'But if you *could* oblige me, I should take it as a kindness. It ain't a long walk, and it's an early one.'

He had done so much for me at various times, that this was very little to do for him. I said I could manage it and he was so very much pleased by my acquiescence, that I was pleased too. At his particular request, I appointed to call for him at the Castle at half-past eight on Monday morning, and so we parted for the time.

Punctual to my appointment, I rang at the Castle gate on the Monday morning, and was received by Wemmick himself: who struck me as looking tighter than usual, and having a sleeker hat on. Within, there were two glasses of rum-and-milk prepared, and two biscuits. The Aged must have been stirring with the lark, for, glancing into the perspective of his bedroom, I observed that his bed was empty.

When we had fortified ourselves with the rum-and-milk and biscuits, and were going out for the walk, I was considerably surprised to see Wemmick take up a fishing-rod, and put it over his shoulder. 'Why, we are not going fishing!' said I. 'No,' returned Wemmick, 'but I like to walk with one.'

I thought this odd; however, I said nothing, and we set off. We went towards Camberwell Green, and when we were thereabouts, Wemmick said suddenly:

'Halloa! Here's a church!'

There was nothing very surprising in that; but again, I was rather surprised, when he said, as if he were animated by a brilliant idea:

'Let's go in!'

We went in, Wemmick leaving his fishing-rod in the porch, and looked all round. In the mean time, Wemmick was diving into his coat-pockets, and getting something out of paper there.

'Halloa!' said he. 'Here's a couple of pair of gloves! Let's put 'em on!'

As the gloves were white kid gloves, I now began to have my strong suspicions. They were strengthened into certainty when I beheld the Aged enter at a side door, escorting a lady.

'Halloa!' said Wemmick. 'Here's Miss Skiffins! Let's have a wedding.'

That discreet damsel was attired as usual, except that she was now engaged in substituting for her green kid gloves, a pair of white.

The clerk and clergyman then appearing, we were ranged in order at those fatal rails. True to his notion of seeming to do it all without preparation, I heard Wemmick say to himself as he took something out of his waistcoat-pocket before the service began, 'Halloa! Here's a ring!'

I acted in the capacity of backer, or best-man, to the bridegroom. The responsibility of giving the lady away, devolved upon the Aged, which led to the clergyman's being unintentionally scandalized, and it happened thus. When he said, 'Who giveth this woman to be married to this man?' the old gentleman, not in the least knowing what point of the ceremony we had arrived at, stood most amiably beaming at the ten commandments. Upon which, the clergyman said again, 'WHO giveth this woman to be married to this man?' The old gentleman being still in a state of most estimable unconsciousness, the bridegroom cried out in his accustomed voice, 'Now Aged P. you know; who giveth?' To which the Aged replied with great briskness, before saying that *he* gave, 'All right, John, all right, my boy!' And the clergyman came to so gloomy a pause upon it, that I had doubts for the moment whether we should get completely married that day.

It was completely done, however, and when we were going out of church, Wemmick took the cover off the font, and put his white gloves in it, and put the cover on again. Mrs Wemmick, more heedful of the future, put her white gloves in her pocket and assumed her green. '*Now*, Mr Pip,' said Wemmick, triumphantly shouldering the fishing-rod as we came out, 'let me ask you whether anybody would suppose this to be a wedding-party!'

Breakfast had been ordered at a pleasant little tavern, a mile or so away upon the rising ground beyond the Green. When any one declined anything on table, Wemmick said, 'Provided by contract, you know; don't be afraid of it!' I drank to the new couple, drank to the Aged, drank to the Castle, saluted the bride at parting, and made myself as agreeable as I could.

Wemmick came down to the door with me, and I again shook hands with him, and wished him joy.

'Thankee!' said Wemmick, rubbing his hands. 'She's such a manager of fowls, you have no idea. You shall have some eggs, and judge for yourself. I say, Mr Pip!' calling me back, and speaking low. 'This is altogether a Walworth sentiment, please.'

'I understand. Not to be mentioned in Little Britain,' said I.

Wemmick nodded. 'After what you let out the other day, Mr Jaggers may as well not know of it. He might think my brain was softening, or something of the kind.'

56

Magwitch lay in prison very ill, during the whole interval between his committal for trial, and the coming round of the Sessions. He breathed with great pain and difficulty, which increased daily. It was a consequence of his hurt, that he spoke so low as to be scarcely audible; therefore, he spoke very little. But, he was ever ready to listen to me, and it became the first duty of my life to say to him, and read to him, what I knew he ought to hear.

Being far too ill to remain in the common prison, he was removed, after the first day or so, into the infirmary.

Although I saw him every day, it was for only a short time; hence, the regularly recurring spaces of our separation were long enough to record on his face any slight changes that occurred in his physical state. He wasted, and became slowly weaker and worse, day by day, from the day when the prison door closed upon him.

It happened on two or three occasions in my presence, that his desperate reputation was alluded to by one or other of the people in attendance on him. A smile crossed his face then, and he turned his eyes on me with a trustful look, as if he were confident that I had seen some small redeeming touch in him, even so long ago as when I was a little child. As to all the rest, he was humble and contrite, and I never knew him complain.

When the Sessions came round, Mr Jaggers caused an application to be made for the postponement of his trial until the following Sessions. It was obviously made with the assurance that he could not live so long, and was refused. The trial came on at once, and, when he was put to the bar, he was seated in a chair. No objection was made to my getting close to the dock, on the outside of it, and holding the hand that he stretched forth to me.

The trial was very short and very clear. Such things as could be said for him, were said – how he had taken to industrious habits, and had thriven lawfully and reputably. But, nothing could unsay the fact that he had returned, and was there in presence of the Judge and Jury. It was impossible to try him for that, and do otherwise than find him guilty.

At that time, it was the custom to devote a concluding day to the passing of Sentences, and to make a finishing effect with the Sentence of Death. But for the indelible picture that my remembrance now holds before me, I could scarcely believe, even as I write these words, that I saw two-and-thirty men and women put before the Judge to receive that sentence together. Foremost among the two-and-thirty, was he; seated, that he might get breath enough to keep life in him.

Penned in the dock, as I again stood outside it at the corner with his hand in mine, were the two-and-thirty men and women; some defiant, some stricken with terror, some sobbing and weeping, some covering their faces, some staring gloomily about. Then, the Judge addressed them. Among the wretched creatures before him whom he must single out for special address, was one who, after repeated imprisonments and punishments, had been at length sentenced to exile for a term of years; and who, under circumstances of great violence and daring had made his escape and been re-sentenced to exile for life. That miserable man would seem for a time to have become convinced of his errors, when far removed from the scenes of his old offences, and to have lived a peaceable and honest life. But in a fatal moment he had quitted his haven of rest and repentance, and had come back to the country where he was proscribed. Being here presently denounced, he had for a time succeeded in evading the officers of Justice, but being at length seized while in the act of flight, he had resisted them, and had caused the death of his denouncer, to whom his whole career was known. The appointed punishment for his return to the land that had cast him out, being Death, and his case being this aggravated case, he must prepare himself to Die.

Rising for a moment, a distinct speck of face in this way of light, the prisoner said, 'My Lord, I have received my sentence of Death from the Almighty, but

I bow to yours,' and sat down again. There was some hushing, and the Judge went on with what he had to say to the rest. Then, they were all formally doomed, and some of them were supported out, and some of them sauntered out with a haggard look of bravery, and a few nodded to the gallery, and two or three shook hands. Magwitch went last of all, because of having to be helped from his chair and to go very slowly; and he held my hand while all the others were removed, and while the audience got up and pointed down at this criminal or at that, and most of all at him and me.

I began that night to write out a petition to the Home Secretary of State, setting forth my knowledge of him, and how it was that he had come back for my sake. I wrote it as fervently and pathetically as I could, and when I had finished it and sent it in, I wrote out other petitions to such men in authority as I hoped were the most merciful, and drew up one to the Crown itself.

The daily visits I could make him were shortened now, and he was more strictly kept. Nobody was hard with him, or with me. There was duty to be done, and it was done, but not harshly.

As the days went on, I noticed more and more that he would lie placidly looking at the white ceiling, with an absence of light in his face, until some word of mine brightened it for an instant, and then it would subside again. Sometimes he was almost, or quite, unable to speak; then, he would answer me with slight pressures on my hand, and I grew to understand his meaning very well.

The number of the days had risen to ten, when I

saw a greater change in him than I had seen yet. His eyes were turned towards the door, and lighted up as I entered.

'Dear boy,' he said, as I sat down by his bed: 'I thought you was late. But I knowed you couldn't be that.'

'It is just the time,' said I. 'I waited for it at the gate.'

'You always waits at the gate; don't you, dear boy?'

'Yes. Not to lose a moment of the time.'

'Thank'ee dear boy, thank'ee. God bless you! You've never deserted me, dear boy.'

I pressed his hand in silence, for I could not forget that I had once meant to desert him.

He lay on his back, breathing with great difficulty. Do what he would, and love me though he did, the light left his face ever and again, and a film came over the placid look at the white ceiling.

'Are you in much pain today?'

'I don't complain of none, dear boy.'

He had spoken his last words. He smiled, and I understood his touch to mean that he wished to lift my hand, and lay it on his breast. I laid it there, and he smiled again, and put both his hands upon it.

The allotted time ran out, while we were thus; but, looking round, I found the governor of the prison standing near me, and he whispered, 'You needn't go yet.' I thanked him gratefully, and asked, 'Might I speak to him, if he can hear me?'

The governor stepped aside. The change, though it was made without noise, drew back the film from the placid look at the white ceiling, and he looked most affectionately at me.

'Dear Magwitch, I must tell you, now at last. You understand what I say?'

A gentle pressure on my hand.

'You had a child once, whom you loved and lost.'

A stronger pressure on my hand.

'She lived and found powerful friends. She is living now. She is a lady and very beautiful. And I love her!'

With a last faint effort he raised my hand to his lips.

Then, he gently let it sink upon his breast again, with his own hands lying on it. The placid look at the white ceiling came back, and passed away, and his head dropped quietly on his breast.

57

Now that I was left wholly to myself, I gave notice of my intention to quit the chambers in the Temple as soon as my tenancy could legally determine, and in the meanwhile to underlet them. At once I put bills up in the windows; for, I was in debt, and had scarcely any money, and began to be seriously alarmed by the state of my affairs. The late stress upon me had enabled me to put off illness, but not to put it away; I knew that it was coming on me now, and I knew very little else, and was even careless as to that.

For a day or two, I lay on the sofa, or on the floor – anywhere, according as I happened to sink down – with a heavy head and aching limbs, and no purpose, and no power. Then there came one night which appeared of great duration, and which teemed with anxiety and horror; and when in the morning I tried to sit up in my bed and think of it, I found I could not do so.

Whether I really had been down in Garden-court in the dead of the night, groping about for the boat that I supposed to be there; whether I had two or three times come to myself on the staircase with great terror, not knowing how I had got out of bed; whether I had found myself lighting the lamp, possessed by the idea that he was coming up the stairs, and that the lights were blown out; whether there had been a closed iron furnace in a dark corner of the room, and a voice had called out over and over again that Miss Havisham was consuming within it; these were things that I tried to settle with myself and get into some order, as I lay that morning on my bed. But, the vapour of a limeklin would come between me and them, disordering them all, and it was through the vapour at last that I saw two men looking at me.

'What do you want?' I asked, starting; 'I don't know you.'

'Well, sir,' returned one of them, bending down and touching me on the shoulder, 'this is a matter that you'll soon arrange, I dare say, but you're arrested.'

'What is the debt?'

'Hundred and twenty-three pound, fifteen, six. Jeweller's account, I think.'

'What is to be done?'

'You had better come to my house,' said the man. 'I keep a very nice house.'

I made some attempt to get up and dress myself. When I next attended to them, they were standing a little off from the bed, looking at me. I still lay there.

'You see my state,' said I. 'I would come with you if I could; but indeed I am quite unable. If you take me from here, I think I shall die by the way.'

Perhaps they replied, or argued the point, or tried to encourage me to believe that I was better than I thought. I don't know what they did, except that they forbore to remove me.

That I had a fever and was avoided, that I suffered greatly, that I often lost my reason, that the time seemed interminable, that I confounded impossible existences with my own identity; that I sometimes struggled with real people, in the belief that they were murderers, and that I would all at once comprehend that they meant to do me good, and would then sink exhausted in their arms, and suffer them to lay me down, I also knew at the time. But, above all, I knew that there was a constant tendency in all these people sooner or later to settle down into the likeness of Joe.

After I had turned the worst point of my illness, I began to notice that while all its other features changed, this one consistent feature did not change. Whoever came about me, still settled down into Joe. I opened my eyes in the night, and I saw in the great chair at the bedside, Joe. I opened my eyes in the day, and, sitting on the window-seat, smoking his pipe in the shaded open window, still I saw Joe.

At last, one day, I took courage, and said, '*Is it Joe?*'

And the dear old home-voice answered, 'Which it air, old chap.'

'O Joe, you break my heart! Look angry at me, Joe. Strike me, Joe. Tell me of my ingratitude. Don't be so good to me!'

For, Joe had actually laid his head down on the

pillow at my side and put his arm round my neck, in his joy that I knew him.

'Which dear old Pip, old chap,' said Joe, 'you and me was ever friends. And when you're well enough to go out for a ride – what larks!'

After which, Joe withdrew to the window, and stood with his back towards me, wiping his eyes. And as my extreme weakness prevented me from getting up and going to him, I lay there, penitently whispering, 'O God bless him! O God bless this gentle Christian man!'

Joe's eyes were red when I next found him beside me; but, I was holding his hand, and we both felt happy.

'How long, dear Joe?'

'Which you meantersay, Pip, how long have your illness lasted, dear old chap?'

'Yes, Joe.'

'It's the end of May, Pip. Tomorrow is the first of June.'

'And have you been here all the time, dear Joe?'

'Pretty nigh, old chap. For, as I says to Biddy when the news of your being ill were brought by letters that how you might be amongst strangers, and that how you and me having been ever friends, a wisit at such a moment might not prove unacceptabobble. And Biddy, her word were, "Go to him, without loss of time."'

There Joe cut himself short, and informed me that I was to be talked to in great moderation and that I was to submit myself to all his orders. So, I kissed his hand, and lay quiet, while he proceeded to indite a note to Biddy, with my love in it.

Evidently, Biddy had taught Joe to write. As I lay in

bed looking at him, it made me, in my weak state, cry again with pleasure to see the pride with which he set about his letter. Occasionally, he was tripped up by some orthographical stumbling-block, but on the whole he got on very well indeed, and when he had signed his name, and had removed a finishing blot from the paper to the crown of his head with his two forefingers, he got up and hovered about the table, trying the effect of his performance from various points of view as it lay there, with unbounded satisfaction.

Not to make Joe uneasy by talking too much, even if I had been able to talk much, I deferred asking him about Miss Havisham until next day. He shook his head when I then asked him if she had recovered.

'Is she dead, Joe?'

'Why you see, old chap,' said Joe, by way of getting at it by degrees, 'I wouldn't go so far as to say that, for that's a deal to say; but she ain't –'

'Living, Joe?'

'That's nigher where it is,' said Joe; 'she ain't living.'

'Did she linger long, Joe?'

'Arter you was took ill, pretty much about what you might call a week,' said Joe; still determined, on my account, to come at everything by degrees.

'Dear Joe, have you heard what becomes of her property?'

'Well, old chap,' said Joe, 'it do appear that she had settled the most of it, which I meantersay tied it up, on Miss Estella. But she had wrote out a little coddle-shell in her own hand a day or two afore the accident, leaving a cool four thousand to Mr Matthew Pocket. And why, do you suppose, above all things, Pip, she left that cool four thousand unto him? "Because of Pip's account of him the said Matthew." I am told by Biddy, that air the writing,' said Joe, repeating the legal turn as if it did him infinite good, '"account of him the said Matthew."'

This account gave me great joy, as it perfected the only good thing I had done. I asked Joe whether he had heard if any of the other relations had any legacies?

'Miss Sarah,' said Joe, 'she have twenty-five pound perannium fur to buy pills, on account of being bilious. Miss Georgiana, she have twenty pound down. Mrs – what's the name of them wild beasts with humps, old chap?'

'Camels?' said I, wondering why he could possibly want to know.

Joe nodded. 'Mrs Camels,' by which I presently understood he meant Camilla, 'she have five pound fur to buy rushlights to put her in spirits when she wake up in the night.'

The accuracy of these recitals was sufficiently obvious to me, to give me great confidence in Joe's information. 'And now,' said Joe, 'you ain't that strong yet, old chap, that you can take in more nor one additional shovel-full today. Old Orlick he's been a bustin' open a dwelling-ouse.'

'Whose?' said I.

'Not, I grant, you, but what his manners is given to blusterous,' said Joe, apologetically; 'still, a Englishman's ouse is his Castle. And wotsume'er the failings on his part, he were a corn and seedsman in his hart.'

'Is it Pumblehook's house that has been broken into, then?'

'That's it, Pip,' said Joe; 'and they took his till, and they took his cash-box, and they drinked his wine, and they partook of his wittles, and they slapped his face, and they tied him up to his bedpust, and they stuffed his mouth full of flowering annuals to prewent his crying out. But he knowed Orlick, and Orlick's in the county gaol.'

By these approaches we arrived at unrestricted conversation. I was slow to gain strength, but I did slowly and surely become less weak, and Joe stayed with me, and I fancied I was little Pip again.

For, the tenderness of Joe was so beautifully proportioned to my need, that I was like a child in his hands. He did everything for me except the household work, for which he had engaged a very decent woman, after paying off the laundress on his first arrival. 'I found her a-carrying away the coals gradiwally in the soup-tureen and wegetable-dishes, and the wine and spirits in your Wellington boots,' said Joe, in explanation of that liberty.

We looked forward to the day when I should go out for a ride. And when the day came, and an open carriage was got into the Lane, Joe wrapped me up, took me in his arms, carried me down to it, and put me in and we drove away together into the country. When I looked on the loveliness around me, and thought how it had grown and changed, and how the little wild flowers had been forming, and the voices of the birds had been strengthening under the sun and under the stars, while poor I lay burning and tossing on my bed, that I was not nearly thankful enough – that I was too weak yet, to be even that – and I laid my head on Joe's shoulder, as I had laid it long ago when he had taken me to the Fair or where not, and it was too much for my young senses.

When we got back again and he lifted me out, and carried me – so easily – across the court and up the stairs, I thought of that eventful Christmas Day when he had carried me over the marshes. We had not yet made any allusion to my change of fortune, nor did I know how much of my late history he was acquainted with. I was so doubtful of myself now, and put so much trust in him, that I could not satisfy myself whether I ought to refer to it when he did not.

'Have you heard, Joe,' I asked him that evening, upon further consideration, as he smoked his pipe at the window, 'who my patron was?'

'I heard,' returned Joe, 'as it were not Miss Havisham, old chap.'

'Did you hear who it was, Joe?'

'Well! I heerd as it were a person what sent the person what giv' you the bank-notes at the Jolly Bargemen, Pip.'

'Did you hear that he was dead, Joe?' I presently asked, with increasing diffidence.

'Which? Him as sent the bank-notes, Pip?'

'Yes.'

'I think,' said Joe, after mediating a long time, and looking rather evasively at the window-seat, 'as I *did* hear tell that how he were something or another in a general way in that direction.'

'Did you hear anything of his circumstances, Joe?'

'Not partickler, Pip.'

'If you would like to hear, Joe –' I was beginning, when I Joe got up and came to my sofa.

'Lookee here, old chap,' said Joe, bending over me. 'Ever the best of friends; ain't us, Pip?'

I was ashamed to answer him.

'Wery good, then,' said Joe, as if I *had* answered; 'that's all right, that's agreed upon. Then why go into subjects, old chap, which as betwixt two sech must be for ever onnecessary? There's subjects enough as betwixt two sech, without onnecessary ones. Lord! To think of your poor sister and her Rampages! And don't you remember Tickler?'

'I do indeed, Joe.'

'Lookee here, old chap,' said Joe. 'I done what I could to keep you and Tickler in sunders, but my power were not always fully equal to my inclinations. For when your poor sister had a mind to drop into you, if I put myself in opposition to her she dropped into you always heavier for it. I noticed that. It ain't a grab at a man's whisker, that 'ud put a man off from getting a little child out of punishment. But when that little child is dropped into, heavier, for that grab of whisker or shaking, then that man naterally up and says to himself, "Where is the good as you are a doing? I grant you I see the 'arm," says the man.'

'The man says?' I observed, as Joe waited for me to speak.

'The man says,' Joe assented. 'Is he right, that man?'

'Dear Joe, he is always right.'

'Well, old chap,' said Joe, 'then abide by your words. If he's always right, he's right when he says this: – Supposing ever you kep any little matter to yourself, when you was a little child, you kep it mostly because you know'd as J. Gargery's power to part you and Tickler in sunders, were not fully equal to his inclinations. Theerfore, think no more of it as betwixt two sech, and do not let us pass remarks upon onnecessary subjects.'

The delicacy with which Joe dismissed this theme, made a deep impression on my mind. But whether Joe knew how poor I was, and how my great expectations had all dissolved, like our own marsh mists before the sun, I could not understand.

Another thing in Joe that I could not understand when it first began to develop itself, was this: As I became stronger and better, Joe became a little less easy with me. In my weakness and entire dependence on him, the dear fellow had fallen into the old tone, and called me by the old names, the dear 'old Pip, old chap', that now were music in my ears. But, imperceptibly, though I held by them fast, Joe's hold upon them began to slacken; and whereas I wondered at this, at first, I soon began to understand that the cause of it was in me, and that the fault of it was all mine.

Ah! Had I given Joe no reason to doubt my constancy, and to think that in prosperity I should grow cold to him and cast him off? Had I given Joe's innocent heart no cause to feel instinctively that as I got stronger, his hold upon me would be weaker, and that he had better loosen it in time and let me go, before I plucked myself away?

It was on the third or fourth occasion of my going out walking in the Temple Gardens leaning on Joe's arm, that I saw this change in him very plainly. We had been sitting in the bright warm sunlight, looking at the river, and I chanced to say as we got up:

'See, Joe! I can walk quite strongly. Now, you shall see me walk back by myself.'

'Which do not over-do it, Pip,' said Joe; 'but I shall be happy fur to see you able, sir.'

I walked no further than the gate of the gardens, and then pretended to be weaker than I was, and asked Joe for his arm. Joe gave it me, but was thoughtful.

I, for my part, was thoughtful too; for, how best to check this growing change in Joe, was a great perplexity to my remorseful thoughts. That I was ashamed to tell him exactly how I was placed, and what I had come down to, I do not seek to conceal; but, I hope my reluctance was not quite an unworthy one. He would want to help me out of his little savings, I knew, and I knew that he ought not to help me, and that I must not suffer him to do it.

We had a quiet day on the Sunday, and we rode out into the country, and then walked in the fields.

'I feel thankful that I have been ill, Joe,' I said.

'Dear old Pip, old chap, you're a'most come round, sir.'

'We have had a time together, Joe, that I can never forget. There were days once, I know, that I did for a while forget; but I never shall forget these.'

'Pip,' said Joe, appearing a little hurried and troubled, 'there has been larks, And, dear sir, what have been betwixt us – have been.'

At night, when I had gone to bed, Joe came into my room, as he had done all through my recovery. He asked me if I felt sure that I was as well as in the morning?

'Yes, dear Joe, quite.'

Joe patted the coverlet on my shoulder with his great good hand, and said, in what I thought a husky voice, 'Good-night!'

When I got up in the morning, refreshed and stronger yet I went to his room, and he was not there. Not only was he not there, but his box was gone.

I hurried then to the breakfast-table, and on it found a letter. These were its brief contents.

Not wishful to intrude I have departured fur you are well again dear Pip and will do better without

$$JO$$

P. S *Ever the best of friends.*

Enclosed in the letter, was a receipt for the debt and costs on which I had been arrested. Down to that moment I had vainly supposed that my creditor had withdrawn or suspended procceedings until I should be quite recovered. I had never dreamed of Joe's having paid the money; but, Joe had paid it, and the receipt was in his name.

What remained for me now, but to follow him to the dear old forge, and there to have out my disclosure to him, and my penitent remonstrance with him, and there to relieve my mind and heart of that reserved. Secondly, which had begun as a vague something lingering in my thoughts, and had formed into a settled purpose?

The purpose was, that I would go to Biddy, that I would tell her how I had lost all I once hoped for, that I would remind her of our old confidences in my first unhappy time. Then, I would say to her, 'Biddy, I think you once liked me very well, when my errant heart, even while it strayed away from you, was quieter and better with you than it ever has been since. If you can like me only half as well once more, if you can receive me like a forgiven child, I hope I am a little worthier of you than I was – not much, but a little. And, Biddy, it shall rest with you to say whether I shall work at the forge with Joe, or whether we shall go away to a distant place where an opportunity awaits me, which I set aside when it was offered, until I knew your answer. And now, dear Biddy, if you can tell me that you will go through the world with me, you will surely make it a better world for me, and me a better man for it.

Such was my purpose. After three days more of recovery, I went down to the old place, to put it in execution; and how I sped in it, is all I have left to tell.

58

It was evening when I arrived, much fatigued by the journey I had so often made so easily. The Boar could not put me into my usual bedroom, which was engaged, and could only assign me a very indifferent chamber among the pigeons and post-chaises up the yard. But, I had as sound a sleep in that lodging as in the most superior accommodation the Boar could have given me, and the quality of my dreams was about the same as in the best bedroom.

Early in the morning while my breakfast was getting ready, I strolled round by Satis House. There were printed bills on the gate, and on bits of carpet hanging out of the windows, announcing a sale by auction of the Household Furniture and Effects, next week. The House itself was to be sold as old building materials and pulled down. Lot 1 was marked in whitewashed knock-knee letters on the brew house; Lot 2 on that part of the main building which had been so long shut up. Stepping in for a moment at the open gate and looking around me with the uncomfortable air of a stranger who had no business there, I saw the auctioneer's clerk walking on the casks and telling them off for the information of a catalogue compiler, who made a temporary desk of the wheeled chair I had so often pushed along to the tune of Old Clem.

When I got back to my breakfast in the Boar's coffee-room, Mr Pumblechook was waiting for me, and addressed me in the following terms.

'Young man, I am sorry to see you brought low. But what else could be expected!'

As he extended his hand with a magnificently forgiving air, and as I was broken by illness and unfit to quarrel, I took it.

'William,' said Mr Pumblechook to the waiter, 'put a muffin on table.'

I frowningly sat down to my breakfast. Mr Pumblechook stood over me and poured out my tea – before I could touch the teapot – with the air of a benefactor who was resolved to be true to the last.

'Little more than skin and bone!' mused Mr Pumblechook, aloud. 'And yet when he went away from here and I spread afore him my humble store, like the Bee, he was as plump as a Peach!'

This reminded me of the wonderful difference between the servile manner in which he had offered his hand in my new prosperity, saying, 'May I?' and the ostentatious clemency with which he had just now exhibited the same fat five fingers.

'Hah!' he went on, handing me the bread-and-butter. 'And air you a-going to Joseph?'

'In Heaven's name,' said I, firing in spite of myself, 'what does it matter to you where I am going? Leave that teapot alone.'

It was the worst course I could have taken, because it gave Pumblechook the opportunity he wanted.

'Yes, young man,' said he, 'I *will* leave that teapot alone. For once, you are right. I forgit myself when I take such an interest in your breakfast, And yet,' said Pumblechook, turning to the landlord and waiter, and pointing me out at arm's length, 'this is him as I ever sported with in his days of happy infancy! This is him as I have seen brought up by hand. Let him deny it if he can!'

The waiter seemed convinced that I could not deny it, and that it gave the case a black look.

'Young man,' said Pumblechook, 'you air a-going to Joseph. What does it matter to me, you ask me, where you air a-going? I say to you, Sir, you air a-going to Joseph. Now, I will tell you what to say to Joseph. Says you, "Joseph, I have this day seen my earliest benefactor and the founder of my fortun's. I will name no names, Joseph, but so they are pleased to call him up-town, and I have seen that man."'

'I swear I don't see him here,' said I.

'Say that likewise,' retorted Pumblechook. 'Say you said that, and even Joseph will probably betray surprise.'

'There you quite mistake him,' said I. 'I know better.'

'Says you,' Pumblechook went on, '"Joseph, I have seen that man, and that man bears you no malice and bears me no malice. He knows my character, Joseph, and he knows my want of gratitoode."'

Windy donkey as he was, it really amazed me that he could have the face to talk thus to mine.

'Says you, "Joseph, he gave me a little message, which I will now repeat. It was, that in my being brought low, he saw the finger of Providence. It pinted out this writing, Joseph. *Reward of ingratitoode to his earliest benefactor, and founder of fortun's.* But that man said that he did not repent of what he had done, Joseph. Not at all. It was right to do it, it was kind to do it, it was benevolent to do it, and he would do it again."'

'It's a pity,' said I, scornfully, as I finished my interrupted breakfast, 'that the man did not say what he had done and would do again.'

'Squires of the Boar!' Pumblechook was now addressing the landlord, 'and William! I have no objections to your mentioning, either up-town or down-town, that it was right to do it, kind to do it, and that I would do it again.'

With those words the Impostor shook them both by the hand, with an air, and left the house; leaving me much more astonished than delighted by the virtues of that same indefinite 'it'.

But, it was only the pleasanter to turn to Biddy and to Joe, whose great forbearance shone more brightly than before, if that could be, contrasted with this brazen pretender. I went towards them slowly, for my limbs were weak, but with a sense of increasing relief as I drew nearer to them, and a sense of leaving arrogance and untruthfulness further and further behind.

The little roundabout lane by which I entered the village for quietness' sake, took me past Biddy's school-house. I was disappointed to find that the day was a holiday; no children were there, and Biddy's house was closed.

But, the forge was a very short distance off, and I went towards it under the sweet green limes, listening for the clink of Joe's hammer. Long after I ought to have heard it, and long after I had fancied I heard it and found it but a fancy, all was still. The limes were there, and the white thorns were there, and the chestnut-trees were there, but, the clink of Joe's hammer was not in the midsummer wind.

Almost fearing, without knowing why, to come in view of the forge, I saw it at last, and saw that it was closed. No gleam of fire, no glittering shower of sparks, no roar of bellows; all shut up, and still.

But, the house was not deserted, and the best parlour seemed to be in use, and the window was open and gay with flowers. I went softly towards it, meaning to peep over the flowers, when Joe and Biddy stood before me, arm in arm.

At first Biddy gave a cry, but in another moment she was in my embrace. I wept to see her, and she wept to see me; I, because she looked so fresh and pleasant; she, because I looked so worn and white.

'But dear Biddy, how smart you are!'

'Yes, dear Pip.'

'And Joe, how smart *you* are!'

'Yes, dear old Pip, old chap.'

I looked at both of them, from one to the other, and then –

'It's my wedding-day,' cried Biddy, in a burst of happiness, 'and I am married to Joe!'

★

They had taken me into the kitchen, and I had laid my head down on the old deal table. Biddy held one of my hands to her lips, and Joe's restoring touch was on my shoulder. 'Which he warn't strong enough, my dear, fur to be surprised,' said Joe. And Biddy said, 'I ought to have thought of it, dear Joe, but I was too happy.'

My first thought was one of great thankfulness that I had never breathed this last baffled hope to Joe. How often, while he was with me in my illness, had it risen to my lips. How irrevocable would have been his knowledge of it, if he had remained with me but another hour!

'Dear Biddy,' said I, 'you have the best husband in the whole world, and if you could have seen him by my bed you would have – But no, you couldn't love him better than you do.'

'No, I couldn't indeed,' said Biddy.

'And, dear Joe, you have the best wife in the whole world, and she will make you as happy as even you deserve to be, you dear, good, noble Joe. And Joe and Biddy both receive my humble thanks for all you have done for me and all I have so ill repaid! And when I say that I am going away within the hour, for I am soon going abroad, and that I shall never rest until I have worked for the money with which you have kept me out of prison, and have sent it to you.'

They were both melted by these words, and both entreated me to say no more.

'But I must say more. Dear Joe, I hope you will have children to love, and that some little fellow will sit in this chimney corner of a winter night, who may remind you of another little fellow gone out of it for ever. And now, though I know you have already done it in your own kind hearts, pray tell me, both, that you forgive me! Pray let me hear you say the words, that I may carry the sound of them away with me, and then I shall be able to believe that you can trust me, and think better of me, in the time to come!'

'O dear old Pip, old chap,' said Joe. 'God knows as I forgive you, if I have anythink to forgive!'

'Amen! And God knows I do!' echoed Biddy.

'Now let me go up and look at my old little room, and rest there a few minutes by myself, and then when I have eaten and drunk with you, go with me as far as the finger-post, dear Joe and Biddy, before we say good-bye!'

I sold all I had, and put aside as much as I could, for a composition with my creditors – who gave me ample time to pay them in full – and I went out and joined Herbert. Within a month, I had quitted England, and within two months I was clerk to Clarriker and Co., and within four months I assumed my first undivided responsibility. For, the beam across the parlour ceiling at Mill Pond Bank, had then ceased to tremble under old Bill Barley's growls and was at peace, and Herbert had gone away to marry Clara, and I was left in sole charge of the Eastern Branch until he brought her back.

Many a year went round, before I was a partner in the House; but, I lived happily with Herbert and his wife, and lived frugally, and paid my debts, and maintained a constant correspondence with Biddy and Joe. It was not until I became third in the Firm, that Clarriker declared that the secret of Herbert's partnership had been long enough upon his conscience, and he must tell it. So, he told it, and Herbert was as much moved as amazed, and the dear fellow and I were not the worse friends for the long concealment. We were not in a grand way of business, but we had a good name, and worked for our profits, and did very well.

59

For eleven years, I had not seen Joe nor Biddy with my bodily eyes, when, upon an evening in December, an hour or two after dark, I laid my hand softly on the latch of the old kitchen door. I touched it so softly that I was not heard, and looked in unseen. There, smoking his pipe in the old place by the kitchen firelight, as hale and as strong as ever though a little grey, sat Joe; and there, fenced into the corner with Joe's leg, and sitting on my own little stool looking at the fire, was – I again!

'We giv' him the name of Pip for your sake, dear old chap,' said Joe, delighted when I took another stool by the child's side, 'and we hoped he might grow a little bit like you, and we think he do.'

I thought so too, and I took him out for a walk next morning. And I took him down to the churchyard, and set him on a certain tombstone there, and he showed me from that elevation which stone was sacred to the memory of Philip Pirrip, late of this Parish, and Also Georgiana, Wife of the Above.

'Biddy,' said I, when I talked with her after dinner, as her other child, a little girl, lay sleeping in her lap, 'you must give Pip to me, one of these days; or lend him, at all events.'

'No, no,' said Biddy, gently. 'You must marry.'

'So Herbert and Clara say, but I don't think I shall, Biddy. I am already quite an old bachelor.'

'Dear Pip,' said Biddy, 'you are sure you don't fret for her?'

'O no – I think not, Biddy.'

'Tell me as an old, old friend. Have you quite forgotten her?'

'My dear Biddy, I have forgotten nothing in my life that ever had a foremost place there, and little that ever had any place there. But that poor dream, as I once used to call it, has all gone by, Biddy, all gone by!'

Nevertheless, I knew while I said those words, that I secretly intended to revisit the site of the old house that evening, alone, for her sake. Yes even so. For Estella's sake.

I had heard of her as leading a most unhappy life, and as being separated from her husband, who had used her with great cruelty, and who had become quite renowned as a compound of pride, avarice, brutality, and meanness. And I had heard of the death of her husband, from an accident consequent on his ill-treatment of a horse.

The early dinner-hour at Joe's, left me abundance of time, without hurrying my talk with Biddy, to walk over to the old spot before dark.

There was no house now, no brewery, no building whatever left, but the wall of the old garden. A gate in the fence standing ajar, I pushed it open, and went in.

I could trace out where every part of the old house

had been, and where the brewery had been, and where the gates, and where the casks. I had done so, and was looking along the desolate garden-walk, when I beheld a solitary figure in it.

The figure showed itself aware of me, as I advanced. As I drew nearer, I saw it to be the figure of a woman. As I drew nearer yet, it was about to turn away, when it stopped, and let me come up with it. Then, it faltered as if much surprised, and uttered my name, and I cried out:

'Estella!'

'I am greatly changed. I wonder you know me.'

The freshness of her beauty was indeed gone, but its indescribable majesty and its indescribable charm remained. Those attractions in it, I had seen before; what I had never seen before, was the saddened softened light of the once proud eyes; what I had never felt before, was the friendly touch of the once insensible hand.

We sat down on a bench that was near, and I said, 'After so many years, it is strange that we should thus meet again, Estella, here where our first meeting was! Do you often come back?'

'I have never been here since.'

'Nor I.'

The moon began to rise, and I thought of the placid look at the white ceiling, which had passed away. The moon began to rise, and I thought of the pressure on my hand when I had spoken the last words he had heard on earth.

Estella was the next to break the silence that ensued between us.

'I have very often hoped and intended to come back,

but have been prevented by many circumstances. Poor, poor old place!'

The silvery mist was touched with the first rays of the moonlight, and the same rays touched the tears that dropped from her eyes. Not knowing that I saw them, and setting herself to get the better of them, she said quietly:

'Were you wondering, as you walked along, how it came to be left in this condition?'

'Yes, Estella.'

'The ground belongs to me. It is the only possession I have not relinquished. Everything else has gone from me, little by little, but I have kept this.'

'Is it to be built on?'

'At last it is. I came here to take leave of it before its change. And you,' she said, in a voice of touching interest to a wanderer, 'you live abroad still?'

'Still.'

'And do well, I am sure?'

'I work pretty hard for a sufficient living, and there-fore – Yes, I do well.'

'I have often thought of you,' said Estella. 'Of late, very often. There was a long hard time when I kept far from me, the remembrance of what I had thrown away when I was quite ignorant of its worth. But, since my duty has not been incompatible with the admission of that remembrance, I have given it a place in my heart.'

'You have always held your place in *my* heart,' I answered.

'I little thought,' said Estella, 'that I should take leave of you in taking leave of this spot. I am very glad to do so.'

'Glad to part again, Estella? To me, the

remembrance of our last parting has been ever mournful and painful.'

'But you said to me,' returned Estella, very earnestly, '"God bless you, God forgive you!" And if you could say that to me then, you will not hesitate to say that to me now – now, when suffering has been stronger than all other teaching, and has taught me to understand what your heart used to be. I have been bent and broken, but – I hope – into a better shape. Be as considerate and good to me as you were, and tell me we are friends.'

'We are friends,' said I, rising and bending over her, as she rose from the bench.

'And will continue friends apart,' said Estella.

I took her hand in mine, and we went out of the ruined place; and, as the morning mists had risen long ago when I first left the forge, so, the evening mists were rising now, and in all the broad expanse of tranquil light they showed to me, I saw no shadow of another parting from her.

A CHRISTMAS CAROL
Charles Dickens

On Christmas Eve Scrooge sits in his counting-house with not a kind word for a soul, just wanting to be left alone until the 'humbug' of Christmas is over. But four ghostly visitors – his partner Marley, followed by the Ghosts of Christmas Past, Christmas Present and Christmas Yet to Come - show him the error of his ways, and by the time Christmas Day dawns, Scrooge is ready to enjoy it!

OLIVER TWIST
Charles Dickens

Until he is nine, Oliver spends his life in a workhouse orphanage where he becomes notorious for daring to ask for more food. When he runs away to London, he falls into the company of a gang of pickpockets including Fagin, Bill Sikes and the Artful Dodger. Oliver's future looks uncertain, until a mysterious plot against him is unravelled by the kind Mr Brownlow.

THE ADVENTURES OF HUCKLEBERRY FINN
Mark Twain

When Huckleberry Finn runs away from his brutal father, he meets up with an old friend, the slave Jim, who is also running away. Together, they travel by raft down the Mississippi, tumbling in and out of amazing experiences – from a floating house to a funeral, a shipwreck to a circus – and learn some of the strange ways of people in the Deep South.

THE ADVENTURES OF TOM SAWYER
Mark Twain

Tom skips school and has some incredible adventures with his friends Huckleberry Finn and Joe Harper – some real enough, others not quite. They go off and live like pirates on an island, are presumed dead, and return just in time for their own funeral. They witness a murder, and discover treasure beyond their wildest dreams.

ALICE'S ADVENTURES IN WONDERLAND
Lewis Carroll

Alice is an ordinary little girl who lives an ordinary
sort of life, until the day she finds herself in the
most wonderful world of mad tea parties and
remarkable characters like the Mad Hatter, the
Duchess, the Cheshire Cat and the Mock Turtle.
As everything grows 'curiouser and curiouser',
Alice is delighted to find that nothing in
Wonderland is the least bit ordinary.

THROUGH THE LOOKING- GLASS
Lewis Carroll

When Alice steps through the looking- glass, she
enters a world of chess pieces and nursery rhyme
characters who behave very oddly. Humpty
Dumpty, the Lion and the Unicorn, Tweedledum
and Tweedledee, the dotty White Knight and the
sharp-tempered Red Queen – none of them are
straightforward. In fact, through the looking-glass
everything is 'contrariwise'.

PUFFIN | **CLASSICS**

AROUND THE WORLD IN EIGHTY DAYS
Jules Verne

For a bet, Phileas Fogg sets out with his servant
Passepartout to achieve an incredible journey –
from London to Paris, Brindisi, Suez, Bombay,
Calcutta, Singapore, Hong Kong, San Francisco,
New York and back to London again, all in just
eighty days! There are many alarms and surprises
along the way – and a last-minute setback that
makes all the difference between winning
and losing.

TWENTY THOUSAND LEAGUES UNDER THE SEA
Jules Verne

A mission to rid the seas of a monster becomes a
nightmare for Professor Aronnax, Conseil and
harpooner Ned Land when they become prisoners
of the 'monster' itself – a spectacular submarine
ship commanded by Captain Nemo. But the
marvels of their underwater journey soon distract
them from their worries – the Professor, at least,
wouldn't have missed this voyage for the world!

THE CALL OF THE WILD
Jack London

Buck is a dog born to luxury, but betrayed and sold to be a sledge dog in the harsh and frozen Yukon. This is the remarkable story of how Buck rises above his enemies to become one of the most feared and admired dogs in the north.

WHITE FANG
Jack London

In the desolate, frozen wilds of north-west Canada, a wolf-cub soon finds himself the sole survivor of the litter. Son of Kiche – half-wolf, half-dog – and the ageing wolf One Eye, he is thrust into a savage world where each day becomes a fight to stay alive.

THE ENCHANTED CASTLE
E. Nesbit

Gerald, Cathy and Jimmy wake a beautiful princess from her hundred year sleep in an enchanted garden. It's really only Mabel, the housekeeper's niece – but the garden really is enchanted, and the ring she slips on really is magic! The children find themselves in some funny, some awkward, some frightening and some absolutely magical situations before everything gets sorted out.

THE FAMILY FROM ONE END STREET
Eve Garnett

The Ruggles family, of Number 1, One End Street, are experts at finding entertainment that costs no money – but often leads to unexpected adventures ... From stout Lily Rose, whose good deeds don't always work as she intends, to baby William, who earns glory at the Baby Show, the seven Ruggles children are lovable and individual – and their adventures are endlessly enjoyable!

THE HOUND OF THE BASKERVILLES
Sir Arthur Conan Doyle

When Sir Charles Baskerville is found
mysteriously dead in the grounds of Baskerville
Hall, everyone remembers the legend of the
monstrous creature that haunts the moor. The
greatest detective in the world, Sherlock Holmes
knows there must be a more rational explanation –
but the difficulty is to find it before the
hell hound finds him'

THE MYSTERIOUS ADVENTURES OF SHERLOCK HOLMES
Sir Arthur Conan Doyle

Sherlock Holmes, the great genius of detection,
with his assistant Dr Watson, once more attempts
to solve the unsolvable. From the extraordinary
case of *The Resident Patient* to the sinister tale of
The Crooked Man, Holmes unravels the most
challenging of mysteries. Using his astounding
methods of deduction, he outwits the most
cunning of thieves and most villainous
of murderers.

THE JUNGLE BOOK
Rudyard Kipling

Here are the famous stories of how Mowgli came
to the wolf pack, learned the law of the jungle
from Baloo the bear, Bagheera the Black Panther,
and Kaa the python, and killed the evil tiger Shere
Khan. And here too are Rikki-Tikki-Tavi, the
snake-fighting mongoose, Little Toomai, who sees
the elephants' secret dance, Kotick the white seal,
and the varied characters in the horse lines of an
army camp.

JUST SO STORIES
Rudyard Kipling

From the 'satiable curiosity of the elephant's child
to the crab who played with the sea, from the
ingenious invention of the alphabet to how the
rhinoceros got his wrinkled skin, these stories of
strange happenings in the High and Far-Off Times
brim with life, humour and magic – a wonderful
collection that will hold you spellbound!

LITTLE LORD FAUNTLEROY
Frances *Hodgson* Burnett

It is quite a shock for a seven-year-old boy to be
whisked away from the New York streets to an
English stately home and be told he is to inherit a
title and a fortune. It is very daunting to have to
face such a crotchety and selfish grandfather. But
then, little Lord Fauntleroy is a very unusual boy.

A LITTLE PRINCESS
Frances Hodgson Burnett

When her father is made bankrup, Sara Crewe is
reduced from cnormous wealth to terrible poverty.
At Miss Minchin's school, where she had been a
privileged student, she is now forced to work as a
servant. But Sara has a loving heart and a quick
imagination, and she knows that with the right
spirit, she can remain a princess inside.

READ MORE IN PUFFIN

For children of all ages, Puffin represents quality and variety – the very best in publishing today around the world.

For complete information about books available from Puffin – and Penguin – and how to order them, contact us at the appropriate address below. Please note that for copyright reasons the selection of books varies from country to country.

On the worldwide web: www.penguin.co.uk

In the United Kingdom: Please write to *Dept. EP, Penguin Books Ltd, Bath Road, Harmondsworth, West Drayton, Middlesex UB7 0DA*

In the United States: Please write to *Penguin Putnam inc., P.O. Box 12289, Dept B, Newark, New Jersey 07101-5289* or call 1-800-788-6262.

In Canada: Please write to *Penguin Books Canada Ltd, 10 Alcorn Avenue, Suite 300, Toronto, Ontario M4V 3B2*

In Australia: Please write to *Penguin Books Australia Ltd, P.O. Box 257, Ringwood, Victoria 3134*

In New Zealand: Please write to *Penguin Books (NZ) Ltd, Private Bag 102902, North Shore Mail Centre, Auckland 10*

In India: Please write to *Penguin Books India Pvt Ltd, 11 Panscheel Shopping Centre, Panscheel Park, New Delhi 110 017*

In the Netherlands: Please write to *Penguin Books Netherlands bv, Postbus 3507, NL-1001 AH Amsterdam*

In Germany: Please write to *Penguin Books Deutschland GmbH, Metzlerstrasse 26, 60594 Frankfurt am Main*

In Spain: Please write to *Penguin Books S. A., Bravo Murillo 19, 1° B, 28015 Madrid*

In Italy: Please write to *Penguin Italia s.r.l., Via Felice Casati 20, I–20124 Milano*

In France: Please write to *Penguin France S. A., 17 rue Lejeune, F–31000 Toulouse*

In Japan: Please write to *Penguin Books Japan, Ishikiribashi Building, 2–5–4, Suido, Bunkyo-ku, Tokyo 112*

In South Africa: Please write to *Longman Penguin Southern Africa (Pty) Ltd, Private Bag X08, Bertsham 2013*